AF429507

Father's Choice

Book One of the Father Series

by

Rhonda Hanson

Father's Choice

Book One of the Father Series

by
Rhonda Hanson

Copyright 2000
ISBN 0-9703817-0-0

2nd Edition 2023
ISBN 979-8-218-26992-0

by

Grace Under Pressure Publishing
P.O. Box 337 Bell Buckle, TN 37020
All Rights Reserved

Those who know me well may find parallels between the main character and myself. This is not unintentional. In order to produce a figure who is believable and tangible to the reader, especially in this, my first attempt at a literary work, I deliberately chose to graft facets of my own personality quirks into Meredith Clark, in order to easily capture her in print.

I chose to write about things that I personally know: music, street ministry, fishing, cats, etc. This, however, is where all likeness ends. Should any reader who is personally acquainted with me discover passages that raise questions, I encourage him or her to simply chalk it off to coincidence. Certain lifestyles breed certain similarities.

There is no depiction of any character in Father's Choice that intentionally mirrors the existence of any living person I have encountered. I have, however, borrowed the best qualities of those who have blessed my life over the years with their love and friendship and of those who have been "Father" to me.

As Father's Choice is being prepared for its second printing, I am taking this opportunity to edit the original text, if only for my own satisfaction. I am never truly done.

Rhonda Hanson

Dedication

This book is dedicated to my mother, Edna Stamper, who read with a passion and who sang, clasping a hymnbook that she never opened. I dedicate it to my dad, Elbridge Stamper, the funniest man I ever knew, with his snuff, bib overalls and his waking me up every morning, singing "In the pines, in the pines..." Sadly, I also dedicate this book to six of us ten "Stamper kids" who have joined Mama and Daddy, three of them, only months from this printing, all within an eleven week period. Now, we are four.

Acknowledgements

Thank you to LuLu Roman, star of "Hee Haw" and, more importantly, my best friend for many years, for her words of encouragement and for her years of staunch support and belief in whatever abilities God has deposited in me.

Thank you to Nancy Alcorn, president and founder of Mercy Multiplied (previously Mercy Ministries of America) for affirming the gifts in me over the course of many years of friendship.

Thank you to Gary and Crystal Schippling, who befriended me at a time in my life when friends were scarce. Gary is with Jesus now but I can still hear him admonishing me to be obedient to all that God has called me to do.

Thank you to the staff of the Hermitage for suffering me to spend long hours under Andrew Jackson's ancient cedars while weaving my story.

Thank you to Officer Wesley Neeley for providing patient technical support and advice regarding matters of law enforcement.

Thank you to Louis Bartet, who taught me about the Father and about the Abraham walk. It is an important mile marker in my life.

A special thank you to my family. You are dwindling in number but are always in my heart. I love you all.

There are three things which are too wonderful for me, four which I do not understand: the way of an eagle in the sky, the way of a serpent on a rock, the way of a ship in the middle of the sea and the way of a man with a maid.

Proverbs 30: 18 – 19

A love story ...

Meredith had always admired a good, clean window. Wherever she went, it was one of the first things she noticed, although she wouldn't be caught dead cleaning one, herself.

She forced her gaze onto the smudged panes of her own upstairs window and away from the trees into which she had been blankly staring. Anyway, it wasn't as if she could actually *see* them.

She looked around her music room, with its paneled walls and rustic hardwood floors, then behind her old upright piano at the faded, ancient wallpaper that she didn't have the heart to take down. Everything about this room was beautifully old, as was the rest of her large Colonial Revival home, nestled on park-like acreage that Meredith loved owning, but rarely ventured out to enjoy. Her manager's firm employed a landscaper to keep it pristine, although she liked to pretend that she would enjoy puttering around out there on a riding mower, herself.

She studied the room's many large windows and skylight and considered how sun-drenched and bright it really *would* be in here if she did cave in and actually wash a glass pane, from time to time. Meredith abandoned that train of thought almost immediately. It certainly wasn't traveling anywhere that she wanted to go.

She twisted her beautiful face into a dark scowl and scrawled a hasty signature across the bottom of a recent set of song lyrics before tossing them to one side. Halfway rising from her desk, she changed her mind, in keeping with her impulsive nature, and snatched them back up for one more critical moment.

Her eyes, almost hostile, scanned her words. They had come a little too easily, which made her suspicious. What in the world had caused her to stroll in here and pen this so effortlessly, almost like taking dictation? *Maybe I had a bad dream,* she suggested sarcastically to herself. She inspected her half-hearted endorsement at the bottom: Meredith Clark. *Big deal.*

"Big deal!" she echoed out loud. She laid the lyrics back down and sighed. She didn't know from where inside her this song had emerged, but it was definitely depressing.

She sniffed and shrugged. That's just what her manager would say. First, he'd dig for an explanation he knew he wouldn't get, then he'd try to make her rewrite it.

Meredith frowned in rebellion. "I'll just keep this one to myself. Some songs are just for me, anyway. Depressing or not, I'm certainly not doing any rewrites today."

Like many of Nashville's writers and musicians, there wasn't much that Meredith *did* do before noon. Only now, at four o' clock, was she slipping into gear. Already the sun seemed to be giving up on trying to penetrate her dirty windows and was toying with the idea of leaving soon and coming back tomorrow for another shot at it.

Meredith chewed on her pen for a moment while she tried to come up with a title for this song. She marked through a couple of idle scratches and then jotted something down with a firm hand.

"There," she announced to no one in general. "The Overflow." She grinned. "A song about my laundry. No wonder it's depressing."

She let her pen drop, then trudged out of her music room and down the stairs, just missing the large cat that was stretched out from wall to banister, at one with the carpet.

"Hey, Speedbump!" Meredith roused the mass of long gray hair with her foot. "What are you trying to do, break my neck? Get up from there!"

Speedbump, whose real name was Hookline, but who was treated to a variety of impulsive nicknames, rolled clumsily down a couple of steps before leaping into the nearest chair. Everyday they went through this same ritual and everyday he managed to look startled.

"You furry blimp." Meredith knelt down in front of the chair and buried her face into his soft gray coat. "You must weigh twenty pounds. You better stay off the stairs, Hook, or I'm gonna stuff a mattress with you!"

She gave the purring mound a quick rap on his hindquarters and pulled him onto her lap.

"Meester Hooksss..." biting her lip and roughing up his coat with a rapid back and forth motion. "Am I rubbing you the wrong way?"

Hookline jabbed his velvet paws playfully at Meredith's hand and turned up his motor.

"Hookers..." Meredith broke off as the telephone rang. She doled out a final caress and a light pop on his head, before eventually making her way over to it.

"Merry?"

"Lucky guess," she returned dryly, recognizing her manager's voice. "Who else lives here?"

Joel Etheridge decided to overlook her sarcasm. It was always best to ignore it when he had to stay focused.

"You didn't forget about tomorrow morning, did you?" he asked.

"Just a minute." Meredith snapped her fingers loudly and shot a glare at her cat, who was blissfully pulling the lining from the bottom of the winged-back chair with his teeth. *"Get out of here! You want me to knock you cross-eyed?"*

Joel lifted his brow. "Are you feeling lucky?"

"Not you, Joel." She gushed out a little stream of laughter. "I meant Hook. He just shredded my chair."

He smiled slightly while rubbing his temples. More often than not, talking to Meredith Clark always seemed to result in his needing a head massage.

"Answer the question."

"Ask me one."

"I asked you if you forgot about tomorrow morning. It's a good thing I called to check. Apparently, you did."

"I did not!" She failed to convince him.

Joel rolled his eyes at his secretary, who flashed him a sympathetic smile and waited in silence.

"Fine, then! What *about* tomorrow morning?" Meredith managed to sound indignant even though it was true that she had no idea what they were talking about.

"Listen, Merry." Joel was speaking slowly and quietly to accommodate his day-long headache. "In fact, grab a pen and write this down."

She muttered something indiscernible and flopped down on the couch. "Go ahead, shoot!"

"Meredith!" Her manager's weary voice began to take on a sharp edge. "Find a pen!"

"Sheesh!" She smirked somewhat wickedly and rolled onto the floor, stretching the curly cord of her old flea market telephone over to the coffee table.

She knew she was aggravating him and she only regretted that she couldn't be a fly on his wall to see the muscles twitch edgily around his firm mouth and watch him drag his hands through his hair.

Those who had known Joel Etheridge for many years recognized this gesture of frustration as a habit he had cultivated only after accepting Meredith Clark as a client. Miraculously, he still had a full head of curly hair but it seemed to have grayed overnight.

The source of his irritation plowed her hands around the coffee table, knocking off stacks of magazines, and a couple of fast food cups, before finally coming up with a pen that would write. "Hang on!" She spotted a long, white piece of paper and dragged it over. "Okay, I'm ready."

Joel seemed satisfied. "Tomorrow morning at nine o' clock," he began and unconsciously lifted a hand to ward off Meredith's explosion. She didn't disappoint him.

"Nine o' clock," he repeated, grinning in spite of the mounting pain behind his eyes. "This is the interview with Robin Masters from Anchor magazine. Read that back to me."

"Robin Masters... Anchor... Freakin' early o' clock..."

Meredith hurled a rejected, dry pen across the room at Hook, who had beat a hasty retreat to the kitchen when she yelled at him, but now risked a peek at her from behind the door. She missed, but he decided to return to his hiding place in case she launched another missile attack.

"Anchor, huh? This isn't one of those girly rags sailors pass around, is it?"

"Hardly!"

"Joel..." Meredith sat up straight and adopted a serious tone. "What's all this for? I mean, I just talked to Anchor magazine. It couldn't have been more than six months ago."

"You've had two number ones since then," Joel pointed out. "But you're right. There *is* a little more to it than that. Not to worry, I'll be there for the whole thing."

She didn't care for the sound of this at all!

"You're coming over here at nine o' clock in the blessed a.m. for a *routine* interview? Since when?"

"Oh, for crying out loud," he muttered, leaning back in his chair and closing his eyes, in an attempt to ground himself. "You're like a case study for anticipatory anxiety, Missy. How about we just deal with things when they actually do *become* things?"

He sounded a little too evasive for Meredith's taste. She stood up and planted one hand firmly on her hip, in an air of defiance that Joel could see, even over the telephone.

"No, *not* okay!" she responded sharply. "You just said there's a little more to it. You want to elaborate?"

"No, I do *not* want to elaborate!" Joel could be as combative as she could. He breathed in and made another effort to take the edge off his temper.

"Look, Merry, you're not being backed into a corner, so stop acting like it. Robin's just coming over for a standard interview. But she also wants to talk to us about a future project Anchor is suggesting and, of course, I intend to be there for that."

"Future project?" she repeated softly, more than a little puzzled. "That *Anchor* is suggesting? Do they own a label, now? 'Cause I'm already on *your* label, hello!"

Joel let out a heavy sigh. "No, it's not that kind of project. Maybe I should have said proposal or something. Maybe I should have just faxed this call, and then shut off all the phones around here." He smiled at his secretary's shriek of laughter.

"Well, why would an interviewer be the one to suggest any kind of project, in the first place?"

"You're quite the interviewer yourself, today. Don't worry about it, Merry and let's just deal with it tomorrow. One more thing. Did you get that plane ticket for Denver?"

"Plane ticket..." More confusion. "Joel, if someone's going to waltz in here tomorrow with some idea that you've already let me know is going to upset me..."

"I never *once* said it would upset you! Get a grip!"

"Joel!" Meredith's voice began to simmer. "I think I have a right to know what's going on and I'd like to know *before* I sit down with Robin Whatever!"

"You act like I'm deliberately trying to pull something over on you!" Joel snapped. "I only have a hint of what it might be, and I see no reason to send you screeching off into orbit, and taking out the solar system, until I'm sure. We can both be sure at the same time. Tomorrow!"

"Am I gonna wind up throwing somebody out of my house?"

Joel shuddered visibly at the thought. "Dear God in Heaven, I hope not!"

Meredith had to laugh at his fervency.

"Merry, let's not joust at windmills right now. Just tell me whether or not you got the plane ticket for Denver."

She sobered up and looked around blankly.

"They messed up and sent it there instead of the office, but it was overnighted three days ago. You should have it by now."

"I'm looking, hold your horses!" She maintained her clueless expression and fumbled impatiently through the sliding avalanche of postal miscellany.

Joel leaned back in the early stages of exhaustion, and listened to the characteristic chaos on the other end of the line.

Of course, she could have just used a digital ticket and let them scan it at the gate, but Merry scorned cell phones.

It was highly unlikely that she would show up at the airport with hers, so he'd had his secretary, Delores, request a hard copy.

He was just flirting with idea of hanging up, and driving over there to search for the ticket himself, when he heard a muted exclamation.

"Did you find it?"

"I sort of... yeah, I sure did!" Meredith finished, a little too brightly.

"You sort of what?" Joel's secretary glanced up at his note of irritation, then pinned her watery eyes resolutely onto her notebook. "You sort of *what*, Merry?"

Meredith shrugged and took the plunge. "I sort of just wrote all over it."

She thought, at first, that her manager was groaning then realized it was a dial tone. She hung up as well, and considered her ticket apathetically. *Robin Masters, nine a.m., Anchor Magazine* followed by several drawings of monkey heads and little houses with Xs in the middle of them.

"I wonder if the airline even cares if I wrote on my ticket," she mused aloud before throwing it back onto the precarious heap.

She had to extricate herself from the twisted phone cord that had managed to become coiled around her waist. All her friends kidded Meredith about having a landline and especially about having an ancient rotary telephone but she was "old school" in many ways, and would dismiss their teasing with an eye-roll or her signature shrug.

Freed from her bondage, Meredith stretched her arms upward and yawned widely, before she padded across the floor and climbed up into the refuge of her window seat to catch the last light of evening.

"Hey, Father!" She waved in the general direction of up and peered into the overhead branches of the shedding oak in the front yard. "I guess I made Joel mad," she confided, then grinned. "Or he *will* be when he sees my plane ticket."

Father smiled at her through the sun-filtered leaves and Meredith cuddled up against the cushions.

Hook came in at the sound of his mistress's voice and decided that what she needed most, was his help sitting on the window seat. He launched his plump body carefully and landed by Meredith's bare foot, pausing as if unsure of his welcome.

"Hey, fat boy." Meredith spoke complacently enough. Hook relaxed. She pulled the curtain back and lifted him up to the glass.

Hook's eyes darted eagerly to and fro, seeking whatsoever bird he might devour. His tail began to whip back and forth, in anticipation. Meredith watched him in lazy amusement for a moment, then leaned wearily against the sill, suddenly reminded of what Joel had said.

"Father..." She had been talking out loud to God ever since she was a small child, long before she actually knew Him; sometimes in petition, sometimes in anger, but always sure that He was listening. She had only begun calling Him "Father" after she had fully committed to walking with Him.

For a while, whenever she ventured to approach Him in conversation, it was hard to do so, without being embarrassed at the memory of some of the ugly things she had spouted off to Him, when she was at odds with Him. Over the years, however, she had simply and naturally come to recognize Him as "Father" and now it was an effort to think of Him as anything else.

"Sometimes I'd like to just smack Joel!" She felt Father's eyes caressing her face and, mistaking His doting for agreement, forged ahead.

"I mean, he's a great guy, don't get me wrong." She laughed, and shook her head at her own silliness. "How dumb is that? Like You're actually gonna misunderstand me!

"Anyway, everybody in Nashville knows that Joel Etheridge is brilliant and I should be glad that he looks out for me, but I wish he wouldn't be so overprotective and, just once, tell me, flat out, what the deal is. But he never does."

"Never?" Father wanted her to think about that one.

She smiled and examined her cuticles. "Okay, not *never*. But now, there's this weird interview thing. I hate that kind of..." Meredith's tongue tripped over a four-letter word. "Yikes!" She grimaced. "Stuff. I meant stuff."

"You meant what you said," Father answered fondly, yet firmly.

"I know," she confessed, always glad to hear His voice, even when He was correcting her. "I wish I *didn't* mean it, but I guess I did, didn't I?   Guilty.   Sorry."

"Forgiven," He replied softly.

Hook leveled inquisitive green eyes at Meredith's face, assuming that her mellow, contented tone was meant for him. She looked down and scratched his ears. "See all the leaves, Hook? It's our favorite time of year."

Hook gently concurred.

"We like fall in Tennessee, don't we, Mister Hooks?" Meredith droned on sleepily. "See how..." She broke off sharply and sat up straight, causing Hook to open his eyes wide in alarm.

"Father!" Meredith squinted and leaned forward for a closer inspection. A slow smile gave way to a big grin.

"Hey, Father!" She tapped the pane happily with her finger. "Did You clean this window?"

Chapter Two

"Get out of here, Hook! I feed you when *I* say, not when *you* say!"

Hook's answer to this was to wrap himself in and out of Meredith's ankles.

In the late afternoon, this may have charmed his owner to the point of grilling him a steak, but at eight-thirty in the morning, he couldn't have chosen a dumber tactic.

"STOP IT!" Hook sprang to one side, narrowly escaping an aimless kick.

Meredith was going to go with this mood. "I train *you*. You don't train me! Beat it!"

The doorbell chimed, in unison with Hook's plaintive meow. Meredith raised her tousled, sleepy head from the kitchen table and stared at her cat in amazement.

"Do that again," she whispered.

She was treated to an encore only this time, Hook participated simply by looking at her stupidly.

"Idiot!" Meredith wasn't sure if she meant this for herself, Hook, or whoever was ringing the doorbell. She sleepwalked out to the front door and, after opening it, made up her mind.

"Good, you're vertical." Joel leaned casually against the door frame, wearing one of those morning person smiles that Meredith personally found sickening. She lumbered away mutely, leaving him where she'd found him.

"But you're not dressed." He ventured in on his own and threw his briefcase onto the couch.

Meredith looked down at her worn-out jeans and her Green Bay Packers sweatshirt. She had cut off the bottom of it. She cut the bottoms off all her sweatshirts. "I'm as dressed as I'm gonna get."

"Well, you might try putting on a personality," her manager remarked. "And while you're at it, do something with this." He fingered her rumpled mass of hair.

Meredith narrowed her eyes and looked at Joel in much the same way one might examine a new species of insect. "Look," she stated, flatly. "Let's make a deal. You won't be amusing, and I won't be absent."

"Absent?" Joel looked down pointedly at his watch.

"Absent, Joel. It means *not here*." She sailed her words over her shoulder, as she moved up the stairs. She paused halfway up. "And no more interviews before two p.m."

Joel was silent. She came back down to the landing and cleared her throat loudly.

"Hey!"

He glanced up from something in his hand he had been frowning at, then back down at whatever it was.

"Nothing after two a.m., and nothing before two p.m." Meredith waited in vain for a response. "And feed the cat, will you?"

He still made no reply.

She rolled her eyes and clubbed the banister with her fist. "Joel! You're not even listening to me. And what *is* that, anyway?"

Joel snapped open his briefcase and tossed something white into it, before crossing the room to the foot of the stairs. He stepped up onto the landing and put his face close to hers, in a successfully intimidating manner.

"Plane ticket." His slow and deliberate reply had its effect. She turned and scampered up the stairs.

Joel waited until she was out of sight before he allowed himself to smile. His eyes scanned the living room. It was clean enough, he guessed. Everything, that was, but the shrine to all things paper that Meredith seemed to be erecting on her coffee table.

"Better not throw anything away," he mused. "She's probably got her will, her car title, and the deed to the house filed in here."

He wandered into the kitchen where Hook was holding a vigil over his feeding dish.

"Captain Hook!" Joel knelt down and scratched the silky ears.

Hook pushed his head against Joel's big hand and purred engagingly. Joel laughed at him and walked over to the utility room.

"Hungry, Hookster?" He rummaged around the shelves for the cat food, then paused thoughtfully. "Is it canned or dry today, Hook?"

"Meow," Hook lied.

"I'd like to believe you, but if I get this wrong, You-Know-Who will throw something at me. Probably *you*."

He walked back out to the living room and called up the stairs for Meredith.

"What?" she yelled back.

"Canned or dry?"

"Dry! Why, what did *he* say?"

Joel chuckled his way into the kitchen where Hook was regarding him hopefully. "Sorry, Captain. But, hey, nice try, though!"

He reached inside the utility room and brought out a box of cat food and grabbed an empty cardboard box for himself. Hook watched him pour the kibble into the dish, disappointment etched all over his disapproving face. He fixed a reproachful eye on Joel's retreating form and flopped down beside his dish in disgust.

Meredith loped downstairs in time to see Joel kneeling beside the coffee table, dragging unopened mail, magazines and papers into the box.

"What are you doing?" she demanded.

"Saving you from yourself, not to mention a possible house fire." Joel looked up at her from his position on the floor. "Meredith, go get some shoes on."

"Why? Is she interviewing my feet, too?" She threw herself into a glider, and covered up with an afghan. "What are you planning to do with all that?"

"I'm going to hide it in the utility room, for now. When Robin leaves, we're gonna sort through it."

Meredith wrinkled her nose distastefully. "Do we have to do all that today?"

"There's no telling what's in this mess. Maybe you have another cat; how would you even know?" Joel stood up with the box and indicated the table with one foot.

"Run a dust rag over that table. Come on now, Missy. Hop to it and I'll get some coffee going."

"There's not enough coffee in the world to make me *hop* to anything," Meredith grumbled.

She watched him take the box out to the kitchen, then stretched and rubbed her eyes. After a couple of minutes, she made herself get up and stood there, looking down at the coffee table in surprise.

"That's actually pretty," she crowed with delight. "I forgot I had that." She could hear Joel coming back. She gave the table a hurried swipe with her afghan and landed back in her chair.

"Hook didn't eat the dry food," he announced, his eyes skimming the tabletop. "That's better."

Meredith shrugged indifferently. "When he gets hungry, he'll eat," she prophesied.

"Want a fire?" Joel nodded toward her afghan.

"No, just a tub of coffee to soak in."

"I'm working on it."

Meredith made some response, but she was trying to speak and yawn at the same time, so Joel let it pass.

"While we're waiting, this would be a good time to talk about..."

The doorbell cut Joel off in mid-sentence. He looked down at his watch, clearly put out.

"She's early! We needed to talk, Merry, before she got here."

His words produced another careless shrug. "If she's early, just leave her out there."

Joel look at her thoughtfully. "Maybe you'd better scoot upstairs and pray for a few minutes. I'll come and get you after I make her comfortable."

Meredith was only too glad to comply. She took the stairs, two at a time, and was seated on the top landing, all set to listen in, when Joel opened the door. She never got to indulge herself, however. Right away, she became aware of Father sending her to her room.

"Your timing is way off," she teased, as she obediently left her perch and came into her bedroom. "Just kidding," she added unnecessarily, flopping on the bed and hugging a pillow.

"I know that." Father spoke lovingly.

"Father, what's going on down there? What do these people want with me? Something about this just feels off."

"Listen, little girl." He had a smile in His voice. "Put all that away. Come sit with Me until Joel comes to get you. We don't often get to visit this early."

Meredith flashed her trademark grin and rolled over onto another pillow.

"Read My Word and see what I have for you," Father continued. "You know how this works. Find My peace and stay in it."

Meredith had bibles all over her room. She passed over all of them, gifts from a lot of sweet people, and pulled an old leather satchel out from under the bed. She sat down on the floor to undo the strap.

Carefully, she slid out an old bible. She had to open it gingerly, because it was falling apart. Her mother had given her this bible years ago. From the first day of her walk with Father, through the years, and to this moment, it served as her friend.

Not that she was good about actually reading it! She wasn't proud of the fact that she would often go months without giving it much thought and then, when a severe trial hit her, devour it to the point of dilapidation. From the looks of it now, one would suppose that Meredith's life had been one long, harrowing experience.

The bible fell open where it had a troubling tendency to: Jeremiah 10: 23.

"Oh Lord," she read aloud in a hushed whisper. "I know the way of a man is not in himself; it is not in man who walks, to direct his own steps."

"I keep forgetting that, Father," she admitted, catching the threat of tears with her fingertips, before they finished forming. She closed her bible with a sad face. This particular verse always seemed to appear right before she came to a difficult crossroads in her life. She felt she could almost see one looming up ahead, in the distance.

"Why do You always do this to me? You know I don't cry pretty." She winked and stepped inside her bathroom to do a quick cosmetic touch up.

Satisfied that she was presentable to a scrutinizing reporter, she raised her bathroom window and leaned out, letting her eyes wander around the idyllic grounds of her property. She breathed in the October morning air that was infused with the rich fragrance of tea olive trees, garden phlox, and southern magnolias.

"It's that Abraham thing, right, Father?"

"It's that Abraham thing," He agreed, blowing her long hair back lightly with His breath.

"So, which is it?" She rested her chin on her folded arms. "Building altars or pitching tents?"

"Would it change things to know ahead of time?" Father asked.

She smiled up at Him coyly. "What do *You* think?" She felt Him smile back.

"You want Me to tell you something good about yourself." He knew His girl completely. "Very well, then. You are loved by the Creator of the universe."

"I know," she whispered, melting in His warmth. "I love You back." She let her eyes feast on the unaccustomed quiet beauty that morning had to offer.

She was still leaning out the window with Father, when she heard Joel tap on the bedroom door.

"Merry?"

"I'll be back later," she promised. She blew Him a kiss and headed back through her room to open the door.

Joel looked at her intuitively. "Are you okay?"

"Am I ever?" Meredith tried to be flippant.

She stepped out of the room and as she moved past him, he caught her gently by the arm and turned her around to face him.

"It's not a rhetorical question."

"I'm just... you know."

"Not unless you tell me."

She never liked for things to become this intense with Joel. It created a closeness between them that caused her to feel nervous and unsure of herself.

She made another attempt at levity and gave his hand a light squeeze. "I'm great, considering how early you made me get up." She leaned toward him dramatically. "Now, where's this lion you've come to throw me to?"

Something like hurt swept across Joel's face, completely throwing Meredith off guard. She pulled back in surprise to look up at him.

"Joel, I was kidding. You're always telling *me* to get a grip. Maybe *you* should get one."

He glanced down the stairway.

"Meredith, I really am here to help you, not to force decisions down your throat." He spoke quietly, his eyes confirming that her lion remark had stung him.

She stood there, wondering where all this was coming from and, even more unsettling, where it was going.

"I hope it doesn't seem like I'm helping Anchor gang up on you, because I'm not. That's not my method."

"Oh, stop it!" Meredith slapped him on the arm lightly. "Come on, Joel, it's early. I don't do early very well. I haven't even had my coffee. Could you pick a worse time to start taking me seriously? That *was* a rhetorical question," she added, when he failed to respond.

"Want I should rough you up?" She whipped out a bad Bogart impression, her eyes dancing with mischief.

Relief spread slowly over Joel's countenance and he gave her a smile. It was faint, however, and it didn't last. He opened the door to Meredith's music room.

"Come in here, please." He stood aside to let her pass.

Meredith raised her eyebrows. "What about the lion?" She gestured downstairs.

Joel caught her hand and tugged her into the room.

"You remember Robin from the last time, right?" He closed the door before turning to look at her.

"Wasn't it a man last time?"

"A man?" Joel's brow furrowed as he thought about it. "No, I don't think so. Anyway, she's anything but a lion."

"Is she pretty, Mister Man?" More dancing eyes.

"She late forty-ish, the mother of three sons with one in college, the wife of a real estate broker, and a free-lance writer that Anchor likes to call in for special assignments."

Meredith opened her eyes wide and belted out a big laugh. Joel grinned at her and shook his head.

"*Man alive*, Joel! You must have sure *enough* made her comfortable to get all that out of her! What did you do, slip some sodium pentothal into her coffee? I'm glad *I* haven't had any yet."

"Why? Keeping things from me?" Joel missed the quick pallor that drained her face as he pulled out the piano bench and patted it suggestively. "Sit down. I want to talk to you."

"Do we have time?" She obeyed with reluctance.

"It's just that I have a better idea now of what Anchor is after and I would *never* send you down there uninformed." He emphasized this with a reproving look.

"I'm sorry." Meredith smiled down at her bare feet in penitence.

"Next time, know better." He pulled the desk chair over and sat down, leaning forward. "Merry, Anchor is hoping to persuade you to write a book."

"A book..." Her pulse started to beat in her ears and the scripture she'd just read began to resurface. "What... what *kind* of book?"

"An autobiography."

"My *life?*" She looked up at the ceiling and then sighed herself into a slumping position. "No, Joel."

"No?" He was watching her closely. "Just like that? No talking about it? No praying about it?"

She hung her head and shook it slowly.

Joel regarded her intently for a long moment, then got up from his chair and knelt in front of her, pulling the curtain of her long hair to one side so that he could read her face.

"Can you tell me why?" he asked gently.

She gave only the merest suggestion of shaking her head again, but said nothing. After a long silence between them, she raised her eyes in an imploring way that gripped his heart.

"Could we just talk about it later? Can I let you know maybe after this trip?" He couldn't possibly know what he was asking her to do! Panic was setting in, causing her to have to fight for composure. She felt dangerously close to tears. There was no way she could talk to Joel about this, and she was hoping to just put him off, at least for now.

He tried in vain to read what was in her eyes.

"Okay, little one," he finally relented. "I'll tell Robin that we'll just have the interview today and we'll give Anchor a call later about this other thing. But only if you agree to wipe off that sad, little cheerleader-for-the-morgue expression." He smiled up at her. "What are the odds of you being on your best behavior, downstairs?"

Meredith forced a grin and let him pull her up as he stood. "Slim to none, I would imagine."

"You little barefoot stinker!" He gave her nose a tweak. "Come on, then. Let's go to the zoo."

Chapter Three

Joel tucked his gate pass back into his jacket pocket, then shifted his weight, in the hope that the airport seat would at least seem more comfortable.

He rested an ankle on one knee, and tapped his fingertips on the chair's padded arm in a bored fashion. The Nashville airport was relatively quiet. He wished all of Meredith's flights could be on weekdays. Neither of them cared for crowds.

Joel smiled at the thought of Meredith's aversion to crowds. For someone who hated them, she sure had picked an odd profession. Topping charts and selling out concerts was not exactly the way to avoid them.

He traveled back in his mind to the day he heard her music for the first time. He had only agreed to listen as a favor for his associate, Marshall Edwards. The last thing he needed, or wanted, was to take on any new clients.

He had, in fact, declined to listen at all, and would have stuck to his guns, if Marshall hadn't assaulted him with CDs, lyrics sheets, and a promo pack, and announced that he was prepared to beg. Joel had reluctantly promised to at least listen, as long as Marshall understood that this was all he was agreeing to.

He had taken the material home that evening. He remembered shuffling through the door, leaving his coat, briefcase, and a stack of promotional merchandise on the floor by the coat rack and throwing himself on the sofa. It had been one of those days he'd like to save in a bottle... so he could smash it later, with a hammer.

He always left his answering machine on, since he was forever leaving his cell phone in odd places. He decided to ignore its furious blinking, as he got up and moved to the kitchen, went through the motions of dinner, then stared at the television for a dull hour before dragging himself up to turn in early. When the machine's infuriating, flashing light caught his eye again, Joel uttered a mild oath, and decided to get it over with.

He halfway listened to the beginnings of each message, jotting down numbers, fast-forwarding through junk, and scowling at hang-ups.

"Joel!" He recognized Marshall's voice. "So, what'd you think? Did you hear it yet? Give me a call, I'm at the house."

"Oh, brother!" Joel grimaced and reset the machine. "I forgot all about that, and Marshall will probably wait up all night, until I call him back."

He rifled through his briefcase and retrieved the manila envelope Marshall had given him.

"This better be good, Edwards." He turned off the lights and went up to his bedroom. Twenty minutes later, he was on the phone.

"Tomorrow at four, Marshall."

"Tomorrow!"

"Is that a problem?"

"Not at all!" Marshall had stuck a jubilant fist up into the air, and pulled it down with a silent 'Yes!'

"Perhaps you'd better check with Miss Clark, first," Joel pointed out mildly.

"Oh, don't you worry about Miss Clark. Miss Clark will be there if I have to hog-tie her!"

Joel looked around at the airport gate area and then at his watch, smiling to himself at the memory of how excited and grateful Marshall had been. "At the very least, I should have received the Citizen's Award for Bravery, for unusual valor," he mumbled. "Or commitment papers."

He glanced up at the monitor that displayed the arrivals and departures. Meredith's plane should be landing any minute.

She'll be cranky as all get-out, he advised himself dryly. He stood up and stretched, then wandered over to the bank of windows overlooking the tarmac. He couldn't go with her to Denver and Meredith had insisted on driving herself to the airport, and leaving her car in the parking lot. Joel had overruled her, not that he was in the habit of personally providing cab service for all of his clients.

I'm just stupid. He pondered his sober reflection in the glass and let out an audible sigh. *Old and stupid.*

Joel Etheridge, at forty, was considered by his peers to be neither old nor stupid, although his friends and colleagues jokingly referred to him as "old man Etheridge" because of the premature gray hair that graced his temples, and mingled in with his brown curls.

Unknown to him, the women at his firm described him in such silly, gushing terms as "lean and mean" and "elegantly rugged" with, as one swooning intern put it, "surprise eyes". They certainly were an unexpected shade of light blue, for such contrasting dark looks. During business negotiations, those eyes could glare narrowly, completely unnerving his opponent like two icy knives. They could flash, like the sky in a summer storm, or remain cold and indifferent, like two stones. Then there were times when they would utterly betray him, usually when penetrated by Meredith's steady gaze.

Meredith's gaze had become more and more unsettling for Joel, lately. Since their very first meeting, they had always been completely at ease with one another. There was a level of comprehension between them, unlike anything experienced with anyone else before, and a comfortable ease of expression that came naturally. Then, why were things so tense and charged between them, lately? Joel sighed bitterly. He knew why.

Just after he met her, Joel sat down with Marshall to try to learn what he could about her, since she wasn't exactly forthcoming. Marshall alluded, albeit vaguely, to a sore spot in Meredith's past that seemed to affect the way she viewed almost everyone. It seemed that she had an unhealthy amount of caution and suspicion toward even the most innocent gesture of caring. He mentioned that he and his wife had always noticed that she beat a hasty retreat, if anyone tried to get too close.

Over the years, Joel had intentionally managed to keep his professional involvement in Meredith's life completely at the helm of all dealings he had with her. Even in the most mundane, superficial things, he maintained a managerial air that never failed to accompany their relationship. He had purposed long ago, when he first suspected what was in his heart for Meredith, to do nothing that would cause her to move away from him. She might never share his life, but at least she would still be in it.

Gradually but surely, Meredith had gravitated toward Joel, in a way that completely surprised Marshall Edwards, and Joel was determined to hold his feelings in check. He had succeeded so admirably, that there were times when Meredith wondered if he could even stand her! He had done well, but he knew that he couldn't hold out much longer.

Joel took in a deep breath and moved idly around the waiting area. He reflected on their last interaction when he brought Meredith to the airport. Normally, he was able to sling her belongings into her arms, and leave her with some dry, sarcastic warning about not getting thrown off the plane. For some reason, he hadn't quite been able to pull it off last Friday.

He knew that he had hugged her too tightly, that he had allowed a tender note to creep into his voice, as he said goodbye and told her to be careful. He saw the anxious way she looked back at him, and he had raked himself over the coals about it all weekend. If he didn't get it together, the next thing he knew, Meredith would be asking to be released from their contract.

That thought hit Joel in the stomach with an unbelievable force. Was that what he had seen in her eyes? Of course, it could be that she was upset with him about that book deal. He had to admit, he had urged her very strongly to go through with it. She had said no initially, but then asked for time to think about it. He had been a little put out with her for keeping Anchor waiting, when all she had to do was give them a firm yes or no, but he'd agreed.

He frowned. Maybe it really was his lack of restraint that had caused her to look at him so strangely, before she boarded the plane last Friday. Marshall had warned him about her tendency to withdraw from any kind of intimacy.

Of course, he had the legal leverage to hold her to their contract. He hoped he wouldn't have to use it. On the other hand, he probably wouldn't force her to remain with his firm if she really wanted to move on. A strange sense of foreboding interrupted his thoughts and draped over him, and he shook it off impatiently.

He would just make sure he was sufficiently indifferent when she arrived. He grated his jaw stubbornly. How long could he be expected to keep that up? If Meredith was going to bolt at the first hint of how he felt about her, then maybe it was for the best. He was running out of patience with keeping up appearances.

"Careful, Etheridge," he muttered under his breath. "Don't be a fool."

The nasal monotone of some anonymous airline employee announced to Joel and a handful of others that flight 1401 had landed. He stepped closer to the arrival area. Meredith was in first class, and would want to be out of that plane immediately, before the fuselage spewed forth its impatient cargo.

Joel was right. Here she came, the poster child for belligerence. She hadn't spotted him yet, so he indulged in an appreciative grin.

Meredith's eyes found him, and she looked at him warily. He checked his countenance and approached her.

"You look terrible." He lifted her carry-on from her tired shoulder, and laid it on his own.

She flashed him a sour expression. "How very nice. How heart-stoppingly sweet. Do you do greeting cards?"

"Come on." Joel glanced over her head, back toward the boarding bridge, where a small cluster of people had stopped to focus on the two of them.

"Let's get out of here, before people start to recognize you." He put his arm around her protectively, and steered her toward the escalators, and down to the baggage claim area.

They stood waiting for Meredith's luggage to come down the conveyer. Joel blocked her from easy viewing with his stance. She turned to face him, summoning every ounce of charm she could manage.

"Mister Man...."

Joel laughed softly. "Oh, is it going to be civil? It must want something!"

"Its shoulders hurt and it's hungry." Meredith wouldn't stoop to an actual pout, but she came pitifully close.

"Spoiled brat." Joel maneuvered her around, pulling her hair to one side and began kneading her neck and shoulders with his hands.

She didn't lapse into the exaggerated and comical expressions of relief and ecstasy she normal responded with. She just stood there, meekly and silently, her head bowed and her muscles tense and strained beneath Joel's fingers.

He looked down at the mass of lovely, long, unruly hair and sighed. *She's exhausted,* he thought solemnly.

He leaned closer to her. "Merry..."

She jumped as she felt his breath on her ear. He turned her around to face him.

"Your bags are out." He knew that she never ate on planes. "Do you want to go home first, or stop to eat?"

"Oh, Joel, if I don't eat soon, I'm gonna cry!"

"Well, let's not resort to that." Joel lifted her bags and nodded toward the door. "Come on, Missy."

Evening was approaching, by the time Joel delivered Meredith to her house.

"I didn't bring Hook by," he explained, when she paused in the living room and searched around with her eyes. "I can run home and pick him up for you or he can just stay another night."

"I've missed him, but he'd drive me up a wall tonight." Meredith crossed the room and curled up in the middle of the couch. Joel left everything by the stairs and settled down beside her.

"Kind of jumpy back at the restaurant, weren't you?"

"Why do you say that?" She picked up a stack of mail and pretended to be interested in it.

"For one thing, you spent a lot of time looking anywhere but at me. You seemed to have difficulty concentrating and forgive me, but I've never known you to be monosyllabic. Here you are now, downright jittery. What gives?"

"Your imagination." She dropped the mail back down and sank into the couch, staring hard at nothing.

"You want to wait?" He leaned his head back and glanced over at her.

"Wait? For the cat? Yes. I said yes."

"No. To talk. Harmless questions at first, like 'How was Denver' and then more important ones."

"Like what?" She allowed her head to rest beside his and waited, knowing what he was about to say, and dreading it.

"You wanted to use this weekend trip to think about that offer from Anchor." Joel kept his voice low and comfortable, sensing her apprehension. "You must have known I would ask."

Meredith lifted tired, emotional eyes to Joel's familiar face. When she was in top form, she could boldly stare him down. Now, her eyes cowered, and she looked helplessly at her hands.

"Tell me this." He was almost whispering. "Is waiting going to make any difference in your answer?"

Joel sounded so much like Father, that Meredith caught her breath sharply. She desperately continued to examine her hands. The evening sunlight exposed the sudden dampness on her cheeks. She knew it, but wiping them would only turn the sun's gentle glow into a spotlight. She remained still, and hoped he wouldn't see.

He did see.

"Look at me."

She turned her face away.

"Meredith." Joel raised himself up, and laid his arm behind her across the back of the couch. "Don't do this."

"Don't do what?"

"What you always do. Start to open up, and then panic and back off. Don't run from me, not this time."

"I want to wait."

"Because you don't know what you want to do, or because you *do* know? I'm not going to play guessing games with you about this, Meredith."

"I want to wait!" she snapped irritably.

He gave her a warning look that never left any doubt as to his seriousness. "I gave you all the time you asked for, and you knew this was coming. I'm getting a little tired of you constantly moving the goalposts. We're not going to wait."

"You just *asked* me if I wanted to wait!"

"Well, we're not going to." He was determined.

"I want to wait, Joel!" she yelled, pushing back from the threat of exposure and opting for anger.

She wasn't the only one who was angry. After years of putting up with Meredith's little quirks and fits of temper, Joel had finally had enough! Dispensing with patience, and surrendering to his frustration, he caught her chin in his hand and forced her to look at him.

"Wait for *what*, Meredith? Wait, to give you time to fortify your walls tonight, and come skipping into my office tomorrow, with your witty, sarcastic load of crap? NO! We are NOT going to wait!"

His temper startled her. She stared at him white-faced, making no further attempts to hide her tears. Her head fell against his chest, and she began sobbing in earnest.

Joel closed his eyes and silently rebuked himself. "Meredith... I'm sorry. Hush, Merry..." He gathered her onto his lap and cradled her like a child. "I'm so sorry."

She buried her face into his neck, and continued to cry softly.

So this was it! Joel steeled himself and blinked back his own tears. She wanted out of their contract! He closed his eyes again, and tried desperately to make it something else.

Had something maybe happened in Colorado? Or maybe... oh, please, let it just be this stupid book deal! Didn't she know that all she had to do was just give him a definite answer, one way or the other, and he'd drop it?

He pulled her damp hair back and stroked her cheek gently. "Merry, let's forget about the book, okay? It's all over. You don't have to do it and I won't bring it up again."

She gripped him tightly and moaned something broken and barely audible.

"I'm sorry," Joel whispered into her hair. "Please forgive me, Merry. I didn't realize it would do this to you."

"Joel... I.. h-have to tell you something." She was struggling for composure.

"It's okay. When you're ready." He brushed the tears from her face. "I'm sorry, little one. I didn't mean to bully you into doing something you're obviously not ready for."

Meredith closed her eyes and let out a long, ragged breath. "It's not about the book." She moved slightly to look up at him, but remained in his arms. "I need to say something to you, now, tonight. I have to get through it."

It's not about the book... Something ominous washed over Joel. He searched through his emotions for one he could deal with. His clear blue eyes scanned every detail of her face and, for the first time since he had known her, Meredith submitted to his scrutiny and even returned his gaze. The sorrow in her eyes was unmistakable. It filled him with a sense of dread, some sort of premonition of being separated from her. He could feel it coming, and he was alarmed.

"I can't do this," he said abruptly.

Still on his lap, she sat up and gripped his shoulders. "I have to say this to you, Joel, and you have to let me!" Her eyes were pleading with him. "I can't put this off, anymore. Please just let me get it over with!"

"And then what?" His voice broke.

She lowered her eyes, and shook her head.

"And *then* what, Merry?" Joel waited a moment before gently lifting her off his lap, and onto the couch beside him.

He stood with his back to her, looked up to the ceiling, and buried his hands in his pockets. It was no use. He knew he could no longer be content to just be her manager, and even *that* was about to end... and he couldn't deal with some speech she rehearsed on the plane, intended to make him feel better about it ending, by her saying they could still be friends. That would never be enough for him. He was all in. If he was to be relegated to nothing more than a friend, the lesser pain would be not have her in his life at all. At least he wouldn't have to deal with fresh grief, every time he saw her.

"I can't do this," he repeated in a dull, lifeless voice.

Meredith jumped up and quickly came around to stand in front of him. Her face was a study in torment.

"Joel!" She tugged at his hands, until he gave them to her. "Joel, you need to listen to me." She broke off, as he looked away. Her brow knitted in confusion, as she forged ahead, trying to make sense of the change that had just come over him. She could actually see him beginning to frost over!

"Joel, *please* listen to me. I have to know something."

He rested his disturbing eyes on hers, and waited in silence.

"When you say you can't do this, are you... do you mean..." She was floundering, and he wasn't going to try to save her.

"What are you saying? I mean, who's talking to me, right now? Is it my manager or my friend?"

A slight wince of pain passed over his handsome face, and then nothing. Absolutely nothing.

"Joel, *talk* to me!"

This time, Joel's eyes did not betray him. Meredith could find no answers in their cold depths.

"Let's have this conversation in my office." His voice, only moments ago laden with tenderness, now took on a stiff formality.

"Joel, don't do this! Please!" Her stunned surprise was in her voice and on her face. "Don't do this!"

"What am I doing, Meredith?" Joel walked over to the door and jerked it open. "You tell me. What am I doing?"

She followed him to the door, and stood there, trembling in a mixture of fatigue and shocked disbelief.

"You're acting like..."

"I'm acting like your manager, alright? Because that's what I am. I mean, those were my choices, were they not? Your manager or your... what was it? *Friend?*" He ground the word out as if it were hateful to him. "Well, that's what I'm doing, Miss Clark. I'm acting like your stupid *manager!*"

Meredith closed her eyes and shuddered, as the door slammed shut behind him. She heard the angry screech of tires, and then the echoing silence that attacked her.

"Oh, Father...." She stumbled blindly across the room and fell onto the couch.

"Joel..."

Chapter Four

Meredith lay staring up at the gray ceiling above her, unaware that it slowly grew lighter in color, as dawn cleared the way for morning.

Her eyes ached. She could tell, without touching them, that they were swollen. She had tried to sleep but kept waking up, intermittently crying and praying.

She pushed herself up from the couch and stood there a moment, looking back at it in a dull stupor. Just hours ago, she and Joel had been sitting there. A rush of warmth flooded her cheeks, as she recalled the way he had nestled her in his arms, speaking gently to her as if she were something precious.

She hugged herself protectively and closed her eyes to block out the vision of Joel lashing out at her in anger. She could still hear the door crashing behind him. Why? What was it she said to make him so furious?

Meredith was jolted out of her trance by the unexpected touch of silk against her feet, and stepped back in alarm, stunned to find Hook nudging her affectionately. She turned on a lamp, lifted her hand to her throat, and looked quickly around the room. He had been here!

Her eyes fell on a small folded piece of paper on the coffee table that Joel had cleaned, only days before. She reached for it with a shaking hand, and something fell out as she opened it. Her heart dropped, as she recognized the extra house key she had given Joel a couple of years ago. Her breath came in shallow, rapid succession as she spread open the note.

Have a full day tomorrow, she mouthed Joel's words silently. *Meetings. May not be around, so call Marshall if you need anything. Brought Hook by. Joel.*

That was all.

Meredith looked down at the key in her hand, slowly realizing what Joel was doing.

"No, you are *not!*"

She grabbed her jacket, groping in the pockets for her keys.

"No you are *not,* Joel!" She ran out, not knowing what she was going to do, once she got to his house. She only knew that she had to get there.

She charged her Jeep down the drive, and onto the boulevard, several car horns blaring at her, before she thought to turn on her headlights. She rolled down her window to let the cool, morning air soothe her burning eyes and looked down at the dashboard clock. Five-forty.

"Oh, Father," Meredith begged out loud. "Please help us get through this. Please help me understand what's going on. I thought..." Her voice broke, and she tried to begin again.

"Joel and I fight sometimes, but we always get past it. Father..." She began mopping away fresh tears with the back of her hand. "He brought back my key. He's leaving me! Does he not want to be my manager, anymore?" Even as she asked this, she knew it was not her real fear.

The image of Joel's stern, hard face as he was leaving, loomed up before Meredith's eyes. As she covered the short distance between their houses, she heard his parting words in her ears. *Those were my choices, were they not? Your manager or your friend?*

What did he mean? What was he saying? Meredith's weary mind was depleted.

She pulled her Jeep into Joel's driveway, almost crying with relief, when she saw that his car was there. "Help me, Father," she begged. She began breathing more and more rapidly.

She hesitated, unsure of what to do next. Joel was a grown man. He could do as he pleased. If he didn't want to continue their association, that was his right.

Association? They weren't just associates, they were friends! There was that word again. Why was it needling at her? And why, as she said it last evening, did Joel's demeanor change into icy hostility? The memory of his hurt, angry voice hammered at her relentlessly.

"Oh, dear God!" Meredith's eyes opened wide in horror. But surely Joel didn't... "Oh, what have I done?"

She laid her head down on the steering wheel and moaned. She had to be wrong about this. She and Joel had been working closely together for several years. Never once, had he given her any indication that he might feel anything for her deeper than respect and friendship.

You know that isn't true. Her heart rebuked her.

"Yes, it is!" She clenched her fist and pounded the steering wheel in frustration. Her conscience rejected her weak argument.

"What are you doing here?"

Meredith jerked her head up, and found Joel standing next to the Jeep, clad in a tee shirt and jeans, the morning paper under one arm.

She searched his face for some small sign of welcome, but found nothing encouraging.

"What are you doing here?" he repeated, stonily.

"I found your note," she began in a small voice.

He frowned and set his jaw, but said nothing.

Meredith took a deep breath, and fingered her keys nervously. "Joel, can I please come in?" She raised her eyes to his, and waited in agony.

She was not alone in her suffering. Joel lowered his head and stared at the ground.

"I have to be leaving for the office soon," he hedged.

"When is soon?"

"I have a nine o' clock and several calls to make before then."

Meredith loosened her grip on the steering wheel. "It's not even six yet," she ventured. "I won't stay long."

Joel looked off into the distance at nothing in particular. After what seemed to be an eternity, he met her eyes. "I'm not trying to be mean to you, Meredith. It's just not a good idea." He began to move away from her car.

He was not going to get away with this! She jumped out of the Jeep, before Joel knew what she was doing. She had spent the entire night with an army of emotions having their way with her, and now it was anger's turn.

She stood up straight, and faced him head on, her closeness threatening his resolve. Temper painted her cheeks, and sparkled in her eyes dangerously.

"Joel Etheridge," she said in a low, trembling voice. "When has it *ever* not been a good idea for us to work things out?"

"Oh, so *that's* why you're here!" Joel's own short fuse began to kindle.

They each stood their ground, smoldering like two beautiful volcanoes. Suddenly, Meredith flowed past him.

"Idiot!" she flung back at him, throwing open his door and making her way straight to his sofa.

Joel stood in the driveway, waiting to calm down before he followed her in.

"Dear God," he sighed. "I don't think I have the strength to go through any more of this. Meredith trips through life, thinking she can just 'fix' things. This isn't a flat tire. She just wants to fast-talk us back into what she calls normal. Never mind that normal for her is hell for me."

Joel cleared his throat, and blinked back hot tears. "Please, Lord Jesus, if You ever loved me, help me!"

He made his way slowly into his house, throwing the paper down on a table, and taking a chair across the room from Meredith.

He waited in silence for her to begin.

Meredith suddenly became aware of her swollen eyes, wild hair, and yesterday's clothes. She looked down and realized she was barefoot, as usual.

Joel watched her covert analysis and then quietly confirmed her fears.

"You look like crap."

She offered a smile, though sadly. Without thinking, she got up and knelt down in front of Joel's chair, raising her eyes to his.

"I miss you," she said simply.

Joel closed his eyes and wished her away.

"Don't, Meredith."

"Don't miss you?"

"Don't say it. Don't say anything."

He opened watery eyes, and looked at her pleadingly.

"Don't stay."

"Don't leave," Meredith countered softly.

She pulled her house key out of her jeans pocket, and laid it on his knee. He stared down at it, glad for an excuse to look away from her.

"Joel..." She touched his hand, and he immediately drew it away. She took a deep breath and continued.

"Yesterday... last night... what was that about? There's
no way that was just about the book."

Joel ran his hand through his hair, and looked at her
vacantly. "The book?"

"Well..." Meredith searched around in her memory.
"It's just that, outside of being tired, you and I were okay,
and then..."

"Then I was yelling at you," he finished for her.

She nodded and opened her mouth to speak, hesitated,
and then went for it. "Then you were holding me."

"I'm sorry about that," he said quickly.

"Why, do I have cooties or something?" She tried to
make him smile and failed.

"That wasn't like you, Joel. I don't mean you don't ever
yell at me. But yelling, and then holding me, and then...
yelling at me again, then... just to storm out like that..." She
reached for his hands again.

He glanced over at the clock.

"You know what, Meredith?" Joel pulled his hands out
of hers, and pushed her gently away. "I'm just not up to a
whole big rehash of last night."

"I think we *need* to rehash it, Joel! I mean, I can't read
your mind. Don't you think I should at least know *why*
you're mad at me? And how long you intend to *stay* mad at
me? And whether or not I'm supposed to clear all my junk
out of your office?"

As soon as the words were out of her mouth, she knew
they were a big mistake! His face lost all color.

"And *that's* what this is really all about, isn't it?" Joel
stood up, almost knocking Meredith down.

She grabbed the chair to steady herself, and got up to
face him.

"That's why you're *really* here!" He was absolutely livid!
"You come over here, acting like you want to lock down

some sort of *friendship* we're supposed to have, telling me that you miss me, and then you start fishing around to see if you're still got a manager! One does not necessitate the other, Miss Clark. It doesn't say in our contract that we have to be friends, in order for me to be your manager. It's all nice and legal, so you can relax and stop trying to manipulate me. Your career is safe!"

"Trying to.... Wait, *what?*"

"Was I not clear? Go back and read your copy of our contract and show me, please, where it states that I will only manage your career, if you agree to hang out with me. How desperate and pathetic do you think I am?"

Shock became grief, then gave way to devastation, and all she could think about was finding some way to make Joel realize the kind of pain he had just inflicted on her! Deeply wounded, and acting purely on instinct, she flew into him, pounding him with her fists, wanting it to *hurt* him, wanting him to feel what she was feeling!

"Stop it!" Joel grabbed her wrists, and she twisted to free herself.

"*I said stop it!*" He pushed her arms behind her back and she fought harder to pull them out of his hands.

"I HATE YOU, JOEL!" Meredith screamed. "I HATE YOU!"

"Be still!" he ordered. He grabbed her fists again, and crushed her against his chest. "I mean it," he warned, when she continued to struggle.

He forced himself to lower his voice. "Meredith, listen to me. I want you to stop this, and I mean right now."

"Let me go!" She was crying bitterly. "I hate your guts, Joel Etheridge!"

"No, honey. You don't mean that, so stop saying it," Joel whispered, into her hair. "Calm down. Just breathe."

"I *do* mean it!"

"No, you don't. Stop it, little one," he commanded softly, gradually relaxing his hold.

She sagged against him. "Yes, I do," she whimpered.

"Be quiet." He guided her head onto his shoulder, and swayed her gently back and forth. "Just hush." He soothed her with a quiet, gentle, rocking motion, until she was silent.

Their storm rolled by, and now they just stood there and clung to each other desperately.

For all Joel knew, he would never be able to hold her like this again, but he was holding her now.

He pressed her closer, and felt himself dangerously verging on tears, when she lifted her arms and wrapped them around his neck, and laid her face against his, weak from too many emotions. She began shivering.

"I'm so sorry," she offered weakly, in a voice filled with shame.

"Let it go."

Meredith looked up at him, her face perilously close to his. "I'm so sorry I hit you. I don't know what's wrong with me. I don't hate you, Joel. I didn't mean it."

"Shhh. I know that." He pulled back to look down at her, and lifted her chin, tracing her lips with his thumb.

"Joel, it's not true." Her eyes were begging him to believe her. "I wasn't trying to manipulate you. You've never been just my manager."

Joel flinched. How much more of this could he take? If she was going to gently define for him the boundaries of their relationship, could he handle it? But ignorance could no longer be bliss for him. Regardless of the outcome, he had to know.

He dropped his eyes for a moment, and then swept them back up to meet hers. "What *am* I then, Merry?"

There was a long, charged silence.

"I thought I knew... until you left me last night. Joel..."
She dared to look into his eyes. "When you left me... when
I came here today... I wasn't thinking about my career. I
wouldn't *want* a career without you. Or anything else..."

She lost some of her bravery, and her voice trailed off
into uncertainty. She was venturing into an unexplored
place with Joel that frightened her. What if she went there
with him, and he left her again? She laid her head back on
his shoulder, and tightened her arms around his neck. "Joel,
what's happening to us?"

He let out a weighty sigh. "I don't know. But things are
changing. Promise me something."

Again, Meredith raised her face to his, and again, his
heart almost stopped.

"Promise me that whatever it is, if it frightens you, you
won't run away from it. Promise me you'll stay and help me
deal with it."

"*Me* stay?" Her wet eyes shimmered. "You're the one
who ran out on me and then, for an encore, sneaked back in
the middle of the night and dropped off your key."

Joel smiled down at her, and lightly brushed her chin
with a gentle fist. "Knock it off."

"I tried to, but you held my arms down."

They both laughed, mostly from weary relief.

Joel led Meredith over to the sofa. He dropped down
and pulled her close to sit beside him. He turned her wrists
up to see if he had held them too tightly.

"You didn't hurt me," she said softly.

He moved his thumbs around to massage her hands
and wrists, and looked up at her. "I need you to listen to *me*
now, Merry."

"Okay."

"Last night, you said you had to tell me something." A shadow crossed Meredith's face and Joel lightly squeezed her hands.

"No. You said you would listen." He was quiet but firm. "You wanted me to know something. I wouldn't stay to hear it, Merry, because I was afraid of what you might say."

"Afraid, why?" She watched him closely.

"I thought you were angry with me about that book deal, but when you said it wasn't about the book, I didn't know *what* to think. It began to sound like you had used the trip to think about asking to be released from our contract."

"And you reacted that strongly?" Meredith shifted herself to sit on her feet and grinned. "You must *really* want to be my manager."

Joel checked his response, then moved on. "The bottom line is that storming out was knee-jerk behavior. I yelled at myself all night about it."

"Why didn't you wake me up last night and yell at me? You do it so well." She reached for a lock of his hair and tugged at it gently.

"I didn't have the heart to. Stop that." He caught her hand and pulled it down, lacing his fingers into hers. "You were so wiped out. I sat down and just watched you sleep for a while."

He lifted her hand and laid it against his scruffy, unshaven cheek. "Did you know that you cry in your sleep?"

"Only when certain people blow up at me and slam out of my house."

Meredith yawned widely against her best efforts. "That's your fault," she added, when he grinned down at her.

He lifted his arm and laid it behind her, leaning dangerously close. Meredith's eyes took in his haggard, morning appearance, and she wondered if she would have to sit on her free hand to keep it out of his silver-streaked hair.

"Tell me something," he said. She looked away. "This question is coming, Merry, so you might as well look at me."

She met his eyes cautiously, and he could see her misgivings.

"Last night, when I wanted to know your decision about the book, you started to cry." His eyes explored her face carefully. "You knew you could just say that your decision was a no, and we'd be done with it, but you didn't. Instead, you started crying.   Why?   Talk to me."

Meredith bit her lip and stared at the floor.

"There's your key," she observed vaguely.

"I see it. You said last night that you had to tell me something. Tell me now."

"You're right, it wasn't about the book." She sighed.

Joel waited, but managed to prod her on with just a look.

"It's just that I don't know how to begin, and it'll be the hardest thing I've ever done. Telling *you*, I mean."

"Am I that difficult to confide in?"

"Only because I care so much about what you think of me. Forget managing me, Joel. You may not even want to *know* me anymore, after we talk."

"Merry, do you really think that anything you tell me could change what I think about you?"

She nodded miserably, a single tear escaping onto her cheek.

Joel was quiet for a moment, then let go of her hand. "Sit tight, Missy," he said, catching the tear with his fingertip and examining her soberly.

He got up, stopping to pick up his key and slip it into his pocket, then looked around for his cell phone. He waved an impatient hand through the air, and reached instead for the house phone, rapidly punching in numbers and looking back to see Meredith closing her eyes, and rubbing her sore temples.

"It's Joel, Delores. Did I wake you? Good. Listen, Dee, I'm not coming in at all today. Sorry about the short notice, but it can't be helped." He paused for her reply. "I can't think about that right now, but thanks for reminding me. Can you juggle?"

He laughed quietly at something his secretary said and replied, "Well, call him up and wave a dinner appointment under his nose. He'll bite on that, I promise you. Hand that other thing off to Marshall."

There was another brief pause. "Not tonight, no. Better try for tomorrow. I'm sorry about springing this on you, Dee, but I'll explain later. We'll talk. Thanks."

Joel hung up the phone and looked around. Meredith had gotten up, and was staring blankly out the front window. He stepped up behind her and pulled her back to lean against him, wrapping his arms around her.

Together, their eyes wandered over the Tennessee hills and autumn colors, each lost in thoughts that neither was bold enough to share.

"Feel like a drive?" Joel knew that hitting the road was an absolutely ridiculous idea, but he also knew Meredith.

She nodded, as he knew she would.

"A long one?"

She couldn't speak, but she managed another nod.

Joel turned her around to assess for himself if she was really up for it. "Neither of us have slept, and we're both exhausted. This wins for the dumbest idea I've ever had, but since I promised long ago to take you, and you accused me of reneging when it never worked out, I was thinking of Gatlinburg."

She gave him a glad smile. "We've done crazier things."

"That we have!" Joel gave her a silent interrogation with his eyes. "Are you fit to drive back now to your place?"

"I can manage."

"How about my picking you up in about an hour? We'll go in my car."

"Thank you, Joel." She wrapped her arms around him and gave him a squeeze.

"My pleasure, brat." He returned the squeeze, then held her at arms length. "I need you to understand how sorry I am about last evening and for getting so angry today."

He checked her protest by laying a finger on her lips. "And about what's happening with us..."

"Joel..." Meredith lifted his hand away and stopped him. "We'd better wait on anything else until we talk. You asked if I was afraid that it would change what you think of me. It's my greatest fear. It's *always* been my greatest fear."

He quietly let her finish.

"I know you'll say that won't happen, but it could. It might. It's why I've tried to keep so much personal distance between us over the years. Next to Father, you're the one who matters most."

She lifted his hand to her cheek and let her tears fall unchecked. "You promise *me* something."

"You can have my life," he said simply.

"Maybe it's the same thing," she answered, closing her eyes to guard against Joel's penetrating gaze. "Promise me..."

"What is it, little one?"

"Please don't walk out on me again. Don't leave me, Joel!" Her voice failed and she began to tremble.

"Come here." Joel took her back into his arms. "I'm so sorry, honey. I wasn't thinking, I was just reacting."

How could he have put her through this?

"I promise you, Merry. Open your eyes."

She obeyed reluctantly.

"I promise. Okay?"

She nodded.

"If I stand on my head, will you smile at me?" It was an old question he'd asked her many times before, right after one of their famous arguments that typically happened just before she was about to walk out on stage. It always worked, and even now, it made her laugh through her tears.

"We're gonna have to install some wipers on you," he quipped. He gave her cheek another soft brush with his thumb.

"Okay, you run home and grab a hot shower and do whatever else you need to do. I'll be there as soon as I call the office again and then get a quick shower, myself."

Joel paused to reassure himself again about her condition. "I'll bring a pillow and a blanket because I want you to sleep in the car."

He steered her out the door and into her Jeep. "You're not going to run off the road on the way back, are you?" He smiled, but he was being serious.

She made a face. "You do realize that it's pretty much walking distance?"

He reached in and pulled her seatbelt across her lap, their faces almost touching. Their eyes locked, and Meredith's heart almost beat her to death.

Joel bore his gaze into hers, and she knew he was trying to unnerve her on purpose.

"Meredith," he said huskily.

"Yes?" she breathed.

He brushed her cheek with his own, and she grabbed the wheel to steady herself, as his mouth met her ear with a whisper.

"Go get some shoes on."

Chapter Five

"Merry?" From a distance she could hear him calling her. She ran down the long, empty corridor toward the sound of his voice, trying every door, frantically searching everywhere, but in vain. His voice seemed to be coming from somewhere else, now. She whirled around in dismay, rows and rows of identical locked doors beckoning to her cruelly.

"Meredith!"

"Where *are* you, Joel?" Desperately, she tugged at every door. Suddenly, one flew open, and she stumbled into an inky black void, falling... falling...

"Joel!" She was caught up in his arms and her eyes flew open.

"I'm here! I'm right here, Merry." Joel lifted the armrest between them and pulled her closer. She looked at him as if in a daze, then around at the car, not understanding.

"I'm here. It was a dream." He brushed her hair back and stroked her brow. "You were dreaming. Everything's okay now."

Comprehension slowly filled her eyes.

"I couldn't find you," she explained in a weak voice.

This is my fault, Joel thought grimly, looking down at her with sad eyes. *This is because of the way I took off last night.*

Meredith stared around slowly, trying to orient herself. "Where..."

"We're almost there," he answered. "But I pulled over to wake you out of your dream, since it seemed to be more of a nightmare."

"Oh. Thank you." She smiled, a little embarrassed and moved over to roll down her window. "It was just..." She paused and smiled again. "I don't think I'll go into it."

"Don't," Joel agreed. "How are you holding up? Do you need anything?"

"If we could stop at that visitor's center on the way," she said, a little self-consciously, "a bathroom would be nice."

"I'm afraid not. You'll just have to go in the woods, like all the rest of God's creatures."

Joel gave a soft laugh at her bewildered expression, but sighed inwardly to himself. Meredith had something she felt she had to say to him, and, even though he was strangely reluctant to hear it, he was hoping to make today as easy for her as he could.

Although their banter was normally dry, he opted now for an openly ludicrous approach, designed to coax her into somehow enjoying any part of this day that she could.

"Hey!" He shot her a fleeting grin. "Where's my little sparring partner? Where is Sister Sarcasm? Come out and play with me."

She willingly took up his labored attempt at comedy, and scowled at his half-serious plea. "You want to play? I'll play *you* like an accordion, if you don't get me to a bathroom!"

Joel raised his brows, in villainous delight. "That would require some squeezing, my dear."

"Fine!" His efforts were paying off and Meredith actually responded with a bit of mock irritation. "Like a pawn shop tuba, then. *That* would require some blasting!"

"Yes! *There* she is!" Joel cheered her on, then stopped short and feigned wide-eyed surprise. "Why, Merry, do you play the tuba?"

"Shut up," she suggested.

"No really, this could be the next big thing. Maybe we can do something with this." He grinned impishly. "Think of it, 'Meredith Clark And Her Rapturous Tuba'. Or you know," he added, thoughtfully, "if the eschatology doesn't 'pan' out, we can always bill you as 'Sister Clark And Her Tribulation Tuba'. Pan out, see what I did there?"

He craned his neck in an attempt to see around Meredith, who was stubbornly donning a severe frown and shifting her seating position into something that felt a little more secure.

"What are you looking for, you crazy ol' coot?" she demanded, her eyes reflecting the effect of Joel's very bizarre brand of wit. "And did I mention that I need to go to the bathroom?"

"A phone," he informed her. "I lost my cell, and I need to get Delores to hit on this, while it's hot."

"I'm gonna hit on *you*, Mr. Etheridge, if you don't get me to a bathroom!"

Joel fixed his eyes on hers and leaned toward her suggestively, lifting his brows again like Casanova. "Is that a promise, Sister Clark?"

She patted her jacket pocket. "You come any closer, and I'll mace you."

"Wait, are you *kidding* me, right now?" He was absolutely astonished. "Seriously? You don't *really* have mace in there!"

"Find out!"

Joel maneuvered his Cadillac back onto the highway, pretending to be acutely offended and sending Meredith off into peals of laughter.

"Please, Joel, stop it!" she begged. "Just knock it off, until I can find a bathroom!"

"What bathroom?" He gave her a sharp sideways glance. "I don't recall agreeing to stop for any bathroom."

"If you don't stop, when we get to that visitor's center, I swear I'm gonna kick this door open and jump!"

"Fine," he relented. "But only because we can't very well have you bailing out of a moving vehicle. You might never play the tuba, again."

"PLEASE stop it!"

"And even if you did, it might never sound the same." He ignored her obvious distress and smirked wickedly. "We might have to change the marquee to 'Meredith Clark And Her Ruptured Tuba'."

"Maybe I *do* hate you!" Meredith rocked back and forth in urgency, completely at Joel's mercy.

His mercy stopped the car at the visitor's center.

It was a little before noon when they reached the mountain village of Gatlinburg. The sidewalks, usually jammed with herds of tourists, seemed almost bare.

"I guess weekdays are the best time to go just about anywhere," Meredith observed.

"Especially women's bathrooms," Joel replied. "On weekends, women go to the bathroom in packs. Or so I've been told." He got out and came around to open her door.

She crossed her arms and fixed him with a disapproving look. "Why don't we just stand outside here, until you get all the bathroom commentary out of your system?"

Joel locked the car and flashed her a grin. "Out of my *system*. That's pretty good. I approve your pun. And since you insist, why do women's bathrooms have those machines on the wall..."

Meredith glared at him. "Get off the stage!"

He gazed down at her with a baby's innocence and shrugged.

"Come on." She tugged at his sleeve and steered him toward a pancake house. "I want food."

They grabbed a corner booth, and a sweet-faced, matronly woman came over with menus and water.

"Good morning!" She stopped and consulted her watch. "Yep! Still morning." She smiled broadly at the sleepy, good-looking faces that returned her greeting. "I'm Gayle, I'll be taking care of you. Anything to drink?"

"Coffee," Joel and Meredith chimed, in unison.

"Real coffee," Joel added. "Black coffee. None of that fake stuff. And we'd like it in clean, hypodermic needles."

The waitress laughed pleasantly and ambled off.

Meredith butted Joel's shoulder with her own. "Why don't you sit across from me, and give yourself more room?"

"Am I bothering you?" He didn't look as if he cared.

"You're the bane of my existence."

"It is my destiny to perturb you," Joel announced solemnly, crossing his muscular arms, and butting her in retaliation. "Besides..." His eyes toyed with hers. "You love it."

She looked away and snorted.

"Oh, *that's* attractive!" he declared.

Meredith reached for the salt shaker, and tossed its contents harmlessly onto Joel's shirt.

The waitress returned with their coffee, and flipped open her pad, expectantly. The two looked at each other, and then down at their salty menus with guilty smiles.

"Do you need a few more minutes?" Their server's sharp eyes took in their flushed cheeks, and she hid an amused smile.

"Oh, no," Joel assured her. "We can do this, watch us. Let's see, this is a pancake house. How about... pancakes?"

"Brilliant." Meredith validated him with sarcasm.

"Good choice," Gayle agreed. "What kind?"

"A whole *house* of pancakes. So, why did I think you'd only have one kind?"

Meredith watched their server fall victim to Joel Etheridge's rare grin, which was always like the sun coming out. It wasn't so much that he never grinned but he was usually so stoic and stern, that when he did suddenly give way to a grin he was actually feeling, it lit up his handsome face and made his eyes all the more captivating. It disarmed their waitress now, and she obliging recited every variety of pancake on the menu.

They made their choices, and were left to sip their coffee alone in their corner. Meredith drowsily rested her head on Joel's shoulder and sighed in relief and contentment.

"Still sleepy?" His low voice throbbed up and down her spine.

She nodded silently and closed her tired eyes. It was so good to have her friend back.

She quickly and firmly squelched out the loud protests her heart was clamoring to make, regarding her choice of words.

I said friend and I meant friend, she insisted, mutely.

Oh yeah? Her heart countered back. *Well, if he's just a friend, how come he can't be out of your life for more than a few hours, without you completely falling apart?*

She shook herself impatiently and felt Joel's strong arm come around her.

"Cold?" he murmured.

"A little." She snuggled closer, and feigned an attempt at a nap.

Joel looked down at her beautiful face, glad that her eyes were closed, unable to discover the depths of passion in his own.

Dear God in Heaven, he breathed silently. *You alone know how much I love this woman. I know You have definite plans for both of our lives. I don't know if You intend for us to ever be anything more to each other than we are at this moment.*

Joel continued to rest his gaze on her unguarded face. *You're such a good Father to Your daughter, and I'm not sure if I'm someone You would even consider for her. I pray for Your perfect will, Father, but...* He laid his cheek against her hair. *I just want You to know that if I could be the one...* He blinked back the results of his desperate emotions. *I would be so honored. I would guard her with my life.*

After slowly climbing the narrow, winding mountain road, Joel pulled his car over into a parking area, and turned off the engine. He glanced over at Meredith, not missing the look of trepidation that clouded her eyes.

"Grotto Falls," he announced, trying to sound casual. "It's a slight uphill hike, but it's very short and easy, if you're up for it."

Meredith nodded, but continued to just sit there, making no preparation to get out of the car.

"Merry." He waited until she looked over at him. "I'm not making you do this."

"I know."

"Are you having second thoughts?" He reached over and caught her hand gently. "You've been through a lot, and this can wait, if it needs to. We can just go back down to the village for a bit, and then head on home."

"No, Joel." She had been looking down at their hands, but she met his eyes and gave him the faintest smile. "It's now or never. And never's not a choice, today."

"Are you sure, Missy?"

She nodded. "Your job is to not let me back out."

"Okay, but no Missy fits when I try to do my job."

"I make no promises."

Joel glanced ahead into the trees with a complex little smile. Finally, he reached back and pulled two windbreakers out of the back seat, before going around to open Meredith's door. He caught her hand and lifted her out, noting that her tense expression had returned.

"You're sure?"

She gave him another brief nod and took one of the jackets as Joel locked the car and pocketed his keys.

They began a steady ascent into the mountain forest. The air was thick with the smell of damp leaves and evergreens. Every now and then, some small, furry creature would scamper out of their way.

This and the warbling of unseen birds were the only sounds, although each was sure the other could hear the betraying beat of a telltale heart.

Gradually, they became aware of the watery music of Grotto Falls, and within minutes, it appeared to them; a breathtaking, wooded cathedral.

Joel took Meredith's hand and guided her carefully over the wet boulders to a sheltered nook behind the falls. They both stood there, acutely aware of the beauty of their surroundings, and of each other. Meredith couldn't hide the look of pure dread on her face, as she realized what all this was leading up to.

Joel noticed. He put his hand into the veil of cold water and brought it back, flicking icy little droplets at her face to tease her out of her dark thoughts.

"Knock it off," she objected, moving out of range and slipping on the loose rocks. She let out a small cry, and caught herself by slamming her hand against the jagged face of a large boulder.

"Merry!" Joel stepped hurriedly over the rocks and took her gently by the arm. "I'm sorry. I didn't mean for you to fall. I shouldn't have been horsing around. I'm so sorry."

He led her back to their place behind the waterfall, and slowly opened her injured hand. "I'm so sorry," he repeated softly. He caught more cold water in his hand, and let the soothing drops spill onto her burning palm.

Meredith stared up at him as if seeing him for the first time, as he reverently tended to her injury, shocked at the sudden revelation that both thrilled and frightened her. *I'm in love with him!*

The thought shook her, and she gasped out loud. He looked up quickly... too quickly for her to mask the truth in her eyes.

Joel immediately pulled her into his arms, claiming her lips with his own, urgently, and with all the force of pent up love suddenly released. Meredith slipped her fingers up into his hair, drawing him even closer.

It was several long moments before she was able to draw back from the kisses that threatened to consume her.

"Meredith..." Joel's eyes were on fire.

"Wait," she breathed, stepping back a little from his embrace. "Wait, don't say it, Joel. Not yet, not until we've talked. Please don't say it!"

Joel gathered her close again, and held her as if she were about to fade away, like the mists from the falls. Whatever her secrets were, he didn't want to know. "You don't have to tell me anything. Or just lie to me, I don't care."

"I can't do that."

"Merry!" He gripped her shoulders desperately, and she looked up at him, startled to find tears in his beautiful eyes. "Why do you have to test me, like this? Why do I have to wait and listen to something you've already said could hurt us, just so I can prove myself to you, when you're done?"

"No, that's not what I'm trying to do, Joel." She lifted her hand to stroke his face tenderly. "I'm not trying to test you. But I can't let you say things to me now, that you may end up wanting to take back. I couldn't bear that! Please, Joel. This is why we came here."

"If you're hell-bent on doing this, then I'm not waiting," he grated out harshly. "I love you, Meredith! I love you!"

Meredith let out a sob, and pushed away from him. "Joel, no! I didn't want you to say it, because I'll *die* when you have to take it back! It would have been better if I'd never heard you say it."

She sank down onto the rocks, unmindful of their wetness, and laid her head on her knees, her long drape of hair shielding her from the anguish on Joel's face.

He turned away, then stepped up to the falls and stood with his back to her, staring into the clear cascade of water, not even seeing it. Meredith raised her head, and watched him, loving him so much she could feel her heart crumbling under the weight of it.

Her eyes took in his perfect form, from his worn leather hiking boots, to his faded jeans and blue plaid flannel shirt, tucked in with the sleeves rolled halfway up, revealing a white thermal undershirt beneath.

She rested her gaze on his silvery brown curls, climbing down his neck, now dancing lightly with the breeze. She continued to appraise him hungrily, as if trying to brand this vision into her mind to take out later like a photograph, when she would no longer have him.

Her heart panicked and cried out to her. *Listen to him and lie! You heard him, he doesn't care. He'll let you get away with it, this time. Tell him anything you have to, but don't lose him!*

I could. Meredith considered it, deception seeming more and more like her friend. *I could just tell him what he wants to hear, and this nightmare would be over.*

"No, sweetheart." Father intervened, rescuing her from herself. "It wouldn't be over. You would only be delaying what you must one day face. Let Me help you with this."

Meredith slowly got up and made her way over to Joel's side. When he continued to stare blankly ahead, not seeming to notice her, she took his hand and cradled it in her own.

"Joel?" She sighed his name, and he turned his flaming eyes onto her face. She caught her breath at their intensity, and silently cried out for the help Father promised her.

"Come sit with me. Please," she added, as he hesitated.

He caught her chin with his free hand and lifted her face, wordlessly surveying her perfect mouth, her vulnerable, fascinating eyes, the color of a dark storm cloud, her beautiful skin. An untamed whip of her hair lashed against him in a burst of autumn wind.

"Take it back?" Joel echoed her words in a voice that laid his heart bare on Meredith's altar. "I *love* you! Do you think I have any choices left? Do you think if I hear something about you that I don't want to hear, I can just... take it back?"

"I don't know," she confessed in a small voice.

Her eyes begged for one more kiss, and Joel gave her what she wanted, over and over again.

"Come here," he said finally. He took her safely back over the rocks to the huge granite wall that supported the overhang above them. He sat down and leaned his back against it, lifting his arms to Meredith.

She sank into them, resting her back against his hard chest, laying her head on his shoulder and realizing, with a quiet sense of wonder, that she had always thought of Joel's shoulder as belonging to her.

Meredith sent up a silent prayer, reminding her Father that He said He would help her with this.

"Now," Joel's deep voice quietly rumbled in and out of her slight frame. "We're going to stay here until you tell me everything. Not because I need to know, but because you need to tell me."

"Father says I have to," she whispered.

"I thought He might have," Joel answered, absently raking his fingertips through her hair. "Talk to me, then. Let's just do this, okay?"

He picked up a windbreaker and spread it over them, holding her close beneath it.

Meredith closed her eyes and secured the fortress of his arms with her own. She took one deep breath and let it out in a shudder.

"Okay." She paused, then braced herself. "Let's just do this."

Chapter Six

Meredith had put this moment off for as long as she could, but here it was, demanding to be dealt with.

"Joel," she began, after a long silence, "haven't you ever wondered why I've never given my testimony at any concerts? Haven't you noticed the way I get a little vague, when a reporter asks about my family, like Robin did?"

"I've thought about it a lot," Joel admitted.

"But you never pushed me."

"No. Not until..." He hesitated then let it go, and Meredith picked it up.

"Not until this book deal. It's okay," she hurried to add. "You couldn't have realized how trapped I was feeling, and right now, you still don't. But you will."

She let a moment or two go by, while she and Joel listened to the soothing waters of Grotto Falls, she for courage and he, for sanity.

Meredith leaned her head back so that she look could up at his face. He gazed down at her and touched her chin with his fingertip, silently waiting.

"I sang one Christmas at a state hospital in Texas. Some of the patients were what they called catatonic. Some were in a vegetative state. I remember thinking what a blessing that could be, to just shut the mind off and be done with it. If that's what it's like, I mean. If it's not, can you imagine the hell of being trapped in your motionless body, with just your thoughts and your ugly memories, and you just have to lie there with them? You can't speak, you can't move. You can't get away."

Joel looked at her with a pained expression.

"I'm sorry. I don't know why I went there," Meredith sighed. "It's just what I remember feeling that night, and I guess I still think about it, sometimes."

Meredith stared back at the falls for so long, that Joel wondered if she was going to be able to get through this, after all.

She shook herself and began again. "Sometimes, people talk about skeletons in their closets... " She broke off with a little laugh, as he silently offered her the hem of a windbreaker to use as a handkerchief. "Oh, what a shocker, the girl's crying again!" She dabbed at her face.

Joel gave her a sad little smile and waited.

"Most people's skeletons are really just something uncomfortable, like an Uncle Bill who drank too much or a cousin who married a Nazi. But *my* skeleton..." She shifted around to completely face him.

"This is the part, Joel," she whispered.

He raised his eyes with misgiving, and she pressed her lips together, and watched him anxiously.

"My skeleton," she repeated, almost too softly to be heard, "is a *real* one... and would be fifteen years old next spring."

Joel could only stare at her, comprehension warring with disbelief. "Did you..." His mouth was dry. "Was it..."

Meredith nodded miserably, and dropped her head toward the ground in disgrace.

Again, there was no sound, other than the laughing waters that had no knowledge of the grief beneath their joyful curtain.

Joel watched Meredith wilt right in front of him. He automatically reached his hand to dry her tears, then checked himself.

"Meredith," His voice sounded strained and unnatural, even to himself. "I guess you *do* need to tell me everything. Start from the beginning. Are you able to do that?"

"I have to." She caught up the windbreaker and hid her face in it for a moment.

"Hang on," she quavered.

Joel closed his eyes and silently called on his God to help him with Meredith. He wanted to pull her into his arms and order her to shut up, to stop destroying everything they had only moments before found in each other.

He loved her more than his very life, but dear God, he was so angry with her right now! Not because she had... he could scarcely bring himself to form the words... had an abortion, but because, without knowing it, she was breaking into a box he had spent years closing and locking.

She had no way of knowing the ripple effect that her confession today was going to have, but she was right. This had to happen, and he couldn't stop it.

Meredith lifted her troubled, tear-stained face from the windbreaker. "I got mascara on it." She held the jacket up for Joel to see. He took it from her and laid it down, waiting in agony for her to continue and just be done with this.

She wrapped her arms around her knees, and began to rock gently back and forth, without realizing it, like a distressed, little girl.

"I know you wonder every year why I don't go home to my family for the holidays. You've asked about it, and I've always managed to avoid getting into it. I've accepted holiday bookings against your advice. Pastors always call me unselfish and sacrificing, but I wonder what they would call me, if they knew that the only reason I was there, under the guise of ministry, was to save my own face. I used those bookings to keep from having to admit that I didn't have a family to go home to."

Meredith interrupted herself and leveled her direct, honest eyes at Joel.

"I'm going to offer you an out today, Joel. When you agreed to manage me... and later came to love me... you had no idea I was bringing so much baggage with me. If you had, you would have made difference choices, I'm sure of that."

Joel shook his head slowly, and Meredith laid a compassionate hand on his knee. Her voice was calm and strangely soothing. "We'll talk about that later."

Joel shook his head again, and Meredith carried on as if she hadn't seen.

"I've been a Christian for about fourteen years. I've never had to revisit my past with Father, since He's always been there. We rarely speak of it, and when we do, some sort of healing always comes out of it. I just wish I'd known Him before everything happened."

Her voice faded and, for a moment, the tumbling waters had their say. She straightened up, as if having received strength from their words.

"You know that I lost my mother when I was twelve."

Joel laid his hand on the small one caressing his knee and nodded.

"She knew Father. She was a beautiful lady. She had a pretty voice. I loved to hear her sing, and sometimes we would sing together and do harmonies. Mom left me her bible when she died. I kept it under my bed. I still do. Back then, no matter where I went, even if it was just to spend a night at a friend's house, I took it with me. It was like having her with me. I never knew my dad. Mom said he was killed in a boating accident, just before I was born. She said

I look like him, but I don't have any pictures, so I don't know. She said I got my love of fishing from my dad."

Joel responded to her sorrowful smile with his own.

"Anyway," she went on, "after my mom died, I had to move in with her sister, who is my Aunt Phyllis and my Uncle Don. Neither of them ever went to church, or anything like that, but they did go to a lot of parties.

"Uncle Don owned an insurance agency, and Aunt Phyllis was in real estate, so they did very well, as far as money goes. They were both gone a lot, which was fine with me, and when they *were* at home, it seemed like all they did was drink and fight. Uncle Don was something of a womanizer, and Aunt Phyllis had decided to fight fire with fire, I guess.

"I never was sure why they took me in. It's not like I had some big inheritance, or anything. In fact, Mom's house and most of her furniture was sold to square her debts away. I have what few pieces were left. I could never figure out their motive. I mean, once I moved in, they all but forgot I was there. I lived there for four years, and, until the end, I hardly ever crossed their paths, especially when things got ugly. And things got really ugly one night."

Joel rubbed her fingers tenderly and gave her the time she needed to begin again. She stared at the ground, as if watching something unfold there.

"I wish I could just say 'the end' now and be done." She smiled such a pitiful little smile, that it was all Joel could do to allow her to continue, but he knew she had to finish, if only for herself. She needed to say things out loud.

Meredith silently urged herself to get on with it. "One night, Aunt Phyllis and Uncle Don came home from one of their parties. I was surprised, because it wasn't that late, about eleven-thirty. I could tell that they must have gotten into a fight and left early, because they got right back into it, as soon as they came in. Aunt Phyllis was screaming at Uncle Don about some woman named Joyce, or something like that. She made it sound like she had walked in on them making out. I could tell they were both pretty much lit.

"Anyway, they yelled and smashed up a few things, and then one of them slammed out and took off in the car. I got back into bed and chalked it off to the booze. I tried to go back to sleep, and I must have at least dozed off because..."

She didn't know she was squeezing Joel's fingers so hard. "Because I didn't hear Uncle Don, when he came into my room."

Joel drew in his breath, as if she'd just kicked him in the gut. "Don't."

"No, listen." She reached for Joel's other hand and brought them up to her heart.

"Joel, he didn't, okay? I hit him with the lamp, hard! It either knocked him out, or he passed out. I don't know. I got dressed and threw as much of my stuff as I could into a duffel bag. I got some cash out of the desk in Uncle Don's study, and I took off."

Meredith rested her eyes lovingly on Joel's distressed face. "He didn't."

"Okay," he said faintly, securing their fingers together.

"I was only sixteen. There's no point in wading through the muck of the following years, as far as how I survived, where I stayed, that sort of thing. Muck is the word for it, but I got by.

"When I was eighteen, I fell in with some people I knew I had no business running with. I got a job singing at a club in Louisiana. New Orleans. You might wonder how a kid from Missouri ended up in a bar, in New Orleans."

She smiled bitterly. "The people I was hanging out with didn't exactly try to shelter me. Anyway, I wound up working there. A lot of scum found their way into this club, Joel.

"I had been singing there for about four months, when I was approached by a man who wanted to know what I was doing singing in clubs, when I could be recording. I don't know if every eighteen-year-old is as gullible as I was, but I bought right into that.

"This guy... his name is Cagle Lawrence, like it matters. Well... it might, later on, but... let me finish this part first."

She stopped and gave Joel's fingers a little tug to make him look at her. "How are we doing?" she asked with a cautious look, searching for any change in his eyes.

"I'm okay." He brought her hand up to his lips. "You?"

She nodded and looked at him tenderly for a moment, before nudging herself forward.

"Cagle started practically living at the club. He pretty well zeroed in on me, and the gifts started pouring in... clothes, perfume, that sort of thing. My stupid little head was turned. He seemed to have a lot of money, and women were almost knocking each other over to get to him, so you can imagine how flattered I was, to have all his attention focused on me.

"After a couple of months, he asked me if I'd ever done any modeling. I just laughed at him, but he kept saying I could do it. He arranged a photo shoot with a friend of his. Just head shots, and I have to admit, it was pretty exciting.

"He came to the club raving over the results and told me that he had some important people lined up, who were considering me for a full lay-out in a cruise line ad. I balked at first, because this meant swimsuit photos, but Cagle chipped away at what he called my puritanical values. When he told me what these people were prepared to pay me, I was stunned. I mean, here I was, all alone in a scary place like New Orleans, living upstairs over a fish market, and not even sure I could afford *that*. I just told all my inhibitions to take a hike, and agreed to do it.

"While all this was going on, Cagle was working overtime to get me to fall for him. He took me to the finest restaurants, hung jewelry on me like a Christmas tree, and declared his love for me about every hour. It wasn't long, before I completely abandoned what little morals I had left, and moved in with him."

Meredith reached up and stroked Joel's face. "I'm so sorry, Joel, for what I'm about to say. For both our sakes, I'm just going to skim the surface, but it's still going to be bad. I can't change that. Okay?"

He nodded, his eyes clouded and full of uneasiness. "But stop, Merry, if it gets to be too much."

She traced the line of his cheek with one finger and marveled at the intensity of her feelings for this man. "Joel," she whispered. "Would you... can I have a hug?"

He gathered her up immediately and laid his kiss on her forehead. She closed her eyes and rested there for another precious moment. Who knew, after today, if he would ever want to hold her again? They sheltered there together, each wishing it could last forever. Finally, she sat up straight, determined to finish.

"Home stretch!" It was a pathetic little attempt at lightness. "Here goes... well, everything, I guess."

Joel gave her a supportive little wink. "You're okay, little one. Take your time."

She nodded and breathed in deeply. "Okay, well... I moved in with Cagle. There were drugs there, Joel. Lots of drugs. It's not something I ever messed with, but still, they were there. Cagle... well, it was something he and his friends got into. His friends, that's another thing. Strange people, coming and going at all hours. They were just creepy!

"I always knew something wrong was going on there. I mean, *besides* the drugs, but I never did find out what it was. I tried asking Cagle, but he just laughed at me and when he got enough of my questions, he'd yell at me to shut up and mind my own business.

"That summer, just before I turned nineteen, I started getting really sick. For weeks, I kept throwing up and finally, I went to a doctor and found out I was... pregnant...."

Meredith closed her eyes and winced.

Joel saw her face go deadly white, and sat up in alarm.

"Merry!" He pulled her close.

"Just a minute." She fought to regain her composure. "Just wait."

"Let's just stop. I mean it, let's just stop."

"No, please don't make me. I'm too close to finishing."

Joel could see that she was breathing in short, sporadic jerks. "Then take a moment to calm down," he ordered, giving her the slightest little shake to make her listen to him.

She did take a few moments and then waved a hand through the air. "I'm good," she said.

He eyed her sharply.

"I'm good, Joel." The ghost of a smile tried to appear. "Let me just finish."

He loosened his grip on her and moved back, leaning against the wall and reaching out for her again. She crept close, but knelt in front of him, taking his hands.

"I have to face you for this," she told him. "I just want to be done. When I found out I was pregnant, I was... well, I guess I thought a baby would make things better between Cagle and me. I thought once he got used to the idea, he might even... well, I don't know what I thought. I finally got up the nerve to tell him. Joel..."

She was looking at the rock wall behind him and speaking in a far-away voice. "He just went ballistic! He started trashing the apartment, and calling me names, and saying it wasn't his, and... hitting me, pretty hard..."

She was still staring past him and didn't see the severe set of Joel's jaw, the clenched muscle that began to move close to his mouth or the hot scarlet that rushed to his angry face.

"It was a bad fight," she continued. "He threatened me with all sorts of... anyway, the first week in September, when I was eight weeks pregnant, he took me to this place and made me..." She burst into hot tears. "It was my *birthday*, Joel!"

Joel sprang to his feet and dragged Meredith up and into his arms. "That's it!"

He wrapped himself around her as if to shield her from the world and covered her flushed, tear-soaked face with his kisses. "That's the end. I mean it, you're done."

They stood that way for many long moments, Joel lifting wet tendrils of hair from her face, and murmuring soft things into her ear. Meredith anchored into his harbor and allowed herself to be loved by Father and Joel.

After a while, the approaching darkness and the cool autumn chill began to invade their haven. He picked up one of the windbreakers and helped Meredith into it.

"Let's get you home."

They made their way down the mountain trail and to the car, without speaking. Joel opened Meredith's door and fully reclined the car seat, insisting that she try to sleep, since she refused anything to eat.

It was after ten o' clock, by the time he got her home. He stopped the car in front of her house, and sat watching her sleep for several minutes.

She had unwittingly opened up the door to a secret, dark room inside of Joel that he desperately wanted to board up again. It wasn't that he had deliberately planned to keep his own secrets from Meredith. It was just that he couldn't bear the pain of having his old wound exposed.

He drew in a deep breath and decided. He would tell her. It was a risk... a big one. But she had taken a risk, herself. Besides, telling her might help her see that not only did he not judge her, but that he understood. When they got inside, he would tell her.

He studied her beautiful face in the moonlight. She was wasted! He hated to wake her up, but the sooner she got to bed, the better.

"Merry..." Joel pulled up the armrest and leaned over to touch her hand. She groaned and slowly opened her eyes.

"Wake up, baby. We're here." He leaned across her to release her seatbelt and raised the car seat back up, before taking her hand again. "Are you alright, Merry?"

She blinked heavily and tried to focus. "I'm... yes."

Joel came around and helped her out of the car. He guided her onto the porch and used his key in the door. He stopped just inside, and Meredith questioned him with her eyes.

"I wanted to talk to you about something," he said, obviously conflicted. "But you need to go to bed, Merry. You're almost asleep on your feet." He seemed to second guess himself, then made a move closer to the door.

"Wait." She stepped up to him and reached for his hands.

"Joel, I said I wanted to offer you an out..."

"Forget it." He cut her off.

"Wait, Joel..."

"Shut up."

"But you didn't know..."

"The last time we were both tired and upset, which, believe it or not, was only this morning, we let things get way out of hand!" Joel set his chin in a way that warned Meredith not to push this. "Let's not do that again, tonight."

"But, Joel..."

"I said NO! You're not LISTENING!"

"Don't yell at me."

"Come here, sweetheart." He immediately relented and brought her close. "Was I yelling? I'm sorry. You just keep on, sometimes, and won't stop. I'm sorry, little one."

He tipped her head back and kissed her softly, then let his eyes travel the beautiful lines of her face. "We're both just wiped out. I'm sorry I yelled. I love you."

She gave him a forgiving smile, and slipped her arms around his waist. "I did it," she breathed. "I got through it!"

"Yes, you did." Joel wondered if this was his moment.

A look of anxiety washed over her face and stopped him. "Are you sure you don't feel differently toward me?"

"I just told you I love you, silly girl. Do I have to put it in the paper?"

She kissed his neck and rested on his shoulder.

Joel closed his eyes and stroked her hair, still struggling. "Maybe we *do* need to talk though, if you're not too tired."

Suddenly, Meredith covered her mouth with her hands, her eyes filled with horror. "No!" she cried out, hoarsely.

He stepped back and stared at her.

"How stupid am I, to just forget? I was going to tell you this today, but I wanted to finish the main part first and come back to it. I can't believe I didn't tell you!"

"Tell me now." He was clearly confused.

"The reason I so was weird at the airport, and so messed up last night, Joel, was because when I had my layover in Dallas, I... saw Cagle Lawrence!"

"You what?"

She shook her head, still unable to believe it, herself. "He tried to stop me and asked me something about living in Nashville, and I just said I was in a hurry, and took off."

"Do you think he knows that you live here?" Joel swept his hand to indicate her house.

Again, Meredith shook her head. "I don't see how he could."

Joel studied her with a sober expression, as thoughts rushed around in his head, colliding with one another. How likely a coincidence was it that Cagle Lawrence just happened to be in the DFW airport the very minute that Meredith Clark, of all people, walked by?

"What is it?" Meredith noted his drawn features, and touched his brow with her fingertips.

Joel reeled himself in and forced himself to relax. "Nothing, sweetie. Just taking it all in."

"It's a lot to *take* in," she admitted. "I dumped a load on you."

She let out a deep breath. "I've tried hard to forgive him, Joel, since becoming a believer. I try not to hate him. But, God help me, I would hate *any* man who would make a woman get an abortion or even just offer to pay for one! I *mean* it!" Her face took on a severity Joel had never seen there before.

He felt an icy chill rush over him. He had to get out of here.

"Meredith..." He pulled her to him and gave her a swift hug. "I want you to go right up to bed. No TV, no laptop. Get some sleep." He managed a smile and ruffled her hair.

"You're leaving?"

"Yes. I need to get some sleep, too."

"But I thought... okay," she finished faintly.

Joel gave a her a long look then laid a tender kiss on her lips.

"Goodnight, little one. We'll talk tomorrow."

He let himself out, almost running to his car.

"Dear God," he rasped, slamming the car door and laying his head back. "You heard what she said. I'm going to lose her. When she tells me she hates me this time, she *will* mean it."

Chapter Seven

A low, steady drone gradually invaded Meredith's deep, cozy slumber. She slowly became aware of a light pressure on her stomach. The drone became a roar. She struggled to open her heavy lids, and pulled the quilt from around her face.

"Hook!"

Hook bestowed a benign, almost regal expression on her, and continued to hum gently.

"Come here, baby boy." Meredith reached down and tugged her cozy, gray buddy closer. "I've missed you, Mister Hooks," she cooed, pulling her fingers through his smoky, mink-soft hair.

Hook pressed his head against her caressing hand. No amount of affection was ever enough, and it was his opinion that his owner had a lot of catching up to do.

Meredith sat up and gathered the big cat into her arms, laughing at the intensity of his purr, and his antics to encourage her affection.

"You're my sweetie." She cradled him lovingly, and a little jolt surged through her, as her eyes discovered Joel's windbreaker laying across the foot of her bed. A tinge of color flooded her cheeks, and her heart gave a lurch, causing her pulse to quicken.

"Hook," she breathed in hushed wonder. "Joel *loves* me! Even after I told him everything, he still says he loves me!"

A swirl of memories danced by to the same tune that carried the leaves, coupled with the wind, past her window. Meredith reached out with her heart, and caught them.

She felt Joel's arms, safe while dangerous, tasted his lips, catering yet hungry, searched his eyes, guarded but defenseless. She was drifting in the overwhelming flood of her love for him.

"My heart's a goner, Hook," she confided, setting her pet to one side, and rolling over onto her pillow. "I'm drowning." Out of nowhere, she suddenly thought of the unusual song she'd penned, only days before.

"Drowning in *The Overflow*," she added, sleepily, then quickly changed her mind, as she remembered what the overflow really was. She didn't want that. "Joel rescued me from drowning." She liked that thought better.

Meredith snuggled back into the drowsiness that was returning to engulf her.

"I love him too, Hook," she whispered. "I haven't said it yet... but I will. I love him so much."

She drifted away to find him in her dreams.

Joel stepped out of the elevator, and made his way into his suite of offices, his face grim and forbidding. His entrance was witnessed with alarm, by a petite woman in her mid-fifties, surrounded by computers, phones, paper work, and pictures of grandchildren.

She raised her eyebrows, as she took in the bleak, weary countenance of a man who clearly had not slept all night.

"Delores!" Joel tossed his coat and briefcase onto a sofa and focused his tired eyes on his secretary.

"Wait." She hurriedly got up from her desk and headed over to the coffee maker. "Just hang on, you need this." She came back to him with a large mug of black coffee in her hands.

Joel smiled gratefully and sank down beside his coat, taking the cup she gave him. "Thanks, Dee," he offered, letting the aromatic steam waft up to his drawn face.

Delores pulled her desk chair over and sat down to face her boss. "Joel, what is it?" She accepted his silence only for a moment, then asked hesitantly, "Is this about you and Meredith?"

He looked up quickly, and read discernment in her face. "You know?" he asked, in mild surprise.

She smiled perceptively and nodded. "I've always known. Doug and I pray for both of you every morning, before we leave the house."

Joel stared into his coffee and let out a deep sigh. "Have I been that obvious?"

"Not to the casual observer."

"Well, Dee," he returned, a faint smile appearing as he sipped his coffee. "You're *anything* but a casual observer."

He combed his fingers through an unkempt mass of curls and closed his eyes, as he settled back into the sofa and rested his feet on the large table in front of him. "I guess I'd better explain about yesterday."

Delores eyed him carefully, before getting up and walking over to her desk. "Let me check first and see if any of the interns are out there."

"Oh, they're out there, alright. I think I may have hurt a few feelings on the way in." Joel opened his eyes and caught his secretary's broad grin.

"And probably broke a few hearts in the process," she declared, picking up the phone and pressing a button.

"Lynn? Or wait, is it Donna?" She paused. "Oh, sorry, Donna. Listen, honey, I'm leaving the machine on for all incoming calls. I want you girls to catch all the inner-office stuff but this office is off-limits until I let you know, okay?" She glanced down at her watch, listening to the intern's question. "No one, not even Marshall. I'll call you in a few minutes."

She laid the receiver down and shook her head at some fleeting thought, then reclaimed her chair and examined Joel's troubled face. "So, yesterday was about Meredith," she opened, simply.

He nodded, lifting himself up to lean forward and rest his coffee on a coaster. "It sounded like you knew that yesterday, when I called you."

"I did," Dee admitted. "I've been watching things come to a head between you two over the past few days. I guess I hoped that yesterday might turn out to be the day that every dog has, if you'll pardon the expression."

"If we're going to start flinging around clichés, Dee, maybe 'what goes around, comes around' would be more fitting," Joel commented quietly, his features revealing a painful surge of emotion. He continued to meet her eyes, as if trying to convey an unspoken message.

"What goes around..." She repeated his words slowly, confusion knitting her brow, then finally giving way to dismay, as she correctly read his tormented face. "Oh, Joel!"

He dropped his gaze and flushed.

She leaned forward intently. "Does Meredith know, then? Did she find out on her own, or did you tell her?"

He shook his head. "She doesn't know."

"But you said 'what goes around'. That *is* what you're talking about, right?"

"Yes."

Her eyes widened in horror. "You don't mean that it's Merry who... had an abortion." She choked on the ugly word, and Joel silently nodded. "Oh, dear God in Heaven," she breathed. "That poor little thing!"

"It's complicated, Dee," Joel began, his tired mind threatening to wander off without him. "It was a long time ago, before she became a Christian. She just turned nineteen, that day, in fact, and this creep she was involved with made her do it. She was afraid of him."

"Poor baby!" Delores's eyes were bright with unshed tears. "And *he* certainly sounds like a big time loser!"

"Cagle Lawrence!" Joel spat out the name, then laughed bitterly. "You know what's so ironic, Dee?" He leaned back again and crossed his arms. "You remember Meredith's flight in from Denver on Tuesday? She had a layover in Dallas. Who do you think, after all these years, she runs right into?"

"No way!"

"Yes! Cagle Lawrence!" Joel leaped up from the sofa and paced restlessly around the office. Delores sat still and tried to absorb everything he was telling her.

He turned and looked at her desperately. "This whole thing started with that Anchor magazine offer. The idea of putting Merry's life into print sent her into a tailspin. She was literally circling the drain, and I couldn't see it. I thought she was just being Meredith. Dear God, I wish I'd never heard of Anchor magazine!"

He grabbed the back of his neck and manipulated a sore muscle. "Merry read a scripture that morning, before the interview, that she felt was telling her that she should at least be willing to go through with it but, for reasons I didn't yet understand, she was miserable about it.

"She asked me not to mention it again, until she got back from Denver. She wanted to use that time to pray about it. Can you imagine what it must have been like for her to walk through the DFW airport and run smack into what she has spent years running *away* from? *Now*, of all times, when she was already feeling cornered?"

Delores looked vacantly at him and shook her head. "That poor little thing," she repeated brokenly, her own mother's heart almost able to imagine the grief that Meredith had been carrying for so many years.

Joel gazed out the window at the city, perfectly still and motionless. No one walking in would have guessed him to be the battlefield he was. His secretary watched him prayerfully, her concern for him mounting. After a bit, she ventured over and joined him at his post.

"You said that Meredith doesn't know about your... situation." She spoke with caution.

"She doesn't," he replied. "You know, Dee..." He turned to face her. "I was all ready to tell her. I was!"

He shook his head and his smile was filled with remorse. "Can you believe it? She and I drove all the way to Gatlinburg yesterday. She loves that place so much and, since she was determined to tell me everything, I was equally determined to make it as pleasant, for lack of a better word, as I could for her.

"I even kept ribbing her, like some sort of lame court jester, just to get her to relax and she seemed to, for a bit. Then we hiked up to this waterfall and it took some time, but she was finally able to get through it. Dee..."

Joel's eyes reflected his sadness. "It was so hard for her, but she toughed it out. When we got back to her house, I intended to tell her about... well, anyway, I thought it would help, if she knew that I was the last person who was going to judge her. But then she said..."

He hung his head and leaned against the windowsill.

"What did she say?" Dee gently prompted.

"That she would hate... she said *hate*... any man who would force a woman to have an abortion, or even just offer to *pay* for one." Joel turned away from the window and his secretary's own eyes filled up at the sight of his tears.

"Oh, Joel!" She laid a consoling hand on his arm. "You have to know she wouldn't mean *you*." She made him look at her. "You have to remember what she's been through the past few days. She was exhausted, Joel, and emotionally strung out. There's no way she would include you in that, if she knew. She didn't mean it."

"Oh she means it, alright!" Joel made his way back to the sofa, and fell into it heavily. "You didn't see her face. She means it."

He looked up at her helplessly. "Who would have thought last week, when I was reminding Meredith about her interview and fussing at her about a stupid plane ticket, that something as routine as a book deal would go off in our faces, like a bomb? And then, on top of that, she has to go and run into that guy! I'd like a shot at running into him, myself," he added darkly.

"Did she say what happened, when she ran into him? Did he approach her?"

"He asked her about living in Nashville, so apparently, he knows she's here, but most of the general public knows that, so I guess I shouldn't read too much into it." Joel crossed his arms and looked at her solemnly. "On the other hand, maybe that's exactly what I should be doing. Part of me reasons that there's no way he could have deliberately set up running into her in Dallas and part of me wonders if he's stalking her."

"Joel!" Delores turned pale and lifted her hand to her face. "Do you really think he could be?"

He let out a breath of exhaustion. "Oh, I don't know, Dee. I'm sure I'm reaching. But then again, Meredith is a celebrity, and her public comings and goings are pretty much plastered over all her fan clubs' social media pages. It might not be too hard to anticipate flight patterns to and from Nashville to Denver."

He removed his feet from the coffee table, and raised himself into a sitting position. "Never mind me, Dee. I'm sure I'm making absolutely no sense, right now. I'm pretty much talking in my sleep."

Delores returned to her desk and regarded him with worried eyes. "What are you going to do?"

He pulled himself up and gathered his coat and briefcase from the sofa. "Pray, I guess," he answered in a hollow voice. "The same thing I've been doing all night."

He opened the door to his private office. "That's about all I can do, at this point, right?" He hesitated. "Thank you, Dee, for listening to all this. It helped."

She smiled sadly and waved him away, still sorting through what she'd been told.

A few minutes later, Joel's labored blend of repentance and petition was interrupted by the sharp buzz of the intercom.

"Joel?" Dee's voice sounded uncertain. "You have a call. It's Meredith."

"Okay. Thanks." Joel looked at the phone, as if unsure of what do to with it. He sent up a silent prayer and took the receiver with an unsteady hand.

"Hi there." He closed his eyes and dared his voice to waver.

"Hi, yourself." Meredith's low, beautiful response thrilled him beyond belief. "Am I interrupting?"

"Never," Joel murmured. "You sound rested. Did you sleep good?"

"I don't even remember lying down, so I guess I must have passed out. Hook woke me up this morning, but I went back under for a little longer."

"You needed it. In fact, you should just sleep all day."

"I can't. Something stinks in my kitchen, and I have to find it. It's probably in the fridge," she added, with a grimace on her face that Joel could see.

He laughed softly and stroked the receiver with one finger. "Silly girl. When's the last time you cleaned it?"

"The fridge?" Meredith sounded surprised. Joel smiled at her muffled giggle. "Well, I've never actually..."

"Merry!"

"Well, Joel, I don't *do* fridges. Fridges or windows. How do you not *know* that? Have we just met?"

"You're hopeless," he breathed, sending tiny little shivers down her spine. "But at least you sound like you feel better. You sound like something else, too."

"Oh yeah? What's that?"

"Oh, I don't know." He somehow managed to seem at ease, and comfortable. "Maybe a little shy, perhaps. Tell me, sweet Merry, what could you possibly have to feel shy about, this morning?"

"I have no clue what you're talking about!" Meredith insisted, her cheeks flushed with color.

"Why, Sister Clark," he grinned. "Are you blushing?"

"How did you... no, I am not!"

Joel chuckled at her sputtering denial. "You have the guilty tremor in your voice of a woman who's been soundly kissed and then re-kissed."

"I do not! I'm coming down with something!"

"Lies, all lies," he persisted. "It's all very well for you to hide behind that phone, Missy, but if I just dropped by to see for myself, what would I discover, besides a thick sludge oozing out the door of your refrigerator?"

Meredith laughed her old laugh and Joel's taut features smoothed into relief. "I can't today, though," he sighed with regret.

"Really, no?" Her disappointment was obvious. "Not at all?"

"I'm playing catch up from yesterday, little one, and I have a dinner appointment at six."

"Not even for lunch?"

"You'll excuse me, please, if I point out that lunch in *your* kitchen sounds a bit unappetizing, to say the least."

"Yeah, well when have you *ever* said the least?" Meredith was in a bantering mood and Joel wanted so badly to play hooky again today.

He reached into his top drawer and pulled out one of her promo pictures. His eyes melted as his fingers traced her lovely face.

"Tell you what. I'm off to a late start, so lunch couldn't happen before two-ish, if even then. Call me, okay?"

"Maybe I will, maybe I won't." She tried for petulance.

"Cut it out," he growled playfully. "You want a smacking?"

"For lunch? Is that anything like a mackerel?"

Joel grinned. Her happy lilt was like a tonic to him.

Meredith barreled ahead, her heart light and careless. "Because I had one of those last Christmas, and I found it to be rather yukky!"

Joel brushed her photo with a kiss and placed it back in the drawer. "Last Christmas, huh? That's probably what's stinking up your kitchen, then."

"Shut up, you," she advised.

"Merry?" He whispered her name, making her go limp.

"Hmm?"

"I love you. Call me around one."

"I will. 'Bye."

"'Bye, sweetheart."

Joel held the receiver to his chest for a moment, before returning it to its base. He laid his head down on his desk and let the memory of Meredith in his arms wash over him.

"Dear God," he prayed anxiously, "I don't want to keep things from her. As far as I'm concerned, that's the same thing as lying, and I don't want to start this phase of our relationship out like that, but telling her now would only hurt her, and I just can't bring myself to do that.

"I admit it, God, my fear of losing her is what's really distressing to me. You heard what she said. But it's not just losing her. I don't want to hurt her. Please protect her heart, Father. Please show me what to do about this."

He sighed and silently rebuked himself for not telling Meredith everything last night, when there was a tenderness between them that might have made it possible for her to forgive him.

Joel sat up and rested his chin on his hands and let himself look into a forbidden place in the back of his mind that he had spent years avoiding. His eyes misted over, as muted angry voices from his past began to intrude and attack him.

He hurried to retreat, as he always did, unable to bear the pain that always felt fresh, that was always ready to stab at him with a vicious glee. Joel had long ago decided that he deserved its bitter sting. Whenever it came, he was again in that moment, and time had done nothing to heal anything.

He silently waited, hoping that God would speak to him. He tried to quiet his spirit and listen, even though he knew that when it was time to lay down your will and face your fears, listening could be a scary thing.

Joel's door opened suddenly, and Delores practically fell through it, making her way to his desk, in a highly agitated state. Joel jumped up, as his startled eyes took in her flushed face and panicked expression.

"Dee, what is it? What's the *matter* with you?"

She simply hurled a white piece of paper at him. He recognized the fluttering scrap as a business card and bent down to retrieve it, turning it over as he stood up.

His jaw rippled and his blood began a slow boil, as he stared at the name embossed on the front: Cagle Lawrence.

Chapter Eight

"He's out there?" Joel demanded, in disbelief.

Dee nodded wildly, unable to speak.

"Better pray with me." Joel came around his desk and caught his secretary's hands in a firm grip.

"Father..." His voice was raw with emotion. "If You don't help me now, I may just beat this man within an inch of his miserable life, and right now, I wouldn't care if I killed him! I'm sorry God, but there it is. I'm so angry, I can't see straight.

"I need Your help. I need You, Holy Spirit, to please control me. You know fully well that I'm a sinful enough creature, as it is, and I admit I'm absolutely carnal here, in this moment. All I can think about is busting his face for him!

"I'm sorry, Lord Jesus, but I can't make a bunch of phony confessions right now, just because they sound spiritual. I can't tell You that I don't hate this man, because I do. All I can do is admit it and ask You to forgive me, and to help me. I need you, Father."

Joel lifted his sleep-starved eyes to look at Delores, with the hint of combat lurking in them.

"What did he say, Dee?"

"That he's not leaving here, until you agree to see him."

He ran a restless hand through his hair and let out a mumbled oath.

"I'm sorry, Dee," he apologized. "I still wrestle with my tongue, sometimes."

"Believe me, I understand!"

Joel sat down at his desk and eyed her soberly over the tips of his compressed fingers. "Well... I guess we'd better not keep Mr. Lawrence waiting."

Delores moved reluctantly to the door, then turned around when he asked her to wait.

"Better hold all calls."

"Even... "

"Especially Meredith. And Dee, if things drag on... well, she's supposed to call at one about lunch. If we're still at it, will you tell her that I'm sorry and that I'll call her the minute I'm free? But that's all, don't say anything else."

She nodded, her hand on the doorknob. "Ready?"

"No. But let him in, anyway."

Delores opened the door and stood in the entrance. "Mr. Lawrence, Mr. Etheridge will see you now."

She stood aside and admitted a blonde, bearded man, about Joel's age but, as Delores noted, when Joel rose from his chair, not nearly as tall or as muscular.

Clearly not Joel's equal, she decided with satisfaction, as she slipped out and closed the door behind her.

Joel nodded curtly to a chair and settled down at his desk, eyeing Cagle Lawrence malevolently, waiting for him to begin.

"Nice digs!" Cagle looked around the large, tastefully furnished office appraisingly, while reaching into his lapel pocket. "Mind if I smoke?"

"Yes."

"Fine." He gave a nonchalant shrug and leaned back in the chair, surveying Joel's stormy countenance. "I can tell from your demeanor, that you know who I am."

"I do."

"She told you, huh?" He grinned unpleasantly and shook his head. "Well, I must say, that surprises me. Did she also tell you that we ran into each other in Dallas, recently?"

"She did." Joel fought back the aggressive impulses that rushed to his head, his face completely unreadable.

"Just how much *did* she tell you?" Cagle asked, evaluating Joel's stoic features.

"She told me everything, Lawrence. Why? Did you think you were going to come in here and drop some bombshell on me?"

Cagle continued to wear his repugnant grin. "Maybe. Something like that. So, she spilled her guts, did she? Never thought she'd go that far, but then she's changed. Physically, too. What an eyeful! Not that I ever complained before!"

The muscles next to Joel's mouth began to twitch, as he struggled with the desire to get up and knock Cagle Lawrence out of his chair.

"Just why are you here?" he demanded quietly, his voice covered with ice.

"Well, yes, that *would* be the question, wouldn't it?" Cagle sized Joel up briefly, before leaning forward. "And since you're obviously a cut-to-the-chase kind of guy, I'll just tell you. I want you to stay away from her!"

Joel, although a little taken aback by such an outrageous statement, recovered smoothly and fixed a sardonic eye on his potential target.

"That's a pretty unrealistic demand, Lawrence, considering the fact that I'm her manager."

"Oh yeah, that's right!" He rolled his eyes and smirked in amusement. "Meredith's done gone and got religion. She's a little songbird, now. Tell me, Etheridge." He leaned back with a fatuous expression. "Are you keeping her for a pet? What does it take to make her sing?"

A loud crash brought Delores running. She stopped short, and gasped at the sight of the overturned chair and Cagle Lawrence doubled up on the floor. Her hands covered her mouth.

"Get Marshall in here!" Joel gritted out tersely.

Delores just stood there in disbelief.

"DO IT NOW!" he thundered.

She turned and raced back to her desk.

"Get up, Lawrence." Joel watched in disgust, as he pulled himself back up and onto the chair.

"So..." Cagle huffed, out of breath, and striving for composure. "So, you've called out for... reinforcements."

"If you mean Marshall," Joel replied, settling back into his chair, "I sent for him to stop me from killing you."

"Tut, tut!" Cagle mocked, still a little winded. "That's not exactly... Christian charity, is it?"

Joel studied him with hostile eyes. "No," he conceded, evenly. "It isn't. But I don't claim to be an example of Christian charity today. It's a good thing my salvation isn't based on my performance."

He leaned toward Cagle threateningly. "I don't adhere to a sin-now-repent-later lifestyle, Lawrence, but let me tell you this. If you say one more suggestive thing about Meredith, I will smash that plate glass window with your face!"

Cagle swallowed hard and wrestled to appear in control. "Then it's just as well that you've sent for your friend. Because you're *really* not gonna like what's coming next!"

"Is that a fact?"

Marshall Edwards opened Joel's door quietly and stood in the frame, uncertain of what he was walking in on.

"Close that door, Marshall, and get in here!" Joel instructed in clipped tones.

Marshall came around to Joel's side of the desk and viewed Cagle Lawrence with a blend of curiosity and distaste.

Cagle returned the evaluation. Either of these men would be more than a match for him physically but, with the card he was about to play, he wouldn't have to rely on muscle. He smiled coolly at Marshall Edwards.

"So, Etheridge... aren't you gonna introduce me to your sidekick?"

Marshall flashed him a dark look. "Marshall Edwards." He furnished the information himself, before looking down at Joel. "What's going on, here? All Dee said was that you wanted me in here."

Joel scanned his face thoroughly. "This is Cagle Lawrence," he informed him, not missing the rising color in his associate's visage, but deciding to be sure.

"Marshall, you've known Meredith for several years, long before I met her. Does his name mean anything to you?"

Marshall met Joel's probing eyes reluctantly and then nodded.

"So you know?"

"Do you?" Marshall hedged, holding back until he was sure.

"I know everything."

"Did *he* tell you?" Marshall indicated Cagle Lawrence with a contemptuous nod.

"Meredith told me."

"Excuse me," Cagle interjected with scorn, "but would you two gentlemen mind working out these tedious details on your own time?"

Joel made an impatient move toward him, and Marshall placed a detaining hand on his shoulder.

"Steady," he advised. "What do you want, Lawrence? Just say it and get out."

"He's already said it." Joel kept his eyes locked on Cagle. "He wants me to stay away from her."

"Stay *away* from her?" Marshall was astounded. "What kind of lame request is that?"

"Oh, it's not a request, I can assure you," Cagle answered, confidently. "It's an order."

"An order!" Marshall exploded. "Where do you get off, buddy, waltzing in here and giving orders? Do you honestly expect to be taken seriously?"

"Why yes I do, my good Marshall." Cagle's eyes took on a wicked gleam. "I expect to be taken *very* seriously! Otherwise, you will all be very sorry... especially your little songbird."

Joel shut his eyes, in an attempt to block out this repulsive wretch, unconsciously making a fist and molding it firmly into his palm. He drew a deep breath and silently called out again for the Holy spirit to harness him.

"Is that supposed to be some kind of threat?"

"That's exactly what it is... some kind of threat." Cagle somehow managed to seem unruffled, in a room with two men who both wanted to rip him to shreds.

As Joel stood to his feet, Marshall caught him by the shoulder again and stepped between him and Cagle Lawrence.

"Just hold it," he muttered to his friend. "Stay where you are."

He turned to confront Cagle and lifted a warning finger.

"Look here, Lawrence! We've had just about enough of this. You're obviously counting on some ace in the hole to clinch what you're after, so out with it!"

"Clever boy!" Cagle extolled tauntingly. "You figured that out all by yourself. Very well," he said, enjoying his moment to the fullest. "I advise you both to be seated."

Joel stood firm, causing Cagle to think of the adage 'if looks could kill'.

"Let's sit down, Joel."

Joel shook off Marshall's compelling hand and deliberately walked around to rest on the front of his desk, next to Cagle Lawrence. Marshall came swiftly around to monitor his slightest move.

"Say it." Joel's words were hissed and full of venom. He seemed ready to strike.

Cagle joined Marshall in surveying him closely.

"Alright," he replied, a little too relaxed to be believed. "If you know anything at all about Meredith, then you know she did some modeling. I got her involved in that. She was quite a looker at eighteen, although nothing like she is now!"

He reached again for a cigarette, then felt Joel's glare and decided it wasn't worth it. "I not only lined her up with some lucrative jobs, I did a little camera work, myself."

He waited for a reaction but was treated to inscrutable silence. "Yes sir," he resumed. "Some extraordinary camera work. You wouldn't believe how kind the lens was to hot little Meredith!"

"You're lying!" Marshall said shortly. "Meredith never posed for anything more risqué than swimsuit photos."

"Did I say she posed?" Cagle donned a self-assured air. "No way! These were candid shots and all natural! In *every* sense of the word," he added meaningfully.

Joel left off praying and made a lunge for him. Marshall grabbed him and literally used every ounce of strength he had to drag him away from Cagle Lawrence.

"Stop it, Joel!" he yelled. "Get back! That's exactly what he *wants* you to do!"

Joel whirled around, and, for a split second, Marshall thought he would hit *him* and for that split second, he would have been correct. That was Joel's instinct and intent. He stopped himself, but gave Marshall a look that accused him of siding with the enemy, then roughly jerked his arm out of Marshall's grasp.

"On the contrary!" Cagle protested, a shudder betraying his bravado. "I don't exactly relish a repeat performance of Etheridge's earlier assault. Don't worry," he admonished, when Marshall stared at Joel in surprise. "No lawsuit, at least not today. Money's not what I'm after."

"Just what *are* you after?" Marshall snarled, angrily.

"Very simple. Meredith!"

Delores grabbed the telephone receiver impatiently, while trying to hear what was being said behind Joel's door.

"Yes, Donna!" she said in a brusque tone. "Oh, it's Lynn, sorry. What is it, honey?"

She let out a sigh at the young intern's response. "Oh dear. No, never mind, ring it through."

She hung up the phone and lifted it again as it began to ring.

"Meredith!" She forced a smile into her voice. "How are you, sweetie?"

"Hi, Dee!" Meredith returned lightly. "I'm good. How 'bout you and Doug?"

"Can't complain, love."

"That's good to hear. Listen, Dee, is Joel around? I'm supposed to call him about lunch."

"Well..." Delores paused, unsure of herself.

"Is something wrong?" Meredith lost some of her brightness.

"Merry, Joel's with someone in his office, right now. It was unexpected, and he asked not to be disturbed. It looks like it might go on for a while."

"Oh." She was silent now.

"He *did* say to tell you that he's sorry, and that he'll call you the minute he's free."

"He did?" She perked up instantly and Delores smiled at her transparency.

"Of course he did, silly! You know Joel wouldn't forget you."

Meredith beamed happily to herself. "I guess not. Thank you, Dee."

"You're very welcome, sweetheart." Delores tone was warm and loving. "I'll tell him you called."

Meredith rang off and Delores hung up, a mixture of relief and dread spreading over her.

She couldn't help thinking about Merry, with her flawless complexion, astonishing gray eyes, perfect white teeth and dark, abundant hair that reached to her waist. She was an extraordinary beauty, and seemed completely unaware of it.

Delores had to smile at the stark contrast between Meredith's stunning features and her old, worn-out jeans, cropped off sweatshirts, and habitual lack of footwear.

She remembered the first year of their involvement with her. Joel had abandoned tact altogether, and informed her that the next time she showed up at a concert dressed like that, he would personally come onstage and pack her off like a twenty pound sack of dog food. So, of course, she had to try him!

It was at an outdoor rally in California. Meredith had no more than approached her microphone, when Joel suddenly materialized, threw her over his shoulder, and marched off, to the delight of the huge crowd, who apparently thought it was all some kind of gag. Meredith pretended to be outraged, but Delores knew she loved every minute of it. In any event, she had abided by Joel's wardrobe policy from then on.

"Sweet Meredith." Delores shook her head sadly. "I love you like one of my own daughters." She lifted troubled eyes to Joel's door and began to offer up prayers for both of them.

Joel hovered over Cagle Lawrence's chair regarding him with unmasked hatred.

"Get out," he advised quietly.

"Sure, I'll leave," Cagle shrugged. "If you're sure that's what you want."

"Joel, wait!" Marshall held up one hand and turned toward Cagle. "Listen, we're not going to coax this out of you, bit by bit. Now, you've insinuated that you have some incriminating photos of Meredith, yet you admit, yourself, that she didn't pose for them.

"First of all, you'd better explain yourself. Then, you'd better deliver your ultimatum and leave. You're a fool, if you think I can stop this man from tearing your head off, once he decides to do it! I'm not the one who's holding him back, so out with it, Lawrence!"

Cagle's eyes darted back and forth from Marshall to Joel.

"Alright," he conceded, nervously. "But if he lays a hand on me one more time, Meredith will be the one to suffer for it!"

Marshall glanced over at Joel who suddenly seemed like a warrior without a weapon.

"Joel, sit down," he urged. "He means it," he added, when Joel hesitated. "For Meredith! For *her* sake, Joel, sit *down* please!"

Joel looked at Marshall as if he didn't know him. Marshall circled the desk and pulled out Joel's chair. "Come on, Joel."

He made his way over to it mechanically and dropped down, to the relief of both Marshall and Cagle Lawrence.

"Much better," Cagle approved, a jeer in his voice. "Alright, gentlemen. You want to know about the pictures? Fine, I'll tell you. Meredith didn't pose for them, because she didn't know they were being taken. I might as well come clean about that.

"I considered trying to make you believe that she went along with it, but Romeo, here, would never go for it and besides, it doesn't matter. She was turning into such a little prude. She even wanted to stop doing the swimsuit photos, but no way were we going to let a body like that go to waste! So we mounted a camera in the dressing room and camouflaged the lens in a painting. Abstract art, it's called. Nothing abstract about the results, though!"

"You say 'we'. Who else?" Marshall asked, pushing down on Joel's shoulder.

"Let's just say my associates. That's all you need to know."

Joel rubbed his burning eyes, rested his head in his hands and stared vacantly down at his desk. "What's the rest of it?"

"The *rest* of it," Cagle replied, "is this. You get out of her life. Period." He looked at Joel with absolute loathing. "Completely."

"She's under contract," Marshall pointed out.

"Yeah, well, I don't give a damn about contracts," Cagle breezed. "At least, not at this point. In fact, *that* might actually be interesting."

He seemed to be rolling some new idea around in his head. "This is a big outfit. Etheridge isn't the only one here who works with singers. So sure, keep her on the books for now, until I say differently. But you'd better find some other flunky to work with her."

He nodded his head toward Joel. "I want you out of it, Etheridge, and I mean in every aspect, both in and out of this office! And if you don't comply, get ready for the biggest scandal this town has ever known, because little Miss Songbird's portfolio will go viral and end up being the cover story for every rag in this country! You think I'm kidding?"

He gave an ugly laugh, then pulled a small, brown envelope out of his pocket and threw it down in front of Joel. "Go on! Feast your eyes! And I *do* mean feast!"

Joel stared down at the envelope for a moment, then slowly picked up the telephone, while the sound of his own blood pressure began to pound in his head. "Dee, come in here, please. Now."

She obeyed instantly and Joel motioned her to his side.

"Take this over to the window," he said, handing her the envelope. "Take the contents out, look at them, and then put them back in."

Delores looked at her boss strangely but obeyed his instructions. Her muffled gasp and look of horror told Joel what he needed to know.

"That's enough, bring them back to me," he said. She returned the envelope to him, tears spilling down her cheeks.

"I'm sorry." Joel got up and took her hand gently. "I'm sorry, Dee. But you had to be the one. You understand?"

She nodded, unable to speak.

Joel squeezed her fingers. "It's not what it looks like. You and I will talk later, okay?"

She nodded again.

"It's not what it looks like," he repeated. "That's all for now."

Delores cast a reproachful eye at Cagle Lawrence and left the room, weeping silently. Joel watched her go then sat back down.

"Oh, come on!" Cagle objected, his face growing more evil by the minute. "They're certainly not as bad as all that! Not much of a review, I'd say!"

"*Why*, Lawrence?" Marshall stepped toward him in a pleading manner. "Why would you do something like this to Meredith? And why is it so important to you that Joel have nothing to do with her?"

"Two very astute questions," Cagle patronized. "Whether or not anything happens to Meredith, well that's entirely up to your friend, here. I'm only the gun. It'll be Etheridge who pulls the trigger. Let me catch him anywhere around Meredith, and it's game over."

He stopped and regarded Joel through narrowed eyes. "You're a praying man, aren't you, Etheridge? Well, you'd better pray that Meredith doesn't get wise to any of this! If I even suspect she knows, all bets are off. She can kiss her little career goodbye, not to mention her... what do you Christians call it... *ministry*.

"Regarding your second question, Edwards... " He leaned forward and his expression became almost wolfish.

"For now, let's just say I've come to claim what's mine! Don't worry, Etheridge." He gave him a mocking grin. "You can have her when I'm done... if you still want her."

He stood up and snatched the envelope from the desk and waved it at Joel. "Want these? I got a great deal on double prints."

Joel began to slowly rise from behind his desk and gave him a look that wiped the foolish grin off his face.

Cagle began inching his way backward to the door, as Joel pushed his chair back and moved stalkingly in his direction.

Marshall edged toward Cagle, keeping a sharp eye on Joel.

"Don't do it, Joel," he warned him, softly.

Joel halted and turned a stricken face to him. His eyes were begging him to get out of his way.

Marshall placed a supportive, but constraining hand on his arm and addressed Cagle Lawrence coldly.

"We'd like some time to talk this over."

"I'll just bet you would! I don't have to give you time, or anything else. However," he added, sneering in triumph, "I'll give you twenty-four hours. See what you can do with that!"

He flicked his hand in a pretend salute and was gone.

Chapter Nine

Meredith rolled around on the living room rug, absently towing a frazzled shoestring. Hook crouched low, shivering with the joy of the hunt and pounced repeatedly at it, only to have it escape him at the last second. After a while, Meredith sat up and tossed Hook's prey onto the couch.

He leaped up onto it, approaching the shoestring with great deliberation.

"Run! Run, little string!" She laughed softly and dragged herself up and onto the glider. Her eyes traveled up to the mantel clock, as they had doing, every few minutes. It was almost four o' clock! What happened to lunch at two?

Would Delores think she was being a pest if she called back? No, she decided. Delores loved her. She would never make her feel that way.

Still, Meredith reasoned to herself, *I know Joel wouldn't just forget. What could be taking so long? Something must have happened.*

She laid her hand on the phone, then drew it away and scolded herself. "Stop it!"

But still, it was four o' clock! He'd be leaving for his dinner meeting before long.

Meredith stood up and began to pace restlessly, all kinds of imaginations coming to play with her mind. Finally, she threw herself onto the window seat and hugged a pillow tightly.

"Hey, Father." She let her worried eyes wander around the yard. "I need You to come talk some sense to me."

"Are you telling Me you're actually going to listen?" He smiled through an evening sunbeam at the girl He loved so much.

Meredith twisted her mouth into a wry grin and shrugged lightly. "You never know!"

She thought about it and laughed. "Well, I guess with You, that's not exactly true, is it?"

"I guess not," He replied, continuing to watch her tenderly. "I love you."

"I love You, too," she returned with feeling. "Know what else?"

She closed her eyes and crushed the pillow closer. "I love Joel."

"I know," Father answered.

"Why didn't You tell me?"

"Because half the fun is finding out," He answered softly. "And thanks for telling Hook before your own Father."

She could feel His smile and giggled. "Is it okay with You?"

"As long as you love Me first."

"Then we've got no problem."

Meredith's expression became indistinct. She opened her mouth to speak again then hesitated, trouble shadowing her face.

"Talk to Me," her Father urged.

"Well..." She wavered. "It's kind of silly."

"Not to Me."

"I know." Her smile was warm, now. "You never get tired of me rambling on. It's Joel." She chewed on a nail without realizing it.

"I don't have anything to base this on, Father, other than the fact that he hasn't called yet, but I just keep getting the weirdest feeling that something's wrong."

"Are you not secure in Joel's love for you?" Father waited patiently, while Meredith worked this out.

"I am," she answered at length. "I can't explain it, but I know Joel loves me like I know You do."

She listened to her own words and sighed heavily. "That's not even true, is it? I really *wanted* that to be true. What's wrong with me?"

"It's just that you're rummaging around in your past and deciding that Joel's love is too good for you, and so it won't last."

"Will it?" Meredith searched her Father's face nervously.

"Listen, My own," He breathed sweetly. "What is from Me will last. Will you accept that for now and bow your will to Mine?"

"Do You promise it won't hurt?"

"I do not," Father replied. "I only promise that I am faithful and completely trustworthy."

Meredith nodded slowly, her eyes sweeping the amber landscape, the whistle of the evening wind causing her to shiver. "I know that, Father."

She set her chin resolutely. "This one's an altar. I surrender, okay?"

"Okay. I love you."

"I love You back." She blew Him a kiss and climbed out of the window seat.

The room was beginning to grow chilly. Meredith piled some wood into the fireplace and nurtured an uncertain flame into a steady blaze.

She sat on the hearth unconsciously stroking Hook's soft coat, so engrossed in her thoughts that the gentle tap on her door caused her to start in surprise.

She hurried to get up, glancing at the clock. Ten after six! She stopped in her tracks and looked at the door curiously. It couldn't be Joel. He had that dinner appointment at six o' clock. A second knock stopped her musing and brought her across the room.

She opened the door slowly to reveal Joel leaning there with one hand up on the frame, the other shoved into his pocket. He lifted his tired eyes and gave her a worn-out smile.

"I'm sorry," he said simply.

"It's okay." Meredith's heart did a flip and she stepped back to let him in. He tossed his coat onto a chair and crossed the room to the fireplace, as she closed the door and came over to join him.

Both of them stared into the flames for a moment before she tugged at his sleeve timidly.

"What's wrong?"

Joel ran a hand through his hair, then rubbed his stiff neck. "Nothing," he said in a dull voice. "Just tired, I guess."

"Did you cancel your appointment?" She brushed his hand away and reached up to massage his sore muscles slowly.

"Hmm?" He glanced around, seeming to be preoccupied. "My... oh. No, I just postponed it until eight-thirty."

"Kind of late for dinner, isn't it?" Meredith commented quietly.

"Just coffee." Joel straightened his shoulders and turned his back to the fire. He gazed longingly into her eyes. "I'm sorry about not calling you."

"If I had any sense, I wouldn't even be speaking to you right now." She made him smile and was glad. "But I seem to have lost all my sense, where you're concerned."

"Is that right?" he murmured, in a low voice, coming in a little closer and causing her head to swim. Their eyes lingered on each other.

"Potatoes," Meredith said, out of the blue.

Joel hesitated. "I don't know what that means."

"Rotten potatoes," she answered. "In the fridge. That smell," she finished, as Joel gave her a soft laugh.

He caught her hands and pulled her into his arms. She pressed close, feeling faint with gladness.

Joel draped himself around her. "I love you, Meredith," he said huskily, the timbre of his voice causing her to tremble.

She lifted her head from his shoulder and traced every line of his face with her adoring gaze, pausing at his firm mouth and stopping as she encountered the intensity of his eyes.

"Joel," she dared, shaken by strange, newborn emotion, "I love you, too. I love you so much."

He brought his hands up into her long, soft hair and lifted her face to his own, dividing her lips and holding her there for a long while, both of them not just reluctant, but strangely afraid to end this embrace.

Gradually and unwillingly, Joel released her, his eyes gleaning every aspect of her face.

There was something about his expression, a kind of deep sorrow that both shocked and triggered fear in Meredith.

Her cautious heart was filled with anxiety. She cradled his handsome, downcast face in her hands and coaxed him gently. "Something's wrong. Please tell me what it is. Is it... what I told you? Are you not able to..." He was scaring her.

"Of *course* not!" Joel cut her off sharply. "What do you take me for?"

"For better or for worse!" Meredith teased, her laughter dying away as an unmistakable look of pain flooded his countenance. He didn't seem to be able to look at her.

Because of that 'for better or for worse' thing? Was it the thought of marrying her that did this to him? Meredith was stung!

"Oh, for crying out loud! It was a *joke,* Joel! What is your problem?" She threw her hands up in frustration and walked a few steps away before turning to look back at him with suspicious eyes.

"Oh. I get it," she said, slowly, her voice becoming cool and brittle. "I get it. It's okay to *love* me but I'm not the kind of girl you take home to Mama."

Joel just stared at her.

"It's starting to make sense, now. Ever since we talked yesterday, you've been like two different men, starting with last night, when you brought me home! 'Oh, we need to talk, Meredith,' and then you couldn't get out of here fast enough!"

It had been an emotionally grueling week for Meredith and it was just too easy to give way to indignation as opposed to dealing with fear. Joel's stunned silence and look of disbelief was quickly misinterpreted as guilt and having no defense.

This only served to fuel her anger. Her eyes flashed with all of her misgivings and her past hurts clamored for attention and cheered her on.

"You know, I never *asked* you to love me! In fact, I tried to stop you from telling me, but no, you just *had* to say it... before you should have, apparently, because now that I turn out to be a different item than the one you bid on, all you can do is send out mixed signals!"

Joel stood frozen to the spot, a vein near his temple beginning to pulsate as his jaw tightened in a firm line.

Meredith ignored all the warning signs and foolishly persisted in her barrage. "If I've ever seen a man torn in two over something, it's you, Joel Etheridge!"

She put her hands on her hips and glowered at him. "Well, don't do me any favors! I wasn't looking for your love in the first place, and now that you know I'm not the pristine little flower you thought I was, maybe you'd just better go shop somewhere else!"

She flew across the room to the door and yanked it open. "I release you from any promises you made about not leaving me! What's a stupid promise from *you* worth, anyway? You're free to go!"

All during Meredith's tirade, Joel tried to breathe evenly and struggled to control his mounting temper. He had almost succeeded until those last spiteful words. The rage that Cagle Lawrence had roused in him today was still alive.

Now, he stormed over to Meredith, jerked the door out of her hand and smashed it into its jamb with a force that rattled the windows and sent Hook bolting up the stairs. He caught her by the arm and made her stay put.

"Shut up!" Joel glared at her with white-hot fury. She opened her mouth to defy him and he gave her an impatient shake. "I mean it! Not one more word! I have been stretched today about as far as I'm going, so I'm warning you, Meredith! If all you can do is talk trash, then just shut up!"

She made a move to head upstairs and he tightened his grip. "Oh, no ma'am, I don't think so! You don't get to shoot from the lip and then just ride off!"

He riveted her with smoldering eyes and challenged her rebellious ones until she finally lowered her lashes and laid her forehead against his chest. His heart was racing so hard, she could feel it slamming against his ribs.

"Why do you constantly pull this crap on me?" He wrapped his arms around her and closed his eyes, breathing out slowly in an effort to calm himself down and lower his voice.

"Something flits through your head, Missy, and you just take off after it. First you tell me what I've waited years to hear, and a few seconds later, you're ordering me to leave. Just yesterday, you were begging me *not* to. You are working on my last nerve!"

He looked down and cupped her face in one hand, staring intently, as if trying to discover the answer in her eyes. "Why are you going off on me like this?"

She barely met his gaze. "Because, Joel, you're being so strange tonight. You act like you're in love with me and then, all at once, you act like it hurts to be with me. If we're okay, it shouldn't hurt."

Her voice broke and her eyes welled up with tears. "And if *does* hurt... that means something's wrong. It's not supposed to hurt."

Joel's exasperated countenance subsided into regret and he lifted her chin.

"Sweetheart," he said wearily, "I *am* in love with you. If something *is* wrong, why do you automatically have to assume that it has anything to do with you? Couldn't you just once consider the possibility that other things might be going on, and that it might only have to do with me?"

Meredith reached up to touch the fingertips that outlined her lips. "And does it?" She watched his face. "*Does it only have to do with you?*"

He couldn't let her pin him down! He knew her, and one question always led to another.

If he admitted the truth, then her next question would be whether or not it had anything do with her past. There would be no way around that.

"This is not what I want to do, tonight." He led her over to the couch and sank into it, pulling her down next to him.

Meredith pressed herself deeply into his arms, laying her head against his neck.

"I only have about an hour before I have to leave for my appointment. I just want to hold you like this," Joel whispered. He seared the love on her face deeply into his memory and secured her lips in a long, meandering kiss.

"I don't want to argue," he finally said. "I don't want to fight. This is all I want, just to be with you. I just need to hold you, Merry, while I can."

He hadn't meant to say that! It just slipped out and there was instant confusion in her eyes. He breathed in deeply and let out a frustrated sigh. "Sweetheart, no matter what happens I'll always love you. I need you to know that."

"What does that mean, 'no matter what happens'? What..."

Joel silenced her with his kisses, as many as it took to make her stop asking questions.

Marshall Edwards lay back in his recliner, staring vacantly into the air, the low sounds of late night television providing nothing more than background noise.

His mind was locked so firmly on his thoughts that he never even heard his wife say his name.

She clicked off the television and shook him gently, laughing as he jumped.

"My goodness," she chided. "What is going on in that head of yours? It must be something enormous!"

Marshall squeezed her hand fondly and grinned. "I didn't realize you were there, Bobbie."

"So I noticed. Did you also not hear the phone ring?"

"The phone?" Marshall looked up at her in surprise.

"I thought not!" His wife laughed and kissed his forehead lightly.

She sat down on the arm of his chair, and he rested his head back on the cushion to look up at her.

"Who was it?"

"Joel," she answered. "I meant to come right down and tell you, but then my cell also rang just as he was hanging up."

A look of worry passed over Marshall's usually peaceful features and Bobbie noted his concern.

"Is Joel alright, Marshall?"

"He's... " Marshall weighed his answer carefully, before meeting her eyes and shaking his head.

"No, Bobbie, he's not. It's very involved. It has to do with Meredith."

"He's in love with her," Bobbie stated, matter-of-factly.

"You know," Marshall replied, "I only realized that for the first time, today. I mean, I've suspected an attraction between the two of them from time to time, but today..." He trailed off.

"What about today?" she prodded.

"Bobbie, do you remember when we first took Meredith under our wings?"

"Almost five years ago."

"Remember that night she broke down after a concert, when a young girl told her that she had once thought about suicide, after an abortion?

"Remember, she told Merry that someone had taken her to one of Merry's earlier concerts, and that she had given her life to the Lord? The girl just wanted to thank her and you and I couldn't understand why she fell apart, when we got her home."

Bobbie rubbed her chin in reflection. "That's when she told us about her own abortion... and that jerk who beat her up and made her do it."

"Bobbie..." Marshall took her hand and just looked at her. "Who, of *all* the people in the world, do you think showed up at Joel's office, today?"

She gasped loudly and stood to her feet.

"Oh, no way! Not him!"

"Him."

"Oh, Marshall!" Her husband's words left her stunned. "After all these years? *Why?* Did he tell Joel?" Her eyes widened. "Does Meredith know?"

"Fortunately, she told Joel, herself, yesterday. And I'm positive she has absolutely no idea that Cagle Lawrence is in town."

"Is that why he came here, to tell Joel? I mean, why would he just show up like that? What does he get out of telling Joel, anyway, especially now that he already knows?

"Honey..." Marshall sighed and pulled her back down onto the arm of the chair. "This is very complicated and I confess, my intentions were not to tell anyone else, not even you, but I realize now that would have been a mistake. You really *should* know, especially since you're a prayer warrior. Remember those cruise line ads Meredith did?"

Bobbie nodded.

"Cagle Lawrence and some others... *associates*, he calls them... concealed a camera and took some photos that Meredith knew nothing about." He swallowed and finished with an effort. "In her dressing room, Bobbie!"

"Dear Lord," she moaned, repulsion sweeping over her.

"Lawrence has ordered Joel to completely stay away from Meredith. We're not clear yet, as to why. He says that if Joel doesn't go along with it, then he's taking the pictures to the Internet and the tabloids. Meredith has absolutely no idea these pictures even exist and she's not to be told. That's one of his conditions. The minute she gets wind of it, he intends to make good on his threat."

Bobbie was too horrified to reply at first. Finally, she said weakly, "Joel's on his way over here, Marshall."

He nodded. "I expected he might show up. He met with the leader of a new band and their rep tonight. I have a feeling I know why he's coming."

"He's giving in?"

Marshall nodded sadly and stared straight ahead. "Bobbie, I know the way I feel about you. I love you with all my ability to love. But today, as I watched Joel in that office... Honey, I've never seen human capacity to love that deeply, that intensely. I was afraid for him!"

A hesitant knock was heard and Marshall looked soberly at his wife and then at the door.

"I still am," he said softly.

Chapter Ten

Marshall waited until his wife went upstairs to bed, before he opened the living room door. He was shaken at Joel's ghastly, hollow-eyed appearance, but managed to cover his reaction.

"Come in, Joel."

Joel dragged wearily in and Marshall laid a bolstering arm across his shoulders. "Are you okay, buddy?"

He nodded his head, then shook it silently.

"Come over here." Marshall led him to the couch and pulled a chair around for himself. "Can I get you anything? Anything at all?"

"No," Joel mumbled. He looked up and attempted a grateful smile. "But thanks."

He leaned forward, elbows on his knees, and supported his head in his hands.

"I'll be alright," he said. "It's just that I haven't slept at all the last two nights, and then today was..." He broke off with a bitter laugh. "Well, I guess I don't have to tell you about today."

Marshall regarded him closely. "You should be home in bed."

Joel studied his palms. "I *will* go home soon, Marshall, but I wanted to talk to you about this meeting I had tonight."

"Kinda late for business, isn't it, Joel?"

"Yeah, I'm sorry. I shouldn't be keeping you up."

"You misunderstand me," Marshall said gently. "It's not me I'm worried about."

Joel rubbed his eyes and shook his head. "No, don't worry. I'll be alright. Let's just talk a few things over, okay, Marshall?"

"Sure. Whatever you need."

Joel meshed his fingers together and rested his chin on his hands. "You're a good friend."

Marshall reached over and patted his arm, but made no reply.

"This band, Surrender... you're right Marshall, they're good. Good people, too."

Marshall nodded, waiting.

"I know that I originally agreed to tonight's meeting to decide if the firm would handle their development and that, if we took them on, you would oversee their career." Joel met Marshall's eyes. "And if that's important to you, I won't interfere."

"Joel." Marshall sat back in his chair and gave him a kind smile. "I know why you're here."

Joel sat motionless, scrutinizing the pattern on the carpet.

Marshall reached over and touched his sleeve. "You want me to take over Meredith."

He focused harder on the floor and Marshall waited a moment before speaking again.

"You love her very much, don't you?"

Joel's face contorted, as he labored to maintain some kind of control. A single tear splashed onto the carpet near Marshall's foot, a symbol of ragged emotions mixed with exhaustion, no sleep, and the tormenting knowledge of what tomorrow would bring.

"It's okay," Marshall reassured him, quietly. "We'll do this any way you want, Joel. Don't worry about it. It'll work out, somehow."

Joel picked up the pillow from the couch and rested his forehead against it, unable to reply.

"Hang on," Marshall said quickly. "You just sit there and rest. I'm gonna go see if I can find us both a cup of something hot."

He used this excuse to allow Joel to be alone to compose himself, realizing how very close to the edge he really was.

He made his way to the kitchen and put the kettle on to boil, then rested his elbows on the counter. He stood there for a while, reliving the day and thinking of his friend.

"Dear God," he whispered. "Joel is completely wiped out. Please give him the strength he needs. You're the only One who can get him through this."

He caught his reflection in the window over the sink, and regarded it soberly. "I guess I'm getting on up there, Lord. Sixty's not too far down the road. Our son has married and given us two grandbabies, and our girls are almost through with college. Lord..."

He breathed out a loud sigh. "When our girls are ready for marriage, please give them Godly men who will love them, the way Joel loves Meredith."

The hissing kettle called for Marshall's attention, and he picked out a couple of mugs and mixed up some instant soup.

He made his way silently back out to the living room and set the mugs on the coffee table.

Joel had slumped into a corner of the couch and clutched the pillow to his chest. His face was flushed and his hair untidy, but he seemed to be a little more composed.

"Thank you, Marshall. This is probably just what I need, after all."

Marshall sat down and looked at Joel with worried eyes. "Drink up. I'll bet you haven't eaten anything all day." He sipped from his own mug and hesitated with what he wanted to say.

"Listen," he finally ventured. "I don't like to bring this up, but Lawrence will be contacting us tomorrow."

"Believe me, I know."

"Is it settled, then? You're really gonna do this?"

"What choice do I *have*, Marshall?" Joel held his mug tightly, needing its warmth.

He raised his eyes, now bloodshot and swollen. "Lawrence says if Merry finds out what he's up to, he's going public, and I believe him. I can't take that chance. Meredith is too much of a hothead for us to explain things to her.

"She might promise to play along, but the more she thinks about it, she'll work herself up into a rage and go after him. Believe me, I know a little bit about Merry and her rages. And when that happens, he'll have those pictures of her uploaded before she even knows what hit her."

He sighed and looked up at the ceiling. "She'll think this is about the abortion, and she'll hate me for it."

"Joel, no, she won't."

"She will! She'll think I couldn't deal with it."

"So she doesn't know..."

"About me? No."

Joel stood up and the pillow rolled onto the floor. He wandered around aimlessly. "I couldn't tell her because of... something she said." He waved a hand through the air to dismiss it.

Marshall took a deep breath. "She's up for a tour, right?"

"Not really a tour. Just a couple of weeks."

"When does she leave?"

"Not until after Thanksgiving. Plenty of time for Lawrence to do some real damage."

"Joel, why do you think Lawrence is so insistent that you stay away from Meredith? He didn't say the *both* of us, he just specified you. What could that possibly have to do with the photos? And why isn't he asking for money?"

"I don't know. Ever since he left this morning, I haven't had one free moment to sit down and reflect on what his motive really is. I've been running around all day. For now, all I can do is guess," he replied, his finger idly tracing a figurine on the mantel. "I've been wondering if he thinks he can lure Meredith back into her old life with him."

"After what he did to her? I seriously doubt it!"

Joel shrugged. "I'm not saying he would succeed. I'm just wondering if that's his plan."

"Surely there are other women in New Orleans. Why, after all this time, come all the way up here for Meredith?"

"Who knows? Who knows *what* demon is driving him?"

"Well, if he thinks he can lure her back, then he doesn't know her!" Marshall declared stoutly.

"No," Joel tried to agree, then contradicted him. "On the other hand..."

Marshall stopped him. "What do you mean?" He stared at him in amazement. "There *is* no other hand!"

Joel said nothing and Marshall made an impatient sound of frustration.

"Joel, you of *all* people should know better than that!"

"I do. I *do* know better." Joel grabbed at his stiff neck and struggled with what he was trying to say.

"It's just this, Marshall. If she thinks I've deserted her, not only after she told me she loves me, but after telling me about her abortion, what do you think that's going to do to her? I felt like I just had to see her one more time, so I went over there earlier tonight. It was a big mistake.

"Her rejection radar was already up, and I guess I wasn't able to ditch the mindset I brought in with me from the office. I had no business going over there in that state. I knew it, but I went, anyway. Of course, she focused on my demeanor, and accused me of being unable to deal with her abortion.

"In fact, she threw down on me, and I guess I was still so angry about Lawrence that I fired back! It ended up getting pretty heated. I had to spend the rest of our remaining time together trying to convince her that she was wrong about any misgivings she thought I had.

"Now, after tomorrow, it's going to look like I just stood right there and lied to her about being able to handle the whole abortion thing. She's going to actively *hate* me!"

Marshall shook his head and Joel gave him a look of impatience and exasperation.

"Listen, I *know* that girl, Marshall, as well as I know myself! On a good day, she's an explosion waiting to happen. I'm telling you!"

Joel clamped onto Marshall's shoulder, in an attempt to make him understand. "We're talking about combining a lifetime of exploitation and violation with what she'll see as complete abandonment, and from me, of all people.

"I'm the one she trusts most, next to Father. What if she takes off with Cagle Lawrence, just to spite me?" His voice was growing hoarse and thin. "Just to hurt me, the way she's going to feel I hurt her? Trust me, Meredith Clark is quite capable of retaliation!"

"I don't know," Marshall admitted, shaking his head in confusion. "I just don't know, Joel. I just hope you're wrong. We'll just have to rely on her relationship with her Father."

"I know she loves Him," he answered, dully. "But she's too impulsive. Her emotions control her, at the drop of a hat. You know that."

Marshall couldn't deny it. He sat in silence for a moment, trying to put everything into some kind of perspective. He only hoped that he could be some kind of real help to Joel, in the days and weeks ahead. Working with a new and up-coming band was one thing, but an artist like Meredith Clark was something else. He wasn't sure he was up to the task of managing someone with Meredith's demanding schedule, and overwhelming popularity, but he didn't want to let Joel down.

"Joel, you know I'll do everything I can to help you with Meredith, but no one can deal with her with the same competency that you can."

"You're the only one I would trust with her, Marshall."

Joel rammed his hands into his pockets, and hung his head, as weariness and emotional fatigue began to bear down on him. "Hopefully, the day will come when I can take the burden of that back off your shoulders, but for now, just knowing that you're onboard to take care of her is about the only thing that makes me think I can get through this."

"It's not a burden, Joel. But I'm looking forward to the day you say 'Marshall, you're fired.' That'll mean she's safely back where she belongs."

Joel smiled sadly down at the floor. "Well, at least for now, it keeps her safe within the confines of her contract, and that's comforting, for as long as it lasts. We can only hope that Lawrence doesn't spend too much time meditating on that aspect of things, and end up demanding her release. That's when things will take an even uglier turn." Something dark and menacing rested on his face.

Joel shook himself out of following after his thoughts, and moved to the door. "Listen." He planted tired, hopeless eyes on Marshall's face. "Maybe you're right. Maybe it's just the lack of sleep talking here. I'm going home and try to crash." He managed a weak smile. "Thank you, Marshall for... you know..."

"You stay awake in the car," Marshall cautioned seriously. "And sleep in. I'll start things rolling for you in the morning."

"Thanks," Joel repeated. "Good night."

Marshall closed the door behind him, and began putting the room in order before he retired.

He pushed his chair back in place and reached for the mugs. "Lord, please don't let Joel be right about Merry. Please protect her from Cagle Lawrence and somehow, some way, work all this out for Your glory."

He returned the mugs to the kitchen, came back to lock the door and turned to go upstairs, noticing, as he did, the pillow that had fallen to the floor. He stooped to pick it up, grief filling his heart as soon as he touched it. It was completely soaked.

Chapter Eleven

Pastor Gary Brenner strolled reluctantly into his secretary's office, frowning down at a handful of telephone message slips.

"Marianne!"

She turned from the copier, in answer to his summons. "Yes?"

"This message from Agnes Dunn..."

Marianne grinned mischievously, and turned back to her project.

"Yes, Pastor?"

"Well, she's not... wanting to drop by, or anything like that, is she?"

He prepared to cringe, should the occasion call for it.

"Well, I don't know. She just said she needed to speak with you." Marianne lifted the stack of copies from the tray and retrieved her original. "Why? Did you want me to set up an appointment?"

She managed a serious face, although her boss's look of terror almost did her in.

"Not on your life!" Pastor Brenner declared fervently. "You remember when she dropped by last week? She wanted to fix me up with one of her Garden Club ladies!"

Marianne erupted with a hearty laugh and slid into her chair. "Are you sure Agnes wouldn't like a shot at you, herself?"

His white hair only accentuated the redness that climbed up his distinguished, good-looking face.

"No, I am not at *all* sure!"

He smiled ironically to himself, and continued shuffling through the rest of his messages. "Holidays are right around the corner. I'm okay with the first few gifts she faithfully brings me every year, but I start freaking out around Christmas. Fruitcake! I thought everyone knew I hate fruitcake," he mumbled.

"Then give it to me, I *love* fruitcake!"

"You can *have* it. Complete with those little green things. Marianne..."

She crossed her arms and waited patiently for the same question he asked her every year, about this time. "What *are* those little green things?"

The telephone interrupted her annual response, and she picked it up gratefully.

"Covenant Fellowship!" She smiled at her pastor's poise for flight. "Oh, hi there, Marshall!"

"Thank You, God!" he said in a loud stage whisper. He held his thumb and pinkie up to the side of his head, motioned to his office, and then headed in that direction. His phone greeted him, as he sank into his chair.

"Marshall!" He was genuinely enthusiastic. "Hey, buddy! What's going on?"

"I hope that's not a casual question, Gary." Marshall returned blandly.

"It might have been, but it doesn't have to be." He spun his chair around and propped his feet up on a bookshelf. "So, what *is* going on?"

"Gary, I need to see you. The sooner, the better."

Marshall's voice, normally light and cheerful, had an edge to it that Gary caught at once. "Can you make some time for me?"

"Sure!" Gary twisted his chair back around and examined his calendar. "Let's see, this is Friday... and from the sound of your voice, we need to get to it before the weekend."

"I'd appreciate it, Gary."

"Tell you what... I was just going to run home for lunch but if you like, I can run down to the Row and meet you somewhere."

"Music Row is so jammed at noon," Marshall reminded him. "Why don't I drive over your way, in about a half hour?"

"That'll work. Remember that place near the mall with the potato cheese soup?"

"Perfect. And thanks, Gary. I really mean it."

Gary could almost see the relief on his friend's face.

"Anytime, you know that. See you soon." Gary hung up the phone and glanced back down at his calendar. He buzzed into Marianne's office.

"Yes?"

"Marianne, would you get the Grants on the phone, and ask Wayne or Sheryl if they mind pushing back their three o' clock? In fact, if they don't have plans, I'll just meet them here in the morning at ten."

"Sure!"

A few minutes later, his secretary stuck her head in his door. "They'll be here at ten, Pastor. I would offer to be here, but Frank and I have already made plans with the kids."

"No, don't worry about that. That's your day off." He gave her a careless wave. "I think I can still manage a coffeepot and the answering machine will be on. I just need to give Marshall some extra time today."

"Okay. Well, speaking of the machine, it's on and I'm off. Have a good meeting and we'll see you Sunday." She paused. "Unless there's something else I can do before I leave?"

"No... I think not."

"Are you sure?" Her face wore an impish look. "I'll be happy to set up that little appointment we talked about earlier."

She giggled and ducked the pencil he lightly tossed in her direction, then vanished.

Pastor Gary lifted his car keys from the drawer and paused, remembering the urgency in Marshall's tone. He wondered, as he locked the doors and climbed into his car, if everything was alright at Etheridge and Associates.

He certainly hope so! He was not only Marshall's pastor, Covenant Fellowship was the church home for Joel, Meredith, Delores and many others within that firm. If trouble sprang up there, it could affect a lot of people.

He steered out onto the street, cautioning himself to wait, and not assume anything. Maybe Marshall was dealing with a personal issue. No point in letting his imagination run off with his head. He'd know soon enough.

Marshall maneuvered his car in and out of the lunch hour traffic, his mind steeped in this morning's episode with Cagle Lawrence.

As if making a point, Cagle had arrived a couple of hours ahead of schedule, full of smugness, and exuding an evil sort of triumph.

Joel had managed to sleep, if only out of sheer exhaustion. He had taken Marshall's advice and not come in until ten o' clock, only moments before Cagle Lawrence had decided to make his appearance.

There was little of a positive nature that Marshall could associate with today's encounter, other than the fact that Joel was able to control his temper and refrain from any further assaults on Lawrence.

Marshall scowled darkly. His own estimation of Cagle Lawrence made him wonder if that was such a positive thing, after all.

It had been a brief session, that was another thing. Cagle had simply sauntered in to hear what he already knew, and was gone.

He did say that Joel could see Meredith one more time, to inform her that Marshall would be managing her, but even then, only at the office. That was scheduled to happen today at four, if Joel could arrange it.

Marshall sighed deeply. "That's one phone call I don't envy Joel," he said bleakly to himself. "It's going to be hell for him." Even as he said it, he knew that he could only guess at how true that statement was.

He pulled into the restaurant's parking lot, and noted that Gary's car was already there. This was a meeting he actually looked forward to.

Everyone at Etheridge and Associates loved and respected Pastor Gary Brenner. Marshall and Gary had been friends for quite some time, long before Gary lost his wife, Carla, some twelve years earlier.

Gary was a wise and gifted teacher, as well as a pastor who actually cared about the people in his congregation. He took a genuine interest in their day to day lives, and made sure he was accessible as their spiritual covering. If anyone could view this situation from a Godly perspective, it was Gary.

Marshall's pastor spotted his entrance and flagged his attention. "Hey, fella!" He stood up and grasped Marshall's hand warmly, then motioned toward the booth.

"Good to see you! How's Bobbie?"

"Oh, she's great, Gary. You know Bobbie." Marshall brightened at the mention of his wife's name, to his friend's great relief.

"Tell her I said hello." Gary handed him a menu and signaled a waiter. "Let's go ahead and get all the preliminary interruptions out of the way so we can cover some ground."

Marshall grinned at his friend appreciatively. "Most efficient. I guess your years of pastoring must have taught you that."

"Actually," Gary replied, his eyes softening as he opened up the menu, "Carla taught me that, among other things."

"Carla was quite a lady," Marshall said sincerely, glancing at his menu, as the waiter approached their table.

They gave their orders and flipped over their cups for coffee. Gary eyed Marshall inquisitively, and waited patiently, although Marshall seemed to be having difficulty getting started.

"Marshall," he finally prompted. "Is anything wrong at the office?"

"Why, what have you heard?"

Gary smiled and shook his head. "Not a thing. Hazarding a guess."

"It was a good guess." Marshall unfolded his napkin and began absently twisting a corner of it around one finger. "Something is very wrong at the office. Horribly wrong. Joel and Meredith are facing something straight out of hell."

Gary raised one eyebrow. "He loves her," he remarked, frankly.

"Now, how come everybody knew that but me?"

"I don't know how you could miss it! Joel wears it like a billboard. He has yet to finish a sentence to me, when *she* drags in. And boy, can that girl drag, on a Sunday morning!"

Marshall couldn't help sharing his pastor's grin, as a vision of the sleepy-eyed Meredith, wandering in, wearing sweat pants and a sour "I hate morning people" expression loomed before him.

"Yeah, she certainly does do that!" he agreed.

He laid his napkin to one side as his manner shifted to graveness. "Gary, there's big trouble ahead for Joel and Meredith. Even though they love each other, it may not be enough to help. But then again," he added, giving his pastor a knowing look, "it may be the only thing that can."

Joel sat woodenly at his desk, staring at the telephone as if it were a snake. His tortured mind was serving no purpose at the moment, other than housing sad thoughts that moved rampantly around, helping his headache to grow.

He looked over at the clock and breathed out a quiet sigh. He wished that he had the power to stop time but instead, it was accelerating, rushing him toward that dreaded moment when Meredith would come to his office today and carelessly plant herself in a chair, kicking her shoes off and demanding to be told why she was there.

He laid his head down on his desk, then raised it up again, at the sound of a timid knock.

Delores opened his door and came halfway into the office. "Joel," she began, in a voice rich with compassion, "would you like for *me* to make the call?"

Joel looked down at the telephone and back up at his secretary. "Thank you for wanting to take it off me, Dee."

His words were rough with feeling and he looked away to ward off the threat of exposure. "No," he answered, after a long moment. "I have to do this myself. But thank you."

He absently set the Newton's Cradle on his desk in motion, then stopped it. "What time is good? Still four?"

"I've left an hour open then. Do you need to give her more time?"

"I wish I could." He straightened up in his chair and cleared his throat. "No." He shook his head. "The more time this takes, the more things will be said that shouldn't be. An hour is fine."

"Okay, Joel." Delores paused, then came closer and gave him a quick, impulsive hug. "I'm so sorry!"

He just sat there, looking down at his hands. She gave his shoulder a quick, kindhearted squeeze and left him to face his task alone.

He stared over toward the large windows, trying to rehearse his words. Finally, he abandoned the effort. "Time to get this over with," he muttered out loud, snatching up the phone and punching in Meredith's number, before he could change his mind.

The line rang several times and Joel was beginning to wonder if she was out, when he heard a sudden fumbling sound and a breathless "Hello?"

His heart raced. "Merry?"

"Hey, Mister Man!" Her words were wrapped in tenderness and threatened to send him over the edge.

"Hey, yourself." He tried to keep his tone light. "I thought maybe you were gone."

"I was just... mopping the downstairs bathroom."

"You were cleaning?" He actually was surprised, but he was really just allowing himself to be drawn into a stolen moment with her.

"Not... not exactly." Meredith stammered in a way that was all too revealing.

He smiled, in spite of his heavy heart. "What did you do, Merry?" he asked, remembering the plane ticket.

"What makes you think I've done anything?"

"Out with it."

"Well..." She stalled for time and then exploded, in a torrent of words.

"I mean, I didn't know what else to do with it, Joel, because it was bad, and I don't have a garbage disposal, and if I gave it to Hook, it would kill him, or at least make him sick..."

"Merry..."

"And if I threw it away, it would just stink everything up..."

"Meredith..." He cut in. "What exactly is it we're talking about?"

She let out a sound of exasperation then confessed lamely. "Some green lunch meat."

Joel was startled that he could laugh. He let himself. "And what, pray tell, does green lunch meat have to do with the downstairs bathroom?"

His question was met with moody silence. "Answer, please?"

"Alright, fine!" she retorted, irritably. "I *flushed* it, so there! Like it's any of *your* business!"

Joel laughed again and Meredith reluctantly joined him.

"I take it your project wasn't too successful?"

"No," she admitted. "It sort of backed up. I had to use the plunger."

"Meredith!"

"Well, who *knew*?"

"*Most* people, I would imagine," he returned, still laughing. "Anyway, is everything okay, now?"

"I guess so."

"Merry..." Joel knew he couldn't continue with much more of this, and the thought that this would probably be their last pleasant conversation was wrecking him. Still, he grasped for one more precious second.

"What have I told you before, about these sorts of situations? We talked about this very recently, in fact."

"I forget," she said, as something vaguely tried to come to her.

"Zip lock bags."

"Oh yeah," she said, with a grin in her voice.

"Oh yeah." Joel was able to imitate her inflection, but his eyes were clouding over, and his heart was sinking fast.

This was it. He prayed for strength and forced himself to get on with it.

"Do you think you could come by the office today, around four, for about an hour?"

"A whole hour, huh?" He could see her playful expression. "Gee, I don't know, Mister Man. Whatever will you and I do, to pass an entire hour?"

He closed his eyes and bit his lip.

"Joel?" Uncertainty crept into her voice, when he didn't tease her back. "What is it?"

"I just... Marshall and I just need to discuss some things with you." Joel tried so hard to sound casual.

"*Marshall* and you?" Meredith's careless lifestyle gave off an impression of perpetual confusion, but she was actually razor sharp and not much got by her. "Maybe you'd better just tell me now."

"Meredith..." Joel left off guarding his tone, and she heard undisguised pleading. "Please don't press me now. Please just say you'll come."

She waited for a long moment, then said, "Joel, I thought we had covered all this on-a-need-to-know-basis mystery crap, before. Why can't you ever just say what the deal is, up front?"

"Sweetheart..." He hadn't meant to call her that, but he did. She instantly softened.

"Yes?"

"Please trust me."

"You know I trust you," she said. "I'm sorry."

"I'm sorry, too," he answered. "I really don't mean to be mysterious."

"But that's one of the reasons I love you," she replied softly.

Joel groaned inwardly, and laid his hand on his chest. "Merry..." he whispered. His voice was breaking up.

He took a deep breath, and got a hold of himself. "I'll see you soon, okay?"

"Okay," she answered. There was a lengthy, awkward pause. "'Bye, then..."

"Goodbye."

Meredith hung up the phone slowly, a threatening sensation creeping over her. There was something very unsettling about the way Joel had just said goodbye.

"He didn't even say 'I love you' back to me," she mused quietly, then shook herself.

"Oh, shut up, Meredith! You're just what Joel says you are... a spoiled brat!"

"I love you, too, Meredith." Joel sat there, gripping the dead receiver tightly, and his breathing became labored.

He made his way over to the windows and stared out at nothing at all. "I love you so much."

Joel dropped his gaze down to the busy Nashville streets, regretting his decision to ever come here. As much as he loved Meredith, maybe it would have been better if he had never established himself on Music Row, to begin with.

It was an accepted, undisputed fact that Joel Etheridge was responsible for launching her career. Her swift rise to the top of the industry now made her an exposed and vulnerable target, and Cagle Lawrence had her in his sights, poised to take her down, in the most humiliating way imaginable.

Joel could feel his heart breaking. His tears would come, so he knelt and let them fall. Father caught them. He was saving them.

Chapter Twelve

"I'm sorry to just dump all this on you, Gary." Marshall fidgeted with a packet of sweetener. "But I'm due back soon, and you needed to know."

Gary Brenner sat rigidly in his seat, and stared at Marshall Edwards in stupefied silence.

"Yes," he said faintly. He felt he should say more, but he just couldn't seem to come up with anything else. He exhaled heavily and continued to just look at his friend.

"Anyway," Marshall added, "as of today, I am officially Meredith's manager, and Joel will be working with a new band."

He wiped up the sweetener he had spilled. "She'll pitch a fit! Joel expects her to demand to be released from her contract. If things get ugly enough, he may even agree."

"No, he won't," Gary assured him quickly. "He won't allow just anybody to work with Meredith, not as long as it's in his power to control it."

"Yeah, I know you're right." Marshall smiled bitterly. "You know, Gary, that sick Cagle Lawrence is actually having her house watched!"

"How do you know?"

He shrugged. "Well, I guess I don't know for sure, but that's what he said. He's certainly not one to be bound by any moral constraints, so I have no problem believing him. He even rattled off her home address for good measure.

"Meredith is supposed to come by the office," he stopped and checked his watch, "in about an hour and a half. It's the last time Joel will see her for a long time, maybe even forever, if Cagle Lawrence has his way.

"I wish this wasn't going to be so traumatic, but it will be. The only memory Joel's going to have of today will be an ugly one." He looked at his friend imploringly.

"Joel doesn't know we're talking but he wouldn't mind. Stay close, Gary. To both of them, but especially to Meredith. Joel expects a pretty drastic reaction from her. I hate to believe that but, other than God, no one knows her better than he does."

"She can be pretty volatile," Gary agreed. "But she always comes around, sooner or later, Marshall. You know that."

"Yeah. Maybe." He remained unconvinced.

Gary studied his friend's nervous busy hands while he mulled over what his brain wanted to reject as too much information.

This sounded so far-fetched, yet so plausible. How smart was this Cagle Lawrence? How dangerous, how powerful, how ready to make good on his threat?

One thing was clear; the man must be pretty well set financially, if he could afford to have someone's house watched. A man who would go to such lengths was obviously determined to get what he was after.

Gary offered Marshall a fresh packet of sweetener to mutilate, and chuckled in amusement at his embarrassed grin.

"Listen," he said as Marshall began clearing away another mess, "this Cagle Lawrence may be resolved to have things go his way, but you and I both know that Joel

Etheridge is a powerful opponent. Few men can be as obstinate, or as unyielding. For instance, this business about having Merry's house watched to make sure Joel stays away. She has to come to the office, from time to time. What's to insure that it's not Joel she sees? And what about her mail? Is he watching that, too?"

Marshall sighed wearily. "You don't understand, Gary. It's not that Joel *can't* find ways to get around Cagle Lawrence. It's that he *won't*. Not even a little. And Lawrence seems to know it. If it were anybody else but Meredith. This is the woman he loves."

Marshall's short laugh was harsh. "*Love!* That word is just not strong enough for what Joel has for that woman."

He put down the sweetener and gave his pastor a look of frustration. "Joel is completely... I've never seen anything like this. It's almost scary. If Cagle Lawrence instructed Joel to die right now, I think I almost believe he would lie down, and just stop breathing. Anything to keep those photos of Meredith from getting out there. He won't do one thing to risk that, even if it means having Merry turn on him."

"Do you really think that could happen?" Gary asked soberly.

He gave a helpless shrug.

"Marshall, why doesn't Joel just tell Meredith what Lawrence is up to?"

"I asked Joel that," Marshall said. "He said there's no way Meredith would remain silent and pretend to go along with everything, that her hot temper would make her confront Cagle Lawrence, and then she'd be done for.

"I guess he would know. Lawrence told us that if he even suspects that Merry knows, the pictures will be out the next day. You know what I think?" He eyed Gary sharply and waited for his negative response.

"I think this is one of the most carefully orchestrated, diabolical puppet shows that ever came out of the pit. This character has covered every base!"

"Then why doesn't he insist that Joel release Meredith from her contract, if he doesn't want Joel anywhere around her?" Gary was clearly puzzled.

"Because it's just what I said it is, a puppet show. Cagle Lawrence hates Joel with a passion, and he just wants to watch him suffer. It's fine with him for Joel to gaze at Meredith through the shop window. In fact, he *wants* him to... as long as Joel knows that it's Cagle's shop, and that he can't come in.

"He'll thoroughly enjoy dangling Meredith right before Joel's eyes, but just out of his reach!"

"That's sick!" Gary declared hotly.

"You said it," Marshall agreed, reaching for his napkin. "This meeting today, for example. It's all a part of Lawrence's script, as far as I'm concerned. We all show up, say our lines and Merry storms out, after calling Joel everything imaginable. And unimaginable," he added, sadly.

"It'll no longer be a question of whether or not they can see each other. If Lawrence has his way, Meredith will refuse, on her own, to ever have anything to do with Joel Etheridge, after today."

Cagle Lawrence signaled the back alley bar's waitress for more drinks, drew deeply on his cigarette, and gave his lunch partner a hostile frown.

"I want your man at his post by six tonight and until I say the word, he'd better have somebody there around the clock, or I'm holding you responsible, Peters. No skirt walks out on me! I don't care how long it takes, I get what's mine.

She goes when I'm through with her and not before. And I don't put up with incompetence!"

The object of his veiled threat had already summed Cagle Lawrence up to be a man who thought that life was a B-movie set and that he was the star, but he wisely kept that assessment to himself. He shifted uneasily in his chair, and tapped his own cigarette against the edge of his plate.

"You don't have to worry about Tony," he said, as convincingly as he could manage, under Cagle's antagonistic scowl. "Tony does just what he's told and nothing else."

He waited for the waitress to replace their empty glasses before he resumed his remarks.

"Listen," he began, his eyes darting around the room. "I know you don't like questions, but I'm curious enough to ask, anyway. How many years has it been? Fourteen? Fifteen? Anyway, why wait until now to come after your girlfriend? Why not back then, when she first skipped out? I don't get it."

"It's not up to you to get it," the would-be gangster returned, irritably. "And you're right, I don't like questions. Let's just say that the girl who took off fifteen years ago was a little nobody. Pretty, sure. Great figure. Still, a dime a dozen and easily replaced.

"It wasn't worth my time to go chasing after her." Cagle ground his cigarette out, almost as if symbolically snuffing out the object of his sick desire. "But now's the perfect time. Little Miss Purity has become a star. One of 'Music City's Own', as they say. Name in all the papers, face plastered all over billboards..." He favored his companion with an ugly sneer. "Mere snapshots. Maybe this town would like to see some *real* art!"

Peters dropped his mouth open in surprise. "You mean, you're gonna sell those pictures either way, no matter what the girl's manager does?"

"Sure, why not?" Cagle shrugged indifferently. "And you can bet the offers will come flooding in! What do I care, what happens to the little Holy Roller? By the time I'm finished, she won't care, either. This born-again trip's just a crutch. She can sing about it, and take care of the rent, but it's not like there's any *real* payout, not like Hollywood.

"And as far as her lover-boy manager's concerned, when I'm done, she won't care if he lives or dies. He'll look like such a hypocrite, she'll hate him with a passion, not to mention his precious religion!"

"How do you know they've got something going on?" Peters asked.

"I played it as a hunch at first. Then I went over to his office yesterday to spell things out for him. Forget the hunch!"

Cagle smirked and drained his glass. "No man gets that riled up over a chick unless he wants her for himself. And knowing Meredith Clark, and I do, I'm betting she's all head-over-heels for him. But not for long. Because you see, Peters, I happen to know that just a couple of days ago, she told him all about getting knocked up and having to take care of it."

He gave a nasty laugh. "Perfect timing! Now, when he suddenly goes cold on her, she's gonna think that's why and before long, all this bull about Christian love and forgiveness will go right out the window, along with Mr. Etheridge. And I'll be there, as repentant as ever a little sinner was, to atone for my foolish, youthful ways and to take her away from all this, and from Joel Etheridge. Believe me, by then, she'll be ready to jump into the first cab outta here... which will be going my way!"

Cagle leaned forward and fixed Peters with a warning look. "I'm paying you good money to see that this goes off without a hitch. If you can't handle the job, say so now."

Peters cleared his throat and toyed with his cigarette butt. "You already checked me out," he said. "You seemed satisfied enough, when you hired me."

"I won't be satisfied until I get what I came for," Cagle answered smoothly. "What about her phone?"

"Well, I have to confess, I haven't tapped a landline in a long while. Most people don't use them in their homes anymore. It'll have to be done from the outside. Not the best way, easier to spot and to remove."

"She never did go in for cell phones. That phone is probably all she has. No matter if the tap *is* spotted. The only one who'll be onto us will be Etheridge, and he won't mess with me. How soon can it be done?"

"I'd better do it late tonight when she's asleep, if the gate's still open. The box is mounted on the house."

"Right, do it tonight." Cagle's face contorted with an unholy pleasure. "Tonight is the first in a series of long, sleepless nights for our sweet couple. No music from the songbird tonight."

He stared into his empty glass with mean delight. "Tonight should be just about perfect."

Delores took a deep breath, as Meredith came through the door, and hurried to come up with a smile.

"Hi, sweetie!" She came forward and caught her in a big hug.

"Hi, Dee!" Meredith gave her a beautiful smile and carelessly tossed her jacket onto the sofa. "You smell good! What *is* that?"

"You ought to know. You gave it to me."

Meredith's eyes widened in appreciation. "Boy, I'm good!"

Delores gave a little laugh. "Yes, you are, honey!"

She slipped into her chair and motioned for Meredith to sit. "They're just finishing up in there. Let me give him a ring."

She picked up the phone and dialed into Joel's office.

"Merry's here, whenever you're ready." She listened for a moment. "Okay, just let me know."

She flashed Meredith an apologetic smile as she hung up. "They just need another minute."

Meredith shrugged. "I guess I'm a little early."

She got up and wandered over to the windows, and idly watched the rush hour traffic below. "You keep a clean window, Dee," she commented lightly, refocusing her eyes to study the glass, as she was prone to do. "What are you guys doing for Thanksgiving?"

"I guess we're all going over to our son's house. You met Julian once, didn't you?"

"I did." Meredith nodded absently.

"What about you, dear?" Delores asked. "Made any plans yet?"

"Well..." she began slowly. "I usually go down to the shelter and do a little music, while they feed the homeless. I probably still should do that, I guess, but..."

A pretty pink touched her cheeks, and she turned to Delores, with her eyes shining. "Maybe I'll do something different this year."

Delores felt her own cheeks go red. Why had she asked such a stupid question? Of *course* Meredith would be pinning new hopes on this holiday season!

Just as she was wishing the floor would swallow her up, the intercom buzzed sharply, causing Meredith's heart to dance and hers to break.

Chapter Thirteen

Pastor Gary hesitated, then drew in his breath and stabbed at the doorbell again. He was just getting ready to repeat his efforts, when the door opened slowly and a slight, disheveled wraith looked up at him with dull, lifeless eyes.

No one spoke and, with deliberate indifference, she moved away from the door, leaving it ajar for him to come or go, as he pleased.

After a moment, he let himself in and stared at the little heap wrapped in an afghan, and draped over the arm of the couch. The word "discarded" instantly came to Gary. She somehow made him think of an unmatched sock lying in the back of a drawer.

He shivered slightly. It was freezing in here!

He looked around for the thermostat and adjusted it, before coming back around to take a seat close to her. He was still searching for a way to begin when a low, shallow voice interrupted his thoughts.

"What do you want, Preach?"

He finally spoke slowly and carefully. "I want you to say things to me. I want you to tell me what you're feeling... if you even know, yet. Whatever you need to say, I want you to hit me with it."

Meredith dragged herself up into a sitting position and raked her long hair to one side, before meeting her pastor's eyes.

"Yeah? And then what?" she asked sharply. "Is that when you start making excuses for him and try to make me understand why people do the things they do?"

Her sad, beautiful face took on a hardness completely foreign to her, and she looked away with bitter eyes. "We're not going to have that conversation."

"Alright," Gary agreed, in an effort to calm her. "We won't talk about him. Right now, I just want to know about you."

"What *about* me?" she bit out harshly. "Am I okay? No, Preach, I am *not* okay! What else do you want to know? Do you wanna bounce a sermon off me about forgiveness? Well, go do a podcast, and leave me alone!"

She wiped a traitor tear away angrily and focused her cold stare onto the floor.

Gary watched her silently and gave her time to reset her emotions, before he spoke again. "Did you sleep at all last night?"

She shrugged.

"Have you talked to Father?"

"Nope!" She chopped the word off in a way that warned him not to pursue that any further.

He left his chair and came and knelt in front of her, taking her small hands in his.

Meredith was about the age his and Carla's little Bethany would be, had she survived her feeble start at life. Gary had so empathized with Meredith over the years that, without knowing it, he had transferred his paternal love over to her. He ached, just seeing the pain in her face.

"Listen." He spoke cautiously, so as not to have her withdraw any further. "I didn't come here to talk you into anything. We won't talk about yesterday if you don't want to. I won't speak of forgiveness. I won't even try to get you to pray with me.

"I just want you to know that I'm hurting for you." His voice wavered and she glanced up to see real sorrow in his eyes. "I wish my Carla could have known you, Merry. She would have loved you as much as I do."

Meredith struggled for restraint before mute sobs began to shake her slight form. She clung to Gary's hand and allowed herself a brief release, before clearing her throat and wiping her face on the afghan.

"Thank you," she whispered, in a voice like wet gravel. She tried again to clear her throat, which was becoming a little sore.

"I know you mean that, Preach, and I love you, too. The thing is..." Here was one of the very few people in the world, possibly the only one, that she didn't want to hurt today. She chose her words with care.

"The thing is, I have to work through this by myself, at least for now. We can't talk yet, okay?"

Gary gave her an understanding smile and caught one of her hands again with a little squeeze.

"Okay," he conceded. "I'll back off, if that's what you want. But you might as well know that I'm gonna keep coming around, from time to time, to make sure for myself that you're making it okay."

"Oh, *I'll* make it okay," Meredith declared with the familiar lift of her defiant chin. "I always make it."

She gathered the afghan tighter and eyed Gary curiously. "How did you find out about all this, Preach?"

"Marshall," he admitted, hoping she wouldn't realize he had known before yesterday's meeting.

"Marshall," she echoed dully. "He was at the office yesterday. I guess he hurried to tell you what went down, in case I came home and did something drastic, like shoot my cat. Good ol' Marshall." Her tone was laced with bitterness.

"Merry, you and Marshall are friends, you *have* been for years." Gary protested, mildly. "You trust Marshall, don't you?"

Meredith stiffened and leveled her heavy gray eyes at him. "Don't be hurt by this, but today I don't know *who* my friends are and I don't care. And as for trust, don't make me laugh! Sorry," she added, seeing his faint reaction. "That's just how it is."

Gary digested this quietly, before rising up and preparing to leave. "People do love you, Merry," he insisted softly. "You know in your heart that Marshall's your friend. And someday, you'll realize that Joel is, too."

Meredith leaped up from the couch and faced him squarely and furiously. "Joel Etheridge was *never* my friend!" Her words were bitter and coated in wrath. "He's nothing but a two-bit liar and for all I care, he can rot in hell!"

"Meredith!" She had finally managed to shock him!

"I don't care! If you're here on some campaign for Joel, you can just forget it! I don't intend to ever see him again, so don't be looking for me at church tomorrow morning!"

She seemed to be having difficulty breathing, and Gary noticed high color in her cheeks. He hesitated, then placed the back of his hand on her forehead. She was burning up!

"Why, you're... your hands were cold when I got here, but you're running a fever now!" He was alarmed.

"My throat," she explained impatiently. "It's just a little hard to swallow, and my ears are starting to ache. I get this from time to time, it's no big deal."

"And you're planning on holing up in this house, that feels like a meat locker, all weekend, and probably won't even think to eat."

"I can turn the heat up if I need to," she answered sullenly. "And I eat when I get hungry."

"Eat what?" he demanded. "Merry, you won't even go to the store unless there's absolutely no food in this house and even then, you come back with frozen corn dogs, or lunch meat you never even bother to open!"

Meredith lifted glazed eyes to her pastor and favored him with a scornful glare. "Well, I guess we both know who furnished you with *that* bit of information. You certainly have been busy today!"

Gary almost choked on his frustration. "Okay, okay! Let's not even go there, if it's going to get you all worked up. The point is that you've got to take better care of yourself. Stop looking at me like that, and listen to me!" He took her hands, pleading with her. "Won't you please see a doctor, Meredith?"

"It's Saturday, Preach."

"Let me take you to the ER, or a walk-in clinic."

"Yeah, right. Like I'm gonna go hang out in some overcrowded waiting room for eight hours, with about a hundred croupy kids! Not to mention a pack of teenagers, pretending they're taking selfies, when they're really just uploading pics of me, looking my absolute finest, to their social media pages. No thanks!"

She saw his genuine concern and offered him a small truce. "Okay, I'll call Doctor Beatty's service and see if he'll call something in for me. Happy?"

Gary relaxed in relief and nodded. "Yes, if you promise to get right on that."

Meredith took a suggestive step toward the door and he took the hint.

"Will you give me a call if you need anything, or if you just want to talk?"

She gave him a slight eye roll, then came up with something like a brief smile. "When it's time."

Gary stopped at bottom of the porch steps and turned, as Meredith spoke again.

"I'll be fine, Preach. And... thanks."

He smiled and waved, before getting into his car and, as the door closed behind her, he sent up a prayer with her name on it.

He was so engrossed in his petition, that he never even noticed the black Suburban just down the road from Meredith's drive, or the two men witnessing his departure.

Joel stopped short and looked at his telephone with startled eyes.

He had forgotten to turn on his answering machine. The last thing he wanted was to talk to anybody right now. He reached over to switch the machine on, then sighed in resignation, and snatched up the receiver.

"Yes!" His voice was thin and abrupt.

"What do you mean *yes*? You don't even know what the question is, yet!" There was a beautiful laugh on the other end of the line, and Joel slumped back into the sofa, in glad relief.

"Mom!"

"Hi, honey!" She chuckled softly. "You actually sound like you've missed me!"

"Mom..." Boyish tears surprised Joel, and he hurried to sound normal. "Of course, I've missed you. How are you?"

"Oh, you know me, honey."

Laura Etheridge spoke lightly, while her mother's ears scanned her son's voice for what she immediately identified to be brokenness. "I'm always fine. More importantly, how are you? And Joel Etheridge, why do you even *have* a cell phone, if you're never going to answer it? I've been calling it for the last two days. Your voicemail is full, by the way."

"Oh, Mom, who knows where the heck that silly thing is? Cell phones are just a big pain. I don't know why I ever thought I needed one." Joel couldn't help remembering that he and Meredith both shared this same viewpoint, and just thinking of her stung him. "I guess I haven't checked house messages lately, either. Anyway, I'm okay. I'm good."

Too quick and too cheerful. Laura wrinkled her brow and swallowed a lump that suddenly formed in her throat.

"Son..." She hesitated for a brief second. "Tell me honestly, if this isn't a good idea. You can't hurt my feelings."

"What is it?"

"Well, I've waited until the last minute as usual, to think about the holidays. I don't know if you've made any plans."

"Mom," Joel cut in gently. "I thought I'd just stay in Nashville, this year. I'm not up for a lot of traveling, if that's okay."

"Sure, it's okay. And then you'll be leaving right after Thanksgiving for one of Meredith's trips, won't you?"

He couldn't manage an answer.

"Joel?"

"Uh... no, Mom, that's... there've been a few changes."

"Oh." She knew she had just stumbled on the cause of her son's heartache. "Well," she hurried on, "if you're going to be home, then you're playing right into my hands."

"Oh yeah?" He rubbed his eyes and tried to be more attentive. "How's that?"

"I thought I'd invade your bachelor pad for a bit."

Hope sprang up in Joel's heart, but he paused before responding. "You're not going to Iris and Jack's?"

"Your sister's been after Jack to go to Florida all year, and he finally caved in," Laura informed him. "So I'm all alone, poor me."

"Mom." Joel lost his battle for composure, as gratitude and a need for his parent overwhelmed him. His voice was pitifully revealing, and Laura's eyes began to spill over.

"Could you?" he asked hoarsely. "Would you really come?"

She forced a bright laugh. "I can and I will."

"When can you?"

Her still lovely face softened, as she heard his faint pleading tone.

"When do you want me, honey?"

"Yesterday."

"I'll get up early tomorrow and head your way. I'm driving, so it'll be late before I get in. Probably eight or nine. Want anything from Oklahoma, Joel?"

"Just you, Mom." He marveled at the effect her coming was already having on him. "Call along the way, okay?"

"Okay, Son. I'll see you tomorrow night. I love you."

"I love you too, Mom." Joel hung up the phone and lay back against the sofa cushions, focusing his eyes blindly on the ceiling. Relief was fleeting and pain found him again.

In defiance to his will, his mind took him back to yesterday's meeting with Meredith.

By the time she left, she ran the gamut on emotions, ending with nothing short of rage. Her beautiful, expressive eyes had burned, as she unleashed her careless tongue in a verbal assault on both him and Marshall.

When she finally realized that no amount of threats or abuse would convince Joel to release her from her contract, she proceeded to spew forth an eruption of curses and insults that had left Marshall white-faced with horror, even though her bullets were aimed at Joel.

She made her exit by snatching a framed photo of herself with Joel, Marshall, and Delores off the wall, and smashing it down onto the pointed top of a Dove award.

Joel reached for a pillow and closed his eyes, as he thought about the one moment that had hurt him more than any other. It wasn't her accusations. It wasn't her threats or her four-letter words.

Nothing had any impact at all, compared with that split second when her shining eyes first dimmed, and her bright smile clouded over with that earliest twinge of fear that something was not right.

All night long and all today, that one change of expression played before Joel's eyes like some kind of cruel hologram.

Now, as it haunted him again, he released a ragged breath and, dispensing with the prescribed rudiments of manhood, gave in to that racking, depleting sort of sobbing that comes in mercy, to stop a man's heart from killing him.

Meredith crouched miserably in the window seat, and identified with the dead, gray, barrenness of November's first Saturday.

Like Joel, her mind had relentlessly forced her to relive yesterday's nightmare, over and over. She had engaged in one early bout of weeping when, as she was waking, she remembered that Joel had asked her in Gatlinburg to spend today with him.

Those tears and the few Gary had induced, and now all was dead. And gray. And barren.

Father sat quietly and watched her, His heart full of her. His arms were so ready to take her, but He knew that this strange child, that He loved so much, wanted to keep hurting. Right or wrong, it was her way. Persistently loving her was His way.

"Meredith."

"Don't," she whispered.

"Merry." Her suffering stung His heart.

"Please, don't."

His eyes rested sadly on her stony countenance, and on the crumpled heap of His son, Joel. His hands caressed the two bottles He carefully guarded.

Almost full, their precious salty contents were not unlike those He had been keeping watch over for His children, since the dawn of their creation.

Chapter Fourteen

Laura Etheridge pushed back her chair and gathered her tall, handsome son into her arms, as he entered the kitchen, clearly looking as if he'd been awake all night.

"Good morning, Mom." Joel dropped a kiss on her head and crossed over to the coffeepot.

"I set out a mug for you," she remarked casually, slipping back into her seat and moving her bible over to one side. "Am I crossing that thin line between mothering and nagging, if I also offer to throw some breakfast together for you?"

Joel gave her the suggestion of a smile and brought his coffee over to the table. "Tell you what..."

He took a chair and gave his hair the characteristic rake with his hand. "How about if I pass on breakfast, and slip in for lunch today, if I can make that happen?"

"Okay. Call me just before." Laura watched him stare blankly into his coffee for several minutes, before she leaned over and tapped his hand fondly.

"Joel?"

"Hmm?" He wouldn't look up.

"When you're ready, I'm here. Okay?"

He blinked quickly and managed to give her a swift glance. "Mom..."

She waited, and he carried on, awkwardly.

"I'm sort of tapped out, right now. I've been on a bender lately. The last few days have been much too hard and fast, and I need..." He swallowed and continued. "I need to return to some level of normalcy, if there *is* such a thing, and control. I'm too unstable now to be much good to anyone. It's too fresh to go into."

He raised his beautiful eyes, so much like his dad's, and let her read them. "I do want to talk with you about it, when I can do it without getting wasted. I can't *afford* to get wasted now, I have meetings all day. But we'll talk soon, Mom."

She let him know with a touch that she understood, and he looked past her at nothing, before finishing.

"I have to be able to concentrate. Something has hit me in the gut that I know the enemy means to destroy me with. I can't let that happen. I know you don't miss anything." He flashed her a wry grin.

"I might as well admit I've been crying like a faucet. For the most part, there's been some healing in that, but I'm starting to cross that line where it stops healing and starts paralyzing. I've got to focus, Mom." He gave a faint laugh.

"If I got into everything with you this morning, I wouldn't even be able to show up at the office, let alone conduct business, and business doesn't care about my personal issues. It doesn't go away, and it demands my attention and clear thinking, which is currently not my strong suit."

Laura reached over and gave his arm a pat. "Okay, Joel. No hurry." She gave him a conspiratorial wink. "I prayed all night for strength to come over you. It looks like God is coming across, huh?"

Joel loved this woman! He didn't even want to imagine what it would have been like to grow up without her. One thing he knew for sure... forty, fifty, sixty, it didn't matter. You never outgrew the need for a Godly mother.

"When do you go in?" Laura asked, scooting back her chair.

"Not until nine. I've got an hour."

She got up and took her cup to the sink, stopping on the way back to pick up her bible and ruffle Joel's hair, before leaving him to finish his coffee alone.

"Joel Michael Etheridge, you are grayer than your mother!" She gave him an affectionate bop on the head. "Just do what you do, honey. I'm going back to my room to do a little unpacking so if you leave before I'm done, I'll see you at lunch."

She laid a light kiss on his cheek and slipped out to give him some space.

Joel recognized the gesture she was making and smiled abstractly to himself. His little mom had so much wisdom and loved the Lord so devotedly. He was greatly relieved to have her here. If anyone could help him keep a clear, level head through all this mess, it was Laura Etheridge.

She was a tiny little thing, even smaller than Meredith, and barely reaching five feet two. No one would ever suspect her sixty-one years. Her short brown hair still had a luster and the few wrinkles she did have had to be looked for. Her eyes were dark and bold, only hiding behind glasses when she was reading or doing close work.

Joel had his father's eyes and tall, muscular frame. Paul Etheridge, before being killed in a car crash some twenty years ago, had been the love of Laura's life, and it never ceased to thrill her that their only son was such a close replica to his father, in so many ways.

Iris, their only daughter, looked very much like Laura. She was four years younger than Joel and living in Kentucky with her husband, Jack. There were no children... anymore.

Joel's heart wrenched at the thought of his sister, who once loved him.

He shook off old remorse and headed for the shower.

Delores put down the telephone for the third time, arguing with herself that it would do absolutely no good, at all, to try and talk with Meredith. She'd probably mumble some vague excuse and hang up on her or, worse yet, be openly hostile to her. She couldn't handle that!

She bit her lip and frowned at the telephone, mulling over what to do. Finally, she lifted up the receiver and rang up Gary Brenner.

"Dee!" He returned her greeting warmly. "I thought you would have had enough of my voice yesterday, the way I rambled on. I must say, I really do have a very patient congregation."

"Well, the fact is, I'm a little worried about something Gary, and I was hoping you could help."

"Sure, I'll try."

"Well, I'm concerned about Meredith," she began and then halted as she realized that Joel had come through the door from the lobby, undetected.

"Oh, shoot," she muttered.

"Hmm..." Gary mused. "Big Guy just stroll in?"

"Yes."

"Did he hear something he wasn't supposed to?"

Delores let out a sigh of resignation. "Unfortunately, yes, so I might as well get on with it."

Joel had approached her desk, and was quizzing her with his eyes.

"Go ahead," Gary prompted with a grin. "Only, don't look at him. That's always a big mistake. Just look down at your desk and go for it. Otherwise, he's going to grill you and you know it!"

Delores knew he was right, so she took his advice. "Well, it's just that Marshall came in this morning, and said you told him that Meredith was sick when you saw her Saturday."

She sensed Joel stiffening, and kept her eyes firmly glued to a stack of papers in front of her.

"Oh, brother! I see now why you didn't want him around for this."

"Yes," she confessed. "But I was wrong. Can you tell me what the deal is?"

"With Merry?" he asked. "Okay. And listen, just save yourself a lot of questions by repeating everything I say."

She smiled at his insight and waited.

"She was running a fever. She complained of a sore throat and an ear ache."

Delores closed her eyes with dread. "You said a fever and a sore throat?"

"And an ear ache."

Why did he have to say that? She cleared her throat. "And an ear ache..."

Joel gritted out something through clenched teeth, and flung his briefcase at the sofa, while Delores winced and leaned protectively over the phone.

"Gary, did she see her doctor?"

"No, since it was Saturday, and I couldn't get her to go to the ER, but she said she'd get Doctor Beatty to call in a prescription for her."

"Do you know if he *did* call in a prescription?"

Delores jumped, as Joel snapped his fingers loudly and, with an imperative gesture, made her surrender the phone.

"Listen, Gary!" His tone was curt, but Gary easily overlooked it, under the circumstances. "Did she happen to mention the fact that this is a recurring problem?"

"She did say that she gets it from time to time, but she also said it was no big deal."

"Well, of *course* she did! That's her official motto, 'No Big Deal'! She probably has it tattooed, somewhere!"

Joel had raised his voice, and now paused long enough to dial it back down. "I suppose she managed to convince you that she'd take care of it right away?"

"Well, she acted as if she knew what to do about it."

"Right!" Joel's eyes were attacking everything in their path. "That why the last episode landed her in the hospital!"

Gary balked for a moment. "When I was in California? Is *this* what that was?"

Joel expelled a long breath in an attempt to cool down. This was hardly Gary's fault.

"Listen," he said, in quiet, measured tones. "I'm sorry, Gary. It's just that Meredith is prone to severe ear infections and last time, she waited so long to have them checked, that her doctor jumped all over her. He said one more episode that critical and she could lose part of her hearing, maybe even completely. Her ears were bleeding, Gary!"

Gary sat up straighter in his chair. "Bleeding!"

"This is very important. I know her well enough to know that, once you left, she just blew it off, especially in the state of mind she was in. I can promise you, Gary, that she was just trying to get you to drop it. She had no intention of making that call.

"I can also promise you that she just laid around in a blanket all weekend. I doubt if she's eaten anything." Joel had been fingering one of the pencils on Dee's desk and now snapped it in half. "That little idiot!"

"I'll go check on her now, Joel." Gary pulled on his shoes and looked around for his keys.

"Do that, Gary, will you? It won't do for anyone from this office to go, not even Dee, not yet. Dee's going to get

Beatty on the phone to see if he can get her on in there and then call you back. Gary, you have to *make* her go."

"I'm on it, Joel. I'll call you when we're back." Gary hung up before Joel could thank him.

He handed the receiver back to Delores with a look of apology. "I'm sorry," he said simply.

"No, Joel, I'm the one who's sorry," she protested. "It wasn't right to try to keep this from you. I see that now. I may have meant well, but it was stupid, not to mention dangerous."

"Well, I really can't blame you." Joel picked up his briefcase. "The way I've been throwing fits lately, crawling down everyone's throats and acting like Meredith..."

He grinned at her raised eyebrows. "It's a wonder you haven't all quit!"

He took the devotional from her desk and headed toward his office. "I need about a half hour."

Laura turned the fire off under the whistling kettle and listened for a moment. It *was* the doorbell, after all!

She wiped her hands on a dishtowel and hurried through the living room to answer it.

The tall, white-haired man, who lifted his eyes expectantly, was unable to conceal his surprise.

"Yes?" She waited pleasantly.

"I'm... sorry," he stammered in wonder. "I'm sure I must be staring. It's just that I expected Joel. I didn't see his car, but he sometimes puts it in the garage."

"I'm afraid *mine* is in the garage." She dimpled slightly, recognizing him from a church bulletin on Joel's coffee table. "He was here for lunch earlier today, but I'm afraid he's not here now. You're Joel's pastor."

"Gary Brenner." He offered his hand and she shook it lightly. "I'm sorry, but surely we've not met?" He would have remembered.

"I'm Laura Etheridge, Joel's mother. No, we haven't met, but I've seen your picture."

She stood to one side and gestured him in. "If you don't mind following me out to the kitchen, I was just about to make some tea. Are you a tea drinker?"

Gary smiled his appreciation. "I am, and that's very definitely the best offer I've had all day."

He followed her trail, and pulled out two chairs, as Laura busied herself at the counter.

"I phoned the office," he explained, watching her quick light movements. "Delores said Joel left around three. He didn't say where he was headed, so she just assumed he was going home early. I have to pass this neighborhood anyway, on my way home, so I thought I'd swing by."

Laura carried a loaded tea tray over and allowed Gary to take it from her, before sitting down.

"Joel called here, just before he left," she explained, pouring the hot water and handing him a tea bag. "He didn't say what his plans were, only that he'd be home around seven for dinner."

She raised her cup and looked at him across the rim with direct, honest eyes. "He said you might try to reach him."

Gary returned her scrutiny, wondering how much she knew of her son's troubles. She read his mind and smiled.

"No, he hasn't filled me in yet." She laughed at his revealing flush of color, and settled back into her chair.

"He will, when it's time. Time is something I have a lot of these days, so I can afford to be patient."

"Are you staying through the holidays?" Gary asked, relaxing into her easy manner.

"I'm staying as long as it takes."

He nodded, understanding, and toyed with his cup. "I told Joel that I would call him about Meredith." He glanced up at her. "Have you ever met Meredith Clark? She's one of Joel's clients."

Laura's eyes sparkled in amusement. "Pastor Brenner..."

"Gary," he corrected.

"Gary, you and I both know that Meredith Clark is *not* just one of Joe's clients!"

He grinned at her frankness.

"I *have* met her, a couple of times, in fact. She's a work of art. I may not know what's happened between them, but I'd have to be a squash not to know that Joel's in love with her."

Gary lifted an eyebrow. "A squash?"

She shrugged. "Pick any vegetable you like."

He laughed in delight, as she popped a cookie into her mouth and offered him the plate.

"A squash will do nicely!" Following the bleak order of the past few days, her naturally good nature was having a revitalizing effect on him. "I know Joel's glad you're here."

"Well, ordinarily, a forty-year-old man wouldn't have too much use for his mother, I'll admit that."

She pointed her spoon absently. "I'm the only parent Joel has left, so he'll just have to make do. I'm pretty much his only family, period."

"That's something that I've always wondered, about Joel. Why hasn't he ever married? Or *has* he been married before? I've never just come out and asked him that."

Laura shook her head. "Never has. I used to nag him about it and then one day, he just looked at me in that sober way he has, and said 'Mom, if it takes the rest of my life, I'm waiting for that once in a lifetime love. If it never comes, I'll die without it, but I'll never settle for anything less.' And he never has."

She smiled tenderly. "And so I've always prayed that God would grant him his desire and give him that special love he's waited all of his life for."

She grinned at Gary. "A lot of women have tried to convince my son that they were the answer to that prayer. This Meredith must be really something!"

Gary burst out with a rich laugh. "Oh, if you only knew!" He leaned forward, shaking his head. "Meredith became sick over the weekend. She said she would call in for some medicine but of course, she didn't. Joel found out about it this morning, and burst into flames!"

Laura giggled softly.

"He asked me... I *guess* it was asking... to take her to the doctor. I literally had to force her, by threatening to get Joel involved, if she didn't come peaceably."

His face clouded over for an instant, at the memory of her cold reception and angry resistance.

Laura gently invaded his thoughts. "What did her doctor say?"

Gary smiled. "Doctor Beatty? You know, he and Joel are the only two people I know of in Nashville that Merry can't intimidate. He yelled at her like a losing football coach, while the nurse rammed a needle the size of the Opryland Hotel into her hip!"

He rolled his eyes. "This did not sit well... pardon the pun... with our Little Miss Sunshine, who grabbed the needle and threatened to make the nurse eat it!"

Laura wiped her swimming eyes and shook with silent laughter.

"She's been ordered to take penicillin at home and I'm supposed to bring her back a week from today."

"Do you think she'll take her medicine?" she asked, studying his face as he looked down into his cup.

He met her eyes, another grin playing around his mouth. "Doctor Beatty said there had better be enough penicillin in her system next Monday to raise the dead! He also told her that if there wasn't a drastic improvement by then, he would personally body-slam her into a hospital bed so hard, they'd have to dig her out of it!"

"Sounds like he learned his bedside manner from Bullies-R-Us!" Laura chuckled, her phantom dimple ghosting her cheek so quickly that Gary wondered if he had imagined it.

"It's what Meredith responds to," he said. "Joel does it best, but Doc Beatty's no slouch. She'll take her medicine. The good news is that she got there in time before any real damage was done. She has Joel to thank for that. She knows it too, which is why she put up such a fight!"

"Not exactly sending out thank you cards, huh?"

"Listen, the real scene came when we got back. While we were gone, Joel gave Marshall his key to her house and made him take a load of groceries over there. You wouldn't believe that girl's eating habits!

"Anyway, he insisted. He even made out a list. Meredith hit the ceiling and threatened to throw it all out in the backyard. That reminds me." He handed Laura a folded check. "Stubborn to the letter N!"

Laura's eyes opened wide in amazement as she took the check and laid it to one side. "So this is what Joel has waited all his life for. My poor lovesick son has finally met his match!" she declared flatly.

"Looks that way." Gary laughed, then looked at her searchingly. "Are you a praying woman, Mrs. Etheridge?"

She widened her eyes expressively.

"Laura," he amended, accepting her silent rebuke.

"I have to be, Gary," she said simply. "And let me tell *you*, it pays to check in!"

"I believe you," he laughed. "Your son and his Meredith are gonna need some no-nonsense intercession."

He opened his hands and gave her a challenging look. "You up for it?"

Laura caught his hands in agreement and right away, they had Father's attention.

Chapter Fifteen

Hailey Fisher leaned back in her chair, making no effort to mask her confusion, and tried to understand what Joel was saying.

"You and Meredith are close, Hailey."

She nodded curiously.

Joel rested his chin in his hands, and weighed his next words.

"That's who Meredith needs in her life right now. Someone she feels very close to."

"Joel, Merry's like a sister to me, but even I don't rank up there with you."

"It can't be me."

"Why not?" she demanded.

He shrugged and she rolled her eyes. "Joel, why don't you do the entire city of Nashville a favor, and just tell that girl that you love her, already?"

She didn't get the shy grin she was expecting.

"I did."

"You did!" She broke into a smile. "Well, finally! It took you long enough. So, whatever's going on in her life right now, you're the one to help her with it, because I happen to know that she loves *you* like crazy!"

Joel picked up a pen and tapped it lightly on his desk. "How do you know that?"

"Well, the fact that I'm not blind comes in handy." She stopped and gave him a searching look. "Wait... what do you mean by 'how do you know that'? Do you mean that you told her how you feel, and she didn't admit that she loves you?"

"She did, but... " He let his words hang in the air.

"But what?"

He shrugged again and she slapped the arm of her chair. "Stop that! You and Meredith are both, hands down, the shoulder-shrugging champions of Tennessee! It's like an Olympic event, with you two. Why can't either one of you ever just give somebody a straight answer?"

"She said she did, but now she doesn't. Satisfied?" He concentrated harder on the pen in his hand.

"Well, I don't know how she managed to make you believe she doesn't love you, but she's lying right through her beautiful teeth."

Joel raised his head with such a hopeful look, that Hailey felt a stab of sympathy for him. "Do you think so, Hailey?"

"Joel Etheridge, how can you be so brilliant and so dumb at the same time?" She grinned at his look of surprise.

"Maybe you're so used to the way most women look at you, that you've built up an immunity to it, and can't see it in Meredith's eyes. Take it from me."

She stabbed the chair arm with her finger for emphasis. "Men run off the road looking at Merry, and she doesn't even know it. She only looks into *your* eyes, Joel, and if you can't see that, you're either blind or you don't *want* to see it."

He stared off at the window. "I *do* want to see it. I did see it. But it's... not there, anymore."

"Did you two have a fight? I mean, other than the recommended daily allowance that you both seem to require from each other? You know... "

She leaned forward and fastened him with a teasing look. "Those constant wars that you two engage in were the big tip off for most of us. You know, *bad* attention is better than no attention at all."

He almost laughed, then returned to a somber mood. "I wish it *was* just a fight. Hailey, how much do you know about Meredith's past?"

"Why?" She looked at him guardedly.

"Because she shared something with me, last Wednesday. Something that happened a long time ago. If you don't know about it, then I won't go into it."

"Are you referring to a situation that involved a man? Excuse me," she added crossly. "I mean a sorry *excuse* for a man! I didn't mean to insult men, in general."

Joel played the next card. "In New Orleans? When she was nineteen?"

Hailey whistled softly. "I can't believe she actually told you about that! I mean, I've tried a hundred times to get her to talk to you about it, but she absolutely would *not*. What made her change her mind?"

Joel leaned back and rubbed his forehead. "It's a long, involved story, Hailey. But it has something to do with why I called you here." He broke off and gave her a direct gaze. "When's the last time you talked to Meredith?"

"Not since before she went to Denver. I just got back from Memphis last night. I started to call her, but someone called *me* before I could, and I didn't think of it again until this morning. I decided to just stop by there, on my way home from here."

Joel sat up straight, and gestured in a way that underscored his need to be listened to very carefully. "I want to say something to you. You're not really going to understand, because I'm going to have to be vague. I have no choice. But try to glean what you can, okay?"

She nodded and waited.

"Merry and I spent the day together last Wednesday. She wanted to tell me about... the abortion." He bit his lip and waited to make sure she really had known about it. Satisfied that she had, he continued.

"She kept on insisting that when I heard what she had to say, I would change toward her. But before she could tell me anything, I told her that I love her. I didn't want to wait. After we talked and she told me everything that had happened, I had to keep reassuring her that nothing had changed; that I really do love her. The next night, she finally told me that she loves me and literally, within minutes, she was trying to hand me my walking papers."

"But Joel, that's just Merry and you *know* it," Hailey argued. "She's just scared. She's told me on more than one occasion that she's never been in love before. But she's in love with *you*, you've got to believe that!"

"I believe she wouldn't say it, if she didn't mean it."

"Exactly!"

"But sometimes, Hailey, a person can experience so much hurt and betrayal that love just gets lost in the shuffle."

Hailey studied him for a long, quiet moment, and he allowed her analysis.

"Did *you* betray her, Joel?"

"No, Hailey, I didn't. But she thinks I did."

She sighed, completely understanding. "Whatever Meredith convinces herself of, is the only truth she will accept, until God finally gets through to her."

Joel nodded. "Hailey, there's something more. This is where it gets vague. I'm not Meredith's manager anymore."

"Say that again?" She blinked in astonishment.

"Oh believe me, you'll hear it again and again... many times and in many different ways. That's why the horse, himself, is speaking to you." Joel indulged in a sarcastic grin. "This will probably become Internet fodder in no time at all, if it hasn't already."

The intercom buzzed and Joel picked up the receiver. "Yes?" His face flickered with approval at something Dee said. "Would you ask him if he would mind waiting for just a very quick minute? I won't be long." He paused, then smiled in relief. "Thanks, Dee."

He hung up and gave Hailey a faint smile. "Sorry. Listen, that's an appointment, so I'd better fish or cut bait."

She grinned at his use of one of Meredith's ultimatums.

"Something's happened that I can't talk about." Joel clasped his fingers together and leaned forward onto the edge of his desk.

"It has to do with Meredith and even *she* doesn't know about it. She can't either, not yet. I'm not trying to play games with you," he added quickly, catching her skepticism. "But I'm under a gag order that I'm not about to violate. Someone is out to get Meredith and he's deadly serious about it. I've been promised that if she gets wind of it, she's going to be hurt. And the kind of hurt this person is talking about won't go away. This kind of hurt, she can't survive."

"Are you saying that if she *doesn't* get wind of it, nothing will happen?"

"I don't believe that for a minute, but supposedly not, if I do what I'm told. Who knows? But I won't risk it and he knows it. I'm behind the eight ball."

"Someone knows about her past!"

"Yes, but that's not... " Joel stopped himself. "That's all I can say for now."

She stared at him dumbly. "Okay, so you're *not* her manager? Officially?"

"She's still under contract with this firm, but I've been ordered out of her life, both professionally and personally.

"Marshall has taken over Meredith's management. For whatever reason, this guy doesn't seem to mind that so, at least for now, she stays in-house, here. We're trying not to rock the boat, because he hasn't made releasing her from her contract a condition. I find that very odd," Joel added in a strange voice, as if he were talking to himself. "What is that about?"

"If someone's out to get *her*, why would he care who her manager is, one way or the other?"

"Who knows? He just does." He got up and came around to sit in a chair next to her.

"Listen. She can't even suspect any of this. You have to understand, Hailey. One false move, and Meredith is destroyed. She has no idea this person is up to anything. All she wants to believe is that I couldn't handle what she told me about her abortion, and that I don't want her, anymore. And, for now, I have to let her think that."

He had managed to stay in control until now. His voice shook, and Hailey suddenly believed him. She didn't understand any of it, but she believed him.

"Then... it really doesn't matter to you? What she told you?" she asked quietly.

Joel's eyes were clear and direct. "I've never been in love before, in my life. Meredith is it for me. She is all there ever will be, and if she won't have me, then I'll do without love. But she's not convinced of that and I can't explain myself to her... not without putting her in danger and I *won't* put her in danger, even if she hates me for the rest of her life. I can't, Hailey. I love her."

Hailey laid her hand on one of Joel's and smiled. "I know you do, Joel. That much is clear. Tell me what I can do."

He pressed his temples in a way that accented the great amount of stress he was under.

"Meredith is targeting almost anybody and everybody right now. I can't prove this, but after talking to Gary, I think even Father's getting a cold shoulder.

"Could you just pray about spending some time with her and seeing what you can do to... I don't know... thaw her out a little? If she would just open up to God, I know He could get her to drop her weapons and surrender.

"They do so well together, when she stops fighting Him. She may not ever have any use for me again, but if she gets hurt at God, she may decide she doesn't have any use for Him, either." Joel's eyes had never been so full of meaning. "Hailey... that would be the end of Meredith."

Hailey propped her cheek in one hand and looked over at him, after a moment. "Well, just sitting here, I'm drawing a blank on what I could possibly do, but I guess the important thing is to just be available. I can certainly do that!"

She rose to leave and Joel joined her.

"Here, I'll walk you out," he offered. He stopped at the door and turned back to her. "I guess I don't have to tell you that something as simple as making yourself available to Merry can put you in line for a lot of abuse."

She smiled and he hesitated.

"Hailey... whatever you do, don't defend me. She'll turn on you. It'll get ugly."

"I know."

"Thanks so much."

She shook her head. "Thanking me might be a little bit premature. Let's just see what happens."

Joel opened the door and escorted her into the outer office. A tall, good-looking, dark-haired man rose up out of his seat as Joel motioned to him.

"Hi, Ross! Thanks for coming." He indicated Hailey with a touch on her arm. "Hailey, this is Ross Decker, a good friend of mine. Hailey Fisher, Ross."

Ross took her hand and spoke a warm greeting. She did a quick appraisal, and filed his name away in her head.

"I'll be right with you, Ross, if you care to grab some coffee and have a seat."

"I'll have yours. It's easily the most comfortable one in the building," Ross joked, giving Hailey another swift glance before heading into Joel's office.

"Good to see you again, Dee," Hailey said on her way to the door.

"You too, Hailey."

Joel opened the lobby door and signaled for someone to hold the elevator. "Thanks again, Hailey, for coming by."

"Thanks for calling me. I'll see you at the wedding."

"The wedding?" He was puzzled.

Hailey laughed and stepped into the elevator. "Joel, you're something else!"

The doors closed and he stood there a second before he realized that she had been teasing him. He almost smiled, then thought better of it.

Meredith dragged out to the porch and pulled a handful of mail out of the box. She stood a moment, looking down her long drive at a field across the main road.

Someone was riding a horse out there. It was a perfect day that not even Meredith could fault. This day wouldn't take criticism.

It was in the high sixties and sunny, with just enough clouds to make the sky interesting, and it was predicted to stay that way most of the week.

Meredith meditated on how much trouble it would be to load the Jeep up and go fishing. It was a weekday, so she wouldn't have to contend with a crowd. She decided to abandon everything, and everybody, and just take off.

In fact, why not just throw a few things into a bag and *really* take off? She didn't have a gig until the weekend. She could easily be back by then. Her producer's parents had a furnished cabin at Center Hill Lake that they offered her the use of, nearly every time they saw her.

She turned around and wandered back into the house, almost stepping on Hook, as she stopped to throw the mail onto the coffee table. She had been letting it pile up again. After all, it was her table, not Joel's.

Hook followed her into the kitchen.

"Don't start!" she mumbled, opening the fridge, staring into it and then shutting it again. Nothing looked good.

Hook gazed up at her with imploring eyes, and she made a face. "Oh come on, Hook, don't look at me like that. You act like you're gonna die, if you don't eat the minute my feet hit the floor."

This was encouraging! She was actually talking to him without yelling! He turned up the charm.

She scooped him up and held his face firmly in front of her own. "Alright! You can eat, just don't stare at me like that. I *hate* that, it's creepy."

She plopped him back down, yanked the pull-ring top off a can of cat food and just sat the whole thing down on the floor.

Hook looked thoughtfully at the can and then at his dish, as she walked off. He decided to leave well enough alone. He would make do.

Meredith flopped down next to the telephone and dialed her producer's number.

"Perry Mitchell Productions!"

She wrinkled her brow. Who, in the world, was this? She shrugged. "Is Perry around?"

"May I ask the nature of the call?"

Meredith rolled her eyes. "Who *is* this?"

"My name is Patty, how may I help you?"

"You're new, aren't you, Patty?"

"Well, yes..."

Meredith smiled, in spite of her displeasure. "Well, you're doing a bang-up job. This is Meredith Clark. The nature of this call is to talk to Perry, so please, just get him on the horn, will you?"

The other voice hesitated. "Is this *really* Meredith Clark?"

"Unfortunately," Meredith admitted dryly.

"Uh... okay..."

She came so close to laughing, that it surprised her. She had forgotten what laughing felt like.

"Meredith!" Perry's voice caught her attention.

"Hey there, Music Man! Got yourself a new guard dog, huh?"

"I hope you were nice."

"I was Miss Manners."

He knew better, and laughed. "What's up?"

"Going fishing."

"Is that right?"

"Yep. Just as soon as you say I can use the cabin."

Perry grinned at her bluntness. "I'm sure that's fine. When are you leaving?"

"An hour?"

"Sure. Stop by, and get the key." He paused. "You know, there's a chance I won't be here. Let me give you directions, and I'll leave the key with the receptionist, in case I'm still out."

"Patty Cake? If she won't give it to me, do I have permission to take it by force?"

"Could I stop you? Get a pen."

Meredith scrawled down his directions. She knew the Cove Hollow community pretty well, so she shouldn't have any problem.

"Merry, Mom and Dad keep a list on the kitchen table with information about the cabin... where things are, how to work gadgets, that sort of thing. I'm not sure if there's still a phone there or not. They talked about taking it out, but with Dad's heart, maybe they decided to leave it. But there's pretty much no cell service out there. A bar, if you're lucky."

"There's no one I want to talk to," Meredith replied.

Perry raised a brow, but decided not to pursue that.

"Perry, can Hook come, or would your parents rather I left him here?"

"Oh sure, take the Hookster, no worries." He hesitated. "Hey, Merry, if there *is* a phone, will you call me either here, or at home. and let me know that you made it there okay?"

"Uh... sure." A thought came to Meredith. "Perry, I need a favor."

"What's that?"

"Can you just not tell anyone where I am? I need some time alone."

He didn't like the sound of that.

"No one? Not even Joel?"

"Especially Joel."

He didn't say anything.

"Perry, please. I just want to be alone. I need to work some things out, and I don't want to have to deal with Joel right now. Please?"

She meant it. He didn't like it, but maybe there was no harm in it.

"On the condition that you check in with me once a day."

"Oh, for crying out loud, Perry! I'm a grown woman!"

"And Joel Etheridge is a grown man. A little *too* grown, for me to want to get on his bad side."

He didn't have to be able to see her, to know that there was a defiant scowl on her face. Her silence spoke volumes.

"That's the deal, Merry, take it or leave it."

"You said there might not even be a phone there."

"Then find one."

"Fine!"

"If you miss one day calling me, I'm gonna come looking for you, and I'm bringing Joel with me."

"No, don't do that. I'll call, I promise."

"Alright," he agreed, greatly relieved. He didn't know what was going on between Joel and Meredith, but he wasn't going to aid and abet her, with whatever it was she was up to.

"So, I'll be around in about an hour, then," Meredith said.

"Yeah, and Merry, there's a little grocery store there, at the cross roads. You can't miss it, you have to turn right by it. You might want to stop by there, on your way to the cabin. There are probably canned goods and frozen stuff there, but you'll still need to get things like milk and bread.

"There are plenty of linens. Don't clean it when you leave, Mom and Dad pay a service for that. Even if you do clean it, Mom will send them over there, anyway. That's just who my mom is."

"Okay. Thanks, Perry."

"Sure. Listen, when you get back in town, why don't you run by the studio? I've got a rough mix of what we did a few weeks ago, if you want to sit and give it a listen."

"Umm... just me?"

He shrugged and decided to let her win this one. "Sure, that's fine. I can call Joel in later to hear it."

"Okay, let's do it, then. Thanks again, for the cabin."

"Remember your promise."

"And you remember yours."

Cagle Lawrence had listened to this exchange with considerable interest. He grinned as both parties hung up.

Center Hill Lake, huh? That sounded inviting. Too inviting to pass up. He might like fishing as well as the next guy.

He handed the headphones back to Peters with a smug look of satisfaction. "Who do you know with property out at Center Hill Lake?"

He looked back at him in surprise then gave it some thought. "I can't think of anyone I personally know with a place out there. But the last time I was ever out that way, there was a sort of lodge or something by the marina there. Seems like there's more than one. So even if there are no cabins available, I guess you could rent a room at one of those."

Cagle grunted, and pulled out his phone. "What town is Center Hill Lake in?"

"I guess start with Smithville, if you're looking for a place to stay."

Cagle spent a moment or two navigating until he found what he wanted, then made a call to put a room on hold.

He ripped a sheet of paper out of the notebook, where Peters had scrawled down the directions Perry had given Meredith to his parents' cabin and to the convenience store.

He had to hurry and grab a few things and get on the road, if he was going to get out to Cove Hollow before Meredith arrived.

"And don't forget, little songbird," he crooned. "You'll want to be sure to call your friend every day and check in. We don't want Mr. Etheridge snooping around our little cabin, do we?"

Chapter Sixteen

Ross Decker settled back and pondered the information Joel had just given him. He pressed the tips of his fingers together and looked at Joel thoughtfully. "Do I understand, money is not the motive here?"

Joel made a small scoffing sound. "He hasn't asked for money but I'm sure that comes later. He's trying to make this look more like some sort of emotional blackmail. He demands certain behavioral concessions, primarily that I have nothing to do with Meredith. At all."

"Not that it matters, but do you know why?"

"I think I do." Joel threw one leg up onto his desk and leaned back. "I'm standing in his way. It's easy to see that's he's a vain, puffed up little guy, full of himself. Meredith did the unthinkable. She not only left him, but she became a success without him. He had been trying to groom her for his own purposes, but that didn't work out for him. I'm sure he had other women in tow, but Meredith is the one that got away, and getting away was a huge blow to his ego.

"I think if she were just some girl no one really knows, it wouldn't be worth his time." Joel leveled his eyes at Ross. "But she managed to not only get free of him, she became a success, and now that she's a celebrity, the little creep just wants the last word."

Ross thought quietly about that. "And the last word is?"

"This is about punishment. There's no way this is just him wanting Meredith back. In fact, if that enters into it at all, I'm sure he only wants her for one last fling and has every intention of kicking her to the curb, when he's done with her. He *said* money wasn't the issue, but he's lying.

"I don't believe for one minute that he'll just throw those photos away, if I'm a good boy. He'll hang onto them a little longer for insurance, but when he's done with Meredith, he'll swap them out for cash so fast, we won't know which way is up. I'm sure that's been his plan from the very beginning. Make a bundle off Meredith after all, and humiliate her at the same time."

Joel's face darkened, and his voice became cold and calculating. "Ross, I won't let that happen. I'll stop him. Whatever I have to do, I'll stop him."

"Careful," his friend cautioned. "Don't let anyone else hear you making little remarks like that, because if anything *should* happen to Cagle Lawrence, you'll be the prime suspect."

"I'm good with that," Joel scowled. "Sometimes I wish I could step outside of my salvation just long enough to do what my flesh wants to do, and then slip back in, when I'm done."

"Why, what does your flesh want to do?"

Joel grinned in a way that would make anyone else besides Ross Decker nervous. "Bag him and tag him."

Ross laughed and shook his head. "Like I said, careful there!" He studied Joel for a moment and his smile faded.

"Joel, I'm just a cop, I'm no lawyer. But I do know that, at least on the surface, this falls outside the realm of criminal law."

"How do you mean?"

"Well, you admit yourself, he's made no demands for money. Until he does, we can't get him for extortion."

Ross stared absently at the wall and thought about it. "He's pretty clever, actually. Even if he *had* asked for money, this is a civil infraction. The photos are of Meredith. She would have to be the one to file charges."

"She doesn't even *know* about them!" Joel gave him a sharp glance. "She can't either, that's part of the deal. And she won't."

"Well," Ross said flatly, "it might be a moot point, anyway. Those pictures were taken over fifteen years ago. I'm sure there's a statute of limitations working here."

Joel let his leg drop to the floor and sat up straight in his chair. "You mean he couldn't even be prosecuted?"

Ross shrugged lightly. "Oh, anybody can be prosecuted but in this case, not very successfully, I'm afraid. Besides," he added, giving Joel a questioning glance, "isn't that exactly the kind of publicity you're trying to avoid?"

Joel looked up at the ceiling and expelled a long breath. "Yeah, and he knows it too, the sorry..."

He stopped himself just in time. He had been praying about his mouth lately, and was being given a lot of chances to practice self-control. This small restraint was the first one he'd managed all week.

Both men were silent for a time. Finally, Ross shifted in his chair and put his thoughts into words.

"Alright. This isn't much, but it's all I have."

Joel waited expectantly.

"There are no guarantees, but I have a couple of friends on the force down there. As a matter of fact, one of my long-time buddies in New Orleans is a U.S. Marshal. Maybe they can all do a little digging for me. Who knows? This Cagle Lawrence might have had a few run-ins with the law, that could work to our advantage."

Joel brightened up instantly. "Man, Ross, that would be great!"

"Well, let's not get too excited. It may turn out to be a dead end street. All we can do at this point is snoop around and see what we can come up with."

"Meredith did mention drugs."

"What did she say?"

"Just that there were all kinds of drugs around and a lot of strange people, coming in and out, at all hours. She never got involved with any of it but from the way she talked, there was never any real effort to hide what they were doing. She just wasn't street savvy enough, back then, to understand much about it."

"Well, that could be something," Ross speculated slowly. "You wouldn't happen to know the name of that club Meredith sang at, would you?"

"She never said." Joel thought about it for a moment. "I guess you could ask Marshall or her friend Hailey."

Ross grinned. "Hailey, as in that brown-eyed, blonde number you just introduced me to, outside?"

Joel laughed and fired a rubber band at him. "Why yes, Officer Decker, that would be the one. Maybe I'd better jot her number for you, so you can contact her. In an official capacity, of course."

"Of course!" Ross picked up the rubber band and shot it back in a counterattack.

Joel scribbled her number down and came around the desk to hand it to Ross. He stopped, as they started to the door.

"Ross, Hailey doesn't know about this. She does knows that someone is blackmailing Meredith, but she has no idea who or why. She can't know. Try to keep Lawrence's name out of it, if you talk to her."

"Okay. I'll handle it."

"Thanks, buddy!" He gave him an affectionate slap on the back, and saw him out.

Dee smiled up at them and waved at Ross, as she caught the ringing telephone.

Joel closed the lobby door behind his friend and turned to look at Dee.

"Is that someone on hold for me?"

"Hailey."

He sat on the corner of Dee's desk and took the call.

"It's Joel, Hailey, what's up?"

"Joel..." She seemed a little agitated.

"What's wrong?" He frowned and waited.

"Maybe nothing," she stammered. "But I thought I'd better say something, in case it does turn out to be something."

"Okay... " Joel looked over at Dee and held up a flat palm in bewilderment.

"I went by Meredith's place on the way home. She wasn't there, and at first, I didn't think too much about it."

Hailey hesitated. "Joel, is Meredith scheduled to be out of town?"

Delores watched his face begin to draw.

"No, she's not. Not until after Thanksgiving. Why are you asking me that?"

Hailey let out a big breath. "Merry and I always leave notes in each other's mailboxes, when one catches the other out. I started to put one in hers, but there was already a note in there. She was asking the mailman to hold her mail, until she contacts the post office."

Joel was silent for so long that Hailey began to wonder if he'd even heard her.

"Joel?"

"I..." He tried to clear his head. "I don't know where she is, Hailey."

"Well, I guess I knew something was wrong. I mean, I told you I was going by there and you didn't say anything to me about her not being there."

"No," he responded slowly. He shook himself. "Let me talk to Marshall or Pastor Gary. Maybe one of them knows something. If you *do* find out anything, please call me."

"Sure! And if you hear from her... "

"I won't hear from her."

She didn't say anything.

Joel suddenly remembered something. "Hailey, the man I introduced you to, this morning, Ross Decker... you remember him?"

She raised her brows. "Sure!"

"Well, besides being a buddy of mine, he's also a cop. I've asked him to look into something that relates to what I mentioned to you this morning."

He paused briefly. "I hope you don't mind, but he asked me something I couldn't answer, and I thought maybe you could. I gave him your number."

Hailey twisted her mouth into a pleased smile. "No, Joel, I don't mind."

"Great. Thanks, Hailey."

Joel hung up and favored Delores with a look of full exasperation. "She's skipped town!"

"Are you sure?"

"I'd bet on it," he answered grimly. "I swear, Delores, if I ever get my hands on that girl..."

Delores cleared her throat loudly, and gave him a wide grin.

"Maybe you'd better not finish that sentence," she advised. "I blush easily!"

He looked down self-consciously and smiled. After a moment, he glanced up to find his secretary still wearing her teasing grin.

"Knock it off, Dee." He shook a harmless fist at her and winked, then wandered back into his office. The familiar frown came back to shadow his worried face, as he wondered where she was, and if she was safe... and alone.

Meredith carried the last of her load in from the Jeep, and stood looking around the cabin. It was easy to see that Perry's parents took pride in it.

Although it had an overall rustic feel, the soft, gray, leather furniture, and brass fixtures suggested a touch of elegance. Meredith had been in their home before, and recognized Mrs. Mitchell's flair for decorating.

She saw, to her great annoyance, that there was, indeed, a telephone at the cabin. "Oh, lovely." She made a face and plopped down on the vast couch.

"Come check this out, Hook," she said to her fluffy companion. "I could live and die on this couch!"

Hook recognized an invitation when he heard one, and vaulted up to lie beside her. Meredith laughed at the way his color so matched the couch, that it caused him to almost disappear.

"Let's get one of these, Hookster. Ours is just about ready for the dump, anyway."

Her heart suddenly stung her, as she remembered the backdrop her old couch made for her and Joel, just the week before. She blinked quickly and set her chin.

"Yeah, Hook, that'll be the very first thing we do when we get home. That old piece of junk is history and what makes history so good, is that it's the past."

Poor stubborn Meredith. The only way she could stop the pain, was to insist on cold indifference. She spent hours on building her wall, meditated on ways to reinforce it, and dared anyone to come near it.

Even Pastor Gary was having increased difficulty. She had been unusually cool to him, ever since he took her to see her doctor. If anyone even remotely connected with Joel made any overtures of kindness, all they got for their trouble was a stiff reception and, in many cases, a sharp tongue.

Even now, alone with no one to see, she wrapped herself in bitterness as if it were her favorite afghan, and refused to let her thoughts wander around, where they might get into trouble. She kept them firmly corralled, along with her heart and her tears.

She let her eyes wander over to the phone again, and with an effort, made herself reach over and call Perry's office.

She smiled cynically at the speed with which she was put through to him.

"Merry!" There was obvious relief in his voice. "Thank God!"

"What do you mean, 'thank God'? For Pete's sake, I just barely got here, Perry. Give me time!" She wrinkled her brow and frowned.

"Joel called here, wanting to know where you are."

She just sat there and he let her digest it.

Finally, he heard her mutter something he really hoped he hadn't heard, and then hit something, probably a table, with her fist.

"What did you tell him, Perry?" she demanded.

"Nothing, yet. I was out, and the receptionist told me what he wanted and that he expects me to call him back."

He wished, with all his heart, that he hadn't wound up in the middle of whatever was going on with those two!

"Merry, if I don't call him, it's just a matter of time before he calls back. If he asks, point blank, if I know where you are, you're not really expecting me to lie, are you?"

"You promised!"

"I didn't promise to *lie.* I said I wouldn't volunteer anything! Being pinned down, especially by a man like Joel, is an awkward position to be put in. You can't really intend for me to just blatantly lie to him, and say I don't know where you are!"

"Perry!" Hot tears, spawned by anger and a feeling of being betrayed, quickly found their way into Meredith's eyes. "Why did you lead me to believe that you'd keep this a secret, if you knew all along that you weren't going to?"

"Shoot, Merry, what do you want me to do?"

"I want you to keep your promise! Or are you like every other so-called Christian in Nashville?"

He drew in his breath sharply. What was wrong with this woman? He had never heard her talk like this! Sure, she had a temper from time to time, but he'd never known her to bag on Christians, and lump them all into a group, as if she wasn't one herself!

"Are you saying, Merry, that you'll view me as a *real* Christian if I agree to lie, but if I don't, you won't?"

She stopped in surprise. "No, Perry, I didn't mean that. But the whole purpose for this trip was so that I could get away by myself, and..." A new tactic occurred to her. "I guess no one's told you this, but Joel's not my manager anymore."

"Maybe not directly, but Marshall is, and it's Joel's firm."

Meredith gritted her teeth in frustration. She groped for more control and managed to ask, in a reasonably calm voice, "So, Perry, how are you wanting to handle this?"

"Personally, I just want to tell him the truth. I mean, why should he have a problem with you spending a few days at my folk's cabin? As long as he knows where you are, and that you're safe, he'll probably even think it's a good idea. I mean, it's not like Center Hill is that far away."

Meredith closed her eyes in resignation. "Does your telling him get me off the hook, as far as having to call you every day?"

He thought about it for a moment. "No."

"You jerk!" she belted out angrily. "I'm sick of everybody treating me like I'm a little girl! I'm not a kid, I'm in my thirties, Perry!"

"You're also a woman alone, in a place where you don't know anyone, but you can bet someone will know *you*. It's the off-season, and everything is practically deserted."

"I *live* alone, do you understand that? I've been alone for years! I've slept alone in the streets!" She was getting hotter by the minute. "And for all I care, I can *die* alone!"

"You see?" Her producer was getting a little miffed, himself. "It's that kind of reckless talk that doesn't exactly make you sound like a responsible adult. Just stop all this, Meredith!

"I thought you understood that the reason I wanted you to stay in touch with me is because I actually care about you. I'm not trying to treat you like a kid, I'm trying to treat you like a good friend. Does that really make me a jerk?"

She bit her lip and decided that he was not her enemy. Joel was, but he was out of firing range, at the moment.

"I'm sorry," she offered, after a bit. "Could you just try this? Could you just tell him that you do know where I am, but that I asked you to keep it to yourself? Could you just try to convince him that I'm in touch with you on a daily basis, and that you know I'm okay? I mean, I'll be home on Friday, anyway."

"Okay," he finally relented. "I'll try that. I'm not guaranteeing that Joel will settle for it. I'm only saying I'll try. You know what he's like, Meredith."

"I thought I did," she said quietly.

"Listen. You can hate me all you want, but if I don't hear from you by this time tomorrow, I intend to make good on my threat. I'll bring Joel right to your door!" He hoped she believed him, because he meant it.

"I know. I'll call, don't worry. Can I go now?"

"Yes... oh wait, one more thing. His message says that if I do hear from you, to find out if you have your meds with you."

"Perry... " Her voice suddenly began to crack. "I've got to go. I'll call tomorrow." She hung up, before he could stop her.

She hopped up and began to pace furiously around the room.

Who does Joel Etheridge think he is? She fumed inwardly. *What business is it of his where I go in my spare time, as long as I show up for my concerts? He doesn't have any use for me anymore, that much is obvious. He doesn't even want to deal with me on a professional level. He just better butt out of my personal business and leave me alone!* She stamped her foot for emphasis.

What are you so upset for? This strange girl would argue with anyone, including herself. *You offered him an out. Now that he's had time to think it through, he's changed his mind. Simple as that.*

"If he wants out, fine," she muttered out loud. "But release me from my contract! It's not like no one else has ever asked to work with me."

Meredith leaned against the kitchen counter and rested her head on one hand. Probably the only reason he forced her to abide by her contract, was because she produced substantial funds for his firm.

"I can't believe I ever let that man get close to me," she said darkly. "I guess that was all just some kind of rush for him. Just wanted to see if he could get to first base with his star client."

Father sat through all this, sadly. Her mouth was so separated from what was really buried deep under her wounds. Meredith had so divorced herself from her heart, that it no longer guided her. She was left to the devices of her mind and they were slowly poisoning her.

He knew that it wasn't that she didn't mean the things she was saying. She did mean them. But He also knew that she didn't *want* to mean them. His arms longed to take her onto His lap and comfort her, but she resisted Him at every turn. He waited patiently, thinking of how He missed her.

She stood there stewing, mentally labeling Joel with every cruel and hateful tag she could invent. She fully intended to continue cultivating a pure hatred for him.

Cagle Lawrence could not have picked a better time to knock on her door.

Laura Etheridge curled up in the corner of Joel's sofa, and waited for her son to finish what he was saying.

Her eyes took in every revealing line on his face, and it gave her a jolt to realize that he had not only given Meredith his heart, but that, if she didn't care to have it, he didn't want it back. It was almost more than she could do, to watch him go through this.

She had remained open but unobtrusive and, after a few days, Joel came to her, as she knew he would, and confided everything, including the situation regarding the photos of Meredith.

Joel half lay and half sat on the other end of the sofa, in a slump that used to get him in trouble, when he was a kid.

"Mom, how can everything come to a boil, all at once, like this? It's like hell just reached down deep and gave us a full load."

"You just answered your own question." Laura raised her brows thoughtfully. "That sounds pretty accurate. We humans are trapped in such a physical world, that we almost never look beyond the obvious things to see what's really behind them."

She met his quick look. "Why would it be so hard to believe that the enemy would go to such extremes to shut down an anointing like the one that rests on Meredith, or the covering God has put in her life to protect her?"

He continued to hold her eyes. "Do you really think I'm meant to be that covering, Mom?"

"What do you think?" she countered, in all seriousness.

Joel glanced down at the pillow and gave it some study. "I guess it really doesn't matter, now. Meredith won't have anything to do with me. I know," he added quickly, predicting the objection she was about to make. "She *can't* have anything to do with me. But staying away because she has to, and staying away because she wants to, are two different things, Mom."

"Son," she said gently. "How many times, over the past few years, have I heard you speak about what an emotionally complex creature Meredith is? Are you really going to let the enemy make you think that she believes all that stuff she's been saying about you?"

She reached over and touched his arm. "She's just doing what she can to keep from hurting, honey. I've listened to a lot of her music since I've been here, and I can tell from her lyrics, that she's no stranger to pain. I can even see where she's made a friend of pain, and let it teach her.

"But she just wasn't ready for this. That girl loves you, Joel, so much that, in her mind, the only way to cope now, is to give in to an emotion that doesn't require her to think or hurt. Anger's just an easy trip for her, right now. It lets her feel like she's still in control. You can see that, can't you, Son?"

Joel sat still and considered his mother's words. He felt a slow comprehension begin to overtake him, and reached over and took her tiny hand in his own. "I see it, Mom," he said quietly. "But I guess I haven't told you what's been bothering me the most."

A dark shade of grief painted his face, and she waited, slightly uncomfortable, knowing where this was headed.

"It's about..." He stopped, and gave Laura a look of raw pain that stung her heart and she gently squeezed his hand. He couldn't get it out and, in spite of his resolution to keep his emotions in check, here came the tears, just a few, to remind him that they were still in there.

These were old ones that could never be dried, that never seemed to stop forming. His mother had shared this particular sorrow with him for several years now, and made no effort to check her own watery eyes. She moved a little closer and he rested his head against her shoulder.

"Mom..." he fumbled. "I wanted to tell her. I tried to tell her, but I couldn't. I wish to God in Heaven that I had!"

He took a rough swipe at his face and tried to smile. "It's kind of funny, when you think about it. I mean, I was afraid if I *did* tell her she'd hate me and now, because I didn't, she hates me."

"Joel..."

"No, Mom. She does hate me. At least she believes she does, and with Meredith, it's the same thing. It has the same effect. She thinks I couldn't deal with her abortion, and that

I just put her out of my life. She thinks I can't love her because of it."

He gripped his mother's hand tightly. "I wish, with all my heart, I had told her!"

His mother sat silently and thoughtfully meditated on what Joel was saying. He gave his face an impatient wipe and cleared his throat.

"Okay, I'm done." He came up with something like a smile and she gave it back. "That's enough of that. I have a lot more sympathy for women who cry all the time, than I ever did, before. Maybe they really can't help it, after all."

She laughed and patted his leg. "Well now, there are real tears and then there are *drama* tears. It's good to be understanding, Joel, but don't be gullible. With women, it's about fifty-fifty."

Joel closed his eyes and gave a little laugh. "Sheesh, Mother, can't you come up with better odds than that?"

She grinned and shook her head. "Sorry! I probably should have made your father have this talk with you, before you started noticing females. Not that you've really ever noticed any, until now. Speaking of that, has anyone checked on *your* female today?"

"She took off."

"Took off what?"

"Took off *where*," he corrected, glumly. He started unraveling a thread on the pillow and Laura lightly popped his hand.

"She went fishing. She's staying at a cabin that her producer's parents own on a lake not far from here."

"You two have gone fishing a few times, right?"

"We have." Joel smiled, remembering. "She's very competent, Mom, with a rod and reel. I suspect she could out-fish me any day of the week. I'm a bit surprised that she would just take off, though, this close to that Ryman thing on Friday."

"Well, this might just be good for her, and you can relax a little, knowing she's enjoying herself. Plus, she probably can't get into too much trouble fishing."

Joel rolled his eyes and donned a sarcastic expression. "Mom, Meredith Clark could get into trouble in the middle of Heaven!"

Chapter Seventeen

Meredith stood in the doorway of the cabin and stared at Cagle Lawrence in utter disbelief.

"Meredith," he said in a rush of words. "If I promise to just stand here outside, would you let me talk to you? Just for a minute, please?"

She closed her eyes and opened them again. He was still there.

She hurried to pick up the pieces of her brain. *Alright, girl.* She mentally braced herself. *Hang on to your hat.*

"How did you find out where I was?" Her voice was remarkably cold and churning, with no hint of the shock she was experiencing.

Cagle was well prepared for this. He certainly wasn't going to say, "Well, I just happened to be bugging your phone..."

He smiled, in what he intended to be a sheepish manner. "I saw you while I was at that little store, back at the crossroads."

This much was true. He had gotten there as quickly as he could, and waited for Meredith's white Jeep to pull in, as Perry Mitchell had suggested she do. He had to know whether or not she stopped there, so he could use it as an excuse.

"I have to confess I followed your Jeep when you left. It was such a surprise finding you here, that I wanted to see where you were staying. I was hoping we could talk."

"Talk." Her voice was as hostile as her glare. "What in the freakin' world could you and I possibly have to talk about? And how do you just happen to be at Center Hill Lake, anyway?"

"Well, when I ran into you at DFW, I told you I was coming to the Nashville area."

"Did you? And you consider *this* to be the Nashville area?" She narrowed her eyes expressively. Cagle had forgotten how beautiful those eyes were.

"No, but one of the guys I've been doing business with, has a place out here. He offered it to me for a couple of days, and I took him up on it."

"Doing *business* with, huh? I just bet." She gauged him critically. "And since when are you a nature lover?"

"Meredith," he said plaintively. "It's been fifteen years. People can change a lot in fifteen years!"

"Oh, so that's why you're here? To tell me you've changed? I've seen that movie."

He lifted his hands, and gave a little shrug. "Well, I can't make you believe me, but I have to at least know that I tried."

Meredith gave a harsh, callous laugh. "Man, that's rich, Cagle! You really *are* a piece of work!"

She crossed her arms, leaned against the doorpost, and carelessly set herself up for deception. "Alright, then. Let's see what you've got! Give it your best shot."

It was all Cagle Lawrence could do, to mask the conquest that he was beginning to feel. He gathered his wits, and played it the way he had rehearsed it.

"I was so stunned to see you at the airport," he began, "that I really wasn't able to say much of anything that made any sense. I mean, you were practically a kid the last time we saw each other, and I was too, if actions are anything to go by."

It was clear that she agreed, but she remained silent.

"Meredith, I haven't been right these past fifteen years. I mean, I've been successful, as far as that goes. But I've never lost that nagging feeling in my gut, that I'm responsible for most of the hardships I'm sure you've had to endure, because of getting involved with someone like me."

Meredith peered at him with a mixture of suspicion and intrigue. "Yeah, well, pay attention to that gut of yours, Cagle. There's probably something *to* that."

"I know there's no excuse for how I treated you, and I'm not trying to make any. You were only nineteen, but I was twenty-five years old. I don't know what I was thinking back then, Meredith. Maybe it was all the drugs and the drinking. I don't know."

"Which, of course, you don't do anymore," she cut in dryly.

"No, I don't!" He managed to sound convincing. "I mean, I do have an occasional glass of wine with a meal, but no, I don't do any of that other stuff anymore. Please believe me!"

"Why, Cagle?" She tilted her head and eyed him probingly. "Why is it so important to you that I believe you now? Why, fifteen years after the fact, do you suddenly need for me to believe you?"

He let out a sigh and tried for an appealing look. "I don't know, Meredith. I just do. I guess it took running into you in Dallas, to make me realize that I need your forgiveness, before I can move on."

"Forgiveness, huh?" Her voice was like acid. "Don't take this personally, Cagle, but you're barking up the wrong tree. I haven't been doing too well in the forgiveness racket lately. What makes you think you'll have better luck than anyone else has?"

"Well..." He seemed uncertain. "I've seen your picture in various magazines since I've been here, Meredith, and read some articles about you. You're involved in the Christian industry, now."

"I am?" She feigned surprise, then smirked. "You let that roll your tongue like the plastics industry, or the produce industry."

He smiled. "I didn't mean it like that. It's just that I know that Christians talk a lot about second chances, and forgiveness. I don't know. I think those articles sort of gave me hope that you might find it in your heart to extend some of that forgiveness to me."

"Yeah, well, don't believe everything you read, Cagle," she admonished coolly. "And there's no telling *what* I'd find in my heart, if I cared to look... which I *don't.*"

She stood there and examined him closely. "Why does this mean so much to you, *really*... if it even does?"

Cagle shook his head. "I don't know if I understand it, myself. I just haven't seemed to be able to find any peace in my life, since we were in New Orleans. I know what I did to you was a filthy, low-down thing, Meredith, and I just wish I could make you believe how sorry I am for it!"

He had the unholy ability to look right into her eyes and convey everything he said as the truth! Meredith hadn't talked to Father in so long, that her discernment was practically non-existent.

"Cagle," she said, in a thorny voice. "What do you want me to do here? What are you waiting for me to say? It was a *baby,* for crying out loud! My son, or my daughter! A *dead* baby, thanks to you! *That's* what we're talking about! It's not like you spilled Bordeaux on my white mink!"

"*Our* son or daughter," he corrected.

"You said it wasn't even yours!" She literally screamed her words at him.

"I know I did!" He appeared to be in anguish. "I was a fool, I know that now! Back then, it didn't seem real to me, Meredith. But I've interacted with enough friends and their children over the last fifteen years, to see that what I did to you was a horrible crime!" He actually achieved a tearful quaver in his voice.

"Please, Meredith, won't you at least think about forgiving me? Won't you at least sleep on it, instead of just flat out refusing? Please!"

She hesitated, completely baffled by his ring of authenticity. "Let me ask you this," she finally said. "What does *forgiveness* look like to you? What does it include? I hope you're not asking for an active role in my life again. You'd better *not* be!"

He shook his head quickly. "No, nothing like that! I hope I wouldn't be so stupid, as to ever hope for anything like that again. I just don't want you to hate me, Meredith. I think if I just knew you had forgiven me, I could go on from here."

"Go on where?"

"I just... I don't know. On with my life..."

Meredith shifted her weight and looked down at her feet for a moment. "You say you'll be around here for a couple of days?"

He nodded.

"I'll think about it, Cagle. That's the best I can do right now, sorry. If you had come to me just a week ago, I might have been able to accommodate, you pretty much right on the spot. But I'm assuming that you want *real* forgiveness, not just my saying so. If that's the case, you need to give me some time. Sorry, that's all I can offer."

"I'm just grateful that you're even considering it! That's so much more than I deserve. I won't keep you. I can see it's getting late," he continued, moving away from the door and smiling in a way that implied gratitude. "May I check in with you on my way back?"

She shrugged. "I guess so, if I'm still around. I mean, you'll want your answer."

"Thank you, Meredith! I'll see you soon, then." He waved and headed back to his car.

Meredith closed the door and fell onto the couch like a rock. A big, heavy rock. She lay staring at the ceiling in astonishment.

When she had seen Cagle Lawrence at the Dallas airport, little more had transpired, other than a garbled response to something he had asked her, and a hurried excuse to move on.

For years, she had been dreading the day she might actually have to dialog with him, but now that it had finally happened, it hadn't been nearly as bad as she had expected. He certainly seemed much different than the man she left behind, in New Orleans.

"Maybe he's right," she mused, mulling over what he had said to her. "Maybe a person really can change a lot in fifteen years."

A crestfallen cast came into her eyes. "I mean, after all, it's only been a few days, and look how much Joel Etheridge has changed."

Cagle Lawrence got into his car and laughed wickedly. "Oh, you beautiful doll," he breathed in satisfaction. "Clever tongue, but still as naive as ever! And prettier... much, *much* prettier! Too pretty to waste on church!"

He eyed her cabin door greedily. "Forgiveness. That was a good one! I did you a favor, songbird, by making you get rid of your little 'mother load'. It would have been a sin to mess up that body over some screaming brat!" He laughed again and drove off into the night, where he belonged.

What was that? Meredith rolled over and fought to open her heavy eyes. Was that a fire alarm? Alarm! That was it! She sent out a scouting hand, and located the dutiful and annoying alarm clock she had set to wake her up.

Slapping it off, she pulled herself up into a sitting position and rubbed her eyes. Hook followed suit, stretching his back out, and assuming a look of instant malnutrition. Meredith fixed him with a glassy stare, and coaxed herself out of bed.

She had never been a morning shower person. In fact, she desired, at all times, to only be as awake as she had to be, in order to function. It was chilly in the room, so she quickly pulled on a pair of cotton tights and slipped into some old jeans. She managed to find the one sweatshirt she hadn't yet mutilated, and pulled it over her head, muttering impatiently, because one sleeve wanted to play.

"Come on!" She stopped in the doorway and gave Hook a nudge with one foot. They ambled into the kitchen, and he took the shortest route to his litter box.

"Cover it up this time!" Meredith advised loudly, sorting through a bag of groceries for his food. Without thinking, she dumped it out while he was still in the litter box and, of course, Hook canceled all appointments and came barreling out to be of assistance.

Meredith opened her mouth to scold him, then shut it again with a shrug. "I guess I brought that on myself," she admitted.

She picked up the litter scoop and buried Captain Hook's treasure for him. "Just this once, big boy. I don't work for you!"

She set the coffeepot into action and gathered the fishing gear she had prepared the night before. Throwing on a heavy jacket, she started the dreaded task of loading the Jeep.

On the way back into the cabin, she spotted a man's footprint on the front stoop and scowled. So much for it all being just a bad dream, then. Cagle Lawrence really *had* been here.

"At least I think he was," she mumbled, heading for the kitchen to fill up her thermos and find something to eat. "Maybe this ear infection has eaten into my brain." She turned a lazy expression onto her cat. "And maybe you're really a garbage disposal with fur."

He looked up at the sound of her voice, and licked his tuna covered face. Meredith laughed at him, as she started slapping sandwiches together and tossing them into a small ice chest. "You missed a spot, Hook."

She stopped by the bathroom and made sure she wasn't hideous, in case some tabloid photographer was hiding out in the bushes, then piled the rest of her things into the Jeep. Leaving Hook to amuse himself, after several stern warnings about taking care of other people's property, she headed down the road to a fishing spot she'd had good luck at, once before.

She had intended to get an early start, but it was already after eight. It was a little colder than she would have liked, but predicted to grow considerably warmer by noon. She grappled with her gear in a way that would have made her dad proud and was soon kicking back.

Meredith was a girl who stayed with it. Fishing was the one thing in which her patience was unparalleled, and she could sit right there until it got dark, if she needed to.

It turned out that she didn't need to. She immediately attracted a school of bream, but wasn't too excited about it. She'd had her sights set on catfish, so much so that she probably would have thrown back a ten pound bass.

She replaced her hook with a bigger one and added a weight to fish more deeply. It took her a while, but after she began using what the locals referred to as blood bait, she finally hit the lottery.

For a short span of time, Meredith forgot all about the abrupt changes in her life. She forgot about concerts, she forgot about her past, she forgot about Cagle Lawrence, she even forgot about Joel... every few moments.

The problem was that they had gone on too many fishing expeditions together, for this one not to call him into her thoughts, as if he needed calling.

She blinked quickly and began doing her psychological exercises, designed to lose the weight of him. What was done was done, and the best thing now was for her to blow it off, and call it a lesson learned.

She set her chin in a determined way and gave her attention to her sport. Within an hour, she decided she had her limit, and set her rod and reel over to one side. She pulled a canister of hand wipes out of her Jeep, and cleaned the smelly stains of her efforts off her fingers.

"Are they biting?"

She spun around to find Cagle Lawrence smiling benignly at her. She wavered a moment, obviously at a loss.

"I saw your Jeep," he explained, coming down the embankment to join her.

Meredith made a mental note to buy a new car.

"So, how's the fishing here?"

"You haven't tried it yet?" She opted to trade a question for a question, a technique she was known for.

"You said it yourself, yesterday." Cagle grinned. "Since when am I a nature lover?"

He sat down on a small boulder and took a look at her catch. "I'm only here for the quiet, and maybe the scenery. But if I could be guaranteed results like this, I might be persuaded to learn how to fish."

Meredith shut the door of her Jeep and came back to assemble her equipment. "Sorry, there are no guarantees. The fish have a mind, for lack of a better word, of their own, and you just have to second guess it."

"Are you actually going to clean these?" he asked.

"Well, I'm certainly not going to eat 'em like this," she replied. "I've skinned plenty of catfish in my lifetime; it's no big deal."

Cagle watched her gather her gear, noting her slim form and her long, beautiful hair. He almost gave her a compliment, but quickly stopped himself. This, coming from him, would only serve to anger her.

He decided to use another angle. "My car is parked over that levee. I was just out for a walk and happened to stumble on you."

This, of course, was not true. He knew she was at Cove Hollow to fish, and he was out early, watching for her departure and strategically timing his arrival.

He looked up at her in a manner designed to generate sympathy.

"I have to confess, I didn't sleep very well at all last night, after we talked."

She made no reply, but continued to return items to her tackle box and look around to see if she was missing anything.

"All I could do was lie awake, wondering if there was any chance you would consider what I asked you," he continued. "If you would be able to forgive me. I know I don't deserve it, but I have to keep hoping."

He got up and crossed his arms against the chill.

"Oh, so you're pulling out today?" Meredith took the cup off the top of her thermos and poured black coffee into it. She sipped it, looking at him with unreadable eyes.

"No, not until Friday. I know I said I'd give you time to think about it, Meredith, and I won't push you. It's just that I..." He tried coming across as apologetic.

"Well, I probably shouldn't have brought it up. I just didn't know how long you were staying and..." He broke off and let his words hang in the air effectively.

Meredith slid one hand into her pocket and looked down at the ground, pursing her lips thoughtfully. It wasn't that she felt she owed this man anything. But he did seem sincere, in a way she had never known him to be before.

Maybe he was right. Maybe his previous lifestyle had prevented him from being able to cope with things, fifteen years ago. Maybe it was time they put this issue to rest. But then again, she couldn't forgive Joel and he certainly hadn't done anything as horrendous as Cagle had done!

Her mind hurried to object to the case her heart was trying to build for Joel. After all, Joel professed to be a Christian. Cagle admitted his faults and wasn't trying to hide behind religion. He was just a man who wanted to account for things and move on. Surely it wouldn't cost her anything to give the guy a break, she mistakenly told herself.

She cleared her throat and glanced up to find Cagle looking at her wistfully. "Cagle, I just wish I had some way of knowing if this was going to come back to bite me," she said quietly. "I mean, I've moved on. I came to Tennessee eight years ago, and I carved out a new life for myself. I don't have to tell you that my relationship with you left me with a lot more than just bad memories."

Meredith felt the old familiar pang at the thought of her unborn child, and her eyes misted over. Cagle took her fingertips lightly.

"I know," he said, in a soft tone. "I know, Meredith, and I hate myself every day I live, for what I did to you. I wish you could believe me."

She pulled her hand out of his, and wiped her face on the sleeve of her sweatshirt.

"Well," she said, after a moment, "I *want* to believe you. I really do. It would probably be a very healing thing for me, if I thought that you honestly regretted what happened."

"That's the most frustrating part for me," he said, studying her shrewdly, as she continued wiping her eyes. "I know the torment I've been experiencing these past few years, but there's no way for me to communicate that to you, without it sounding rehearsed."

He only hoped he could keep a straight face!

Meredith studied the ground again, trying to count the cost of what he was asking of her. "We've got a lot of muddy water under our bridge, don't we, Cagle?"

He nodded silently.

"Shoot!" She gazed out across the lake, while her searching eyes reflected the rapid thoughts that were moving through her head. She sighed and turned back around to face him. "Fine, then, Cagle. You stand forgiven."

How could he manage the look of glorious rebirth he instantly wore? He even contrived a couple of tears!

"Thank you, Meredith!" He clasped her hands, as if in reverence. "Thank you so much! You have no idea what this means!"

And it's a good thing you don't, he added mutely, all the while maintaining the face of an exalted choirboy.

He released her hands and appeared to be leaving, when he stopped suddenly, and looked back at her. "You know, I was wondering if... no, it's a bad idea."

"What?" she stupidly asked, just as he hoped she would.

"Oh, it's dumb. It's just that once you get back to Nashville, you'll probably be really busy with your music and... that's going well, isn't it?"

He switched topics rapidly and deliberately, in an attempt to confuse her and, at the same time, renew her bitterness toward Joel. It worked.

"I guess," she said, with a sullen shrug. "Whatever."

"How does that work? Are you sort of representing yourself, or do you have some kind of manager?"

Meredith coughed out a hard, dry laugh. "Some kind of manager! That's priceless. Yeah, he's some kind of manager, alright. I just don't know what kind! Well, that's not true. I know *exactly* what kind."

Cagle smiled and donned a pleasantly confused facade. "But if you're not happy with one manager, you just get another one, right?"

She frowned. "Not always. That firm is also my label. There's a nasty, little thing called a contract, that ensures the nervous breakdown that every musician is entitled to."

She tossed her hair in a way she didn't realize was very attractive. "Doesn't matter. I'm actually being managed now by his associate, who I find much more to my liking. As soon as my contract expires, I'm out the door."

Cagle arrested his smile and let his gaze wander around the landscape.

She watched him curiously. "What were you going to ask me?"

He found a charming, almost shy grin and put it on. "Oh, I was just wondering if you would consider having dinner with me tonight, at that little restaurant on the marina... for new times' sake. See? Bad idea. And besides..."

He cleverly pushed the right button. "Your manager probably wouldn't be too thrilled at the prospect of his highly visible Christian recording artist being seen in the company of an old reprobate, like me."

Meredith's eyes flashed quietly. "Joel Etheridge may hold the papers on my career, but what I do in my personal life is none of his business!"

"But what if somebody recognized you? I wouldn't want to get you into trouble." He was moving in for the kill.

"Maybe you should let *me* worry about any trouble that man thinks he wants to start with me! Good grief, it's just dinner! I'll meet you there at seven." She resumed loading her equipment into the Jeep.

"Want a hand with any of that?"

"Nope. Got it."

"Okay, if you're sure. Guess I'd better shuffle off, so you can get going." Cagle turned to leave. "Thank you again, Meredith, for everything."

"Don't mention it." She hopped into the Jeep.

He waited to watch her drive away and gave her a little wave. "No, really, sweet Meredith. Thanks for everything. And I do mean everything!"

Chapter Eighteen

Ross Decker accepted the coffee Delores offered him, and smiled gratefully.

She dropped a handful of messages on Joel's desk. "Want me to hold your calls, Joel?"

"Sure, Dee," he answered slowly, sifting through the stack of pink papers. "Hold it a minute."

He finished his perusal and glanced back up at her. "Perry didn't call?"

Delores wrinkled her brow. "I didn't give you that?"

He lifted the stack of message forms up, and shook his head.

"Sorry, Joel. The phones were all going off at once. I must not have written it down."

Joel gave her a mock frown. "Well, then you're just fired, aren't you?"

Ross gulped his coffee and looked up quickly, then mellowed, when he saw the bantering look on his secretary's face.

"Guess so," she volleyed, obviously not worried. "My, my, what *will* I do with my day?"

"How about getting Marshall on the phone for me?"

"Before or after you find out what Perry had to say?"

Joel tapped the back of one of the forms. "Know what other vital office memo comes in pink, Dee?"

He shot Ross a sideways wink and waved the square of paper at her menacingly. "I wouldn't count on Secretary's Day, if I were you."

She laughed at his empty threat. "Well, he didn't say much. She's been fishing. She told him she was heading back today. She's probably home by now, because she's got that thing at the Ryman tonight."

Joel nodded. Neither Delores nor Ross realized just how anxious he had been, until they saw him visibly relax.

"Okay. You can stay, but the next time you forget a message, you'll be in a bread line down by the river."

Delores rolled her eyes and strolled out humming. That's just how concerned she was.

Ross laughed and shook his head. "I was getting all ready to feel sorry for Dee, but I can see now that you two deserve each other."

"You got *that* right."

Joel snatched up the telephone before it even finished ringing. "No, you can *not* have a raise!" He chuckled at something Delores said. "Careful on that thin ice, Dee."

He listened to her reply and grinned lazily. "Put him through."

Ross sipped his coffee and thought about how good it was to see Joel laugh, even if it was a little forced. He was trying to stay on top of things, and that was going to be very important.

"Marshall!" Joel turned the speaker on and hung up. "Are you upstairs?"

"I'm back in my office. What's up?"

"Just wondering if you're going to be around in about an hour. I need to talk to you about this benefit Meredith is doing after her trip."

There was a pause on the other end and Joel's face changed. "Is that a problem, Marshall?"

"No," he returned quickly. "I'm just leaving to run down the Row, and I'm wondering if I can be back in an hour."

"Just whenever you can. Holler at me."

"Sure, old man." Marshall hung up and Joel punched off the line with a relieved expression.

"I thought for a minute that he might resent my wanting to stay involved with her concerts," he said, by way of explanation to Ross, as he caught his puzzled expression. "Because technically, Marshall is Merry's manager, now."

"Marshall knows that's just a formality to appease Cagle Lawrence." Ross waved a dismissing hand in the air. "You know he doesn't mind your input. In fact, I'm sure he appreciates it."

"I guess. Speaking of the devil, have you managed to learn anything useful about Lawrence?"

Ross leaned back and presented Joel with a smug look.

Joel gave him a careful smile. "What?"

"Coke."

"We're not talking about something to wash a burger down with, are we?"

"We are not. Got popped, too."

Joel's grin spread slowly. "You don't say? Did they put him in time out?"

"He 'done a nickel', as they say, in all good gangster movies."

"Five years? That's all?"

"Possession with intent to distribute." Ross gave a light shrug. "Actually, that could be considered a lot, these days. Especially since he actually served the whole thing."

Joel thought about that. "When was all this?"

"Apparently, right around the time Meredith would have been in the picture. It's possible she bailed on him, right before he was arrested."

"It's probable. She would have told me about it."

Joel caught hold of one wrist and raised his arms above his head, leaning back and giving his friend a searching look. "Has he been clean since then?"

Ross laughed shortly. "Oh, Brother Etheridge... life is good."

"Yeah?" His eyes lit up. "How good?"

"Very, *very* good!"

Joel's adrenaline began to kick in. "He's still dealing?"

"Dealing would only be good. Trafficking would be very, *very* good." Ross smiled cryptically at his friend. "Wanna get him?"

"Can we?"

"With the New Orleans PD's blessing and cooperation, in a round about way. He still lives there."

"You're kidding!"

"I'm happy to say I am *not*."

"What an idiot!" Joel couldn't believe his ears. "To go right back to the place where you were busted before, and still be involved in what sent you away in the first place!"

Ross chuckled. "Well, he may be an idiot, but he's *our* idiot. As to why he still lives in New Orleans, let's just say the plot thickens."

Joel just sat there, hardly daring to breathe.

Ross held him in suspense only for a second.

"Parole."

"I thought you said he served the whole sentence."

"Oh, he did... the first time."

Ross laughed at Joel's startled expression. "Our boy just won't quit playing with the riff raff. Three years later, he did another year and three months on a four year sentence.

Same charge, less dope. Fell through the cracks and hit the streets. His parole is still in effect."

He watched Joel absorb all of this tentatively.

"How can he even be in Tennessee then, Ross? Surely he's not the kind to notify his parole officer that he's hightailing it out of town."

"Oh, I'm sure you're right," Ross commented. "But why crowd him for a little thing like parole violation, when we can pop him for something with a much bigger bang?"

Joel raised his eyes with a cautious hope. "Ross, do you really think we can get him?"

"I really think we can, Joel," he answered softly. "I really do."

Meredith opened her door and instantly lit up at the sight of her best friend.

"Get in here!" she said gruffly, pulling Hailey in and giving her a hug.

"I was on my way home from the mall," Hailey explained. She stopped and inspected Meredith's face.

"Girl, how, in the world, did you manage to get sun in the middle of November?"

"Fishing," she responded, motioning her toward a chair and plopping down on the couch, forgetting that she had promised herself not to ever sit on it again. "Hours and hours of non-stop fishing."

"Well, I must say, it looks good on you."

"Why, thank you, dahlink!" she said glamorously.

"So," Hailey sat down. "Where'd you go?"

"To Perry Mitchell's parents' cabin. It's out on Center Hill Lake."

"Oh, I love that place! I went water skiing there last summer."

"Yeah," Meredith stretched. "It's pretty okay."

"So did you catch anything?"

"Loads. I ate 'em all too, baby cakes."

"Well, it's about *time* you ate something." Hailey declared.

Hook came loping in and promptly enlisted her aid in scratching behind his ears.

"Hookers!"

"He heard us talking about fishing and eating," Meredith said, looking over at her spoiled pet fondly, in spite of the disapproving remarks she was prone to make about him.

Hailey pulled him onto her lap and began giving him a gentle massage. Hook closed his eyes and purred loudly, a look of subtle ecstasy on his gray face.

"I need one of these," Hailey decided, watching his obvious enjoyment.

"Don't forget his litter box, when you leave."

"Yeah, right. Like you would ever give him up."

Meredith shrugged vexingly, and Hailey suppressed a complaint.

She left off focusing on Hook and rested inquisitive brown eyes on her friend for a long moment.

"Just say it, whatever it is!" Meredith ordered, a little brusquely.

"Say what?"

"Whatever that is on your face."

Hailey decided to go for it. "I guess I just want to know what the deal is with you. And don't even try it," she warned as she recognized Meredith's forthcoming denial. "You're talking to me here, not some star-struck reporter. I want to know what's changed since I saw you before Denver, because I can see that something has."

Meredith looked away, frowning at the sudden turn the conversation was taking. "Let's not do this."

"Since when are we not able to talk?"

"Since right now. I've got a gig tonight and I really don't want to get all hot and bothered." Meredith looked down at her bare feet. "I would, too. Believe me."

Hailey stared at her intently. After a moment, she laid Hook to one side and came over to the couch to sit beside her.

"Merry, listen. You've got to have at least one person in your life, that you can dump stuff on."

Meredith remained still and Hailey chose to hit the sore spot.

"I'm not saying it has to be me. But whatever it is, you have to be able to talk to someone about it. If not me, then what about Joel?"

"I love you, Hailey, but if you mention that man's name to me one more time, you are out of here." Her voice was like cold steel.

"So that's it," Hailey said gently, simply stating what she had already known. "It's Joel."

Meredith's head came up and she flashed her a look of warning.

"I know, I know. You're going to throw me out. But not until I find out what's going on around here."

"Why do you need to know?"

"Because I love you, silly goose, and I'm worried about you."

Meredith made no effort to mask the fact that she was clearly beginning to simmer. "He sent you over here, didn't he?"

"I saw him, but he didn't send me over here. He didn't tell me what's wrong but I can see he's worried about you."

"Well, tell him for me to drop dead."

"Merry, don't talk like that! You know better than that!"

Meredith sagged against the back of the couch and fixed her with an icy glare.

"Oh great, the silent treatment," Hailey mumbled. "You must want me to send for my things and move in, since you know that I'm not leaving until we talk."

After a long, rebellious moment, Meredith closed her eyes and took a breath.

"Why are you doing this to me?" she whispered. "Can't you see that I'm just not able to do this?"

"You really want to know what I see?" Hailey asked softly.

"No," she returned. "No, Hailey, I don't."

Hailey picked up her hand and held it fondly. "What did he do to you, Merry?"

Meredith's chin began to quiver, and tears forced their way through her tightly closed lids.

Hailey blinked back her own tears. "What did Joel do, honey?" she repeated.

"He said... he told me he loved me... and then..." Meredith began to shake. "Then he left me."

Hailey wrapped her arms around her and let her cry.

"He just *left* me, Hailey! He lied and said he loved me and he promised he wouldn't leave me, but he did, anyway!"

"Do you know why?" she asked, stroking her hair, and rubbing her back with a consoling hand.

Meredith sat up, and Hailey could see the suffering in her eyes. "I told him about the abortion."

"You did? And you really believe that's why?"

"That's when everything changed. That has to be it."

"Why?" Hailey surveyed her face thoroughly. "Why does that have to be it?"

Meredith leaned over on her, engulfed in a fresh wave of weeping. "I don't know, Hailey! I don't know anything, anymore!"

She had devoted all week to a cold denial of any expression of sorrow, and probably would do so again, but for now, in the presence of her cherished friend, she let her grief consume her. Hailey, being a good and wise woman, let her take all the time she needed, and simply served as loving support.

After several moments, Meredith became very quiet, and just sat there in the strange peace that a flood can bring. "Thank you, Hailey," she mumbled. She gave her a weak smile. "I guess I've been needing to do that."

"Yes, you have," Hailey agreed kindly. "Listen to me, girlfriend, and listen good. You and I are the closest thing to sisters that either one of us has. Don't you ever try that dodging number of yours on me again. I'm in your life because God put me here, and it wasn't so you could pull stunts like that."

"I know," Meredith answered meekly. "I'm sorry."

"Now, how well do I know you?"

"Very well," she admitted.

"Well enough to look you in the eyes and know that you're still not telling me everything. Right?"

Meredith hung her head. "You're not going to like it."

"Not the point," her friend replied. "If I don't like it, I can lump it, but you spit it out."

Meredith gave a loud sigh. "Nothing's sacred, I guess?"

"Not today."

She drew her knees up to her chest and wrapped her arms around them. "*He* showed up."

Hailey was startled. "Joel?"

She shook her head and reached for a tissue.

"He..." Hailey repeated slowly. "Who are we talking about?"

Meredith just looked at her.

Hailey watched her fidgeting uncomfortably. It took a minute, but she remembered that they had just been talking about the abortion. It finally hit her, like a rogue wave, and she gasped.

"No way!"

Meredith nodded but said nothing.

"At the cabin?"

She nodded again.

Hailey gripped her arm in shock. "I have so many questions! How did he know you were there? What did he want?" She stopped and gave her friend a look of terror.

"Merry, did he hurt you?" she asked in a tight voice.

Meredith shook her head. "In fact, to tell you the truth, Hailey, he was actually nice."

Hailey closed her eyes. "Nice," she repeated flatly.

"He was! He came to ask me to forgive him."

She rolled her eyes and groaned.

"I know," Meredith said quickly. "I felt the same way. But it turned out to be true. He came by the same evening I got there, and we talked at the door. I saw him down at the lake the next morning, and we spoke again. Hailey, if he were up to something, I think I would have seen it. I mean, we talked a good bit. I even had dinner with him and..."

"NO!" Hailey jumped up and put her hands up to her face in horror. "No, Meredith!"

"It was just dinner, for Pete's sake, and it's a little late to be getting upset about it, now. I already did it. The point is, he didn't try anything. He was a perfect gentleman and I believe he's just trying to get on with his life.

"I mean, it's been fifteen years. Anyone can change and if he's changing, I think the least I can do is forgive him."

"What do you mean, the least *you* can do?" Hailey shouted. "You don't owe that man anything! Merry, have you lost your mind?"

Meredith opened her eyes wide, in innocent surprise. "I don't think so."

"Well, *I* do. *I* think so! Okay? *I* think so!" Hailey was starting to steam. "You are not a naive little girl, Meredith Clark! That man is bad news all the way around, and you *know* that!"

Meredith blew out a deep breath. "Man, all we ever hear about in church is that we're supposed to forgive our brother, and when I do, you jump all over me."

Hailey sat back down and pointed her finger at Meredith in anger. "In the first place, that creep is *not* your brother! In the second, if he were really seeking forgiveness, that would be one thing, but 'that dog don't hunt', Meredith! You can't tell me that he's not up to something!"

She stopped and narrowed her eyes at Meredith. "And in the third place, please... *please* try to make me understand how this guy forced you to kill your own child, and you can just forgive him, but you can't or won't forgive Joel!" Her voice snapped in hot indignation. "*Explain* that!"

Meredith sat and stared at her. She had never known Hailey to blow up like this. She didn't even know she was capable of getting so worked up.

"I probably couldn't make you understand," she finally said in a small, but somewhat cool voice. "I will just say *this*. It's true that Cagle is not a Christian. And for that reason, maybe I can cut him a little slack. What he did, he did in ignorance..."

"Ignorance!"

Meredith cut her off. "Yes, ignorance! Besides, his crime is over. Why should he have to pay for it the rest of his life? But as for Joel Etheridge..."

Her face took on a severe look. "That man has no excuse. He *is* a Christian, or at least that's what he would have us all believe. His crime is ongoing. He hasn't even *asked* for forgiveness! He hasn't even... called..."

Her voice broke but she girded herself in anger. "So don't come around here, championing the cause of Joel, because if you do, I will bounce you out on your butt!"

"Are you really going to sit there and tell me you don't love him?" Hailey demanded.

"I *hate* him!" Meredith was yelling, banging the couch for emphasis. "There! Satisfied?"

Hailey just sat there and looked at her with sad eyes.

"Oh, don't do that," Meredith said in a ragged tone, when she saw her friend's eyes begin to well up. "Don't, Hailey! Please don't cry, you'll get me started again, and I just can't. Not anymore. I need to be done with crying."

"I'm just... I just..." She sniffed and took the tissue Meredith offered her.

"You just what?"

Hailey met her eyes and gave Meredith a look that almost tore her heart in two.

"It's just that you're so... anointed, Meredith. Your music is... it changes so many lives. Please don't let anger and bitterness do this to you. Please don't keep saying things like 'hate' and 'drop dead'... "

She couldn't finish, and wept with no restraint.

Her words stung. Meredith looked at her remorsefully, then hung her head.

"I'm sorry, Hailey. I know I shouldn't talk like that. I'll try to do better." She smiled a little shakily and took her hand. "Okay?"

Hailey nodded and squeezed her fingers. "I need a promise."

She winced but waited in silence, unwilling to commit.

"I need you to promise me, Meredith, that you won't let Cagle Lawrence back in your life again."

"Hailey, he hasn't made any move to indicate that he's after that. Even the dinner was just a dinner, I swear."

"Please, Merry," she persisted. "Please don't see him again!"

"I can't very well stop him from just dropping by."

Hailey cringed. "He... knows where you live, then?"

"He wanted an address to let me know how he's making it, from time to time. I couldn't very well give him the office address. I'm not gonna put up with Joel's interference!"

"But why did you feel like you had to give him any address, at all? If you were ever going to tell *anyone* to drop dead..."

Hailey left off finishing and just looked down at the tissue in her hand helplessly.

"Please be careful, Merry," she begged brokenly.

"I will. That much, I *can* promise you. I'll be careful. I'll also be late for my gig, if you don't get out of here." She smiled to take the edge off her words.

Hailey got up and Meredith walked her to the door.

"Listen," she said as Hailey opened it to leave. "I'm sorry I'm such a jerk. I do love you, Sissy. I didn't mean to make you cry."

"I know. I love you, too." Hailey gave her a tight hug. "Do good tonight."

She waved and Meredith flashed her another brief smile, before turning away and heading back inside.

Joel closed the refrigerator door and hurried to grab the phone, before it woke his mother up.

"Hello!" He brought the phone back with him over to the counter.

"This is Hailey."

"Hailey..." He grabbed a paper towel and began dabbing at the milk that had just sloshed over the sides of his glass. "How are you?"

"Not good at *all*, that's how I am!" She was agitated, and sounded as if she'd been crying. She spoke sharply to him.

"No more being vague! I'm going to ask you a question and I want a straight answer. The last thing I can handle right now, is somebody else shooting me a line of bull!"

He put down his glass and waited. "What is it?"

"And I don't want to hear anything about gag orders!" She barreled ahead, as if not even hearing him.

"Wait!" he interrupted sharply. "Stop! Hang up and let me call you back."

"Joel!"

"Stop, I said! Are you at home?"

"Yes!"

"Hang up."

He replaced the receiver, and went into the living room to fish his cell phone out of his briefcase. He rested on the arm of the sofa and punched her number in, waiting impatiently for her to answer.

"Joel?"

"What is this about?"

"Why are you being so weird?" She was exasperated.

"Just be careful what you say over the phone, when you call me or Meredith. I'm not sure if my phone here is tapped or not, but hers definitely is."

"Are you serious?"

"Deadly serious." He moved his hand through his hair. "What's going on?"

"What I just said. I want some straight answers!"

"What's your question?" He countered gruffly.

"Just tell me this. Is Cagle Lawrence the man who's threatening Merry?"

Joel didn't say anything.

"Don't you dare act like you didn't hear me, Joel Etheridge! I mean it!"

"Hailey, please don't force this."

"The truth! Now!"

"Listen..."

"He's *seen* her, Joel!" Hailey was actually shouting at him. "Several times! Do you understand me? They had dinner together at Center Hill Lake!"

Joel was unable to move, let alone respond.

"Now, you listen to me and you listen good!" Hailey was seething. "I know you love her. I know you are trying to protect her. But you asked me to get involved and, doggone it, Joel, if that fiend is the one who's threatening her, you'd better tell me, and tell me now!"

Joel laid his forehead on his palm and stared down at the floor. "Did he... do anything..."

"She said he didn't, but that doesn't mean he won't. Answer me!"

Joel stopped being evasive and breathed out heavily. "It's him."

"Oh, dear God," she wailed. "I knew it! I just *knew* it!" She gripped the phone in a desperate manner. "Joel, what are we gonna do?"

"I don't know," he answered in a weak voice. "God help me, Hailey, I just...   Pray.   Pray hard."

Joel pressed his hand against his chest in distress. "And, please, whatever you do, you can't warn her. You can't, Hailey!"

"I don't see why not! I think she deserves to know!"

"I *told* you!" He spat the words out as if he'd like to choke her. "He's having her house watched! Her phone is tapped! Do you think he's not serious about what he'll do, if she finds out what he's up to? He's promised us that if he even suspects she knows, she's going down.

"You don't know what this man has on her, Hailey. This has nothing to do with the abortion."

"But I'm her best friend! How can I know this and not tell her?"

"She's not the same submissive teenager she was in New Orleans, Hailey. If you're her best friend, then I don't have to tell you that the effects of those years have turned her into a hotheaded gunslinger. If you say one word to warn her about Lawrence, she'll swear herself in, like a posse of one, and go after him and when that happens, Meredith is done! If you love her at all, you won't say a word. I'm begging you! Hailey, listen to me, now. I know you're upset, but you have to listen to me. I am *begging* you!"

"Alright!" She responded to the alarm in his voice. "Okay, then. But as soon as it can happen, you and your buddy Ross are gonna come clean with me."

"We will. I'll call you as soon as I can arrange it."

She hung up and Joel held the phone, motionless for a long moment, then he made his way down the hall. He knocked softly on the door at the end.

"Mom?" he opened it slightly. "Will you pray with me?"

Chapter Nineteen

Thanksgiving Day dawned clear and cold. Joel was submerged deep into the sofa, one leg dangling off the side, arms up over his head.

The Macy's Thanksgiving Day parade gave it a valiant effort but could do nothing to stir him out of his lethargy.

Laura paused on her way through the living room and considered him. He looked like a man who had died with his eyes open. She silently passed on to the kitchen and after a few minutes, emerged carrying a hot, steaming mug.

"Son?"

"Hmm?" He kept watching some unseen thing.

"Cocoa."

He nodded, but stayed fixed on whatever he was focused on.

Laura sat the drink on a coaster and knelt down beside him. She stroked his hair and he looked over at her.

"Don't let it consume you," she said gently.

He gave her a weak smile and touched her face. "I know. I won't."

"Here." She moved back and reached for his cocoa. "Sit up and take this. I bet you haven't even had any coffee this morning."

Joel pulled himself up into a sitting position and reached for the cocoa. "Thanks, Mom."

"How long have you been out here?"

"Daylight, I guess."

"Joel!" She chided him in a soft voice. "You have to stay on top of it. Ross has been telling you that. Don't let it bury you, not now, when you're so close."

"Oh, I know, Mom. It's not that. I mean, it's not the situation itself."

He tried some of his cocoa and leaned his head back.

"Then what?"

"Well... it's Merry, but not what you're thinking. Not the Cagle Lawrence thing."

"Thanksgiving?"

He nodded.

"Is she alone?"

"She's going to spend it like she does every year. Singing down at the homeless shelter, while they have their Thanksgiving meal."

"But she loves doing that."

"She loves those *people*, Mom, and she would do that for them any day of the year. But Thanksgiving and Christmas are a time to be with family. I guess I was just hoping..."

He let it drop.

Laura waited, partly because she didn't know what to say, and partly because it would only be something he already knew.

Joel seemed to be thinking deeply. After a moment, he lifted his eyes to hers.

"Mom, I need a favor. Could I use your car, for just an hour or so, today?"

"Sure," she replied automatically. "Is there something wrong with yours?"

He shook his head. "No, it's just that mine might be recognized."

"You want to drive down to the shelter."

"Is that wrong?"

"Is it safe?" she returned, quietly.

He put down his drink and leaned forward, resting his elbows on his knees.

"I think it'd be okay. I could slip inside the door after I hear her start singing, and then leave before she's done."

She could see the longing in his eyes.

"I just have to see her, Mom. It's been so long. I just want to look at her, just for a moment."

She gave him a long, steady gaze before slowly nodding. "But you have to be careful, Son. You don't want to blow it."

Joel touched her cheek. "What time is it?"

"A little after ten. Good thing I did most of the cooking last night. Now I can just relax."

"When's Gary coming?"

"Probably a little over an hour."

"Okay. I'm gonna hit the shower, Mom. If I'm not back by noon, why don't you guys start without me?"

"Not on your life! We're not gonna drop dead from starvation if you're a few minutes late. You just take your time."

Joel pushed himself up out of the sofa, gave his mother a hug, then headed for the shower.

Shortly after eleven, he slid into Laura's silver Buick and drove to the downtown area of Nashville. He parked the car a couple of blocks down from the shelter and began walking in that direction.

He had asked Delores to call the administrator earlier in the week, as if she were just somebody who had heard that Meredith might be singing there today, and she was able to find out that she was scheduled to begin around eleven thirty.

Joel rounded the curb, clad in a Redskins Starter jacket and jeans, a baseball cap and dark glasses. Anyone knowing him and expecting his arrival would have been able to recognize him, if only because of his hair. All he could do was hope that he would blend in, and that no one would look too closely.

He stepped a little faster, as he heard Meredith's beautiful throaty voice and her strong, aggressive touch on the piano. He stood back from the entrance for a minute.

The last of the food line was shuffling slowly into the door. Maybe he could just move along with it. If he waited until the doorway was clear and then came in, Meredith might look up and see him. She would recognize Joel, if he were wrapped in swaddling clothes. He felt a small rush of pleasure as he realized this about her, and held the thought for a moment, like a flower.

Just as the last man was moving in, Joel fell in behind him. As he entered the large room, he immediately ducked behind a portable partition, normally used to section off the area, but now standing against the wall to make space for everyone.

He moved closer in behind its fold and peered through the gap the hinges created. Joel stared at the object of all his love and devotion, drinking in her lovely face as if he were dehydrated.

She was so beautiful! Her voice and her presence were forming a canopy that these neglected and hurting people were harboring under. They claimed Meredith as if she were one of them, and maybe she was. In her own way, maybe she was just as homeless as they were.

He blinked furiously and tried to clear his eyes, so that he could see her better. He stood still, not daring to move, taking in every small thing about her and tucking it deeply into his heart. He let her voice wash over him, especially now, as she sat on the piano stool and chatted with the crowd.

Gone was the angry edge of her tongue, the sharp glare in her eyes, the bitter gall that she had been soaking her feelings in.

Meredith loved these downtrodden people. Whatever was going on in her own life right now, it was not their fault and they would receive all the care and compassion that it was a natural part of her to want to give. She had checked her weapons at the door, and had come to pour out of herself whatever kindness might still be left.

If there were only some way for Joel to let her know that he had been here! He knew that it wasn't a smart thing to do, that it would only infuriate her. But maybe it would touch another part of her, a hidden part that maybe missed him and wondered if he ever thought about her.

Joel racked his brain, trying to think. His heart surged hopefully as he remembered that he had a key to Meredith's Jeep on his key ring, then fell when he realized that he was in Laura's car. Maybe he was supposed to just leave it alone.

He couldn't. Common sense was going to lose this round. It was Thanksgiving and he had to let her know that she had been on his mind, and in his heart.

He grappled fiercely with his thoughts, sending up a quick prayer. Suddenly it came to him. He took out his wallet and sorted through it, being as careful and as quiet as possible. He found it! His hand shook as he retrieved an old movie ticket stub.

Somewhere In Time. Joel smiled tenderly. He had never felt foolish for hanging onto this stub, although it would have embarrassed him at the time, if Meredith had found out.

A couple of years ago, after a grueling day in the studio, they both decided that what they really needed was an expensive Coke and a good movie. Meredith mentioned that the Sarratt Cinema at Vanderbilt University was having a revival of classic romance. Joel had provided the expected sarcasm, but was secretly more than willing to take her.

It was the first time he had ever seen tears in those lovely, gray eyes. She didn't have a tissue, and had unconsciously fished around in the dark for what she thought was the hem of her jacket. It turned out to be the hem of Joel's jacket, instead. He sat there, quietly watching her dabbing away at her sweet face, completely oblivious to what she was doing. Finally, she became aware of him watching her, and looked up in surprised consternation.

Joel's heart churned, as he remembered the day at Grotto Falls, when she glanced up with those eyes, and again lifted up his jacket to say "I got mascara on it". He had never managed to take either jacket to the cleaners.

He let go of his memories as he heard Meredith announce her last song. He waited until her eyes closed, as he knew they would, once she got into the music, and after one more hungry look at her, quietly went outside.

A couple of guys were still sitting on the sidewalk with their backs against the building. Another was leaning against the wall on the other side of the door, his hands up under his shirt to keep them warm.

Joel glanced down at his own Starter jacket. It was easily worth several hundred bucks, a gift from a friend on the team. Joel smiled to himself. Meredith was worth anything and everything. He knew, as he approached this cold young man, that he would give him the jacket, whether or not he helped him, but the man didn't know that.

"Hi." Joel smiled at him in a way that endeared him to all his friends and the man smiled back with uncertainty.

"Hi."

"Can I ask you something?"

The man sized Joel up, then nodded and looked down.

"Well... first, what's your name?"

"Pockets." He grinned. "They call me Pockets 'cause I used to keep all my stuff in my pockets. Everybody said I looked like a kangaroo."

He looked off down the street and laughed ruefully. "Don't got no pockets no more. Somebody stole my pants, when I was washin' off down yonder."

He gestured toward the river, then looked back down at his worn old sweatpants and blinked. "Had all my stuff in them pants..."

Joel almost reeled with the impact this man's words had on him. He purposed firmly in his heart to come down here more often and to get to know these people.

Meredith had never asked him. Maybe she wasn't sure that he'd fit in. He was sorry to say that maybe he wouldn't have. But his broken spirit had caused a deeper compassion to awaken in him, and he was feeling it now.

He cleared his throat and looked steadily at the young man. "Pockets, do you know the girl who's singing inside?"

He smiled broadly. "Miss Meredith? She's a angel!"

Joel couldn't both agree and disagree, more.

"If you don't mind doing something for me, I'll give you this jacket."

Pockets dropped his jaw and stared at him in disbelief. He reached out a grimy hand and fingered the satiny material almost reverently. Then he looked up at Joel with wary eyes.

"I won't do nothin' to hurt Miss Meredith!" He looked around nervously. "She's goin' to eat with us. She's goin' to save me a chair. She said I could sit by her."

"No," Joel said hurriedly. "I don't want to hurt Miss Meredith either, Pockets. I love Miss Meredith!"

Pockets gave him an open-faced, semi-toothless grin. "Me too!"

Joel grinned back and pulled the ticket stub out of his wallet again. He held it up for Pockets to see.

"I just want you to give this to her. That's all. Would you do that for me?"

Pockets looked at the jacket longingly.

"I promise you, Pockets, I'll still be here when you're done. I won't go anywhere, until you come back and tell me you gave it to her." Joel laid his hand on the man's shoulder. "I give you my word."

Pockets hesitated only an instant, then took the stub in his dirty fingers and went inside.

Joel stood just outside the door and watched. He realized that if Meredith later saw Pockets wearing his jacket, she would certainly be curious to know where he'd gotten it.

One of the reasons he had grabbed it this morning was because it wasn't something he wore often, and the whole point was to not be spotted. He reflected on it, but couldn't remember that he'd ever had it on when she was with him.

The thought deflated him a little. If only he'd known he was going to do this, he would have worn something she would have been sure to recognize, when she saw it on Pockets. Well, it couldn't be helped. If she saw the ticket stub, that should be enough.

Meredith had finished her concert and was squatting down, talking to someone who had come up to the edge of the stage and was reaching for her hand.

Pockets dragged a chair up to the stage and used it as a stair. He went over and hunched down beside Meredith. She listened to him intently, and even held out her hand and let him drop the stub into it, but stuck it inside her jeans pocket, without looking at it. She probably thought it was just something Pockets had found on the ground, Joel decided, feeling a bit dejected.

Pockets scrambled down off the stage and headed for the door. Joel stepped to one side, taking his keys out and pulling off his jacket. He was holding it out to Pockets when he came outside, and smiled at the look of surprise on his face when he found that Joel was still there.

"Here, let's see how you look, Pockets."

He was beaming as Joel helped him into the very nice jacket. He turned this way and that, as Joel gave a low whistle.

"You look great, man." He slapped his back in a friendly manner. "Did she ask if you knew who sent the piece of paper?"

He turned and glanced up at Joel before looking back down at his new jacket.

"No. I jes' said 'Here, I got somethin' for ya'. She said she's gonna read it later."

A spark of hope kindled inside Joel. "Oh, did she? That's good news."

It was cold, and Joel was in his tee shirt now. He shook the young man's hand heartily. "Listen, I know you guys are ready to eat so I'll let you go do that. I need to go."

"You hungry?" Pockets asked generously. "If you are, we got plenty! You can sit at mine and Miss Meredith's table, prob'ly. We can move over."

"Pockets," Joel looked him straight in the eyes and gripped his shoulder lightly.

"I want to tell you from the bottom of my heart, that that's the best invitation I've had in years. You don't know how much I wish I *could* come in and eat with you and Miss Meredith. But I have to be somewhere else.

"You go on in and have a happy Thanksgiving. And thank you for helping me." He gave his arm a couple of light pats and then walked away.

He turned back around as he heard Pockets calling him.

"Hey there, Mister! Thanks for this fine coat! I'm gonna take real good care of it!"

Joel grinned and waved again, as he headed to the car. He sat there for a moment, basking in the memory of the last half hour. After a while, he started the engine and drove off in the direction of his house.

"Thank you, Father," he whispered. "Thanks for letting me see her. And thanks for letting me meet Pockets."

Gary let Laura take his coat and stopped to inhale deeply. He looked at her and smiled, and she laughed at him.

"You hungry, Gary?"

"Starving!"

"Well, gee, I hope you're not going to keel over before Joel gets back."

Gary looked confused. "Isn't that his car out there?"

"He's in my car," she explained. "Come on, let's get some coffee."

She led him into the kitchen, a place that lately seemed very dear and familiar to him. He had really enjoyed the few times over the past weeks, that he and Laura had just sat, and talked, in here.

He strolled over to the coffee maker as comfortably as if he were in his own home, and poured two cups, then brought them over to the table.

"Very good, Jeeves," Laura quipped, taking her coffee and gesturing toward a chair. He grinned and sat down.

"Is Joel's car not running?"

"It's fine." Laura gave a little sigh. "He just didn't want to take a chance on someone recognizing him."

"Oh, then it has something to do with Meredith."

"Yep!" She cradled the warm cup in her hands. "Right or wrong, good idea or bad, he just had to see her, Gary."

He looked at her in surprise. "He went over there? He can't do that, Laura, even if he *is* in someone else's car!"

"Not to her house," she said. "She's at the homeless shelter today. She agreed to sing there for their Thanksgiving dinner and Joel... well, he couldn't seem to stop himself. He had to sneak off down there, even if he only got a glimpse of her."

She flashed him a grin. "I think junkies call it a fix."

Gary traced the rim of his cup soberly. "Laura, I personally don't know if I can watch much more of this. Those two are killing me."

"Well, you old romantic!" She laughed, but then looked down at her coffee, with a sigh. It was obvious that something troubling had just occurred to her, to bring this shadow to her face.

Gary touched her hand for an instant. "What is it, Laura?"

She lifted her dark eyes and met his with a frank look. "Gary I don't know if Joel has talked to you in the past few days, so you may not know this. Cagle Lawrence has been seeing Meredith."

He just sat there and shook his head.

She nodded and his brow drew in concern.

"He showed up at Center Hill Lake when she was there last week." Laura gave him a despairing look. "She even had dinner with him!"

"Has she gone completely mad?" Gary couldn't even fathom this! "What, in the world, could she possibly be thinking?"

He sat his cup down and studied her closely. "You know, Marshall said that Joel thought this might happen. He seems to have called it right."

Laura's eyes misted over. "Gary, you should have seen Joel, when he found out. Meredith's friend Hailey called him last Friday night and told him. After he talked to her, he knocked on my door and asked if we could pray." Her face was very revealing. "He knelt down by my bed and just grieved. All I could do was kneel down beside him, and pray for him."

Gary looked at her grimly. "How long do we put up with the enemy, Laura, before we say it's enough?"

She sat up a little straighter, and waited expectantly for him to continue.

He spread his forefinger and thumb apart. "We have a book that thick, that tells us over and over again about all this authority we have as believers, but authority is like a parachute. It's comforting to know you've got it, but it serves no real purpose until you're forced to use it."

She studied him carefully, as her eyes began to clear. "Go on."

"Well, it's just this. I know Joel and Meredith certainly aren't kids but to *me* they are, and both of them seem like mine. I'm getting just a little sick of watching a creature like Cagle Lawrence run around, with the devil's hand up his back, terrorizing a whole town.

"I believe I've had just about enough of it, and I'm sure *you* have. I guarantee you I can come up with at least ten other people who feel the same way. I want us all to get together and pray this mess off of those two. I mean, hit our knees, and don't stop until we get heard!"

Laura surveyed Gary with respect, and their eyes met in agreement as Joel let himself in the front door.

She gave him a slow smile. "You're on, Man o' War!"

Gary drove slowly up the circle drive, then got out of his car and paused in front of Meredith's large house. He frowned, as he noted the black BMW with Louisiana tags. He hoped he was wrong, but he knew he wasn't.

He stepped up onto her porch and knocked firmly. After a few seconds, Meredith came to the door and looked up at him in surprise.

"Hey, Preach." Her voice sounded tense, and she made no move to open the door any wider.

"Hi, Merry! Just wanted to drop by before I head home for the night and check on you."

"Well, I'm fine. You didn't have to go out of your way."

"You're never out of my way, you know that, kiddo." He smiled at her in a way that usually brought a similar response. This one wasn't as convincing as it might have been. He gave her a searching look. "You okay?"

"Sure." She gave him the characteristic shrug. "Why wouldn't I be?"

"Well, normally you'd ask me in." Gary didn't like to make her feel uncomfortable, but seeing Cagle Lawrence's car was a little unsettling, even though Laura had warned him that he might. He tempered his words with a light pat on her shoulder.

She looked behind her then back at Gary. "Well, the thing is, I have company right now, so it's probably not the best time for us to visit. Would you take a rain check?"

Gary could see that she really felt badly about saying this to him, but was not going to ask him in. He didn't want to make it more awkward than it already was.

"Alright, Missy. No worries."

Her eyes flickered. She stepped onto the porch and pulled the door to, behind her. "Why did you call me that?"

"Call you what?" He drew his brows together, not understanding.

"Missy. You just called me Missy. You never have."

He thought about it. "Now that you mention it, no, I guess I never have. Didn't realize I said it now, and I can't tell you why I did." He watched her expressive face. "Why, honey? Does that name mean something to you?"

Her eyes filled with sadness and her gaze dropped to her feet. "No."

Gary touched her arm. "Well, I'm sorry, Merry, if I just made a major blunder. Forgive me?"

She hinted at a smile and nodded.

"You all better? The ears, I mean?"

Another nod.

"Well, your doctor seemed pleased last Monday, so I guess I am. If you need me, you'll call me?"

"Yeah, I will, Preach. I'm sorry about..." she nodded toward the door.

"Like I said, no worries." He gave her a light, swift hug then moved toward his car. "I'll talk to you soon."

Meredith felt strangely like talking to him tonight, but Cagle was here and she wasn't up to the conflict.

As if hearing his name, Cagle Lawrence opened the door and came out onto the porch.

"Meredith? Is your visitor gone?"

She nodded silently.

"Are you alright? It's cold out here!"

She closed her eyes and rubbed her forehead with her fingertips.

"I'm alright, Cagle, except that I've been fighting a sinus headache all afternoon, and it's just getting worse. Would you mind if we called it a night, and I took something for it and went on to bed?"

He looked down the road at Gary's departing taillights and back at her, thoughtfully. "No, not at all. I probably need to turn in, myself."

He gave her elbow a squeeze, then stepped off the porch and out to his car. "Take care of yourself!"

Meredith returned his wave and then wearily headed back inside. She locked up, and shut the house down for the night, then climbed the stairs to her bedroom, a heavy loneliness settling over her.

She took a brief hot shower and slipped into an old tee shirt and gym shorts. Hook was lying on her discarded clothes, and she ran him off impatiently and jerked them up. Something red was peeking out of her jeans and it caught her eye.

Meredith sighed and pulled it out. Pockets! She was so busy after her concert, that she really wasn't understanding what he was telling her, even though she had tried to look as if she was. She never wanted to make any of those people at the shelter feel unimportant to her.

She laid the bit of paper on her nightstand and threw most of the pillows off her bed, before climbing up onto it and sitting cross-legged with one pillow on her lap.

"Okay, Mister Pockets," she mumbled. "What's this all about?" She twisted her mouth in annoyance. It was just a blank bit of cardboard.

Meredith turned it over and gasped out loud. She laid her hand on her throat, where her heart seemed to be beating.

"Oh, Joel," she whispered, as her breathing became labored and tears sprang from her eyes. "You kept this."

She gave a little sob, as another realization came to her. "You were there!"

All at once it dawned on her, that indefinable thing that had been needling her all day. That jacket Pockets had on! She knew he could never had afforded something like that, not even from a thrift store.

An outdoor rally, three years ago, suddenly inserted itself into her memory. She had an instant vision of Joel wearing that jacket.

He had been there! A faint moan escaped her.

"No, you don't!" She instantly scolded herself. "You can just stop it! You are *not* gonna let him mess with you!"

Meredith crumpled the ticket up and threw it down on the floor, then turned the lamp off and rolled over. A minute later, the lamp came back on. She sat up and looked despondently down at the ticket.

Finally, she picked it up and smoothed it out. Her eyes lingered on it, as she slowly went over to a dresser and opened the top drawer. She traced it tenderly with one finger, then laid it in the drawer beside its mate.

She stood there, swaying with emotion. After several long minutes she carried herself back to bed and once again turned off the light.

Her wet eyes stared up into the darkness. "Joel," she breathed softly. "You were there. You were right there. Why, Joel?" She was alone in the dark, with no one to see her tears. She gave them free course. "Why did you come, if you don't love me anymore?"

She buried her face in her pillow and fell asleep crying his name.

<h1 style="text-align:center">Chapter Twenty</h1>

Meredith threw her bags just inside the door and dragged in, closing it firmly behind her. Leaving everything in a pile, she sprawled wearily on the couch she still had not replaced.

"Phew!" She pulled her hair up in one hand and let it drop over the arm of the couch. "I guess I'd better call Hailey and see about picking Hook up."

No, wait, she had that benefit concert downtown, tonight. She'd have to do that later, she decided.

She closed her eyes and tried to relax. The airport had been a madhouse! She had been spotted by a youth group at the baggage claim area, and was promptly besieged. She was forced to sign her name on every conceivable item, from gym bags to sneakers, and even someone's arm.

She smiled to herself. That kid's mom was gonna have a fit. She was pretty sure he'd handed her a laundry marker.

She rolled over into a fetal position and curled around a pillow. Two weeks. Not the longest stretch on the road by any means, but it still took it out of her, especially since she had insisted on traveling alone, and fending for herself.

Meredith snuggled into the pillow and reflected on her trip. It had been good to get out there with people. They had been kind to her. All those smiles, and hugs, and the nice things they wanted to say to her had somehow started a slow melting in her heart.

If she were going to be honest with herself, the melting probably began when she found Joel's ticket stub in her pocket, but she was *not* going to be honest with herself.

She had, in fact, taken herself to task the following morning. She had strictly pulled her emotions back in line and given herself a vigorous, harsh lecture, until she had Joel Etheridge anchored at bay.

Even now, as he came into her thoughts, she scowled and pushed him away. He wasn't going to do this. He wasn't going to just beam out of her life and then amuse himself by dropping her little crumbs, whenever he got bored.

Meredith looked up at the mantel clock. She'd better take a shower and get ready for tonight's benefit. It was an invitation only acoustic event, featuring area musicians who were glad to lend their talents to her charitable cause. As tired as she was, she was excited about this. It was for the homeless shelter.

Delores had arranged for special tickets to be printed and distributed to the staff, volunteers and beneficiaries of the shelter. Meredith had asked for the first four center rows to be reserved for them and, since she was top billing, her request was promptly carried out.

She got up with great reluctance, and began loading herself down with her luggage. Marshall would be here at five to take her to her sound check, so she'd better get in gear. She stared down at her bags, and then up at the stairs. There was nothing for it, but to start climbing.

Joel slammed his car door and started resolutely across the back parking lot. If Delores had been thinking at the time, she never would have let it slip that Marshall had confided to her, in a moment of frustration, the fact that Meredith was over at the CMA Theater in her old, everyday clothes, apparently with no extra ones.

Joel set his jaw in a hard line and banged impatiently on the backstage door. *Marshall was the one who picked her up,* he fumed. *Why did he even let her get in his car like that?*

He hit the door harder with the side of his fist and a young teenager with an important looking clipboard and an arm band opened it curiously, then stepped back in surprise.

"Mr. Etheridge!"

Joel clapped his hand on the boy's shoulder and grunted as he moved past him, probably a rude gesture, but one of the highlights of the awestruck kid's evening. "Which room is Meredith Clark in?"

The boy led him up some stairs and pointed. "She's at the end of the hall." Joel Etheridge had spoken to him! Maybe later, he would accept a demo from him!

"Thanks, kid." Joel sailed his words at him and aimed himself in the direction the boy had pointed. He slowed his steps, as he approached her door. It was slightly open. Meredith was just sitting there, staring at herself in the mirror, an empty expression on her face.

"Just what do you think you're doing here, dressed like that?" He spoke in a quiet, yet volatile manner, and she hopped up from her chair and looked at him with startled eyes that very quickly began to smolder.

Anger rushed to her beautiful face. Her heart, banished as a traitor since Thanksgiving night, leaped up at the sight of him and even made a move to run to him. This further enraged Meredith, who caught it tightly and made it stay put.

"I made it clear that I didn't want to be disturbed!"

"*Did* you now? Well, chances are that I'm about to disturb you, after all." Joel threw his coat down on a chair and speared her with his eyes. "I asked you a question."

"Mr. Etheridge, if you have any problems with my attire, I suggest you take it up with my manager, Marshall Edwards." Her voice was an iceberg. "Close the door on your way out."

Joel's face began to twitch with too many emotions coming at him, all at once. He floundered between overwhelming love for this creature, and a searing irritation at having his policy so blatantly rebelled against, and thrown back in his face.

The truth would force him to admit that much of his anger was really nothing more than an excuse for him to interact with her. Since security was tight, and there was no possibility of Cagle Lawrence gaining access to the backstage area, Joel had seized on what Delores told him as a reason to confront Meredith, and having to admit it to himself made him all the more turbulent.

He complied with her request and closed the door, but remained inside, his presence filling the room. He began to move toward her purposefully, and she backed away, repeating over and over to her disobedient heart that she hated him.

Joel's stormy eyes grazed her face. "You will do well to remember, Miss Clark, who it is that signs Mr. Edwards' paycheck and who generates the predominant funds that support yours. You will get out of that lawn mowing garb and into what you know to be acceptable attire or you *will* be cut from the program."

They stood there and faced each other squarely. No matter how she felt about it, Meredith knew that Joel meant it. She *couldn't* be cut from the program! All her friends from the shelter were coming just to see her. She was planning to recognize them from the stage. This whole evening was for them. But he would cut her in a heartbeat if she continued to defy him. She hadn't brought any other clothes, but she didn't admit this. Instead, she lifted her chin and tried to keep her voice steady.

"These are street people, Joel. I don't have to try to dress up for them. And they're the only reason I'm here."

"You are here, Meredith, to raise money for these people you say you love so much. Well, the vast majority of the audience is *not* made up of street people. They were invited because they have money and you want it."

He moved closer, grimly determined that she yield to him. "Even if the whole crowd was nothing but a bunch of transients, don't you think they deserve to be treated with the same respect and consideration everyone else gets? You are their princess, and you're going to dress like one."

He turned abruptly and crossed over to the telephone, snatching it up and pounding one of the extensions written on the base.

"This is Joel Etheridge! Any gofers standing around out there?" He returned her hot glare. "Kenny. Well, get Kenny back here, to Meredith Clark's room. Right now."

He hung up the phone and pinned her with a look that held her motionless and silent, but not for long.

Meredith jerked up a hairbrush and aimed it at his head. He moved quickly to one side, then began to slowly close the distance between them. She looked around and grabbed a heavy tray, flinging it at him and hitting him in the ribs.

Joel gripped her shoulders and pressed her firmly against the wall. His face was just inches from hers when he grated out in a scathing voice, "Sometimes I wish you were a man, Meredith! If you were, I'd teach you a vital lesson about these little fits of yours!"

"Oh yeah?" she spat back, quickly. "Well, as long as you're fantasizing, Joel, try to imagine what life would be like, if *you* were a man!"

Joel held her securely in place, wrestling with one impulse after another. A knock on Meredith's door was the only thing that stopped their battle from escalating. He pointed with a warning finger, before crossing the room to answer it.

His eyes fell on the young boy who had let him in the back door. "So you're Kenny."

"Yes sir!"

"Kenny, do you think you'd know my car? It's out back."

His eyes opened wide. "That black Cadillac? Sure!"

Joel handed him the keys and smiled dryly at his enthusiasm. "I need you to get the garment bag and the small carry-on from the back seat. Lock it up, and bring those to Miss Clark. If I'm not here, give my keys to Marshall Edwards. You know Marshall?"

Kenny nodded. "Yes, sir."

"By the way, Kenny," Joel added curiously. "Where *is* Marshall?"

"There's a short or something in one of the stage monitors. It's buzzing. He went to see if it can be fixed in time, or if they should just do without it."

Joel looked at his watch. "No, we can't do either. Tell him I'm calling Perry Mitchell to get one over here, and to meet me in the Green Room in about ten minutes."

Kenny straightened up importantly. "Yes sir, Mr. Etheridge!"

He took Joel's keys and hurried off.

Joel closed the door again and returned to address Meredith, who was still leaning against the wall, mentally flinging daggers at him.

"I knew you would try something like this, Missy. That's why I sent Delores over to your house, to get your clothes. Comply quietly, or I'll personally remove you from the stage. I don't make idle threats, so don't test me."

She raised her combative chin. "I think now would be an excellent time for you to turn over that key, Mr. Etheridge. You give it back tonight, or I'm having the locks changed."

Joel came very close and looked down at her for a long, unsettling moment.

"Alright," he agreed stoically. "I'll leave it with Marshall, when I see him in the green room."

Surprise quickly passed over her features, then rapidly turned into contempt. "See that you do! I should have left well enough alone, and kept it when you gave it back before, you two-faced liar!"

Meredith expected an angry reply, a veiled threat, a reemphasizing of his ultimatum. What she got completely shook her.

Joel lifted his hand and brushed the back of his fingers gently across her face. She couldn't move. He stroked her cheek with his thumb, and gazed deeply and longingly into her eyes, with that same tragic sadness she had seen the night she told him she loved him.

"Shine, little one," he said, softly and unevenly. He rested tender, adoring eyes on her, then turned away and swiftly left the room.

Meredith collapsed against the support of the wall and trembled violently. She fought with everything she had to keep from crying. Kenny's hesitant knock on the door saved her.

She took the items Joel had instructed him to bring and thanked him meekly. She locked the door behind him and slowly opened the garment bag.

Her reaction was not unlike the one Joel's movie stub had induced. She uttered a low, weak moan and lifted out a black, Leavers lace, midi-length dress. Joel had bought it for her once in Los Angeles.

She knew, without opening the carry-on, that the soft, black, suede slouch boots and carefully chosen jewelry would be inside.

Why had Joel asked Delores to bring *this* dress? Her cheeks were flushed, as she slipped it on. She stood in front of the mirror, and stared solemnly at her breathtaking reflection.

Before she could stop herself, she remembered the look on Joel's face, when she stepped out of the shop's fitting room, wearing it.

She closed her eyes tightly. It was the same look he had given her at Grotto Falls, that he gave her just moments ago, before leaving the room.

"Okay, Meredith, you can stop it now." She hurried to push away the memory of Joel's expressive eyes, and the sensation of his fingertips on her cheek. "Maybe he did mean what he said at one time, but once he found out about you, he just couldn't handle it, so there it is. You have to let it go." She coached herself sternly. "You just focus on your music, and remember why you're here. Don't you dare let Joel Etheridge get into your head tonight, of all nights!"

After some time of waiting and pacing, she heard a knock and Marshall calling for her. She let him in.

He showed no reaction to her change of clothes.

"You're on, Merry," he said quietly. "Oh, wait... I'm supposed to give this to you." He reached into his coat pocket, then clenched his hand, with a look of regret and self-consciousness.

"Well, this is dumb. I couldn't have picked a worse time to do this, but I guess it's too late, now."

Meredith looked down at her key and then up at Marshall, in stunned silence. She glanced back down at it, as she held out her shaking hand.

Marshall dropped it into her palm and gave her a kind smile. "Not right now," he said, reading her eyes. "Let it go until later, sweetie."

She let the key fall into her carry-on and followed him out, as if going to the guillotine.

The musical fare of the evening had been a little bit of everything. The backstage area was packed with various country singers, blues and jazz performers, gospel artists, and a rock band.

Marshall stood with his hand on Meredith's shoulder. He gave her a fatherly pat, as she was introduced and she took the stage to the tumultuous delight of the packed house.

She was a vision! The floor lights bathed her in a warm, golden luster. Her long hair danced in the strong current of an overhead vent, and the people from the homeless shelter ignorantly worshiped her. She was the closest thing to royalty that any of them could imagine.

Meredith stood at the center of the stage and began to talk to the audience about her friends in the first four rows, especially recognizing the military veterans. She had them stand to a loud ovation, and made them feel special.

Finally, she took her place at the piano. She traveled through her set, taking the audience with her on her journey. To their regret, all too soon, she announced that the next song was her last, and thanked them for coming.

Meredith couldn't stop herself from looking up, past the end of the grand piano, and into the darkness of the offstage area. She couldn't see Joel, but she knew he was there, concealed behind the curtains, hidden away from the detection and unwanted attention of others, and carefully watching over her performance, as he always did. She could feel his eyes on her.

She sat there timidly, looking down at the keys, and all became still. Joel could tell, from her long hesitation, that this was an unplanned moment. After another long silence, she tentatively touched a few hushed notes and when her voice came, it was husky and laced with emotion.

"I wrote this... I guess, a couple of months ago..." She paused, then began again, with an effort. "I've never actually sung it before, so..." She let out a deep breath.

"It's called The Overflow."

Joel focused on her intently, from his secluded position in the wings. He'd never heard this! She was replacing her most popular song, that she always sang at the end of her concerts, with this one. He knew that her eyes had searched for him, before she chose it. What did she need to tell him?

Her piano opened up a path for her and she stepped out onto it, as if afraid of where it might lead her. A soft, slow, minor melody called her forth, and she followed after it, fearfully and reluctantly, but obediently, her low, quiet voice beautiful, but broken.

"My heart is like a fragile boat,
Aimlessly drifting, pitched and tossed.
If life's a storm, I have no hope.
If faith is blind, then I am lost.
I am lost.

"My heart is like a graveyard flower,
Solemnly fingered, left alone.
If time's my foe, this is my hour.
If peace a dwelling, no one is home.
No one is home."

Joel lowered his head, hardly breathing, and stared hard at the floor. The pain in her words were being felt in his own heart. He didn't know if either of them could bear it.

"Love stops by my window each morning at dawn.
He calls my name, He lingers there.
I draw back, ashamed of the gown I have on.
He is a gentleman.
I am not fair.

My heart is like a tiny seed,
Buried alive, waiting to grow.
If pain's a gardener, there is no weed.
If tears are rain,
I drown beneath
The overflow."

Meredith had been so completely at the mercy of what the song was doing to her, that her heart lay exposed and helpless, in the wake of her emotional performance. People throughout the audience were quietly beginning to weep.

Joel stood there in pieces, tears falling freely, as only he understood the suffering of Meredith's fragile heart. For the past two months, she had kept this song hidden from him, but he knew that tonight, in this moment, she had sung it to him, alone. She had dared to come out from her deepest hiding place. She needed him to know. He did know.

Meredith rose, without realizing it, and was just standing there, as the crowd erupted into deafening applause. The massive curtain closed and Marshall came and gently led her offstage.

She was immediately accosted by a surge of individuals with backstage passes. Cameras were going off furiously, and she was jostled back and forth between clusters of people, all wanting some kind of consideration from her.

In the midst of clamor and confusion, she was swept past Joel. Their eyes collided and Meredith was jarred as she witnessed both pure love and intense grief shadowing his sad, handsome face. She felt a slip of paper being tucked into her hand. He gave it a gentle pressure, then took himself away.

She looked down at the little note and then back up to see Joel moving through the crowd, and down the long hallway, apparently leaving the theater. She stared after him, not even hearing the voices calling her name and asking her for photos and autographs.

Normally, Meredith was very approachable after a performance and always tried to be congenial to the ones who sought her out but tonight, she was overwhelmed. She just needed to get to a quiet place. She needed to be alone.

"Marshall!" She began to panic, and looked around desperately.

He shoved past the tight crowd and reached for her.

"Marshall, get me out of here, please!"

He mumbled a series of standard apologies to no one in particular, and guided Meredith away from the offstage area and to her dressing room. He stopped at the door.

"Do you want to take the time to change, Merry, or should we just gather your things?"

"Let's just go!" She gripped his arm tightly. "Please just get me out of here."

Marshall flagged Kenny. He came running and they hurriedly piled everything together.

Meredith looked down at the crumpled paper crushed tightly in her hand. She fingered it for a moment, then suddenly, she had to know.

She spread it out, as Marshall searched around to see if they were leaving anything. Her eyes filled up so quickly, she could hardly finish reading it.

You were never more beautiful. <u>Never more fair</u>. I knew you would shine. You always do.   Joel.

There was something else.

P.S. <u>I love you</u> in old blue jeans, little one. You know that.

She made a small, painful sound.

Marshall saw her clutching the note to her heart and came over to her. "Are you alright, Merry?"

She closed her eyes and shook her head.

"What can I do?" he asked, kindly.

"I just need to go home, Marshall, please. Can you just take me home?"

He took her arm. "Let's get moving, Kenny!"

"Wait!" She halted suddenly. "My friends from the shelter! They're all expecting to see me after the show!" She turned stricken eyes to Marshall. "Oh, no... I can't stay here! I just... I have to go... "

He signaled his helper. "Kenny, has Joel left?"

"I saw him in the Green Room, when I came down the hall."

Marshall looked back at her cautiously. "I guess I know how you feel about this, honey, but you know Joel can fix it."

She hung her head. "Let's just go by there, then."

"Are you sure?"

She nodded miserably.

Marshall sent Kenny on to his car and led Meredith to the Green Room.

Joel was standing alone in front of a painting, his hands on his hips and his head down.

"Joel?"

He turned around at the small sound of her voice.

Meredith was still clenching his note tightly. She bit her lip, then approached him nervously.

"I need to go... but..."

Joel's tortured eyes lingered on her. He looked down at his note and then back up into her sad eyes.

"Would you like for me to go talk to your friends from the shelter, Missy?"

She nodded, then dared to look up at him. "Would you?"

"You know I will," he whispered, with a faint little smile.

He looked over her head at Marshall, then back down into her hollow eyes.

"Go home, little one, and get some rest. I'll take care of it."

"Thank you." She blinked rapidly and her words caught in her throat.

Joel lifted her chin with his fingertips, trying to convey his feelings without words. Silently, he spoke to her, as tears betrayed and exposed both of them. He closed his eyes and touched his forehead to hers. After a moment, he pulled back to read her face, and to let her read his.

"Marshall, take good care of her for me," he said quietly, without looking away from her.

"I will, Joel."

Meredith choked on a muffled sob and turned and ran out.

Joel watched his heart run after her.

Chapter Twenty-One

"Joel, I thought you'd be a little more enthusiastic about this!" Ross gave his friend a look of bewilderment. "Haven't you heard anything at all I've said?"

Joel slowly raised his eyes until they were level with Ross Decker's. He looked at him as if he was waiting for something.

"Should I come back?"

He tried to focus. "Sorry. I was just..."

"You were just thinking about last night." Ross finished his sentence for him, then smiled at the question on Joel's face.

"I was there. In fact, and I have you to thank for this, I was there with Hailey."

Joel rubbed his neck and lifted one side of his mouth in an accommodating smile.

"That reminds me. Hailey called me one night a little while back and demanded that you and I come clean with her. I said I'd try to set it up, but I guess I dropped the ball. To be honest, I just forgot."

"Oh, I know, believe me!" Ross grinned. "Hailey was more than a little bit put out with you! After Meredith's last song, she threatened both of us with bodily injury."

He stopped and studied Joel's somber face. "She was really something special last night, that girl of yours."

251

"That girl of *mine,* huh?" He drew something invisible on the top of his desk with his finger.

Ross didn't answer but continued to regard him prudently.

Joel turned his head and stared out the window with an unreadable expression.

Finally, Ross pulled his chair up to the desk and leaned closer. "I need you to listen to me. Joel?"

He waited until Joel pulled his eyes away from whatever he'd been gazing at, and acknowledged him.

"Joel, I need you to put everything else away, and give me your attention. Are you with me on this thing, or not? Because if you are, I need you fully engaged and present. If you're not, we can do this later."

Joel shifted his weight in the chair and turned to face him. "No, I don't want to do this later. I want to take care of Cagle Lawrence as soon as possible."

"Good man. Then listen to this. That friend of mine in New Orleans? Felix Brasseaux. He's that U.S. Marshal I told you about. He's flying out here next week."

Ross crossed his ankle over his knee and watched to make sure Joel was really listening. "He's gonna help us set this thing up, Joel."

Joel began to take in what he was saying. "Does he have any idea what Lawrence is really doing in Tennessee or does he think it's only about Meredith? You talked about all this only being a civil infraction."

"He not only knows what he's doing here, he knows who he's doing it with."

Joel looked at him sharply. "How?"

Ross shrugged. "You have to remember, the boys in New Orleans are very well acquainted with Mr. Lawrence. They've had their eye on him for years. They even know who his little playmates are. It turns out Lawrence is in over his head. He's been playing around with some pretty heavy hitters. He's in debt to people that you do *not* want to be in debt to, and he's made some pretty wild promises. Now he's going to have to make good on all that, and he knows it."

Joel gave him a surprised look. "Felix told you this? How does he know all these details?"

"It's his job to know." Ross looked around carefully, simply from habit, and leaned forward, lowering his voice before he continued.

"Cagle Lawrence should have invested as much time as Felix Brasseaux has invested, in knowing who his playmates really are. Especially when one of them is ours."

"One of them is... "

"A plant."

For the first time in a long while, Joel really smiled. "Don't toy with me, buddy."

"I would never."   Ross relaxed back into his chair. "The stakes are a lot bigger than I first thought. This is no simple possession with intent. This is big league stuff. Lawrence's days are numbered."

Joel looked at him wistfully. "I wish all this could go down before Christmas."

"Well, you never know. If I understand Felix correctly, our guy on the inside says Lawrence is planning a little holiday party. So, maybe." Ross smiled encouragingly.

"Let's hope for best," he added. "It does urge us to get a move on, though. That's not even a full two weeks away."

Joel nodded and lapsed back into his earlier study.

"Joel?"

He glanced up.

"Get that girl with the delicate, transparent heart something special for Christmas." He held up his hand to curb Joel's response.

"No, don't even stop to think about whether or not she'll accept it. Buy it as if she will. Christmas is a time for miracles." He emphasized his words with a knowing look. "Just do it, buddy."

Joel bit his lip and a steady glimmer of hope slowly began to burn in his eyes. "I hate to rush you off, Ross but... I have an errand downtown." He broke off with a roguish grin, as Ross began to laugh quietly.

Laura Etheridge mentally reached inside and just shut her mind off. It had been yammering at her, ever since she got into her car and she was sick of it. She was going with her heart on this one.

She would just face the consequences when they came around, but she had made her decision last night, as she and Gary sat and witnessed the raw baring of Meredith's soul.

She was going through with this, even if Joel never spoke to her again. She knew she was being rash, but she was tired of being careful.

She drove her Buick up Meredith's long drive and stopped it in front of her house, noting with relief that her white Jeep was the only vehicle there. If she had seen that black BMW Gary had told her about, she felt she would have just marched into that house, snatched Cagle Lawrence up by the hair of his head, and thrown him out into the yard.

She smiled at herself. "You're so scary."

She looked up at the beautiful, old, Colonial Revival house before stepping onto the porch. There were some lights on upstairs, so Meredith must still be up.

She rang the doorbell. There was movement in the house almost immediately, but Meredith seemed to be taking her time about coming to the door.

She hesitated, then rang again. After another minute or so, the door opened slightly. Meredith's face appeared cautiously from around it and her eyes widened in surprise. She stepped back and stared.

"Mrs. Etheridge!"

Laura beamed at her. "You remember me!"

"I..." Meredith continued to stare. "Of course I remember you, I just... what are you doing in Tennessee?" She blushed becomingly. "Oh, that was stupid. Your son."

Laura gave a soft little laugh. "I don't mean to intrude, Merry, but would you let me come in for a few minutes?"

She saw Meredith hesitate and laid a motherly hand on her arm. "I promise to wipe my feet and be on my best behavior."

Meredith looked down and grinned. "I didn't mean to make you feel like you're not welcome. It's just... I thought you might be someone else, at first." She pulled the door all the way open and Laura slipped in.

"Oh, this is great, honey!" She glanced around at Meredith's large, beautiful home appreciatively then turned back to look at her. "How long have you had this place?"

Meredith thought a second. "I guess almost three years. I had a condo on West End, before this. Come sit down, Mrs. Etheridge."

Laura joined her on the couch. "You probably won't remember this, Merry, but the two times we've met before, I crawled all over you about that 'Mrs. Etheridge' stuff and you promised to knock it off."

"Sorry." She smiled shyly and wondered why, in the world, Joel's mother was here. One thing she knew for sure, Joel wouldn't have sent her, under any circumstances! Laura sat and watched her ponder all of this, before reading her mind out loud.

"I know, it seems kind of weird, doesn't it? Here it is, almost eight o' clock at night and your manager's mother just shows up at your house."

"He's not my..." Meredith stopped. Maybe she didn't know.

"Oh yes he is, no matter what it looks like." Laura caught her swift look. "I know about it, Merry."

"Mrs. Etheridge..." She got up on her knees in the middle of the couch and clasped her hands together imploringly, like a bewildered little girl.

"Laura... please tell me why Joel made Marshall take over my management. Why doesn't he want to have anything to do with me?" She hung her head and sighed softly. "Never mind," she finished in a dull voice. "I know why he did it."

"He did it because he loves you."

Meredith shook her head in sad denial.

"Sweetheart!" Laura took her hands gently. "Didn't you see Joel backstage, last night?"

"Yes." Her eyes were beginning to spill over.

"Well, you must not have looked at him too closely, if you're telling me you couldn't find love in those eyes."

She looked down and shook her head again. "I can't afford to keep finding love there, Laura."

"I know, baby." She squeezed Meredith's hands a little. "It hurts. It hurts Joel, too. You're looking at me like you don't want to believe that, but it's true. That man has cried a river of tears over you!"

Meredith couldn't keep her emotions in check, so she kept her head down and focused furiously on her jeans.

Laura reached up and pulled her long hair out of her eyes. "Merry, if Joel knew why I was here, he might never forgive me. It's a chance I'm willing to take. After last night, I can't sit by and watch you two kids suffer any longer."

Meredith sniffed and accepted the tissue Laura pulled from the box on the table.

"Now, you sit back and listen. I'm going to tell you something that Joel should have told you a long time ago. He wanted to. He even tried to tell you one night, but he couldn't go through with it."

Meredith looked up hungrily. If she just knew *something*. Anything!

Laura looked at her revealing eyes with her own warm, loving ones, and gripped her hand firmly. "Honey, don't be embarrassed by this, but I have to say it, before I can say anything else. I know about the abortion you had."

She bowed her head, too ashamed to look at her.

"Baby, that's all in the past. I don't love you one bit less because of it. But you think Joel does."

She nodded slightly, and kept her eyes shut.

"I can't tell you the real reason Joel's having to stay away from you right now. Only Joel can tell you that and even then, only when the time is right. But I *can* tell you something else. Something that I think will show you that you've been wrong about him. Merry, if anything, he loves you more every day.

"Just lean back and I'm going to try to get through this. It's going to be hard for me, but that can't be helped. This is something that happened years ago. Do you know, Merry, that Joel has a sister?"

Meredith's eyes opened wide and she shook her head. "He never said..."

"No," Laura said. "I guess I know he never would have mentioned her to you. It hurts him to talk about her. Her name is Iris. She's a lot like me. Joel is like his father was.

"Iris is four years younger than Joel. Joel packed her around everywhere, almost as soon as we brought her home from the hospital. He thought Iris was his. Even when they were both old enough to go to school, Joel was still trying to carry her everywhere they went. He was so heartbroken when Paul and I sat him down and explained that Iris could walk now, and that he needed to stop trying to carry her."

Laura laughed softly at the memory, and Meredith smiled at the picture she was painting.

"One of the hardest things we ever went through as a family... not the hardest, as you'll see, but *one* of the hardest things was the day Iris came home from school and went straight up to her room. She was a junior in high school, only sixteen. *Barely* sixteen. Joel was home from college for Spring Break. He heard her crying in her room. He went in and was literally with her for hours. Paul and I decided to wait and just let them be. Iris would open up to Joel, before she would confide in anyone else.

"I remember it got really late. It was after eleven before Joel came downstairs. We asked him if Iris was okay and he told us she was sleeping. Then he pulled up a chair and sat down and looked Paul and me both right in the eyes, in that direct way he has, and said, very bluntly, 'Mom and Dad, Iris is pregnant. And if either one of you are thinking about going upstairs and jumping on her, then I'm taking her with me when I leave, which will be tonight.'

"Well, Paul and I were devastated! I mean, we raised her with all the love and attention we had to give. It's not like we weren't close. It just happened.

"The baby's father was a boy from school, a senior named Jack Foley. He was bound and determined to marry Iris and she wanted to marry him, and not just to give the baby his name. She really was in love with him. Jack's parents were just as shocked and thrown by this thing as we were, but we all sat down and talked it out. Jack and Iris were married just shortly before the baby was born. It was a girl. Paul never got to see her before we lost him in a car crash."

Laura pulled a tissue out for herself and began tending to her own tears. "The baby's name was Kayla. Oh, Meredith!" She laid a hand on her knee and gave her a watery smile. "You should have seen Joel and that baby! It was like having Iris to carry around, all over again. He fed her, he diapered her, he baby-sat her, he took her to fairs, and malls, and football games..." She stared off into the past for a moment.

"You would think that Jack and Iris might have resented the time those two spent together, but they didn't. Kayla and her 'Uncle J' were a joy to watch. We had to fuss at him all the time though, because he would have turned her into a tomboy. He even taught her how to shoot and fish."

Laura fanned her eyes furiously to dry them. Meredith was moved by a sudden urge to reach over and take her hand, as Laura braced herself for the rest of it.

"Meredith, if you can picture that relationship, and if you can see how closely it paralleled the one Joel had with Iris, then you'll be able to understand the devastating impact this next thing I'm going to tell you had on Joel. In fact, he's never gotten over it... and I'm afraid he never will."

"Are you sure you can do this, Laura?" Meredith's eyes were tender with concern.

"I have to, sweetheart. For Joel. And for you." She patted her hand and plunged back in.

"Kayla grew up to be the prettiest little thing you could imagine. She had impish, little dimples and long, red curls and the clearest, most beautiful, blue eyes... almost exactly like Joel's. She was head cheerleader and the envy of most fifteen-year-olds, I guess. Joel loved her, as if she were his own daughter. He was having to fly back and forth between Nashville and Oklahoma pretty regularly back then, but he made sure he was around, every free moment he had, to spend time with her.

"I can't describe for you the tragedy it was for Joel, when the flower of his heart came to him and told him she was pregnant, just as his other flower had done fifteen years earlier. None of us knew. Kayla told him in a park one day after school, and made him swear he wouldn't say anything. For some reason, she was deathly afraid of what Jack's reaction would be. Not that Jack was ever mean to her in any way," she added hastily. "Jack adored his little girl. Everyone did.

"What Joel didn't know at the time, was that Kayla had gotten some of her friends to snoop around an abortion clinic to find out what it would cost her to have one. When she got all of her information, she went to Joel and asked him if he would loan her the money. He flatly refused. He offered to tell her parents for her, just like he did for Iris years before. Merry..."

Laura's eyes were streaming now and so were Meredith's. "They would have understood! It happened to them. Joel knew they would, but..."

She hesitated. "For one thing, Kayla had never been told that her parents had to get married because of her, and for another... well, Kayla convinced Joel that if he went to her parents, she would run away. In fact, she told him she had it all arranged, through a friend she'd made at cheerleading camp.

"Joel continued to beg her not to go through with the abortion. He got her to promise him she would at least think about it a while longer. Honey... a few days later, Joel was driving through the downtown area, and there was his precious Kayla, standing on the corner. She was trying to... she was there to turn tricks."

"Oh, Laura, no!" Meredith's hands flew up to her face as she gasped.

Laura crumpled her tissue tightly. "He was a wild man, Merry! He jumped out of the car and grabbed her. A cop saw them and pulled up. At first, he thought Joel was just some guy attacking a young girl, but he soon understood that he was a man in pain, who had just found his niece trying to pick up men on a street corner. He didn't arrest her; he let Joel leave with her. Joel drove her out to the park, and made her talk to him.

"She told Joel that she had never done anything like that before, but that she would try it again if she had to, because she was going to have this abortion, whether Joel helped her pay for it, or not. Meredith, he just felt his back was up against the wall. He couldn't let her turn to prostitution, on top of everything else. Threatening to do something drastic was one thing, young girls will do that. But actually finding Kayla on a street corner, with almost nothing on, prepared to make good on her threat was another. Merry, darling, I'm afraid Joel gave her the money for the abortion. In fact, he took her."

Meredith fell heavily against the back of the couch, and covered her eyes with both hands. There was a muted sound of deep pain and then she was silent.

Laura watched her carefully. "Sweetie..."

She finally looked up at her.

"I wish I was done. I'm not."

"You mean... there's more?"

"I'm sorry, there is." Laura closed her eyes tightly, reliving this particular grief all over again. "I wish I didn't have to say any of this, but you need to understand. Sweetheart, if anyone is able to have compassion for you, it's Joel. If anything, what you told him would have only deepened his feelings for you."

She looked blankly around the room. "Let me just get through with all this. This is the hardest part."

She shifted her position on the couch, and waited a moment, before beginning again. "The thing is, Meredith, that when Joel took Kayla to this clinic, none of us even knew she was pregnant. So you can imagine our shock when... well, there was an accident.

"No," she corrected herself darkly. "It wasn't an accident. It was just blatant negligence, by a bunch of people who couldn't have cared less about Kayla, once they got their blood money. Anyway...."

She cleared her throat and pushed on. "Joel brought Kayla home after the procedure. Both her parents were still at work. Joel wanted to stay with her, but Kayla said it would arouse their suspicions, if they came home and found him just hanging out there, with her upstairs, lying down. She seemed okay, other than being a little weak and jittery, which was understandable. He let her talk him into leaving, thinking she was okay.

"He came on back to the house and just sat over in a corner, staring at the floor for the longest time, not talking. Sometime that evening, we got a call from Iris. She was screaming hysterically that something was wrong with Kayla. Joel leaped up and tore over there. I followed after him, and the ambulance was there when we arrived. I remember the sick feeling that washed over me when I saw that the paramedics had all moved back, and were just standing there, looking at us. And then I saw her..."

Laura's face was washed in pain, and a soft moan escaped her lips. Meredith just stared at her in horror, frozen in place.

"She was gone, Merry. Those monsters at that clinic had punctured her womb and our baby just... lay in that bed and bled to death!"

"Laura!" Meredith slipped down onto the floor and began crying bitterly into the couch.

Laura reached down and stroked her hair. "Honey, I don't want to hurt you, but I need you to get this image in your head. I want you to see the Joel that I saw... the one who fell across his little Kayla, screaming and begging God to take him instead of her. Sweetheart..."

She got off the couch and knelt beside Meredith. "You remember, I said that none of us knew. So just think of the shock that hit Iris, when she realized the things that Joel was saying... that her brother, who she adored and looked up to all her life, was involved in the death of her only child!

"Merry, it's been years, but Iris and Jack have never spoken to Joel since that night. They wouldn't even allow him to come to the funeral. Iris told him, there by Kayla's dead little body, that as far as she was concerned, he was dead too. She told him that she would never forgive him. She never has."

"Meredith..." Laura gathered her in her arms. "That man comes as close to adoring you as God will allow. He's done nothing but suffer, ever since you two have parted ways. He *does* have reasons, serious valid reasons for staying away from you, but it isn't what you think, and it isn't forever. You're precious to him. You have to believe me."

"I'm so ashamed," she whispered, resting on Laura's shoulder, as if she were her own mother. "I just feel so... hateful! I've said so many disgusting, ugly things about him and to his face."

"And you wish you could fix it, don't you?"

She nodded, miserably.

"Honey, you won't understand this, but you can't. You can't go to him and tell him what I've told you. It's not time. And there's a good reason why you can't, but Joel is the only one who can tell you what that reason is. I need you to just trust me enough to believe that I'm telling you the truth."

"It's not that I don't believe you," she answered in a feeble voice. "Laura... I just miss him so much!"

"Oh, sweetie, he misses *you*, don't you doubt that! Why do you think he sneaked down to the shelter on Thanksgiving, and hid there, so he could just watch you? Why do you think he picked a fight with you backstage, last night?"

Meredith smiled in spite of her tears.

"I just wish I could see him," she said wistfully. She looked over at her telephone and Laura read her mind.

"Oh, honey, you can't call him."

Meredith looked at her with sorrow in her eyes. "Is he not ready to even talk to me, then?"

"It's not that he's not ready," Laura assured her. "My goodness, that man would do anything humanly possible to be with you, Meredith. It's not at all that he's not ready to talk to you. It's that he can't. It's the situation he finds himself in. That's as much as I can say about that, honey."

Meredith knew that Joel's mother was telling her the truth, but she just didn't understand any of it. She looked down at the floor, her hair in her eyes, and her shoulders drooping, then shook her head. "No one can make Joel do anything he doesn't want to do," she said, in a small voice.

"These are..." Laura stopped and groped for what to say. "These are very trying circumstances, ones that he can't control and that's why it's especially hard for him. Joel has lived his entire life in a sort of 'master of my own fate' way, but this thing has knocked the wind out of his sails."

"You're asking me to wait." Meredith answered, quietly."

"I am, sweetheart. Can you do that?"

Meredith had been so sure that telling Joel about her abortion was what had driven this wedge between them, but tonight, after finding out about his own tragic experience, she could no longer claim that. Instead, she was being told that it was some mysterious "something" but, other than that, she had nothing to cling to.

Now, she looked directly into Laura's sweet, brown eyes and could see that whatever the secret was that Joel's mother was guarding, it was something that she was just going to have to trust was in her best interest to remain a secret for now.

"I can wait, Laura," she finally said. "I just don't understand."

"No, I know you don't, and I'm sorry I can't make it any clearer. You can't approach him, yet, Meredith. In fact, it would be better if people just continue to think that you two are still at odds. And honey, don't talk about this to anyone, especially not over your phone. I'm seeing that big question in your eyes and I wish I could just tell you everything, but if you can manage to hang tough a little bit longer, everything will make sense. It has to be this way."

"I can wait," Meredith repeated. "I can do anything, if Joel really loves me." She colored slightly, and Laura grinned.

"Well, he does, Merry. He loves you so much, that it gets downright embarrassing for the rest of us!"

Meredith's eyes lit up, but then dimmed again. "I'm so sorry about Kayla."

"Yes. We all are. But we have to move on. I'm just so glad, baby, that the same thing didn't happen to you. Joel has waited all his life for you. You *had* to be here."

She stood up and held out her hands to Meredith. She took them and pulled herself up then threw her arms around Laura's neck. "I love you so much," she offered impulsively.

"I love you too, sweet girl. Now, I need to get back, before Joel and his buddy Ross get in from... wherever they went."

Meredith walked with her to the door.

"Just sit tight, Merry, and he'll come to you. I promise you that, with everything that's in me. My son will come to you."

She smiled unsteadily and nodded.

"One more thing," Laura added, brushing back Meredith's damp hair and looking intently into her eyes. "I pray for you a lot and whenever I do, Someone says to tell you that He misses you. He misses you very much."

Here came the real flood.

"Now, I'm not going to give you a tissue for those, little girl. Those are for Him."

Laura kissed her on the cheek and gave her a warm smile, then left her to work things out with her Father.

Chapter Twenty-Two

Joel swept hurriedly through the front office, not even stopping to acknowledge Delores. She watched him open his door and slam it shut behind him, with an expression of wonder.

He snatched up the phone on his desk and punched in the number on his pager, looking around irritably for his cell phone. "If I'm lucky, I lost it for good, this time," He muttered with a scowl.

"Ross! Sorry it took me so long, but I was just pulling up and I don't have my cell with me. Whatcha got?"

"Plenty," Ross replied. "Your phone got left in my car, that's why I paged you. Plus, I wasn't sure if you've ever had the phones at your office checked for taps."

"Several times. We're clean."

"Okay. This is the story. Felix got into town last night. He's moving fast, Joel. He's already managed to connect with our guy on the inside. It looks like you're gonna get your wish. Sort of."

"What does that mean?"

It means it's going to hit the fan on Christmas day."

"You are *kidding* me!"

"I am not. Actually, think about it. Cagle has. Metro will be running a skeleton crew because of the holiday. How many narcs would *you* expect to be hiding in the bushes on Christmas day?"

"I see your point."

"Joel, we've got a time, we've got a place. Now, listen to me. This is where you and I butt heads. For that reason, I'm glad I'm not there in person. We'd probably come to blows over this."

"If you're planning on telling me to just step back now and let the law handle it, you're right. We definitely *will* come to blows. I don't care about the drugs, that's your department. But he's got those pictures of Meredith, and that's *my* department. I'm sorry, Ross, but if you want to stop me from being there when this thing goes down, you're going to have to shoot me."

Ross sat there and thought that one over. Joel Etheridge was so crazy in love, he probably *would* take a bullet, before he'd trust anyone else to get their hands on those pictures of Meredith, even law enforcement. Arguing with him was just a waste of time.

"Alright, *fine*," he growled irritably. "Have it your own way, even though I'm gonna have a pretty hard time convincing Felix to go along with it, not to mention the chief. I may not even have a job, after this."

"If it all goes pear-shaped, nobody's getting sued," Joel assured him, sarcastically.

Ross made a scoffing sound. "Listen, I need you to meet me over here, as quick as you can make it. Felix... well, he brought something for you."

Joel raised his brows. "Ten minutes?"

"I'll be waiting."

Joel hung up and grabbed his coat. He dashed out as rapidly as he had come in, and Delores was left with her curiosity intact.

He nearly knocked someone over in the ground floor lobby, and would have stopped to apologize, if he had even noticed them.

He was at Ross's condo within minutes. He pounded impatiently and Ross opened the door with surprised amusement.

"I didn't mean break the law to get here!" He motioned for Joel to take a seat, and bent down to get his briefcase.

"There's your phone, Joel." He nodded over at the coffee table and Joel pocketed it, before it could get away.

"Felix isn't here, he's..." Ross waved his hand at nothing. "Doing stuff. Anyway..."

He pulled a large, sealed envelope out of his briefcase and sat down, facing Joel with a serious expression.

"Felix did something for you, Joel, that goes beyond the pale of law enforcement. It took several days to accomplish. He went to bat for a complete stranger."

Joel held his breath, and waited.

"Felix went to a judge, and he managed to secure a search warrant for Lawrence's New Orleans apartment. He went in, and pretty much tore the place apart. It turned out to be very much worth the effort, for a lot of reasons."

Ross looked down at the envelope in his hands for a moment, before holding it out to Joel.

Joel took it and stared at Ross with uncertainty, before starting to open it.

"No, don't do that, Joel!" Ross reached out a hand to stop him, adding even more confusion to Joel's face. "Don't open it. It's... those are the negatives."

Joel pulled the envelope to his chest, and swallowed hard. The muscles in his face tensed in and out, and he looked as if he were about to break down. Ross leaned toward him, compassionately.

"It's not over, yet. You'll still need those copies that Lawrence has, before you can finally breathe easy. But you're closer. You're a lot closer, buddy!"

"How..." Joel looked up at Ross, with a stunned expression, completely dumbfounded.

Ross read his mind. "The fact that he's a U.S. Marshal and the warrant was drug-related... well, it wasn't that difficult to obtain. For you, the important thing is that he did a clean sweep. *Clean.*"

He gave Joel a meaningful look then favored him with a little grin. "How's the weather out there?"

Nothing was making any sense at all to Joel, today!

"Because," Ross continued, smiling at his friend's blank expression, "it's been chilly in here all morning. I've been thinking of building a fire."

His smile became contagious, and Joel looked down at the envelope and then back up, with a smile of his own.

"You need anything to light it with?"

Hook didn't know what the deal was with his owner, but he hoped it stayed that way, for a long time. She had been really nice to him all day!

She fed him faster than she ever had, she scooped his litter box, without making disparaging remarks about his personal hygiene, and best of all, she climbed up in the front window and stayed there all almost all day, talking to Someone in that loving, comfortable tone, the way she used to. Life was good!

He stretched out full length in front of the fireplace, and Meredith came over and joined him. She sat on the floor, absently running her fingers through his soft, gray coat, and staring at the fire.

It has been an annoying day. Cagle had shown up right at lunch time, and insisted on coming in with some Chinese take-out that Meredith neither wanted, nor appreciated.

He chatted away incessantly, and for two solid hours, she pretended to listen to him, nodding when it seemed appropriate. She had been tempted to just tell him that he was pushing this forgiveness thing a little too far.

"Mmmm!" She stood up and stretched really big and she made it sound so good, that Hook tried it. She was right! It was great!

Meredith laughed at him, while she pushed all the coals and ashes back, and secured the fire screen for the night. "I'm beat," she announced. "I'm cashing in my chips."

Hook recognized her ritualistic procedures for shutting down the house for bed time, and scampered up the stairs, to meet her at the top. She beat her own record for speed showering, and tumbled into bed. After saying goodnight to Father, she fell into a deep and heavy sleep. It was the first one in a long time, and she needed it.

At first, she thought she was having a dream. She finally sat up and listened, and heard it again. She grabbed up the phone, but there was nothing but a dial tone. That wasn't it.

The sound stopped for a few seconds, then started up again. She snapped on a reading lamp and looked around. Her eyes traveled over the room, then fell on her briefcase. What, in the world?

She jumped up and opened it, and found her cell phone going off. She had forgotten that Marshall had charged it for her, and after he'd left, she had just tossed it back in there. She hadn't exactly been looking for it.

She picked it up now, as if it might blow up in her hand, then answered it cautiously. "Yes?"

"Meredith."

She drew in her breath sharply. It was *him!*

"Joel?" She looked at the clock. It was two-thirty in the morning. Something had to be wrong! "What is it?"

"First of all, whatever you do, don't turn on any lights. Turn that one off."

She snapped the lamp off without even stopping to think about it, then halted in surprise. "How did you know my light was on?"

"Because I'm standing out back, on your property, near the guesthouse. I can see your window from here. Listen to me. Merry, are you listening?"

"Yes."

"I'm going to let myself in the back door with my key."

"You gave it back to me."

"I had a copy made. You can yell at me about it later. Listen. I'll be inside in a couple of minutes. I didn't want you to hear someone moving around downstairs, and be afraid. I want you to get dressed, and meet me at the top of the stairs. Just sit tight. Don't go banging around in the dark, and wind up breaking your neck."

"But, Joel..."

"Hush. You can fight with me in person, in a few minutes."

He hung up and Meredith felt around for her flashlight. She laid it on the bed, and hurriedly pulled on her jeans.

She found a candle to light and, snapping off the flashlight, carried it with her to the top of the landing, and set it down in a corner. She waited on the top stair, shaking with the impact of strong emotion.

She heard the door open, and her heart began its usual frenzy. She could see the small glow from the tiny penlight he was using. He clicked it off, and came up the stairs to sit beside her. He was in black sweats, and she could hardly see him, until he sat down.

"Joel, why did you call me on my cell phone? And why are you sneaking in the back door, in the middle of the night..."

He cut her off by finding her mouth with his own, and kissing her as she had never been kissed before, in her entire life, very deliberately taking his own sweet time about it.

Laura's words rang in Meredith's ears. When, at last, he stopped to look at her, she was staring up at him in awe. "You did," she breathed, in a hushed voice. Her heart was in her eyes. "You came to me. You *came* to me, Joel."

"Yes," he whispered, brushing her hair back with his hands, and resting his gaze on the face he loved. "I had to. I couldn't stop myself, not this time. Let me look at you."

Their hungry eyes fed eagerly on each other. The candlelight only served to enhance the natural beauty these two had in common.

Meredith closed her eyes and swayed against him. "I think I'm gonna faint."

Joel laughed gently, and watched her smile up at him. "Go ahead, little one. I've got you."

She suddenly threw her arms around his neck. "Oh, Joel, where have you been?"

He gathered her closer. "I'm so sorry, baby. I know what you must think about me. I don't blame you."

"No." She sat up and took his face in her hands. "I don't think that, anymore. Joel, I know about it." She touched his lips and looked up at him with soft, gentle eyes. "I know about Kayla."

Joel released her from his embrace, and pulled back, then stared at her in dismay.

"Joel, it's okay."

Just hearing Kayla's name spoken out loud devastated him. He turned his face away from her, and she heard a muted sound of anguish.

He braced his elbow on his knee, and let his head rest on his palm, closing his eyes tightly, and fighting to keep those old tears that haunted him from escaping.

Meredith laid her hand on his shoulder and tried to get him to look at her. "Sweetheart, I would have wanted to share the burden of that with you, as much as I could. I would have understood. Why didn't you just tell me?"

He jerked slightly, suppressing a silent sob. "I couldn't."

She watched him with a painful stab of compassion. She had never seen Joel like this, and it broke her heart.

"Honey, *please* tell me why you couldn't."

When he finally looked at her, his eyes were filled with dread. "Because, when I brought you back home from Gatlinburg, you said..." He couldn't finish.

She slipped a finger under his chin. "What did I say?" Meredith tried urgently to remember.

She saw how distressed he was, when he began rubbing at the back of his neck, and reached to lift his hand away. She held it tenderly, watching him with grave concern.

"Please tell me what I said, Joel."

He waited for a long moment, before speaking. "You said you would hate any man who would..."

Her sharp gasp stopped him from continuing. She grabbed her stomach, as if she'd been kicked, and turned white.

"Oh, Joel... I didn't..." She moaned, and took his other hand, tears springing forth, all at once. "I wouldn't have meant *you*. I mean, I didn't know about Kayla, but I never *ever* could have meant you. I *love* you, Joel."

Joel let out a breath that he felt he had been holding for years... many long, dark, grief-filled years. He grabbed her desperately, as if she were a life preserver, and he, a drowning man.

She sank into him with a relief she had never known. Joel needed her! He needed *her* and God alone knew how much she needed Joel.

It was her turn to whisper comfort into his ear, the way he had done for her at Grotto Falls.

When the clock downstairs chimed out that a full hour had passed, still they lingered in an embrace, whispering secrets, and confessions, and making promises that no one else would ever hear, before Joel sat up straighter, calmed and consoled, and took her hands in his.

"Merry, I need to say some things to you, because I'm running out of time."

She looked at him in alarm. "What do you mean, running out of time?"

"It'll be getting daylight soon. I have to be out of here, before then."

"I don't understand."

"No." He kissed her hands. "I know you don't, and I can't do much to fix that just now, without taking more risks than I've already taken, just by coming here. Even calling you on your cell phone might not have been too bright."

"Why?" She gazed up at him in a way she didn't realize was causing his heart to pound.

"I can't answer a lot of questions right now. Let me just say what I can. You are going to have to be careful about things you say over the phone."

"That's what your mother said."

Joel looked baffled. "You've seen my mother?"

Meredith nodded.

"Then it was Mom who told you about... Kayla."

She nodded again, and his face cleared.

"You're not going to fuss at her, are you, Joel?" Meredith sounded worried.

"Yes. Just a little. And then I'm going to give her a big kiss."

"Can I have one of those?"

Joel was feeling generous.

"Okay, we have to stop this," he announced, after a bit. Meredith sighed, and he smiled at her, with simple joy in his eyes.

"Meredith, I have loved you from the first moment I saw your face."

"You should have said something." She grinned playfully. "We could have had a picket fence, a Volvo, and two-point-five children, by now!"

"Well, as soon as I get this other mess cleared up, you and I can do something about that. Meredith Clark, are you going to marry me, or not? Hurry up, the meter's running."

Meredith looked up at him, her beautiful eyes radiant in the candlelight. "Joel Etheridge, I'd like to see you try to *not* marry me, after all the grief you've put me through! Marry me you will, or I'll make your life one long row to hoe!"

Joel wrinkled his brow. "You do that, anyway. I just figured that came with the package." He kissed her lightly and smiled at her petulant expression.

"Cut it out. I want to say this to you, and then I have to get out of here."

She recognized that he was serious and waited.

"I know that Cagle Lawrence is in town, and that you've had occasion to see him, from time to time."

"I kinda figured Hailey would tell you. He just showed up, when I was at Center Hill Lake. He said he needed me to forgive him."

Something dreadful showed up in Joel's eyes. "Did he... did he say how he knew you were there?"

"He just said he was there using a friend's cabin, and that he saw me when I stopped at that convenience store, at the..."

She broke off, finally realizing what that expression on Joel's face was. "It's him, isn't it? Whatever's going on, it has something to do with him!"

"Merry, listen to me and I need you to really hear me."

He paused, unsure if he should tell her anything, after all. She wasn't supposed to know. He'd already been informed of what he could expect, if she found out. He'd kept her from knowing, this far.

He hadn't wanted to bring this up, but he also didn't want Meredith innocently mentioning to Cagle Lawrence, during small talk, that things were good between them, now. That would immediately light the fuse on Lawrence's bomb.

Joel weighed it all out silently, before he allowed himself to continue.

"Sweetheart, it's vitally important that you don't change whatever your behavior has been around Cagle Lawrence. If you two have been able to talk as friends, then you need to keep doing that. If you've formed a tolerance for him, then you have to keep on implying that tolerance. No matter what, you can't give him any reason to suddenly think that you suspect him of anything."

"Joel, what has he done?"

"That's the one thing I can't tell you, not yet. I will, very soon. But if you care about our future, you have to do what I'm asking you, or there might not *be* a future. We're so close, baby, to being able to start our life together, but you have to do what I ask. You've told him that Marshall has taken over your management, and let him know that you were angry with me, haven't you?"

"Yes," she admitted, sadly. "I was so messed up, Joel. I guess I said all *kinds* of things about that to him."

"I'm not upset with you, little one, I just needed to know how much you've said. Sweetie, he needs to think that you're still angry with me. That's crucial. He can't know that we're together."

"Why, Joel?"

"Not the time to explain it," he said, simply. "Okay?"

She gave him a look of exasperation.

"Honey, your phone is tapped, your house is being watched. This is serious."

She just frowned and blinked.

"Promise me, sweetheart, that you'll do what I ask. Don't try to understand it. Timing is so important, right now."

He captured her face in his hands and looked at her intently. "Merry, will you do what I ask? Will you trust me? Will you believe that I love you?"

She nodded, her love for him reflected in her eyes.

Joel caught her close for another long kiss. He knew he had to leave her, and that it would be a while before he could ever hold her again, and maybe never, if things went wrong on Christmas day.

His kiss took on an urgency that she completely yielded herself to. Finally, he drew back in frustration. Meredith reached for him and he gathered her up to sit beside him.

There was confusion on her face, but he lifted her hands to his lips and smiled at her. "Father is also gonna be my Father-in-law, so I'm not about to compromise His daughter, at the top of the stairs."

She twisted her mouth into a happy pout. "Oh, so we're back to you taking care of me, again."

"I hope I am. I want to do that for the rest of my life. Plan our wedding, Merry. I'm coming back for you."

She gave a soft, little laugh. "Joel, you sound like Jesus."

"Well, I've never been accused of that, before."

His eyes danced, and she knew he was about to zing her.

"I wish I could say it was the company I keep, but from all accounts... well, I hear you've been sounding like a lot of different influences over the past few weeks, but I think it's safe to say that Jesus has hardly been one of them."

She giggled and frogged him in the arm. He didn't have the heart to tell her that he didn't feel it. That tray-flinging episode though, that was another matter. His ribs were still bruised from that one!

She looked at his secret grin curiously. "What is it?"

He shook his head. "Nothing, sweetie. I've run out of time. I have to go."

She gripped him tightly. "Joel?"

He read her eyes. "I don't know, Merry. Hopefully by Christmas, but I don't know. Listen to me. We can't talk or call each other before then, but it doesn't mean that there's anything wrong between us. It's just the circumstances, and they'll go away soon. Then I'm going to marry you, before God and the whole world, and then I'll kiss you any ol' way I want."

She blushed and it made him laugh. "I need you to stay up here. I don't want you falling over something in the dark. I'm just gonna let myself out, and lock you in. Help make this easy on me, by not gazing at me with those big, sad eyes and tell me that you love me."

"I do love you. I love you, Joel!" Oh, and she did, too! It was all over her, and she wore it beautifully. Joel couldn't stop looking at her.

"I love you, too, little one. I love you, forever. And not only that..."

Here came that gorgeous grin that she couldn't resist!

"I know what you're getting for Christmas."

Her eyes sparkled.

"Don't look at me like that, I have to go." He stood up, and reached down to pull her up into his arms.

"Merry, I don't think we'll get to be together on Christmas day, but I think we might, on Christmas night. I'm going to do my best. Will that do?"

She nodded. "Anything will do."

"Listen, I know how tight you and Hailey are, so if you want to tell her about our engagement, which I intend to make official very soon, you can, but not on the phone. And I'm gonna tell Mom but, other than that, let's just lock this up, okay? She can't tell anyone."

He caught both her hands and brushed them against his rough, unshaven chin, while waiting for her response to his words. "I'm serious, Missy, this can't get out!"

"I know. She won't tell, I promise."

Joel mirrored the look in her eyes. "Are you ready for this?"

She shook her head, but smiled up at him, anyway.

"Standing up will definitely help," he quipped, before branding himself on her lips.

"Scoot!" he said roughly, when he finally released her. "Get in there, so I can go."

Meredith gave him one more kiss. "I love you, Joel."

"I love *you*, Meredith."

She picked up the flickering candle, which would soon be melted away. She took one more starved look at him, then went into her room.

He closed the door, and was gone.

Chapter Twenty-Three

Meredith pulled back the edge of the curtain and scowled. Cagle! What the heck was he doing here? She wished she'd parked her Jeep inside the garage. That way, she could sit tight, and just not answer the door. He was starting toward the porch.

She remembered what Joel had said to her a few nights ago, about not letting Cagle Lawrence sense that she had changed toward him, in any way.

"Father, I need You to help me get through this, okay?" She felt His hand on her shoulder, and straightened her back, lifting her chin. She knew she could do this.

Cagle knocked briskly and confidently, as if sure of his welcome. Meredith bristled. Had he just started that, or had he been doing it all along, and she just hadn't noticed?

She made herself answer the door, and even managed a casual greeting.

"Oh, hi there, Cagle."

"Hi, yourself! Hope it's okay to just drop by." He pulled out a small bunch of flowers from behind his back.

She didn't have to fake the surprised look. This used to be Cagle's method of operation, but she hadn't expected him to try it on her again!

"Wow, Cagle, those are pretty." She wanted to gag. "Where in the world did you find these?" She took the mixed bouquet, and stood back so that he could come in.

"A little shop on Elliston," he informed her, waving his hand, in a cavalier manner. "I was downtown on business and just picked them up, on an impulse."

Speaking of impulses, Meredith thought dourly to herself, *I'm having one of those, right now.* She stifled a giggle, then smiled at him brightly.

"Well, thanks. Grab a seat and I'll go find something to put these in."

She turned and headed out to the kitchen, passing Hook on the way in. She eyed him thoughtfully, and tried to imagine him as a huge, Cagle-Lawrence-eating jungle cat. "I guess not," she muttered, with a disappointed shrug. "Even Hook would be too picky for that."

She spied the trash can. Well, she *was* looking for something to put these flowers in. She twisted her mouth into a grimace, and cheerfully let them drop.

"Oops." She lacked sincerity.

Meredith took down a small glass, and caught some water from the tap. She took a sip, made a face, then poured it out. She stood there another moment, tapping her nails on the counter. What else could she find to do in here to kill some time? Maybe Joel was right, maybe she should clean out her fridge. *Let's not get crazy,* she thought dryly.

"I guess I'd better get back out there."

She forced herself back into the living room, where Cagle had made himself comfortable on the couch. She settled into the glider, masking her disgust. That couch was not meant for him!

"So, Cagle, what brings you out to Old Hickory Boulevard?"

"Just finished up a meeting earlier than I thought, and dropped in to check on you." He eyed her a little more boldly than he had been doing, and she noticed it. She was seeing everything much more clearly than she had, in a long while.

"Say, your cat's not a very friendly animal, is he?"

"Hook?" Meredith looked over at him, in surprise. His eyes were slits, and he seemed to have his hackles up, just slightly. She was silently impressed.

"I wish I could have come by a little earlier," he remarked, picking up a pillow and squeezing it. "I would like to have watched that football game I was asking you about, the other day. But I heard the score on the radio. It looks like your Packers were upset!"

Meredith shrugged and failed to give him the hot retort, and flash of angry, gray eyes that she would have given him, in years past, if he had said anything critical about her team.

"They're not my Packers, anymore. I haven't really watched them play, since Brett Favre left. In fact, I haven't watched *any* NFL games, since he left. He made football exciting and fun. Now, it's all politically correct and lame. I've completely lost interest. I only watch college and even then, pretty much only SEC, except for the bowl games."

Cagle grinned at her. "I stand rebuked." He laid the pillow down and leaned forward. "I read in the Sunday paper about a benefit you put on. I think it was last Friday night?"

"Was that in the paper?"

"It sure was, a huge spread. Great picture of you onstage, too. That dress was a knock out! Did that come from one of the boutiques around here?"

"You always did have an eye for fashion, Cagle." She forced a quick laugh. "Actually, it *is* a designer dress but I got it once, when I was in Los Angeles."

"Yeah, actually that doesn't surprise me," he said smoothly. "It just had those special lines you don't see a lot, here, in the east."

Meredith nodded again, a serious look of perplexity on her face. Surely he hadn't come all the way out here to discuss her wardrobe! What did he want?

"The article mentioned your manager, quite a bit. So I guess he was pretty much all over the place, huh?"

Okay, now we're gettin' somewhere, she thought to herself. She tried to remember her early years of high school drama and came up with the most hostile, surly face anyone could imagine.

"He was a little *too* much all over the place, if you want my opinion. Marshall Edwards is as capable as anyone in this town, and as far as I'm concerned, Joel Etheridge should have just stayed home Friday night, counting his money, and let Marshall handle everything!"

"Didn't you tell me that his associate was taking care of your affairs, now?"

"That's Marshall."

"Oh, I see," Cagle said, in a conversational tone. "So you really don't even interact with your former manager, anymore?"

"Let's just say that Joel Etheridge and I have said everything to each other that *needs* to be said," she hedged, in a scalding tone. "Anyway, he's taken on some new band."

She produced a very effective sneer. "Maybe I should save them a lot of grief, by warning them about what they can expect, in this back-stabbing industry."

"Did you and your former manager have a fight?" He asked, with an innocent expression. "You seem rather put out with him. I noticed it when we talked out at the lake too, but I didn't like to ask."

Since when, she challenged him, silently.

"A fight?" she repeated. "Well, yeah, we had words. But that was only after he pulled a switch on me and took over that new band. Anyway, it's not like we haven't fought before. I've just finally had enough. I get offers all the time from other management firms. As soon as I can find a loophole in my contract, he can eat his copy and mine, too!"

Meredith turned on the belligerent glare that won her the coveted title of "Poster Child" from Joel. Maybe she had picked the wrong career! She sent up a mental prayer, apologizing to Father for using acting as an excuse to lie, and for enjoying it so much.

Cagle leaned back and smiled complacently. "Maybe you should consider basing yourself somewhere else, other than Nashville. I mean, it's mostly Country music here anyway, right?"

"Most outsiders think that but you wouldn't believe the musical diversity in this place. There's a forum for just about every genre. Besides, I love Tennessee. Even the name is pretty and it looks good on signs, when you're driving back in from a long road trip, and cross the state line."

"So you wouldn't even consider moving to another place?"

She frowned. What was he after?

"No way! Tennessee suits me just fine. Well, maybe not as fine as it's going to suit me, once I manage a successful little legal maneuver."

That reminds me, I need to write my vows and start looking at wedding dresses, she thought to herself, skillfully managing to keep the smile off her face, that this thought generated.

He nodded, slowly and thoughtfully, then, after a few seconds, he put on an expression of humble solicitude, not unlike the one he had worn on the cabin porch at Center Hill Lake.

He must have a whole trunk full of all those faces, Meredith mused to herself.

The telephone rang, cutting off whatever he had been about to say, and Meredith sprang to answer it, glad for a chance to talk to anyone at all, besides Cagle Lawrence.

"Hello!"

"Merry, dear, this is Delores."

"Well, hi there!"

"Hi yourself, sugar. You doing okay?"

"Couldn't be better. What's up?"

"I'm calling to invite you to spend Christmas with us this year."

"You are!" Meredith couldn't keep the pleasure out of her voice.

Cagle looked up quickly, wondering who she was talking to.

"Pretty much everybody will be there. Marshall and Bobbie, Laura and Pastor Gary..."

Meredith's eyes widened. "Oh, are they a *couple,* now?"

Delores laughed. "Well, I guess you wouldn't call them that yet, but all the key ingredients are there. Your friend Hailey might stop by that evening."

"Hailey!" She caught Cagle's curiosity out of the corner of her eye and decided to play an ace. She knew that Joel would explain it to Dee, if she asked him about it.

"Listen, I hope I don't seem ungrateful or anything, because I really would like to come. But Joel Etheridge is not gonna be anywhere around there, is he? Because if that's the case, I'm afraid I'm going to have to decline."

"Well, no..." Her brow puckered. Didn't Joel say he and Merry had talked? "He's having his Christmas with Laura the night before, because he has to be gone all the next day."

"So he won't be anywhere around there, then. You're sure?"

Delores was lost. "Well, no dear, he won't be."

"Then, if that's the case, I would love to spend Christmas with you and thank you so much for inviting me! Can I bring anything?"

"Just your pretty face and that voice. We're not exchanging gifts, or anything like that."

"Okay, I'm there. What time?"

"Oh, I think around one."

"Works for me. Love you!"

"I love you too, sweetie!" Meredith hadn't said that in a long time, Delores mused. She must be alright, then. So why was she asking about Joel and... oh! She remembered about the phone. That was it! "Well, don't let me keep you, honey. I'll see you soon."

Meredith rang off and came back to the glider with a thoughtful look on her face. Cagle saw it and wondered what it meant.

"Going to spend Christmas with friends?"

"Yeah, I think I will, this year. I usually go down to the shelter but this sounds like a nice change. Anyway," she added, "I could always run down to the shelter first."

"I heard you asking about Joel Etheridge. I remember you mentioning him at the lake. That's your manager's name, right? That was the name in the paper."

She was surprised at his direct question but recovered smoothly. "He owns my label and the firm that takes care of my management and booking and... well, they pretty much handle everything that concerns me. That's why you

287

can't be too careful when you're signing contracts, I guess, so..." She gave a sullen little shrug. "Lesson learned."

Her remarks were interrupted by the musical tolling of her old grandfather clock and both she and Cagle noted the hour before she continued.

"He's not my manager now, so I don't have to deal directly with him, anymore. Anyway, he's definitely not coming to this Christmas get-together, so I guess it won't hurt to at least run by there. I'll probably go to the shelter first, though. I *know* I'll enjoy that."

Cagle personally didn't care what she did, as long as it didn't involve Joel Etheridge. It didn't look as if it did, so he relaxed.

"What are you doing for Christmas this year, Cagle?" Meredith sounded every bit as casual as he did. "Or will you be headed back to New Orleans before then?"

He grinned lazily. "Oh, no, I'm going to spend it here. Having a few colleagues over for a party, maybe watch a little football. Guy stuff."

"A little male bonding, huh? So what do you guys have planned? Gonna lay around with your beer and pizza, playing poker and scratching and burping?"

He laughed at her inelegance. "Something like that!"

"Well, if I don't see you before then, Merry Christmas, Cagle. If you've been a good boy, that is." Merry intended this to be his cue to leave, but she said it with a grin and he naturally took the hint.

"No coal for me," he returned, picking up his jacket. "I'm the very model of goodwill."

"I wish I could say the same about me, but not this Christmas, I guess." A happy thought flashed through her mind and brought a secret smile. *But, maybe Christmas night...*

"Oh, I wouldn't worry about it," Cagle assured her, indulging in his *own* secret smile. "I'm sure you'll get everything you deserve. I'd be willing to bet on it." He put his jacket on and felt around in the pocket for his keys.

"I won't keep you, Meredith. I've got to be somewhere in an hour, and I need to run by my room first. Just wanted to say hello and give you the flowers."

"Well, I've been feeling a little low the past few weeks, Cagle, and they really hit the spot." She decided not to tell him that she had just named her trash can "Spot".

"That's good. I'll be seeing you soon. Take care!"

"You, too, take care."

Especially when Joel gets a hold of you! Talk about getting what you deserve! She added this as a silent warning and both her mind and her heart, friends again, applauded her wildly.

"Thank you, thank you!" She locked the door and took a bow with a happy grin. "I'm ready for my close up!"

Joel sat on the side of his bed, one foot tucked up under him and the other one resting on the floor. He picked up his coat and took the little box out of the pocket, yet again. He'd been doing this every few minutes, since he'd gotten home.

He'd wasted no time, once Ross urged him to buy a ring for Meredith. The owner of one of the oldest jewelry stores in downtown Nashville was a long-time friend of Joel's, and was not only an artist in designing custom jewelry, but very discreet. Nothing would ever induce him to reveal the upcoming engagements and nuptials of the city's celebrity residents to anyone.

He had put a hold on all other commissions, and had focused exclusively on Joel's request, in order to have the set ready in time for Christmas.

Joel smiled in a distant, dreamy way and fingered the velvet lid with loving hands. The sound of an uncertain knocking brought him out of his reverie.

He stood up and tucked the box into his top drawer, then opened the door.

Laura stood there looking up at him, with what he called her "doe" eyes.

"Can I talk to you about something, Son? It's... really bothering me."

Joel smiled to himself. Here it was, her big confession! He had wondered when this was coming. He decided to see how much mileage he could get out of it.

"Sure, Mom, get in here." He dropped back down on the side of the bed and patted a space for her to sit next to him.

"There's nothing to do, but just blurt this out," she began nervously. "I was going to wait until after Christmas, but that wouldn't be fair to you. Besides, you should know this in case you decide you'd rather I not stay here for Christmas."

Joel lifted one brow in surprise. He had intended to string her along and have a little fun with her, but he could see that his mother was really anguishing over this. He certainly didn't want that!

"Mom, of course you'll stay here."

"Just let me finish." She touched his arm briefly, then took a deep breath. "Son, I don't blame you if you throw me out for this, and maybe I deserve it. But I can't go another day without admitting something I did. Whatever happens, I will at least have gotten it out of my system."

"If not, they have stuff at the pharmacy for that, Mother." His blue eyes sparkled and almost gave him away, in spite of the note of concern in his voice.

She started to resume, then stopped and looked at him cluelessly. "Stuff at the pharmacy for *what?*"

"Getting *it* out of your system."

She continued to look bewildered, and he smiled. "Never mind, Mom. It's not important."

"Well, then don't interrupt me, because this is hard enough, as it is." She looked down at her hands and sorted out how to start over.

Joel grinned and looked off out the window. *Okay, then, let's play,* he decided. *This outta be good.*

"Joel, I know I should have talked to you first, but I knew you'd tell me to mind my own business."

"When have I *ever* said those words to you, Mother?" he interrupted gently.

She gave him a little smile. "I know. But there's a first time for everything."

"I've heard that." He nodded in a deadpan way and she punched him on the arm.

"Stop it, now, I'm trying to be serious."

"Are you? Then you need to do this." He pulled the corners of her mouth down into a little frown and she slapped his hand.

"Stop that! Please just let me say this and I'll get out of your hair!"

"Ah, so you've come to confess to me that you're a flake."

She didn't want to laugh! That was the problem; Joel had always been able to make her laugh, but this was not the time for that. She *had* to tell him about her talk with Meredith!

"Because they also have stuff at the pharmacy for *that,*" he counseled in all sincerity, or so it seemed. "Flakes," he added, with a sober nod.

"Joel Michael Etheridge, if you don't stop it, I'm gonna cook you wet, slimy, boiled okra and feed it to you with a trowel and a funnel!" Her first born was starting to tick her off! "I swear, sometimes you make my head spin!"

"Now, *there's* a pretty picture."

"Joel!"

He stood up and laughed. It was a happy laugh, full of joy, not one of the forced ones he had been obliging her with ever since she had arrived.

She eyed him with suspicion and he reached down and gathered her up into his big arms, squeezing her just enough to annoy her.

"Mother, let me spare you this long, drawn-out act of penance you feel compelled to offer. I already know you talked to Meredith last Saturday night."

She crossed her arms and tilted her head to one side, not sure if she should be relieved or downright mad!

"I really outta give it to you, too, you meddlesome ol' biddy! In fact, I think I will." He caught her face in his hands and gave her a big, wet, exaggerated smack on the cheek, before depositing her back onto the side of the bed.

Laura's hand flew up to her face and she continued to gape at him. "How did you find out?" she demanded.

"She told me."

"*She* told you? When were you able to talk to her?"

"Monday night. Well, technically, the wee hours of Tuesday morning. I went over there."

She gasped. "You did not!"

"Oh yes, I did, Dear Abby, so there!"

"But, Joel... how did you get past that big Suburban that stays parked out there? You said there's always someone watching her house and I saw them there, myself!"

"Mommy, a man in love will crawl through barbed wire backwards, in his birthday suit. He will forge his way barefoot through miles of upturned bottle caps, in the blazing noonday sun. He will eat his way through rivers, yea, even oceans of slimy, wet, boiled okra!"

Laura rolled her eyes in exasperation. "Yeah, well how did *you* do it, hot shot?"

"Me? I walked up to her back door and used a key. But I'm still in love," he added hastily. "Dig a moat around sweet Merry and fill it with boiled okra, and I'm there with two forks and a bib."

Laura kept her arms crossed and tried to glare at him. "You rat!"

"What?" He lifted his palms and gave her a deceptively innocent look.

"Don't you *what* me!"

"Mother, I would never *what* you. They lock people up for less than that, especially us Christians."

"You've known since last Monday night..."

"Tuesday morning..."

"I'm talking!"

"Yes, ma'am!"

He struggled not to laugh. She wanted to be mad and as a good son, the least he could do was to not laugh. He was not a good son, he decided, as he wiped his eyes and gave in to a long, healing bout of mirth.

Laura continued to just gape at him, with a frustrating blend of amazement and disapproval.

"I'm sorry, Mom," he said, his eyes brimming over with happiness. "You're right. I did know and maybe I should have said something, but I didn't. Besides, you deserved it."

He looked down at her mysteriously. "Can you keep a secret?"

Without waiting for an answer, Joel pulled the drawer open and lifted out the tiny black box reverently. Laura stood on trembling legs, and let him lay it into her hands.

She lifted the lid and caught her breath. She had never seen anything so beautiful!

She looked back up into her son's handsome face and exercised her mother's right to cry.

Joel scooped her up into a tight hug. "Thank you so much, Mom, for what you did for Meredith and me. I love you so much for that!"

"You're lying!" Hailey accused Meredith, surveying her face carefully. She stopped and grinned. "Wait! No, you're not!" She screamed with happiness, and grabbed Meredith, dancing her around the room.

"Oh, I can't stand it," she panted, wild with joy for her friend. "When, Merry? When are you guys getting married?"

Meredith laughed and bounced up and down on her bed, like a four-year-old. "We're not sure. Joel wants to do it yesterday but I think I can talk him into waiting until spring. I'd really like it to be outdoors."

"Are you guys going to use Belle Meade mansion? Or Cheekwood, or something like that?"

Meredith stopped bouncing and lifted Hook up to her shoulder. He gurgled softly in her ear. She raised eyes to Hailey that had never been more beautiful and smiled. "The Hermitage."

"Oh, yes!" Hailey's own eyes began to shine. "The Hermitage!"

Meredith sat Hook back down and looked at her friend in amusement. "I promise not to put you in some yukky shade of apricot, or anemic lavender."

"Me?" She stopped and stared.

"Of course, silly. Who else would be my maid of honor?"

Hailey hugged her tightly. "Oh, I love you, Missy!"

"I love you too, Sissy!"

They giggled at the nicknames Joel had hung on the both of them, years ago. It was better than Heckle and Jeckle, or Mutt and Jeff, or Frick and Frack, so they had decided not to complain about it, and give him a chance to come up with something *really* hideous.

Meredith lifted a gentle warning finger. "Now, Hailey... no one... absolutely *no* one else can know about this. Joel said I could tell you and he's telling Laura, but that's it, until we announce it on Christmas. At least, we hope to on Christmas. We have to wait for some other things to work out first."

"What kind of things?"

"Well," Meredith said, a serious frown overshadowing the joy she had been wearing for days. "I'm not exactly sure. Joel wouldn't talk about it. He just said that we would try for Christmas night, because he has to be tied up all day Christmas."

"That's odd," Hailey said.

"So it's not just me, then?" Meredith asked her. "It sounds odd to you, too?"

"It does, but don't borrow trouble," Hailey hurried to reassure her. "Joel knows what he's doing."

"You're right. That's probably good advice," Meredith decided. She smiled slowly. "And now..."

She opened her closet door and dragged out a huge, heavy box, overflowing with bridal magazines. Hailey shrieked with laughter and ran over to help her.

They dragged and pushed until they had it where they could dive in, and dive in they did! Magazines went flying through the air in all directions.

A very startled Hook leaped up and ran in place, like a cartoon kitty, before digging in and propelling himself out of this dangerous den of lunacy.

Missy and Sissy giggled, as if they were a couple of school girls at a slumber party.

"How long have you been keeping all this?" Hailey demanded.

"Since the day I met Joel Etheridge," Meredith joked, with a happy laugh.

"And now..." She whipped open one of the magazines, with a flourish. "Help me pick out a dress." Her cheeks were glowing and her eyes were radiant with joy.

"Let's find something that will make old man Etheridge reach for the Prozac!"

Christmas day had never seemed so long in coming, but it was here now. Meredith threw her head back and sang her heart out, as she climbed into her Jeep.

She had just come back by her house from the shelter, to give Hook his bag of goodies and a seafood sampler she had been hiding from him in the fridge. Hook was in kitty heaven, and she was on her way to finally spend Christmas with a real family! And then tonight...

Meredith could feel the rush of color flood her cheeks, and she smiled happily and thought of Joel, as she did every few minutes. He was never far from her.

She pulled into the McGee's driveway and noted with pleasure that Laura's car was already there, as well as Gary's and Marshall's. This was already starting to feel really good!

Doug McGee opened the door before she could even knock, and laughed when she jumped.

"I saw you out the window," he grinned. He looked down at a large shopping bag in her hands. "Is that for me?"

"Well, you might say that." Meredith gave him a hug. "Have you been good?"

"Maybe you'd better ask *me* that." Delores hurried over and gave her a kiss.

Doug rolled his eyes and tweaked his wife's cheek.

"Well, I'm outta here!" He winked at Meredith and lumbered off into the den, toward the sounds of a football game in progress.

Delores had Meredith put her things down by a pile of coats and brought her into the kitchen, to the delight of Laura and Bobbie. She gave Bobbie a tight squeeze and turned to find Laura smiling at her with so much love, she thought she might cry. Laura came over and wrapped her up in a big, motherly embrace.

"I love you, little lamb," she whispered into Meredith's ear.

"I love you, too, Mrs... Laura!" she answered from a full heart.

Laura gave her a significant look. "We might need to run over that list of names for me again," she said in a low voice. "I have a new suggestion."

"Hey, no whispering over there!" Bobbie protested.

"Who's whispering?" Marshall inquired, having realized that Meredith was in the kitchen and coming in to greet her.

"No one is whispering," Meredith giggled, reaching up to give Marshall a hug. "We were just saying hello."

"How do you get 'hello' out of all that?" Bobbie demanded, her green eyes sparkling in fun.

"You know what you are, Bobbie?" Laura pointed at her. "You're a troublemaker!"

"Amen to that!" her husband declared fervently.

Gary wandered in to speak to Meredith, then the women ran them out of the kitchen.

"Come on, Gary!" Marshall shot them all a withering look. "Woman have taken over the world. Let's go talk about beefing up the space program."

Meredith was eating all this up!

Next Christmas, she thought dreamily, *Joel and I will invite everybody to come over to our house.*

She didn't realize she was standing there with such a revealing look in her luminous eyes, until Laura strolled by and leaned over with a grin.

"Careful there, kiddo. Unless there's something you want to announce here and now, you'd better wipe that 'I love Joel' look off your face."

"Joel!" Bobbie squealed triumphantly. "I heard the word 'Joel'. Now we're gettin' down to the nitty gritty!"

"Bobbie, will you put a sock in it?" Laura asked, with an amused smile.

"Bobbie *sock*... I see what you did there." Bobbie observed, and the others joined her in laughing.

"Get over here, and help me put some ice in these glasses," Laura admonished her, with a grin and a little crook of her finger.

Meredith dropped her head to hide her telling blush, and wandered over to the sink, where Delores was dicing tomatoes.

"Congratulations," Dee whispered, smiling, but not taking her eyes off her chore.

"Did Joel tell you?" Meredith whispered back, in surprise.

"He didn't have to," she returned quietly. "It's written all over his happy face."

Meredith hugged herself in awe. "Sometimes I think I'm just gonna explode, Dee!"

She chuckled softly. "Well, don't do that in here. I'm out of paper towels."

For some reason, this struck Meredith as funny. She began to shake with silent laughter and tried to suppress it, but it was like trying not to laugh in church.

All at once, she burst into an uncontrollable shriek, sliding down against the counter and landing on the floor.

Laura and Bobbie turned and stared at her in amazement while Delores purposefully chopped through another tomato, struggling to keep a straight face.

"Look at Dee," Bobbie instructed, with a nod. "She had something to do with that."

"I didn't do anything!" Delores protested, her mouth twisting itself to control a grin, as Meredith's laugh became infectious.

"HEY!" Doug's voice came bellowing in from the den. "You hens stop cackling in there, and lay some eggs! We're getting hungry, out here!"

Bobbie pulled a piece of ice out of one of the glasses and spat on it, before dropping it back in, and shaking the glass. "This one is Doug's," she informed everyone.

Meredith went down for the count, and Delores wiped her hands on her apron and reached down to pull her up.

Laura looked on with happy eyes. She had just seen this happen to her son. Meredith's heart was getting healed!

"I'm sorry," she panted, using Delores as a rope and hoisting herself up. "Nobody say anything to me and I'll stop. Somebody give me something to do."

Bobbie shook the glass of ice in her hand again, and raised her brows suggestively, with the look of a rascal.

"Stop!" Meredith begged, grabbing her stomach. She whirled around to Delores. "Where's the bathroom?"

"Come here, girly." Laura held her hand out. "I'll aim you in the right direction."

Meredith followed her out into the hall and started toward the bathroom door, when Laura stopped her.

"Merry," she said fondly, her features softening with emotion. "I could never have picked anyone more perfect for my son. I want you to know that Joel has never loved any woman, before you. You're his one and only.

"I know you haven't had your mother around for a long time. I could never take her place, and I wouldn't try, but as much as I *can* be a mother to you... well..." She finished sweetly. "You know."

Meredith nodded, then gave her a tight, impulsive hug. "Thank you!" She closed her eyes and let joy wash over her.

Laura smiled at her lovingly, then gave her a swift pat. "Here's your stop," she announced.

She started back to the kitchen, but took a detour and caught Gary's eye, as she paused outside the door to the den. He read her face and came out to join her.

"Gary," she began, hesitantly. "I told you that Joel and Meredith talked."

He nodded and waited.

"But it's clear from Meredith's countenance, that she has absolutely no clue what Joel is doing today." She kept her voice low, and looked back down the hall where she had left Meredith, and back up to Gary with sober concern.

"I know," he said. He took her hands in his and gave her a tender smile. "Let's pray."

They bowed their heads together.

"Father," he said in a husky voice. "Please protect our Joel today. Please send Your angels to keep watch over him, and please keep Ross and the others from harm. Thank You, dear Lord, that Meredith is here, safe with us, and that she and the others here are spared from worrying about what Joel is involved in today."

He felt a little squeeze on his hands and opened his eyes to find Laura questioning him with her own.

"Gary, Joel didn't tell Marshall and Delores about today, either?"

"I asked him," he said quietly. "He just told them that he and Ross were checking into something that had to do with Cagle Lawrence. He didn't tell them the rest. He said he didn't want to ruin Christmas for everyone."

"Dear God," Laura breathed.

She gave a little shiver and Gary folded her into his arms.

Felix Brasseaux looked around hurriedly, then back at Joel and Ross with an intent expression.

"This is the way it goes down," he said quietly, in his faint Cajun accent. "We just hang back here behind this van until we get the word, which should be any minute, just as soon as the boys finish securin' the area." His busy eyes darted back and forth, making mental notes, as he continued his remarks.

"It's a good thing it's Christmas. No nervous motel manager around to give us fits about marrin' one of these doors. Because we're fixin' to mar the heck out of it." He turned around and sized Joel up. "I doubt you've been involved in too many of these."

Joel looked over at Felix and gave him a little shrug. "I admit it; all my drug busts are experienced vicariously, through episodes of 'Cops'. I'm not looking to be a hero. I care about one thing, and that's all I'm after."

Felix studied him with a curious expression. "What does that feel like, Etheridge? To be that caught up in a woman, I mean?"

"You don't know?" Joel asked mildly.

He shook his head and searched the parking lot with a steady gaze that missed nothing, before turning back to Joel with a rueful grin. "Nah. That kind of fairy tale romance wouldn't know how to survive around an ol' cob like me. I'm probably better off playin' the field. Trouble is..." He lifted his head to catch a better look at a black car with darkened windows moving into the area. "Trouble is that the field has gotten so overgrown with weeds nowadays, you can't find the flowers."

He lifted his radio and secured his earpiece. "Harris!"

"Right here."

"What's the hold up? What's with the mafia staff car?"

"Got a late arrival. Soon as they're in, we're ready."

"Right!"

Ross peered around the back of the van. "Who *is* that?"

He nodded toward a large, portly man getting out of the black Lincoln, after someone opened the door for him.

"He looks familiar. Not sure where, but I've seen him before."

Felix broke into a pleased grin. "Well, praise the Lord, and pass the ammunition! Ol' Lawrence's guest list is pretty impressive. Ross, you're looking at the arrival of one of the most notorious kingpins in Memphis. Mr. Leon Waters!"

"No way!" Ross smiled with delight. "Well, Ho Ho Ho! Merry Christmas, Mr. Waters. Wait 'til you see what Santa brings bad little boys."

He leaned over to Joel confidentially. "We been after that big fish for years. We've thrown back a lot of little guppies, holding out for this one. I'm surprised you'd know him, though, Felix," he said to his colleague. "I've seen him, up close and personal, and even I didn't recognize him."

Felix shrugged nonchalantly. "Let's just say we've had our occasional run-in. In fact..." He couldn't grin any wider. "I wish I could have an eight by ten glossy of ol' Waters' mouth flyin' open, when he sees *my* friendly mug smilin' at him!" He laughed in quiet pleasure. "Yeah, I just love Christmas!"

Ross chuckled at his friend's lack of sympathy for the unsuspecting crime boss. "Who's got the big red key?"

"Vance and Hiller are gonna ram us in. They'll be skirted by Holmes and his men. That's who we'll move in behind." He darted sharp eyes at Joel. "You're not packin', or anything crazy like that, are you, Etheridge?"

He opened his jacket and shook his head.

"Good. Don't need any lovesick tough guy dashin' in with a piece, and gettin' us all killed. I may not have a steady girlfriend, but my mama kinda likes me."

Ross snickered at Joel's light tinge of color. "Go easy on him, Felix. If you saw his girl, you'd loan him your gun!"

"Is that right?" Felix laughed and shook his head.

Ross laid a hand on Joel's sleeve and gave him a look of caution. "He's right, though, Joel. My chief just about put my butt in a sling, when he got wind of you being in on this. He yelled at me like a stepchild! You hang back behind us, now, or I could end losing both my friend *and* my job."

"No worries," Joel returned. "Again, I'm only here to make sure those photos end up in my hands, and no one else's. As to the rest of it, I have no dog in this fight."

Ross looked relieved and patted his friend's shoulder. "Brasseaux!"

Felix snapped up his unit. "Yeah!"

"Roll out!"

"Buckle up, boys!" He crouched low and led them bolting across the parking lot. They fell in behind a line of heavily armed officers, and positioned themselves around the motel door.

Ross stifled a laugh. "Well, would you look at that?" he whispered, pointing at the number on the door. "Thirteen!"

Felix almost choked. "Ain't life grand?" He held up his left arm and secured his weapon in his right. They stood there listening for a minute or two, before he threw his arm forward. "Don't be shy!"

Vance and Hiller pulled back on the battering ram, and crashed through the door with an unbelievable force. A third officer simultaneously threw in a percussion grenade.

The air was filled with bellows of "Police! Everybody on the floor! Move and you're dead!" Bodies were ramming into bodies.

There was a profusion of cursing and wrestling. A wall of SWAT team members had packed the doorway, and no one was going anywhere.

When Cagle Lawrence saw Joel Etheridge, his face turned an ugly shade of purple. He spewed out a stream of filth and pounced at him. No one saw his gun until it went off.

"You need to get some new socks," Hailey declared to Meredith, whose feet were plopped onto Hailey's lap. "Do you think I dropped by today just to hold your ol' stinkin' feet, with these flea market socks you put on?"

She poked her finger through a hole in one toe. "Look at this, girl! I mean, you're not exactly poor. This is pitiful!"

Everyone was still over at the McGee's, even though it was well after dark. They were all bunched up in front of the TV in the den, watching a local network's presentation of "It's A Wonderful Life".

Meredith, who had landed on the couch with a thud and presented her feet to her friend, complaining that they were cold, looked down at them now and back up to Hailey with a languid smile.

"Just be happy she's wearing anything at *all* on her feet," Marshall advised, with a knowing look at Meredith.

"You people leave me alone," she said, with a happy pout. "I'm trying to watch a movie, here!"

And she was! This was her favorite part, where Jimmy Stewart and Donna Reed were forced to stand closer together and share the downstairs telephone, so that they could both hear their friend, Sam Wainright.

"This is so romantic," she sighed.

Everyone starting laughing and she flushed with hot color. She didn't realize she'd spoken out loud.

"Alright!" Hailey came to her rescue. "Y'all leave her alone. This girl's in love, and she's at that stage where even prime rib is romantic."

"Well, I was at the gym last week, with the object of your affection, Merry," Gary said, his eyes glittering with fun. "I can't say for sure, being a guy, but his ribs looked pretty prime to me."

Laura punched him and giggled, and Meredith slapped a pillow over her red face.

"Listen!" Marshall jumped up and cut in loudly. "Turn that up!" He pointed to a news crawler that had begun to creep across the bottom of the screen.

Doug grabbed the remote and raised the volume, as the station cut away from the movie and the voice of a local news anchor began explaining the interruption.

"We have an exclusive, late-breaking story just in, concerning a major drug bust at an area motel, just off Briley Parkway, in Nashville. Undercover officers and a U.S. Marshal have raided one of the units, in what early reports are calling one of the largest drug busts in the state's history, with an estimated hundred kilograms of heroin, fentanyl and cocaine, plus fifty pounds of a substance believed to be crystal meth and possibly more than fifty thousand counterfeit pills, also believed to contain fentanyl. An early estimated street value is upwards of twenty million dollars.

"Although details are sketchy, our reporter tells us that well-known music mogul, Joel Etheridge, is said to have arrived at the location, during a ride-along with law enforcement, and was with them at the time of the raid. He is reported to be the victim of at least one gunshot wound. He was taken by ambulance to a local hospital, but that is all we know, at this time. At least one fatality is being reported, as well. This, however is unconfirmed. Events are still unfolding, and we are standing by, awaiting further updates from our reporter at the scene, and will pass the information along, as soon as new details become available."

Meredith had scrambled up as soon as she heard Joel's name, and was running through the house knocking into everything, searching frantically for her keys.

"Merry, stop!" Marshall started toward her.

"I have to go!" She looked around wildly and pushed out of his grasp. "I have to go to the hospital!"

"Wait!"

"Let me go!" She fought to get away from him, and rummaged wildly through the pile of everyone's coats and jackets.

"Merry, wait!" Hailey rushed to her side. "Stop, honey! Look at me!" She shook her roughly. "LOOK AT ME!"

Meredith stopped trying to fight her off, but stared around the room hystcrically.

"Honey, you don't know which hospital." Hailey spoke to her in a calm, soothing voice. "Okay, baby? You don't know where to go."

"I don't know where he is!" Meredith echoed, wringing her hands desperately, as she realized Hailey was telling her the truth, and not just trying to stop her.

"Doug," Gary moved toward the door with his arm around Laura, who seemed to be in shock. "I'm taking Laura back to Joel's house, in case anyone shows up there. We'll get her car, later."

"Okay, drive carefully." He opened the door and saw them out.

"Home," Meredith repeated, her eyes wide and vacant, obviously in shock, herself. "I have to go *home*. Someone might... I have to go home!"

"Marshall, if I drive Meredith's Jeep, would you follow me?" Hailey had found the keys.

"Let's go."

They gathered up Meredith's belongings and put her inside the Jeep. She sat as still as a stone all the way, not moving or speaking, just staring out into the darkness.

When they pulled up, Hailey made a move to go inside with her, but Meredith shook her head and held out her hand for her keys, her face a churning tempest.

Hailey looked at Marshall and he nodded. She threw her arms about Meredith. "It'll be okay," she whispered. "I'll be praying."

Meredith moved toward the door, and Hailey got into Marshall's car. She laid a hand on his arm, as he started the engine.

"Marshall." She sounded a little strained. "Is there any way we could try to find out about Ross?"

Marshall sighed. "Hailey, none of us were thinking. Of course, we'll go make some calls."

Meredith fumbled clumsily with the keys, before she could finally get in. She dropped everything by the open door, and ran over to throw herself down on the floor, in front of the fireplace hearth, which had sometimes served as an altar.

Her attempt to pray became, instead, a low, painful whimpering, like a wounded animal, then her small frame began thrashing with severe sobbing. She knelt there hugging herself, and rocking back and forth in agony.

After a while, she threw her head back in anguish and screamed for him, in a hoarse, ragged voice. "JOEL!"

Her grieving was violent, and she was beginning to collapse under its force. It was a long while, before exhaustion insisted on a slow tapering off. Meredith rolled up into a little ball and just lay there on the floor, shaking with small, jagged gasps.

The abrupt sound of heavy running across her porch made her leap up quickly, to find him standing in her doorway. He opened his arms and she flew into them.

Joel picked her up and carried her over to the couch. He sat down and nestled her close, murmuring quiet things and kissing the tears from her face. She broke into a fresh wave of intense weeping.

He closed his eyes and held her as close to himself as he could, letting her cry it all out. She seemed to be unable to control it. Finally, he determined that she was going to make herself sick, if he didn't convince her to stop.

"Merry, sweetheart," he breathed into her hair. "It's okay. It's all over, baby. I'm here. Hush, it's all over." He caught her chin gently and persuaded her to look at him. "Hush, now. You have to stop."

"I love you!" Meredith sobbed, clutching him tightly. "I love you, Joel!"

"I love *you*, little one. And I need you to calm down."

He gave her a slow, sweet kiss before lifting her up into a sitting position. She was still shaking, but quieter.

"Ross has gone to call everyone and have them all meet back over here. Then we'll explain what happened, because I only want to tell this story once, and be done with it."

"Joel, weren't you shot?"

He smiled and touched his left shoulder. Meredith pulled open his jacket, and gasped in horror at the sight of his bloodstained shirt. "I should have gone by the house to change first, but once I realized the reporters were already breaking the story, I just hurried to get here. I'm sorry it wasn't in time, before you found out, sweetie."

He stopped her before she could get to the bandages. That would just kick off another round of crying, and he couldn't let that happen.

"Just grazed, that's all. You've inflicted more serious injuries on me than this. You almost did me in with that tray you hit me with. I'm still bruised from that, you little vixen!"

Joel kissed off whatever she had been about to say, then slipped her from his lap, onto the couch beside him, and stood up. "I need to talk to you before the others get here."

He walked over and reached into a gym bag he had left by the door. He pulled out a small, brown envelope and came back over to kneel in front of the fireplace.

Meredith stayed where she was and watched him in wonder, as he stoked some sleeping coals back into a fire, and added a log. He turned to her and held up the envelope.

"Come over here, honey."

She left the couch and knelt on the floor beside him.

"These are the last of pictures and negatives. These were taken of you back when you were in New Orleans... by Cagle Lawrence."

She looked at him ignorantly. "What do you mean? I don't remember that."

"Merry, Cagle had a hidden camera mounted in your dressing room."

Meredith opened her eyes wide, as a feeling of nausea washed over her. She put her hands over her face in shame.

Joel reached up and gently pulled them down.

"Watch me," he said quietly. He held the envelope in the flames until it began to burn freely, then laid it on the logs to be consumed.

"That's the last of them. They're all gone."

She stared at them burning, in sick shock.

"No one except a police officer saw them, Merry, not even me," he reassured her. "Once he realized what they were, he sealed them up and gave them to me."

He saw relief slowly come to her. "You weren't the only one. There were other women, it turns out. I only hope he never made theirs public, the way he threatened to do with yours."

Meredith swallowed hard and closed her eyes, as she finally began to comprehend.

"Joel..." She was ashamed to look at him, but she made herself do it, anyway. "Was he threatening you? Is that why you acted the way you did, after Gatlinburg?"

"He told me to stay away from you, Merry. I had to. I couldn't take any chances on those pictures getting out."

"Oh, Joel!" She threw her arms around his neck. "Joel, I've said the most horrible things about you! Oh dear God, I'm so ashamed! Joel, I'm just... so ashamed! Please forgive me!" Tears crowded into her eyes. "I'm just so sorry, Joel."

Joel pulled her away to smile down at her, and said the same old thing he had wearily been saying to her, for the past few years. "Next time, know better."

He kissed her lightly and reached inside his jacket pocket. "Meredith, you *are* planning our wedding, aren't you?"

She caught her breath and nodded, then looked down as Joel opened a small box, while keeping it close to his chest to keep her from seeing inside. He removed part of the set, and put the box back into his pocket.

"I told you that I knew what you were getting for Christmas," he teased. He held it up and she sank down on the floor, in a weak little heap. It was a perfect, two-carat, white diamond, cut as a teardrop.

She began to tremble.

"Our Father knows that we've shed enough of these to last a lifetime. This is to remind us of what our love is made of, and Who is holding our tears."

Meredith looked up and saw that Joel's eyes were filled with the impact of all those tears.

"Your song broke my heart," he said quietly, looking at her with a sorrowful smile.

"I didn't mean to hurt you," she said, hanging her head. "I just needed..."

He raised her chin with a gentle fingertip. "You needed to tell me."

She nodded.

Joel brushed her hair back, and rested his eyes on her sweet face. "I heard you," he whispered.

He rose to his feet and lifted her up with him.

"Will you trust me with that fragile heart of yours, little one?" he asked softly.

"Yes, Joel."

Joel lifted her left hand and kissed it, before slipping the ring onto her finger. "Merry, never doubt my love for you." He pulled her into the shelter of his embrace. "Never again. Always know that I'll guard our love with my very life."

"Joel." Meredith lifted her head and gave him a long, meaningful look. "I promise right now, here in this moment, that I will never doubt your love, again."

She clung to him, and he tightened his arms more securely around her and just held her for a long while, until the first of many expected cars began to arrive.

Chapter Twenty-Five

Meredith opened the door and Joel's mother ran into her son's arms, alternately laughing and crying. He gave her a little grin, and gathered her up snugly.

Meredith and Gary stood there watching them, with quiet joy.

"Praise God!" Gary came over and gave Joel a bear hug. "We thought we lost you."

Meredith almost cautioned him to watch out for Joel's shoulder, but Joel winked at her that he was okay, so she let it go.

"I just might be that proverbial bad penny," he teased Gary, then lifted his brows at Meredith and nodded toward Laura. Meredith grabbed the box of tissues from the table and brought them over.

"Yes, please! Let me just hang onto these," Laura suggested through her happy tears. "Bobbie and Delores will be as bad as I am."

They were, too. By the time everyone had assembled, the room was filled with sniffling women.

Meredith was done with crying, and was resting securely under the protection of Joel's arm, gazing up at him with adoring eyes. He was trying to concentrate on the things people were saying to him, but she was making it impossible.

He searched around in his mind for an excuse to get her alone for a quick minute, then decided he would just have to wait.

He looked down and winked privately at her and she read his mind and gave him a shy smile. This goaded him to silently torment her with his eyes, until she became so flustered that he laughed quietly.

"Will you two knock it off?" Hailey demanded, in mock irritation. "Surely you didn't call us all over here, so you two could be alone!"

Ross had to laugh at that. "Absolutely, I move we get on with it. If I want an evening of romance, I'll go rent Casablanca."

"Why don't you do the honors, Officer Decker?" Joel offered generously. "Try to do it in that crisp cop voice of yours, that never fails to impress me. The same one that always sounds like Dragnet, even when you're ordering pizza."

Hailey giggled and Ross gouged her in the side. He leaned forward and pulled out a tissue.

"Here," he said, tossing it at her. "Everybody's got a girl to cry over him, except me. Once you've realized the perils I've faced tonight, you may express your appreciation with a little gratuitous weeping."

She grinned and rolled her eyes, but held on to the tissue.

"Well, the most *serious* peril was facing the police chief after Joel, here, took a bullet." He laughed at Joel's abashed grin. "He was waiting for us at Baptist ER, and he didn't exactly bring flowers. Mr. Etheridge whipped out his Music Row charm, and single-handedly saved my job."

He shared in the laughter that burst forth, then began to be a little more serious. "I'm pretty sure all of you know by now what Cagle Lawrence was up to, as far as Meredith was concerned." He glanced over at Joel. "I explained it to Hailey, on the way over."

He nodded.

"Joel first called me about this back in November, not long after Lawrence showed up. I wasn't able to be much of an encouragement to him, since Lawrence had gone to great lengths to steer clear of litigation. The only hope we had was to look for another angle, something else to nail him with, anything that he might be involved in, that would put him at odds with the law, and possibly gain us access to both him and the photos.

"I called a friend of mine, who's a U.S. Marshal in New Orleans. Felix Brasseaux." He chuckled. "Man, I wish Felix could have gotten over here tonight, but he's up to his eyes in paper work, and all *kinds* of stuff. He'll be up all night! Marshal Brasseaux, now *there's* a character, right, Joel?"

Joel laughed heartily at just the thought of Ross's friend, Felix. "They should make a movie about that guy," he stated. "Talk about original material." He glanced down at Meredith. "He is so right up your alley, Missy."

She grinned and Ross continued.

"Well, of course, Lawrence is from the New Orleans area. Still had an apartment there, in fact. When I mentioned his name to Felix, he was already familiar with him. It didn't take much to convince him to help us out.

"His office had already been watching Lawrence and his *associates*..." Ross added air quotes... "for quite a while and were just hoping for a chance to get them all cornered, but they were holding back until they could determine what his business in Tennessee was."

He leaned back and picked up Hailey's hand, without realizing it. "Turns out Lawrence had drawn a five year sentence for a prior offense and had served the whole thing. He got out about nine years ago."

Joel saw the look of surprise on Meredith's face.

"He got caught doing a little dope shuffling," Ross went on. "After he got out, he appeared to stay clean for a while, then messed up and landed back in for a little over a year. Got out on parole, which was still in effect when he came here. I notified my chief about his presence here and he, in turn, notified NOPD. Felix had already been in touch with them, and they agreed to hold off hauling him in for a simple parole violation, and just wait to see what he was up to here.

"It wasn't long at all, before Felix was able to come up with exactly what we needed. Metro had a man go undercover and get chummy with one of Lawrence's contacts. Our plant was able to gain recognition as a desirable client, especially with the thick slab of cash they gave him to flash around.

"The undercover found out that Lawrence was planning what he cleverly billed as a Christmas 'celebration' at his no-security, no-background-check, 'no-tell motel' room... by all accounts just a cozy little meet-up with a few business affiliates. He was supposed to try and wrangle an invitation, but he didn't even have to. Somehow, it dropped right into his lap."

Meredith's face flushed in anger, as she realized what a gullible little wimp she had been. He stood right there on that cabin porch and swore that he no longer did that kind of stuff, and she had just believed him! She was mortified.

Joel squeezed her fingers then shook his head slightly. She sighed and let it go.

"Anyway," Ross continued, "our guy was able to tip Felix off on what was about to go down. We arranged for a stake-out, if you'll pardon the official cop lingo," he said, grinning over at Joel.

"We set up a perimeter around the motel where Lawrence was staying, and just sat back and watched the party file in. When it was time to hit, Felix had us move in behind the entry and front line. We forced the door open and, as the official report states, chaos ensued.

"Everything was going down pretty much as we expected, until Lawrence got a look at Joel and whipped out a gun."

Meredith shuddered and Joel tightened his arm around her.

"None of us realized it, until it went off, and I have to tell you..." Ross almost crushed Hailey's hand, in his excitement. "If that crazy Cajun hadn't been so doggone fast, this would be an entirely different gathering! As soon as we heard the first pop, Felix had already drawn on him and shot his hand pretty much off, which was just Felix's way of warning him. I never saw anything like it!"

He shook his head in amazement. "And *then*, even while he was bleeding out, Lawrence *still* used his other hand to get the gun and try to get another shot off at Joel, knowing that he, himself, was a dead man, if he went for it! This time, Felix put him out of commission. Lawrence died before the ambulance was even en route."

Meredith knew Joel was safe, but this was too much for her. She buried her face in his chest. He whispered something to her and drew his fingers through her hair.

"We did a sweep of the place, and an officer found the pictures he was using to threaten Meredith with. Those, and there were some of other women. The guy was sick! Anyway, it was a good bust. A *great* bust, actually, one for the books. A lot of long-time career criminals went down in this one. I tell you, it was just God that Joel called me back in November."

"It sure sounds like it," Gary agreed softly. "You hate to think of anyone getting killed, but it looks like Cagle Lawrence set himself up for it. Even knowing he'd get mowed down if he pulled a gun out and started shooting, he did it anyway. His hatred for Joel must have been greater than even his greed."

"You can't realize how true that statement is, without having looked into his face. I thought I had seen it all, but I guess I never realized before what complete hatred looks like. It was demonic!" Ross commented soberly.

"Incidentally, Joel, I stopped out by the box and took care of that tap, after I took a few photos of it. Merry's phone is clean. You remember that little redheaded guy, who was crouching down in the corner, and just kept ducking? Did you notice him?"

Joel lifted his brows and nodded. "After things died down."

"That was Alvin Peters. He's a private eye out of Dickson. He's the one Lawrence hired to watch this house. He's up for some simple charges... illegal tap, that sort of thing. He still has to account for his presence at a drug raid, so we'll see where that goes.

"I also took care of those reporters," he added. "I said you and I were out driving around, 'like a ride-along', when I got the call to report, and that I had to get there in a hurry, so you ended up at the scene. That must have made a lot more sense to them than it did to me, because *they* actually bought it."

"Thank you, Ross," Joel said. "And Marshall, thank you for stepping in to be Meredith's manager. You're fired, by the way," he added, with a happy grin.

Marshall laughed joyfully. "Hallelujah! She's all yours!"

Meredith made a face at Marshall, as everyone joined him in laughing. She winked at him happily.

Joel eased Meredith out of his embrace and sat up straight, smiling at her and taking her hands in his.

"I've waited all my life to say these words."

Laura touched Gary's arm and drew in a quick breath, her face shining.

Joel looked down at Meredith and cherished her with his eyes. "This is the woman I have searched through my entire life to find. I've loved her since the moment I saw her, and I have Marshall to thank for that."

Marshall reached up and swiped at his cheeks, and Bobbie took his hand and gave him a happy smile.

"I have hoped, for so long, that Father would share her with me. It didn't seem as if it would ever happen. Our relationship has not had one easy day, since we met. Besides..." He tugged at her fingers and grinned at her. "We all know how Meredith can be!"

Hailey hooted at that, and the whole room joined her.

Meredith gave a little pout, then smiled down at Hook, who had wandered in from sleeping somewhere upstairs. He sat staring around the room with a curious, groggy expression, wondering who let all these people in here, and if any of them brought anything to eat.

He claimed a place up against Meredith, and let his motor idle quietly, while Joel finished what he was saying.

"I just want to announce privately here tonight, that I love this woman with everything that's in me, and that I intend to meet her at the Hermitage in April, to publicly take her to be my wife." He leaned over for a kiss, then Meredith held her hand up to show off her ring.

Even though everyone had suspected this was coming, there was just something about hearing Joel say it, and witnessing the look of joy on Meredith's face, that sent them into a happy frenzy.

Laura leaped up and pulled her off the couch for a big hug, to the extreme displeasure of Hook, who had just found his comfort zone.

Hailey claimed her left hand, and she and Bobbie and Delores had a collective fit over her ring.

Ross took Joel's hand and pulled him around for a brotherly hug, that was duplicated in varying degrees by Marshall, Gary and Doug.

Gary waited until the bedlam had died down, then lifted his hand for silence. He smiled at Laura.

"I can't tell you how happy it makes me, to see how God has come through for these two. I also want to say that these have been the longest two months of my life and Joel, I'm sorry to be the one to have to point this out, but I'm afraid they have done nothing to impede the accelerated graying of your hair."

Joel flashed him a sour grin as everyone laughed.

"Merry, I hope you like *my* hair," he added, touching his own snowy head, "because it looks like this is a pretty good representation of what you're going to get. And I don't want to hear you complaining either, because I've known Joel for a long time, and he didn't look like that until *you* blew into town!"

Gary waited until more laughter finally faded, then gave them all a loving smile. "Before we leave, let's take time to offer thanks to God for being the champion He always is, and let's also gather around and lay hands on Joel and Meredith and give them our blessings and prayers."

Joel looked into Meredith's eyes and discovered the same grateful tears that were spilling from his own. He touched the diamond on her finger and she understood.

Chapter Twenty-Six

It was a spring day. It was a perfect day. It was the Hermitage and Meredith was the most beautiful bride Joel could ever have hoped to find.

His eyes filled up immediately, at the sight of her coming toward him on Marshall's arm. Marshall was softly whispering heartfelt sentiments to her, as he led her to the one she loved and, like Joel, her lovely eyes brimmed over with gladness.

This was the only setting that could almost do justice to Meredith's beauty.

The dignified, old home of President Andrew Jackson was very dear to Meredith's heart. It lay nestled among massive and ancient, gnarled trees, and soft, green grasses that stretched as far as one cared to look.

Its peaceful and poetically sad grounds had provided Meredith with a quiet haven for a lot of writing, a lot of daydreaming, and a lot of soul searching.

Meredith's off-the-shoulder gown was like something to be found among the ladies of Shakespeare's passion, light and simple, flowing and free.

Her dark, abundant hair fell in abandon below her waist, loose tendrils lifting in the breeze, confined only by a simple circlet of white flowers, that her friends from the shelter regarded as the halo that gilded their angel.

In deference to the day, her feet consented to be shod by only the merest suggestion of satin slippers.

As soon as the stately, horse-drawn carriage had pulled up to the main gates of the Hermitage, Meredith stepped down with Marshall's assistance, and began her walk up the carpeted drive, between the towering rows of bordering, archaic trees. She moved with a grace that was almost music.

Now she stood beside him, the one whose eyes called her to come.

Ross and Hailey looked on from their respective attending positions, and Laura, Bobbie, Delores, and Doug watched from the front row, the joy of the day reflected on their faces.

Marshall kissed her cheek and surrendered her hand to Gary, who reached for Joel's, and fused them together.

Laughter erupted from all around, when Joel blatantly scorned tradition, and immediately and thoroughly kissed his bride.

"Joel, we haven't gotten to that part, yet," Gary protested, laughing heartily, along with everyone else.

Joel grinned and obediently faced his minister, but failed to look repentant.

After an opening prayer, Gary began to share earnestly, from his heart, the deep and stirring things that had settled there, during the past few months of observing not only the revelation of love between these two, but the forging of that love in the flame.

He paralleled what he had witnessed as a hint and a shadow of the love that Christ has for His Bride, and the unselfish lengths He went to, that enabled Him to claim Her for Himself.

He led Joel and Meredith in the traditional vows, then asked for the rings. Joel removed Meredith's teardrop from her left hand, and she looked up at him curiously. He gave her a caressing smile and turned to Ross, who offered him its mate.

Meredith looked down as he paired them together, then gave a little gasp, as he slid their union onto her finger. The wedding band was styled as a ring guard. Its diamonds formed a beautiful heart that, when fitted together with the engagement ring, sheltered the teardrop that now rested inside.

"Meredith," Joel said, in a voice rich with emotion. He gazed down into her eyes, with love in its purest form. "Our tears have been many... some of them bitter, some happy... some wounding, some healing... but all captured inside the heart of God. I love you, Meredith, with all that is within me. I am so honored that Father would allow me to not only love His daughter, but to take her to be my wife. I pledge to cherish you, to cover you, and to devote my life to being Father's provision for you."

Father looked down at His children, with His heart full and His face wreathed in smiles. He lifted the two bottles He had been so carefully tending, and poured their cherished, salty volumes into a single larger one. His smile broadened at the glow on His daughter's face. He was happy. She was getting a good man.

Meredith drank deeply from Joel's eyes, before turning to Hailey and taking his ring. She looked at him with all that burned in her heart, then lifted his hand tenderly. He glanced down at the simple wide band and tears immediately rushed to his eyes. Engraved on its surface, for Joel and all the world to see, were the words that poured over him like an anointing: *Father's Choice*

Meredith reached up and touched his chin with a gentle hand.

"Joel... I take you as my Father's choice for me. I take you as my covering, as my shield, as my companion, and as the great love of my life. I promise to be by your side, for the rest of our time on earth. I promise to love you, to care for you, to trust you... "

She paused and leaned in dramatically. "To *obey* you..."

She grinned, as the crowd ruffled in quiet laughter. "What do you think about that?"

Joel gave her a happy smile. "I think it's about time."

Gary had to halt the ceremony, and laugh at that one. "Well, a little humor is just what we needed," he declared. "These two were about to do me in." He wiped his moist eyes and lifted his bible.

"I wavered over sharing this scripture today, because of man's willful attempt to misinterpret it, remove it from context, and to pervert it, but beholding the bond of love between this precious couple calls it to mind again, remote and obscure, yet beautiful and untarnished.

"There are three things which are too wonderful for me, four which I do not understand: the way of an eagle in the air, the way of a serpent on a rock, the way of a ship in the middle of the sea and the way of a man with a maid."

He smiled at the look of devotion that passed between them.

"In as much as Joel and Meredith have consented to the vows of matrimony, and have pledged themselves to one another in the giving and receiving of rings, in the presence of God and these witnesses, it gives me great pleasure to pronounce that they are man and wife. What Father has joined together, let no man take apart." He winked at Joel. "I think you can take it from here."

Joel didn't need to be told twice. He pulled his wife into his arms and again claimed her lips with his own. It wasn't until Gary cleared his throat, and gave an exaggerated cough, that he reluctantly released her.

"Hold that thought," he whispered in her ear. She blushed and he laughed softly.

"Ladies and gentlemen!" Gary turned them around to face their family and friends. "It is both my joy and my honor to present to you Mr. and Mrs. Joel Michael Etheridge!"

Music burst forth from the stringed quartet, and Joel and Meredith were immediately set upon by a happy swarm of well-wishers. Laura was able to pick her way through the throng, to her son. She caught him around the neck in a tight embrace.

"I love you so much, Joel," she said, in a weepy voice.

"I love you so much too, little Mother." He kissed her face and gave her another hug.

"Son, she's everything I could ever want for you," Laura declared, as she and Joel watched Meredith reacting comically to something Marshall had just said to her. "Even the bad parts."

He smiled quietly. "*Pray* for me, Mom!"

The crowd eventually allowed Joel and Meredith to proceed to a huge white tent, that housed the reception. The musicians had already relocated into position, and music was flowing over the grounds in much the same way that it did long ago, when the late president and his bride danced under the limbs of some of these same trees.

For a while, the couple was caught up in various demands to cut cake, receive toasts, pose for pictures and whatever else was expected. Finally, they were able to break free of the confines of protocol, and mingle around, chatting with their friends.

A big, dark, burly giant of a man tapped Joel on the shoulder. His eyes lit up and he grabbed the man's hand, and slapped him on the back.

"Felix!" Joel turned to Meredith. "Sweetheart, if it wasn't for Felix Brasseaux, this day would never have happened. Felix, this is my... *wife!*" He broke off and laughed. "You heard it here first!"

Felix reached for Meredith's hand but instead, she threw her arms around him.

"Thank you!" she said earnestly, her voice breaking. "Thank you so much, Felix!"

Ross caught his eye and winked, and Felix grinned and hung his head.

"Turns out Ross was right, Etheridge. I'd have loaned you my gun!"

Meredith looked from Felix and Ross to Joel with a confused smile, when they all began to laugh.

She grinned and turned to lift the hem of her dress from the pull of someone's foot, and found Pockets and a few of his cohorts beaming at her in awestruck joy.

"Sorry, Miss Meredith!" He stepped back quickly and looked down to inspect the damage, which was minimal.

Meredith caught him around the neck, to his great surprise and delight.

"Oh, Pockets, what do I care about some silly dress? You know I'd rather be in jeans."

He continued to glow, while she distributed more hugs to the rest of the group.

Joel looked over and smiled, watching his little bride go to great lengths to make her friends from the shelter feel welcome.

"Pockets!" He filtered through the people and gave the man a swift embrace. "Man, it's good to see you!"

"We came to see Miss Meredith, in her white dress and flowers. She's a angel," he reminded Joel confidentially.

"Did *she* tell you that?"

Meredith jabbed him, then patted her friend's arm. "Don't you listen to him, Pockets, he's just teasing you. Listen, if you guys want to eat the best cake in the world, follow me."

They were only too happy to oblige.

Perry Mitchell came up and shook Joel's hand. "Long time coming, but it looks like you finally hit pay dirt, Joel."

Joel happily agreed. He began talking with Perry and as Meredith was returning from the cake table, she noticed a woman approach Joel and lay a tentative hand on his back.

Laura came up, and put her arm lovingly around her new daughter-in-law, her face glistening with tears.

"Watch this," she whispered, nodding toward Joel.

Joel knew Meredith's touch so well, that he instantly realized it wasn't her. He excused himself and turned around, expecting to see Delores or Bobbie. He stared in shocked disbelief.

"Hi there," the woman began in a nervous voice. She was shaking and her smile was unsteady. "Remember me?"

"Oh, dear God!" Joel clutched at his chest to control his heart and tears, fast and furious, rained down his face. "Iris!" he breathed in wonder. "Oh, Iris..."

He seized her and folded her into his arms, saying her name over and over again, repeating that he loved her and that he was sorry.

A man who had been standing to one side, stepped into Joel's view. Joel lifted his head and saw reconciliation in the man's eyes. His embrace spread to include Iris's husband, and the three of them huddled together, being healed.

Meredith hugged Laura and helped her cry tears of thanksgiving.

"Did you know they were coming, Laura?" she finally asked. Laura nodded, wiping her face.

"When I went back home after Christmas, I got a call from Iris. She and Jack had just rededicated their lives to the Lord, and they wanted to forgive Joel and to make things right again. This is how they chose to do it."

She grinned over at Meredith. "Girl, can I keep a secret or what!"

"You sure can, lady!"

Laura watched her children for another happy moment, before taking Meredith by the hand.

"Come and meet your family."

Chapter Twenty-Seven

Joel lay on the couch and playfully roughed up Hook's coat. The *real* boss of the home, who graciously allowed boarders, landed on Joel's stomach, and wrapped all four limbs around his arm, wildly excited to have someone in the house who knew how to have a good time!

Joel lifted his arm and laughed as Hook hung on and took a ride.

"You're flat out dopey, Captain Hook," he chided. "It's not too hard to figure out who raised you."

He caught his little playmate by the hindquarters, and held him upside down, so that his head was suspended just inches above Joel's.

Hook took a swat at his unshaven face, and began to purr loudly. He reacted swiftly to the sound of a new arrival, and immediately jumped down and bolted for the kitchen.

Meredith watched him go, in sleepy-eyed amusement, then came over and tugged her husband up, and crawled onto his lap for her kiss.

Joel rumpled her disarrayed hair and grinned. "Nice of you to drop by, Lady Grunge."

She flashed him a sour expression then gave it to Hook, as he marched back in to see what was taking her so long.

"Get out of here," she advised peevishly.

She buried her face in Joel's neck and sighed. "You know, it's perfectly fine with me, if you want to feed him in the morning, instead of waiting for me to do it."

"I did."

"You did?" She jerked her head up and glared at Hook, who interpreted correctly, and moseyed off to pursue other interests.

Joel chuckled and pulled her face around, so that he could see her. "Good morning, Mrs. Etheridge."

"I don't do mornings."

"Gee, that's too bad."

He gave her a lingering look.

She picked up a pillow and crowned him with it.

Joel caught the pillow and returned fire, then wrapped his arms around her.

"When do you think our wedding pictures will be ready, sweetie?" he asked.

"I think he said something like four to six weeks. I reminded him that we have to see them first, before he can upload to his site or send anything to the papers."

Meredith yawned and stretched. "When is Laura coming back or did she say?"

"As soon as the house in Oklahoma finishes closing. I should probably run over from time to time, and air my old place out, so it won't be all musty, when she moves in."

"Do you think she'll really like Nashville enough to want to stay here? Maybe she should have just rented her house out, until she was sure."

"Well..." He shifted his weight and toyed with a strand of her hair. "I've been noticing the furtive glances between Mom and Gary, lately. I think it's a pretty safe bet that she'll like it here, just fine. In fact, if there wasn't something brewing there, she never would have sold her house, I can promise you that."

Meredith grinned. "What about Hailey and Ross?"

"What about them?"

She lifted her palms expressively. *"Hello!"*

He laughed. "You just want to partner everybody up, you old married woman!" He tweaked her nose.

"You're the one who made that match, so don't lay that trip on me." She pouted attractively.

Joel smiled at her failed attempt to scowl at him. "Well, it was just a matter of making the proper introductions. The minute they saw each other at the office, the rest was pretty much text book chemistry."

"What would you know about chemistry?" She baited him with her eyes.

"Well, I admit, I don't stack up against the Queen of Refrigerator Mutations, but I do know my way around the medicine cabinet of love."

"Is that a fact?" Meredith commented dryly. "Well, next time you're rummaging around in there, try to come up with something for this."

She caught a handful of his silvery brown locks. "I'm getting tired of taking the rap for this geriatric thing you're working on."

"You should have thought about that before you set out to wing me in the heart, you cruel wench!"

Meredith studied him for a long, slow moment, then caressed his face in her hands.

His blue eyes sparkled. "Wanna kiss and make up?"

She playfully dropped a small peck on his forehead.

"Not exactly what I was going for..."

She grinned and let that pass. "Listen, I want to ask you something and I'm serious now, so give me a straight answer."

Joel raised his eyebrows and put on his listening face.

She looked at him pointedly before continuing.

"Do you have any weird habits I should know about?"

"What do you mean, habits?"

"You know! Habits. Things you just sort of do over and over, without thinking. *Habits,* Joel!"

Joel creased his brow and tried not to smile. "Well... I do pick my toenails whenever I watch Mystery Science Theater. And I stand up straight with my hand over my heart, all during reruns of Black Sheep Squadron and Patton... except during commercials. That's when I run into the kitchen and look for things to spread peanut butter on."

Meredith seemed to accept this as a serious answer. "What about toilet paper?"

"Never tried it."

She grinned and punched him. "No, dummy! I mean how do you hang your toilet paper?"

"*My* toilet paper?" Joel sat up straighter and gave her a puzzled look. "Honey, come on, are we really having this conversation?"

She looked exasperated. "For crying out loud, Joel! Just answer the question!"

"Why? Is there something unseemly about the way you found *my* toilet paper hanging this morning?"

"Yes!" she replied, a little put out. "I had to pull from *under!*"

He just blinked.

"Joel, you're supposed to hang it so you pull from over the top!"

"Am I?" He returned evenly, deciding that she was very pretty this morning.

"Yes!" She flicked her hair impatiently and thumped him on the chest. "Why do you think the manufacturers go to so much trouble to put designs on toilet paper, if you're just gonna hang it backwards?"

She stopped and narrowed her eyes curiously. "Why are you looking at me like that?"

"I'm worried," he said quietly.

"Why?"

"Because that actually made sense."

She let out a big sigh and rolled her eyes.

Joel leaned back and fastened her with a look of lazy amusement. "I can't believe you get so worked up over toilet paper, when our refrigerator is in there being held hostage by militant lunch meat. And let's not even *mention* the windows in this place."

"That's your job, now."

"Now," he repeated emphatically. "When was it ever *your* job?" Meredith gave him a full dose of big, gray eyes.

"Stop that."

She turned on all her charm and smiled at the effect she was having on him.

"You wouldn't wash a few windows for your wife?"

"Not on your life, Wife."

He tried to steel himself against those eyes.

Next, she pulled out all the stops and hovered just inches from his face, deliberately reeling him in.

"I need a big strong man to help me."

"Help you what? Help you sit and watch?"

She began tracing his face with her fingertip. "Please, Mister Man?"

"Why should I?" her husband demanded. "What's in it for me?"

Meredith picked up the afghan and grinned slowly. She lifted it over their heads.

By noon, every window in the house was shining.

Coming soon from

Rhonda Hanson
and
Grace Under Pressure Publishing

Father's Wings

the much anticipated sequel to

Father's Choice

Enjoy the return of the characters you came to know so well in the first chronicling of the love story of Joel and Meredith. Get to know new ones as the lives of Joel and Meredith continue forward into a season of intercession and spiritual warfare that can only be survived under the protection of a loving Father.

Father's Wings

Expected release December 2023

www.ingramcontent.com/pod-product-compliance
Lightning Source LLC
Chambersburg PA
CBHW050315160726
48002CB00001B/43